T0245533

CARL'S DOOMSDAY SCENARIO

Titles by Matt Dinniman

Dungeon Crawler Carl Series

DUNGEON CRAWLER CARL

CARL'S DOOMSDAY SCENARIO

THE DUNGEON ANARCHIST'S COOKBOOK

THE GATE OF THE FERAL GODS

THE BUTCHER'S MASQUERADE

THE EYE OF THE BEDLAM BRIDE

KAIJU: BATTLEFIELD SURGEON

The Shivered Sky Series

EVERY GRAIN OF SAND

IN THE CITY OF DEMONS

THE GREAT DEVOURING DARKNESS

Dominion of Blades Series

DOMINION OF BLADES

THE HOBGOBLIN RIOT

THE GRINDING

TRAILER PARK FAIRY TALES

CARL'S DOOMSDAY SCENARIO

DUNGEON CRAWLER CARL BOOK TWO

MATT DINNIMAN

ACE

New York

ACE
Published by Berkley
An imprint of Penguin Random House LLC
penguinrandomhouse.com

Copyright © 2021 by Matt Dinniman
"Backstage at the Pineapple Cabaret" copyright © 2024 by Matt Dinniman
Penguin Random House values and supports copyright. Copyright fuels creativity, encourages diverse
voices, promotes free speech, and creates a vibrant culture. Thank you for buying an authorized edition
of this book and for complying with copyright laws by not reproducing, scanning, or distributing any
part of it in any form without permission. You are supporting writers and allowing Penguin Random
House to continue to publish books for every reader. Please note that no part of this book may be used
or reproduced in any manner for the purpose of training artificial intelligence technologies or systems.

ACE is a registered trademark and the A colophon is a trademark of
Penguin Random House LLC.

Library of Congress Cataloging-in-Publication Data
Names: Dinniman, Matt, author.
Title: Carl's doomsday scenario / Matt Dinniman.
Description: First Ace edition. | New York: Ace, 2024. |
Series: Dungeon crawler Carl
Identifiers: LCCN 2024013570 | ISBN 9780593820261 (hardcover)
Subjects: LCGFT: LitRPG (Fiction) | Novels.
Classification: LCC PS3604.I49 C37 2024 | DDC 813/.6—dc23/eng/20240423
LC record available at https://lccn.loc.gov/2024013570

Carl's Doomsday Scenario was originally self-published, in different form, in 2021.

First Ace Edition: September 2024

Printed in the United States of America
1st Printing

Book design by George Towne
Interior art on pages v, 356: Vintage Black Texture © 316pixel/Shutterstock
All other interior art by Erik Wilson (erikwilsonart.com)

If you hold a cat by the tail you learn things

you cannot learn any other way.

Mark Twain

CARL'S DOOMSDAY SCENARIO

1

WELCOME, CRAWLER, TO THE THIRD FLOOR.

THE PREVIOUS LEVEL WILL COLLAPSE IN 3 HOURS AND 35 MINUTES.

WE TELEPORTED STRAIGHT FROM THE GREENROOM TO A LONG golden hallway reminiscent of the first hallway we had entered.

"Carl, look! We're outside!" Donut said, looking up into the air. Next to her, Mongo gave an uncertain squawk.

Sure enough, a dark sky rose above us, dotted with stars. A colorful nebula, reminiscent of the background image on Odette's stage, covered the sky.

The air still felt stale. I pulled my slingshot, aimed it at the stars, and I fired.

Plink. Sure enough, the rock bounced off the ceiling, about 25 feet up.

"It's an illusion," I said. "It's like that mall in Las Vegas. They make it look like you're outside, but you're really not."

"Well, that's disappointing," Donut said.

The walls and the ground were made of golden-colored bricks. A plush red carpet led to a familiar door at the end of the hallway. As we approached, the door opened on its own. A tall figure stepped out, and all three of us stopped.

A well-built, young, and disgustingly handsome man wearing a tuxedo waited for us. His skin was a dusky gray, and he had a short pair of devil horns jutting from his forehead. The man stood about my height, and he had long gray-and-black hair that was held back in a ponytail. A barbed tail poked from the rear of his tuxedo. A pair of black bat-like wings sat folded tightly against his back.

"Hello, Mordecai," I said, examining his new form. "Jesus, dude. Looking good."

"Wow," Donut said, looking him up and down. "I wouldn't kick you out of bed for eating crackers."

Even Mongo's customary screech sounded as if he was in awe.

> Mordecai—Incubus. Level 50.
>> Guildmaster of this guildhall.
>> This is a Non-Combatant NPC.
>> Also known as the Gigachad of the Over City, Incubi are the male counterparts of the infamous Succubus. The smooth, seductive, and ultimately deadly Incubus can be identified by his stunning good looks, exquisite charm, and sensuous feet. They can only be found on the urban levels of the dungeon. They give new meaning to the phrase "hit it and quit it."

"Princess Donut, Carl, little Mongo, welcome to the third floor. The training levels have concluded. Now the games may truly begin," Mordecai said, bowing slightly. Even his voice had gotten deeper. He indicated for us to enter.

We walked inside, and the door closed behind us.

"Training levels?" I said. "For fuck's sake. You call those training levels?"

"Oh, thank goodness," Mordecai said once the door closed. He ripped the jacket off and pulled off the tie, unbuttoning the top three buttons. The jacket was odd, with a pair of long slits along the back to accommodate his wings. "I thought you two were never going to show up. I've been in this thing for three hours, waiting for you. I hate formal wear."

"The interview ran long," I said. "I take it the general public can't watch this part?"

"Nope," he said. "They'll watch you go in, and they'll watch you come out, but they don't get to see what's going on inside. It's like a jury room."

His room was exactly the same as it had always been, but he'd cleaned up even further. A pair of beds had magically appeared since the last time we'd been in here.

"Those are for the transformation, if required," he said. "Remember what happened with Donut when she took that enhanced pet biscuit?"

I swallowed, remembering the weird, gooey blob thing she'd transformed into before.

"So," Mordecai said, "have you decided who wants to go first? I suggest Princess—"

"Me," Donut said, jumping up on one of the beds. "Let's get this rolling."

"Okay, Carl, take a seat," Mordecai said. I sat in one of the chairs. Mongo jumped into my lap and squeaked, sounding concerned.

"Mommy will be okay," Donut said. "You hang out with Uncle Carl for a few minutes while I get some work done. Behave yourself."

The baby velociraptor settled into my lap. I suddenly felt uncomfortable having that many teeth so close to my crotch. If he bit me now, I didn't know what would happen. I suspected he wouldn't teleport away. Instead, he'd get frozen like Frank and Maggie had that one time. Hopefully, I wouldn't find out.

"Okay," Mordecai said. He waved his hand and a screen appeared floating in the air, like we were on Odette's show. "Your current race is 'cat.' This is a list of all the available races you may choose. It looks like you've been given 320 different choices. It is in alphabetical order, and you may click on any of them to drill down to a very specific set of details. Also, the system AI has narrowed it down to a set of three recommendations. We will spend the next hour or so going over these choices, and then I will—"

"I choose cat. Next."

Mordecai took a deep breath. "Donut, there are a few choices on here where you'll actually look mostly—"

"Cat. Final answer. Let's move on."

Mordecai looked at me. I shrugged. She'd made it clear from the start that she wasn't going to change. I was just happy she'd dropped the idea of me turning into a cat also.

"Okay, then," he said. "A message will pop up, and you have to confirm your choice by clicking on it."

"Wait," I said, a horrific thought coming to me. "It's not going to, you know, change her back to the way she was before, is it?"

"Too late," Donut said. She glowed for a moment. "I clicked it." She looked at her paw. "I feel the same."

"No," Mordecai said. He looked pointedly at Donut. "But it is important to ask questions like that. I made it so she actually chose to not make a choice. Nothing will change, but she will now have access to a few racial benefits she didn't have before."

"Benefits? What are they?" Donut asked.

"I don't know, Princess Donut," Mordecai said, sounding exasperated. "We never got to examine the cat choice in the menu. You'll be able to see when we're done. And you wouldn't have changed yet anyway. The change doesn't happen until the end of the process."

"Okay, Donut," I said. "We need to think carefully about this next choice. Let's see what the AI suggests. Okay?"

"Let's do this," she said. "Show me anything with the word 'princess' or 'queen' in the title."

"Okay, moving on," Mordecai said. A list of items appeared on the screen, though the list appeared to be much shorter than the last one.

Mordecai paused, his eyes flashing as he quickly looked over the selections. "Okay, Princess Donut. It looks as if you've been given 34 class choices. That's a pretty short list. In fact, it's the shortest I've ever seen, but I think that's a combination of your racial choice and a result of your stats. Your base constitution is still two." He paused. "No, actually it's four now, thanks to your racial choice of cat." He again searched through his unseen menus. "Oh, I see now. It's actually a combination of four things. You both also have that Desperado pass, which precludes several of the classes right off the bat. And Donut has that tiara on her head, which narrows it even further. But that's all right. There are still a few great choices on there."

"So what's good?" Donut asked, looking at the list. "Ohh, that one sounds cool. It sounds menacing yet mysterious and fun. I pick that one."

"Wait," I said, jumping to my feet. I caught the now-asleep Mongo in the crook of my arm and rushed to the screen. "Do *not* pick anything yet until we've looked it over carefully."

Donut pointed at something entitled **NecroBard**.

Mordecai grunted. "That's actually not a bad choice. It's one of the three recommendations."

I looked over the list. The only base classes available to her were **Bard**, **Magic User**, and **Barbarian**. Each of the base classes had a few additional items under them, including **Necromancer**, **Wind Mage**, and **Warlock**. The **NecroBard** subclass was listed under both **Bard** and **Necromancer**. There was also an **Earth Class** heading, and the majority of the available items were listed under there. Included on that list were several interesting items, including **Feral Cat Berserker**, **Animal Test Subject**, and **Roller Derby Jammer**.

I looked at the list of the three AI-picked recommendations. They were:

Artist Alley Mogul.
NecroBard.

and

Former Child Actor.

I said a silent thank-you to the game gods that they hadn't named the roller derby one "Derby Queen." She probably would've insisted upon picking it without reading anything. We'd discussed this, and we had a loose plan based on Odette's advice. But Donut was also prone to go off the rails from time to time.

"Donut," I said. "Click on each of the three recommendations so we can see the information."

"I'm telling you right now I am absolutely not choosing this one," Donut said as she clicked on the first choice.

Artist Alley Mogul.

This Charisma- and Intelligence-based class is the modern-day merchant. Using your superior artistic talent to entertain and entice fellow nerds, the Artist Alley Mogul travels the world to sell her copyright-infringing wares. While not particularly menacing physically, this plucky merchant is extremely difficult to hurt. Members of this class receive the following benefits:

+5 Dexterity.

Instant access to the level 5 *Shield* spell.

A 25% discount at all stores plus a 15% bonus to money earned from sales.

10% interest earned on all coins upon descent to the next level.

Level 5 Pathfinder skill.

Access to Enhanced Dodge, which allows the Dodge skill to train to level 20.

Level 5 Dodge skill. (Already obtained.)

Additional subclasses become available on the sixth floor.

This is an Earth Class. As an incentive to choose an Earth Class, you will receive a Silver Earth Box upon choosing this class.

Mordecai grunted. "That incentive is a little weak compared to what they usually do. It's usually a gold box and a couple stat points."

"I'm not surprised," I muttered. My eyes immediately focused on that Pathfinder skill. Odette had said I needed to find something with that skill. But we were looking for something else, too.

"Still," Mordecai said. "This is a very good choice for her. If she can get Dodge over level 15, she will be almost impossible to hit. And a 25% discount at stores is great, too. That'll be on top of the bonus she already gets from her charisma. Stuff will be half-price for her, and that's a huge deal. But most importantly, you'd have access to the Pathfinder skill. It'll make finding stairwells, shops, and guilds much easier."

"Yeah, no," Donut said. "Artist Alley? Really? Aren't those the nerds that like *Star Wars* and draw pictures of cats dressed like the guys from *The A-Team* and stuff?" She shuddered.

"It's a good choice," I said. "Let's look at the other two."

NecroBard.

This unusual class combines one of the most loved occupations with one of the most reviled. Necromancers specialize in magic related to raising the dead. Bards must choose an entertainment-based skill. Depending on this choice, whether it be singing, the kazoo, or storytelling, the resulting crawler will use this skill to either entertain, protect, or glamour both the living and the dead.

The NecroBard receives the following benefits:

Instant access to a level 5 entertainment-based skill of their choice.

Access to all membership-based clubs, regardless of current memberships.

Free rooms at all safe rooms.

A 10% mana cost penalty on all non-Necromancer or non-Bard spells.

Instant access to the level 3 *Turn Undead* spell.

Instant access to the level 3 *Panty Dropper* spell.

+5 to Constitution, Charisma, and Intelligence.

−2 Strength.

Additional benefits depending on entertainment-based skill choice.

"So help me god," I said, "I will abandon you right here and right now if you choose to take up the kazoo."

"I could play an instrument," Donut said, voice full of wonder. "I could be a singer!"

"We want to keep viewers, remember?" I said.

"What this description doesn't say is that a lot of the necromancer spells will be cast with her instrument," Mordecai said. "And that means she won't have to use spell points to cast them. That's pretty huge. Plus each instrument has a long list of additional benefits. This is a solid choice if you end up picking a DPS class. Something that does a lot of damage. She'll have a wide range of both protection and other support skills."

"Carl, look! I could get a harmonica!" Donut said. She'd pulled up the submenu of entertainment skills. She gasped. "Bongos. They have bongos, Carl."

"Harmonica? How would that even work?" I said. "You don't have thumbs."

"You don't need thumbs for the harmonica, Carl. Not if I get one of those neck thingies."

I had a quick vision of tiny Zev attempting to strangle me after I allowed Donut to take up a ridiculous instrument. "Please, let's just look at that third choice."

Former Child Actor.

This rare subclass is an offshoot of the Character Actor class. It can only be obtained by crawlers who have both received the Cut! achievement and have obtained at least one trillion views.

Once a spoiled brat superstar, then addicted to drugs, you have crawled back from the brink stronger than ever. You are ready for your comeback. This Charisma- and Chance-based class could go either way. You'll either rise to the top, or you'll be dead in a ditch in a week.

This unique Earth Class is based on the Bard/Rogue Jack-of-All-Trades subclass, but with a few distinctive differences.

In addition to the following benefits, the most distinct aspect of this multifaceted class is the level 3 Character Actor skill. This skill increases in level only upon descent to the next floor.

Additional benefits:

Immunity to all poisons and diseases.

Level 5 Cockroach skill.

+10 to Charisma.

+15% faster growth in all Charisma-based skills.

The Manager Benefit.

This is an Earth Class. As an incentive to choose an Earth Class, you will receive a Silver Earth Box upon choosing this class.

I watched Donut's eyes get huge upon reading this one.

"What the hell is the Character Actor skill? Or the Cockroach skill?" I asked. "And what was the Cut! achievement? I don't remember that one."

"I got it for being a good actress," Donut said. "When we tricked the goblin shamankas."

"Okay, but it doesn't explain what the 'character actor' part means. Mordecai?"

Mordecai didn't say anything for several moments. His lip was curled in displeasure. On that incubus face of his, it looked downright menacing.

"What?" he said. "Oh, so 'character actor.' It's a bit complicated. Basically every floor, Donut has to pick a specialty."

"Specialty?" I asked.

"She can basically pick a new class each floor. Each floor from now on will have a theme. So it would be somewhat useful. If it's a floor filled with ice monsters, she can pick a fire class, and so forth. But it's also a chance-based skill. So if she chooses it, and then she chooses a fire mage, the system AI basically rolls the dice and decides how many fire mage spells and skills to give to her. And as soon as she's done with the floor, she loses the skills and starts over. Each higher level of the Character Actor skill, however, gives better skills. It makes it so she is pretty weak for the early levels, but once you get higher, it can be quite powerful depending on her class choices."

"I don't think I like that," I said. "It leaves too much to chance. What about her existing spells, like *Magic Missile* and the like?"

"Those are untouched. But if she chooses a class that has a penalty for those skills or spells, they will apply. For example, if she chooses a necromancer specialty, that *Magic Missile* spell will cost 10% more to cast, but just for the length of that floor. Or if she chooses warlock, her constitution will go down one point for the length of that floor."

I liked that she would be immune to poison and diseases. "What's the Cockroach skill?"

"Basically, it gives a chance to survive a fatal attack. At level five she's guaranteed one free lethal hit a fight, though she'd be near death afterward. At level ten, your health doesn't go down at all after the first fatal strike. The problem is, the only way to train that skill is by using it. Or with potions, or a training guild if you can find one, but that can get expensive."

"I like it," Donut said. "If I pick it, then I can just choose Necro-Bard as my specialty every floor, but pick a different instrument every time. Wouldn't that be neat? It's the best of both worlds!"

"Not necessarily, Donut," I said. "If you get a bad roll from the AI, you might get stuck with underpowered skills and spells until the next floor."

"Exactly," Mordecai said.

"Let's spend some time looking at the other choices," I said. "But of the three, I think I like the Artist Alley one the best."

"I agree," Mordecai said. "I think the NecroBard *might* be better. But you're right, Carl. It's a . . . dangerous choice for your social numbers."

We spent some time going over the other choices, carefully looking at all the abilities. The Feral Cat Berserker was basically a barbarian that'd end up getting her killed immediately thanks to her low health, and the Animal Test Subject was a mage that specialized in using poison. It also caused the crawler to glow green. Warlock was a solid choice in terms of skills, but it caused her to lose one point of constitution, which would make her just too fragile. The others used mostly melee-based attacks and weren't really suitable.

I took a deep breath. "Donut, I know you're not excited about it. But I really think you should go with the Artist Alley Mogul class. It's not perfect, but it's the most well-rounded."

"Okay," she said.

I exchanged a look with Mordecai to see if he was buying it. He appeared skeptical. "Really?" I said.

She approximated a shrug. "We gotta do what's best for the team, right? You want me to be a nerd, I'll be a nerd."

DONUT: CARL, ARE YOU SURE ABOUT THIS? HE IS GOING TO
     BE REALLY MAD.
CARL: Do it.

"Okay, then," Mordecai said. "The menu is going to pop up now, and you have to scroll down and choose it."

Donut glowed for a moment. A moment later, she glowed again. "Done. I am now a stupid Artist Alley Mogul."

"Goddamnit, Donut!" Mordecai cried. "God-fucking-damnit!"

"And scene," Donut said, waving her paw.

"Whoa," I said. Mongo stirred in my arms. "What's happening?"

"Mordecai, dear, that's Carl's line. You should pick something else. Carl, he's upset because I chose the Former Child Actor class. I was acting! Isn't it great?"

"That not acting," I said. "It's called lying."

"It wasn't a lie. Not technically. I picked the Artist Alley Mogul as my third-floor specialty. It's basically the same thing anyway, so I don't see why he's so upset. It said I received all the benefits except the 25% discount. Or the *Shield* spell. Or that Pathfinder skill."

"That's like all of the usable benefits, Donut." I sighed. "At least your charisma is now higher. And you have that Cockroach skill."

"And I'm immune to poison and disease!"

"Yeah," Mordecai said drily. "And you've received the manager benefit."

"Oh yeah," I said. "What *is* that?"

I already knew exactly what the manager benefit was. Odette had explained it in detail.

"That's me," Mordecai said. "*I'm* the manager. From now on, for the remainder of your time in this godsforsaken place, I will instantly teleport to any safe room you are in."

"Yay!" Donut cried.

"No, not yay," Mordecai said. "I was supposed to transfer to a magic guild after this floor. I *like* running the magic guild. My room gets bigger, and I have access to my potions and more spells. Now every time you sleep or eat or stop to brush your teeth, I'll be forced to spend my time with you. Away from my room and my clothes and food. Oh gods, and I've lost my tunnel access. No more television. No more access to the information codex. And since I can no longer watch you stumbling around the dungeon, I will have no warning for when I'm to be teleported away. And if you buy a personal space . . ." He started grumbling under his breath.

"That wasn't cool, Donut," I said.

DONUT: I TOLD YOU HE'D BE MAD. I DON'T LIKE PEOPLE MAD
     AT ME, CARL.
CARL: Yeah, he's pissed. Sorry about that.

"If you do pick the manager benefit, and it's not attached to an obvious choice, you'll want to make it look like a mistake," Odette had said. "Don't ask him about it, because once he tells you what it is, it'll be too late. He won't be allowed to tell you unless you ask. Make it look like it was all Donut's idea, and you didn't have anything to do with it. Mordecai can hold a grudge, but he still sees Donut as a child. He'll forgive her. If he ever found out you did this on purpose, he would never forgive you."

"What if that manager benefit is attached to a class that isn't as good?" I said. "I like having him around, but it doesn't seem like that great of a trade-off if it hobbles Donut."

"There's a lot he can't tell you or help you with as a game guide. As a manager, that's all out the window. He'll lose access to the codex, and everything he tells you will have to be from his own memory. But Mordecai has been in the dungeon for a very long time, and that brain of his is the single greatest resource any crawler can have. As long as he *wants* to help you, it'll be the next best thing to having him in the party. He'll be able to use the chat feature. He is an alchemical master. Get him in front of an alchemy table, and he'll be able to make you potions. Surely you can see the benefit in that."

I did, indeed, see the benefit in it. So we'd decided to take Odette's advice. I didn't like lying or tricking Mordecai. He was as close to a friend as I could get with an alien, and I knew this could irreparably harm that trust and friendship if he ever found out. Furthermore, I didn't trust Odette. We now owed her, and she potentially held something over us. But I did trust that she wanted us to survive for as long as possible.

After quickly discussing it with Donut, we'd decided the risk was worth it. We would pick that benefit if it was available.

Mordecai's well-chiseled face groused. His smoldering eyes focused on Donut. "Well, congratulations, Crawler. You are now Princess Donut the Level 13 Former Child Actor Cat. Welcome to the third fucking floor."

Mordecai glared at me.

"Your turn," he said.

2

MORDECAI TOOK A DEEP BREATH, AND I WATCHED HIM CALM himself.

"Okay," he said. "Let's take a look at your race selections, Carl."

I sat on the bed. I'd transferred the still-sleeping Mongo to the seat. Donut sat next to the baby velociraptor and rested a paw on his tiny head.

Lines and lines populated the screen.

"It looks as if you have 398 choices. That's a good amount," the incubus said.

I focused on the line of the three AI-recommended choices and laughed.

Hobgoblin.
Human.

and

Sasquatch.

"Huh, that's odd," Mordecai said. "I've never seen the system recommend the existing race before."

"The AI loves Carl's tootsies," Donut said.

Mordecai made a face. He opened his mouth as if to say something, then closed it.

I clicked on the first one, the Hobgoblin.

A spinning 3D model of a large creature appeared in the air. It was basically a large, more muscular goblin, but with festering sores on its face. My stomach lurched at the sight of the monster, and for the first time, what was happening here really hit me.

I can say the word, and I will turn into that thing. Forever. Holy shit.

"Ew," Donut said. "Carl, you are not picking that. If you're going to change, you should pick what he chose." She waved at Mordecai. "An incubus. Or a Changeling. Yes, a Changeling! You can alter yourself to fit my current class. Carl, wouldn't that be great?"

"Neither of those are on the list," I said. I didn't like the idea of the Changeling anyway. Mordecai had said—like with Donut's Character Actor skill—the facsimile wasn't always as good as the original. Extreme versatility came with a price.

Hobgoblin.

This limited race is only available to crawlers who have obtained a level five Explosives Handling skill by the time race selection becomes available.

A Hobgoblin is what happens when a lady troll manages to get a goblin drunk enough to talk herself into his pants. Large, muscular, and smart, Hobgoblins excel at trap making, explosives management, and all-out mayhem. Unfortunately, these guys are so ugly, even Gorgons lose their lunch looking upon them. This race is best suited for Rogue- and Fighter-based classes.

Automatic +3 to all trap-based and explosive-based skills.

+5% faster skill progression in all trap-based and explosive-based skills.

Unlocks higher-tier explosives and trap-making abilities, allowing one to raise these skills to 20.

Free access to all Hobgoblin Sapper Workshops.

−5 to Charisma. Charisma is capped at 10.

+1 to Dexterity.

+2 to Intelligence.

Adds the Regeneration skill. (Already obtained via Trollskin Shirt)

This was a good race. In fact, it was almost perfect for the build I had in my mind. But there was no way I was going to turn myself into that thing. Absolutely not. The bonuses were great, but I would lose all of our viewers. They really were ugly. And not cute ugly like Mongo. These guys were genuinely unsettling to look at.

I was curious what the system had to say about humans.

Human.
    You're already a human. I'm going to go out on a limb here and guess you don't need a description. If you choose this, nothing will change. Except for these racial benefits:
    +2 to all base stats.
    Adaptability. +2% faster skill progression.
    Choosing this race unlocks multiple exclusive Earth-based classes.

I cringed a little as I clicked on my last choice.

A large, hairy humanoid with massive feet started spinning. It looked almost identical to the creature in those beef jerky commercials. It was a stereotypical, hair-covered bigfoot creature with fangs and a giant forehead.

Sasquatch.
    This limited race is only available to crawlers who have obtained a level five Smush skill by the time race selection becomes available.
    Bigfoot. Yeti (if you choose an ice-based class). Skunk Ape. The list of nicknames for these things is almost endless, but in the end, the result is the same. First, you take a human, you cross it with a gorilla, you make them a foot and a half taller,

cover them with hair, and then give them size 24 feet. The resulting behemoth is a monstrous melee fighter and tank.

+3 to Bash Skill.

+3 to Smush Skill.

−3 to Intelligence.

−1 to Charisma.

+6 to Strength.

+6 to Constitution.

+2 to Dexterity.

Unlocks higher-tier Smush Skill.

I eyed the spinning 3D bigfoot creature with distaste. I focused
on the creature's massive sparkling feet. That was not going to happen. I didn't want to become a joke or a fucking parody of an Earth
creature. I thought of what that orc had said, that I was the AI's pet.
No. No way.

"Advice?" I asked Mordecai.

"Keep looking," he said. "There are a few additional races available that still give you access to the exclusive Earth-based classes.
Based on Donut's offerings, it appears the Earth classes are going to
be the best ones this year."

For the next two hours, I read through every available race. There
was a wide variety of choices, from short, squat, purple-skinned little
people called Night Dwarves to tall, thin gazelle-like fighters called
Lyrx Elves to monstrous rock creatures with molten centers called
Coal Engines. There was even a finger-sized parasitic worm creature
called an Intellect Hunter. I wondered if they were the same creatures who ran the Valtay Corporation, but I was afraid to ask. They
could take over the bodies of any creature they killed, though the
bodies would immediately start to rot. Mordecai said that was
actually a solid choice, but I couldn't imagine losing myself to
that form.

Most of the creatures were fairly balanced with one another. Generally the stats adjusted for a net gain of about 10 stat points, and if

they didn't, it came with a skill bonus or a few random abilities, like night vision, the ability to fly short distances, or inherent racial spells. The exclusive races, like Hobgoblin and Sasquatch, usually added an extra bonus or two making them slightly better.

I found one odd choice hidden amongst the others. A Primal. I clicked on it, and the 3D image was empty.

Primal.

For the first several seasons of *Dungeon Crawler World*, all contestants started off as Primals. Primals are blank slates. You will look the same as before. You will obtain all skills associated with your current race, with the following exceptions:

–1 to all base stats.

All higher-tier skills are unlocked and are able to train to 20.

Choosing this race unlocks multiple exclusive Earth-based classes.

I thought about this for several moments, trying to decide if this was better or worse than a straight human.

"How hard is it to train a skill above 15?" I asked Mordecai.

"Getting skills up to 10 or 11 is relatively easy as long as you use them regularly. Look at Donut's *Magic Missile* spell. It's only the third floor, and it's already at level nine. But each level after that is a slog unless you really dedicate yourself to training. There are multiple ways to train skills up. There are guilds, equipment boosts, expensive potions, and unreliable spells. If you get a particularly generous sponsor, they might grant you something that'll also raise a skill. But it can be done with dedication and a lot of strategic planning. Every season, a few crawlers choose this race. It usually doesn't pay off. Only a rare few crawlers manage to train one or two skills above 15."

"Is it worth it, to get a skill above 15?"

"Absolutely," he said. "A level 15 *Fireball* is a powerful spell that can ruin the day of most mobs. A level 16 *Fireball* is literally four

times as potent. A level 20 can turn a mountain into an active volcano. If you manage to train one of your punching skills above 15,
you will be unstoppable. But you'd have to get there first. If you
choose this instead of human, you'll miss out on the extra 10 stat
points you obtain, and you'll lose five additional points. It's like starting five levels behind. That's a big deal. But it's not insurmountable.
It's well worth it if you plan your build carefully and dedicate yourself to a few core skills."

"Let me ask you something else," I said. "The Maestro guy gifted
something called a Legendary Skill Potion to Maggie during his
show. Are those things common?"

"I can't . . ." He paused, looking at Donut. His expression soured,
as if he just remembered everything had changed thanks to that
Manager skill. "They're not common at all, and if you can find one
for sale somewhere, it would cost many million gold. If that Maggie
crawler has half a brain, she'll sell it. But during the Faction Wars
segment on the ninth floor, each clan can bring a war chest of supplies. That's a specific unit of measurement based on volume. Each
clan will usually fill these chests with such potions and magical rings
and other small but powerful items. I'll have to explain how that
works later."

"So, they'll have a bunch of these potions?"

"The ninth floor is going to open up in about a half hour. And
about fifteen minutes after that, most of those potions will have already been used up. But not all of them. Again, it's a lot to explain."

"What's your take?" I asked. "Human or Primal?"

"You *should* pick Hobgoblin or Coal Engine, but both will probably lose you viewers. People hate hobgoblins. Interviewers don't like
them on their shows."

I looked over at Donut, who had fallen asleep. She'd curled up
with Mongo.

"What is a Primal anyway?" I asked. "It doesn't say. Is it just
something made up for the dungeon?"

"Yes and no," Mordecai said. "The Primals are the progenitors, the first known species to conquer the universe. They are the boogey-men of the cosmos. Nobody knows what they looked like or any-thing about them other than that they spread across the galaxy, and then one day, they just vanished. There was a great war that spanned all corners of the galaxies. We can see the remnants of the battles. If they were fighting a species other than themselves, we don't know who they were. When someone comes across an abandoned remnant of their civilization, the resident AI, if it is still sane, usually takes the form of the race of the species who discovered it. That is why they look like whoever chooses them. It is said one day they will re-turn. Mothers call upon Primals to instill fear into their young ones. Some systems worship them as gods."

I opened up the menu, scrolled all the way to the bottom, and I picked **Primal** as my race.

MY LIST OF AVAILABLE CLASSES CONSISTED OF OVER 650 CHOICES.

"You'd have even more if you didn't have that tattoo on your neck," Mordecai said.

"Why? And what sort of classes are excluded?"

"The Desperado Club doesn't allow . . . What is the word? Goody Two-shoes? It doesn't allow those sorts. So no Cleric classes and Pal-adin classes," Mordecai said. "Along with a few monk classes, which is unfortunate as they would've been worth a look. But I think all three of your suggested choices are good ones."

I looked over the AI's recommended choices. All three were from the pool of Earth-based classes.

Bomb Squad Tech.
Prizefighter.

and

Compensated Anarchist.

"Hmm," I said. I pulled up each one in turn.

Bomb Squad Tech.

This exclusive class is only available to crawlers who have obtained the Boom! achievement.

People who actually choose to work with explosives are the craziest bastards around. You excel at making things blow up. And while you're good at keeping the bombs from going off in your own hands, Bomb Squad Techs still tend to lose both friends and limbs at alarming rates. Luckily this class comes with a benefit that can fix 50% of that problem.

All explosive-based traps will mark themselves as you approach.

All armor is 10% more effective.

The handling of explosives no longer degrades them.

Automatic +2 to all explosive-based skills.

+5 Bomb Surgeon skill.

+2 to Dexterity.

+2 to Constitution.

−2 to Intelligence. (After all, only dumbasses would choose to do this for a living.)

Plus the Limb Regeneration Benefit.

This is an Earth Class. As an incentive to choose an Earth Class, you will receive a Silver Earth Box upon choosing this class.

This was good, very good in fact, but it was missing some of the key benefits I was looking for. The next class had the same issues.

Prizefighter.

This exclusive class is only available to crawlers who have obtained a level five in the Pugilism skill.

This is a Monk subclass.

Sweaty, half-naked men circling each other in a ring, turning their faces into raw pulp as the crowd roars. The people in this audience don't care who is fighting whom, as long as one of them ends up a crumpled, bloody heap on the mat before the night is done. Prizefighters don't do it for the glory, or for honor. They do it to put food on the table. It's nothing personal.

Prizefighters receive the following benefits:

+5 to Constitution.

+2 to Strength.

−2 to Intelligence.

−2 to Charisma.

+3 to the Pugilism Skill.

+1 to the Unarmed Combat Skill.

+1 to the Iron Punch Skill.

+5 to the Knockout Skill.

+(1 × Floor Number) gold for every mob killed with a punch.

Unlocks higher-tier Pugilism Skill benefit. (Benefit already received)

This is an Earth Class. As an incentive to choose an Earth Class, you will receive a Silver Earth Box upon choosing this class.

That +3 in Pugilism was a huge bonus, considering I'd already managed to get it to 10 thanks to that Cheat Code potion. I'd pick this class in a second if I thought I could just punch my way through the dungeon. I knew already that wasn't going to happen. I needed something that was more versatile.

I sighed and pulled up the description on the third suggested class.

Compensated Anarchist.

This rare and exclusive class is only available to crawlers who have obtained level five in the Explosives Handling skill and have received at least 500 billion views by the time they've reached the third floor.

When the oligarchs want to manufacture a social movement or, better yet, stop one in its tracks, they must first bring in the big guns. The paid protesters. The Agent Provocateur. This Monk/Rogue hybrid class is a trap-making, bomb-making, social-media dynamo. The Compensated Anarchist will happily throw a Molotov through a window one moment and step in front of a camera to plead for the violence to stop the next. Expert in hand-to-hand and dirty tactics, the Compensated Anarchist only suffers when it comes to more traditional fighting techniques.

+1 to the Bomb Surgeon Skill.

+1 to the Trap Engineer Skill.

+1 to Unarmed Combat Skill.

−25% damage when using bladed weapons.

+25% mana cost for damage-dealing spells.

+5% skill progression speed in all trap-making and bomb-making skills.

+2 Hide in Shadows Skill.

+ *Fear* spell.

+1 Intelligence.

+5 Charisma.

+5 to the Find Trap Skill.

+5 to the Backfire Skill.

+5 to the Escape Plan Skill.

Access to the Desperado Club. (Already obtained)

Access to the Naughty Boys Employment Agency.

This is an Earth Class. As an incentive to choose an Earth Class, you will receive a Silver Earth Box upon choosing this class.

Compensated Anarchists must choose a subclass upon descent to the sixth floor.

"Holy shit. That seems like a winner," I said. "This one has a ton of stuff attached to it. Though Compensated Anarchist is kind of an oxymoron. I guess that's the point."

"Yeah, all those classes with view-count minimums are usually really good. They do it on purpose to give the more popular players a boost. This one definitely seems tailored for you. Let me look deeper into it while you peruse some of the others. There's probably a few issues hidden under the hood."

I started sorting through the mass of other classes. I could hide all the ones that didn't have any special requirements, as they generally weren't nearly as good.

I didn't get very far before the world rumbled. I glanced up, surprised. The second floor had collapsed.

The new countdown appeared. We only had eight days to complete this next level.

Welcome, Crawlers, to the third floor! We have just over 700,000 crawlers remaining. You will have eight full days to complete this floor. We will have a longer announcement later, but we know most of you are currently dealing with your game guides. We are looking forward to seeing what races and classes everyone picks. We have some new, exciting classes available this season! Good luck to everyone!

"Eight days," Mordecai said, looking up at the ceiling. He shook his head. "If they keep this up, the sixth floor is only going to be open 11 or 12 days. The factions are going to be pissed. It's usually open for 30."

I went back to work. There were multiple classes that seemed really good on the surface. Many were similar to the Bomb Squad one, like **Riot Forces Support** and **Trebuchet Commander**. And a few of the non-Earth ones were interesting as well, including the **Rogue Trapmaster** and **Trickster** class.

Donut and Mongo snored loudly in unison as Mordecai and I discussed the ins and outs of each class.

"Just a warning," Mordecai said. "Donut didn't have to worry about this, but some of these classes have strict stat minimums. The charisma minimum for the Compensated Anarchist is 25. You'll have 36 points to distribute, but you'll be forced to spend 17 of them on your charisma right away, even with that plus five. And then another six to get your base dexterity up to 10, though I'd recommend that anyway."

"Yikes," I said. "That kind of sucks."

"But several of the skills that it comes with are pretty rare. The Backfire skill, for example," Mordecai said. "It allows you to pick up a trap and deconstruct it. You'll be able to use the materials for your own purposes. The triggering mechanisms alone are quite valuable. You could make a living just by farming traps."

We went over a few of the other skills. Bomb Surgeon, which came with a few of my choices, allowed me to basically take a stick of dynamite and cut it into pieces, making smaller, less potent bombs. Or I could deconstruct smoke bombs and utilize the individual parts for traps. Hide in Shadows was self-explanatory, though with Donut and Mongo in tow, I imagined it wouldn't be too useful.

Multiple classes had a Pathfinder skill, including the Trickster class. But I soon learned the Compensated Anarchist had the next best thing.

"What's this Escape Plan skill?"

Mordecai nodded, looking it over. "Odd. It looks like it's an old skill, but I've never come across it before. You learn something new every day. It shows hidden doors more readily, but more importantly, there's a secret benefit." Mordecai grunted. "You can thank your cat for this one. It says it offers access to the dungeon locator, but it doesn't say what that is or how to access it. Luckily for you, I do know how to find and read it. Before, I wouldn't have been able to tell you."

"What is it?"

"At every major intersection of the dungeon is a concealed map legend that intelligent and wandering mobs can utilize. It gives a very general overview of what's in every direction. You know how at the zoo there's arrows that say, 'Monkeys this way, lions that way'? It's the same concept. It'll point you toward exits and city bosses and so forth. It's not quite as good as the Pathfinder skill, which basically opens up the map in a very wide area, but this might be even more useful in some ways."

"Okay, what about this Naughty Boys Employment Agency?"

He shrugged. "I have no idea what that is. It sounds like a quest-giving guild."

"And the subclasses? It says I have to pick one on the sixth floor."

"We can't see what they are yet. It's pretty rare that you're required to choose one, but I've seen it a few times. You'll likely have to specialize further in one of the three skills. Bombs, traps, or hand-to-hand."

"Okay, then," I said after a moment. "So what do you think?"

"If you were in a more well-rounded party, I'd tell you to go with the Prizefighter class," Mordecai said. "If you were in an even larger group, I'd suggest the Bomb Squad. All three of those are good. The Compensated Anarchist is potentially the best, but like with your race, it requires a lot of work. You're going to need to grind and grind and focus on gaining as much experience as possible. With these shortened timers, it's going to be a lot harder."

I grinned. "I guess it's a good thing we now have a group member who knows what he's doing."

Mordecai narrowed his eyes at me as I scrolled down and picked **Compensated Anarchist** as my class.

———

I NEXT HAD TO FIGURE OUT MY STATS. DONUT ENDED UP WITH THE following:

Strength: 20.
Intelligence: 23 + 5 (Tiara) +1 (Charm) = 29.
Constitution: 4 + 2 (Brush) = 6.
Dexterity: 12 + 2 (Crupper) +2 (Bracelet) +5 (temp. floor bonus) = 21.
Charisma: 70.

Her strength had taken a minus-three hit, but her dexterity had risen by four, her constitution by two, and her charisma by another single point thanks to her cat racial choice. Her constitution was still worryingly low. Finding items to get that up would be one of our first priorities.

She'd only gained a net of four stat points by choosing the cat race, but she had received a ton of new skills. **Night Vision, Slash Attack, Catlike Reflexes,** and a benefit called **9 Lives.**

The 9 Lives benefit was similar to her Cockroach skill, but it wasn't as good. It halved the damage received for the first nine physical attacks she received per day. That was helpful, especially considering her low constitution. But if we were going to be facing superpowerful monsters, a half attack would still likely cut her in half.

She eventually awakened. "What'd I miss? Did you grow elf ears?" She looked me up and down. "You're still human. That's boring."

"I'm not human. I'm a Primal."

"Is that like a caveman?" She made a show of sniffing me. "You smell the same."

"If you had remained awake, you would have learned what all this meant."

She shrugged and stretched. Mongo yawned loudly, also stretching. He made a purring noise that sounded suspiciously catlike.

I was going to have to continue to be the party's tank. I received three stat points on level up, and I had a pool of 36 points, though more than half of them were chosen for me thanks to the class's minimums. After everything settled, I ended up with the following:

Strength: 10 + 3 (Toe Ring) = 13 +3 (When Gauntlet Formed).
   Intelligence: 5.
   Constitution: 10 + 4 (Shirt) +1 (Ring) +2 (Ring) +2 (Boxers) = 19.
   Dexterity: 10 + 1 (Gauntlet) = 11.
   Charisma: 25.

I'd given myself enough intelligence to read that *Wisp Armor* spell book, but I didn't do it quite yet. I was still on the fence about using it for myself, giving it to Donut, or selling it. I wanted to see what its actual monetary value was first. The *Fear* spell I now had cost three points to cast.

I wasn't too happy yet with this build. Donut was still way more powerful than me. For the hundredth time in as many seconds, I wondered if I was an idiot for choosing this path. I'd been forced to spend a ton on charisma. The stat was mostly useless, especially since Donut was already deity-like with hers. I was going to have to level as quickly as possible. In my head, I originally was hoping for much more strength and constitution. From now on, all my points were going to go into those two until their base was at least 20.

Donut had ended up with a skill set that allowed her to pretty much make it up as she went along. My chosen path required very deliberate planning and rigorous training. But if I managed to excel—and survive—I could mold myself into something very powerful. *Was* I an idiot? I knew some people would definitely think so.

"Only one thing is going to make this work," Mordecai said. It seemed as if he'd been reading my mind.

"Training?" I asked.

"No," he said. "Money. And lots of it. Come on. Let's go outside." He started buttoning his tuxedo shirt back up. "Where did I put that tie? Oh, there it is."

"Wait, you can leave your room?"

"Of course I can leave my room. I'm your manager now. Plus I have to present you two. It's part of the whole deal." He straightened his bow tie and rubbed the front of his jacket.

"Technically you're *my* manager," Donut grumbled. Mongo screeched.

That was actually a good point, but neither Mordecai nor I wanted to broach that subject just yet. He ignored it for now. "I'm not allowed to directly fight with you, but I can still occasionally step outside. Especially on the urban levels. Let's go. I'm going to present you, and then I need to show you something. Carl first, then Donut and Mongo."

All of us stood and lined up at the door. He opened it with a flourish.

When we'd entered the room, we'd been in a long golden hallway with tall walls. But now spread before us was a bustling village with dozens of creatures of all types walking about. The stenches of sulfur and smoke filled the polluted air. Dozens of medieval-style shops filled the area. The ground appeared to be made of wooden slats with wide spaces in some areas. Smoke drifted lazily from the holes. Above, on the fake ceiling, a blazing red sun rose, filling the area with a crimson-hued light.

Mordecai looked out at the village. None of the denizens gave him any heed. He waved for me to step outside, and I did. My feet echoed on the slats. The temperature out here was much higher than the previous level.

"I'd like to present Dungeon Crawler Carl, the level 13 Compensated Anarchist Primal. Welcome, Carl, to the third floor."

3

"THIS IS CALLED THE OVER CITY," MORDECAI SAID AS WE WALKED along the wooden street. My minimap was awash in the white dots of NPCs. Mordecai's dot had turned to a yellow star. A few blue dots of other crawlers were scattered about, but not many. "Where you exited the second floor has no bearing on where you enter this floor. It is completely random, so you will now be mixed in with crawlers from around the world."

"So Brandon and crew could be anywhere?" I asked. "How big is this place?"

Donut sat on my shoulder and Mongo stood on her back, like we were a goddamned vaudeville act. With my increased strength, I barely felt their presence. Many of the NPCs stopped and gawked at us as we passed. Most of the NPCs in this area were humanoid dwarves, but a mix of regular humans and orcs and elf-like creatures also walked about. All wore medieval-style clothing. Large armored guards with obscured faces also strolled about.

"Yes, they could be anywhere," Mordecai said. "Their location is based on the location of their game guide. You can talk to them directly, but they probably don't know where they are in relation to you. They had someone called Mistress Tiatha as their guide. I don't know her that well, but I can try to figure out where she is if you'd like."

"Is this one giant city?"

He nodded. "The Over City levels are a tradition in *Dungeon Crawler World*. There are hundreds of small scattered villages surrounded by wide swaths of abandoned city. It's all connected. As far as you're concerned, these urban areas appear every three levels." He stomped his foot on the rickety ground. "Most of this is just window dressing. You're still below the surface of your planet. That isn't really the sky of some distant world. There isn't really a massive volcano under our feet."

"Volcano?" I asked, looking down.

"We'll get to that. Think of this as a stage set for the benefit of the viewers. This and all the following floors will be significantly smaller than the first two, with the exception of the ninth floor. This one is probably about the size of the state of Arizona. About 300,000 square kilometers. Most of that is the ruins."

"What about these NPCs?" I asked.

A pair of dwarven girls, no older than teenagers, was practically swooning at the sight of Mordecai. They said something, trying to get his attention. He growled at them, and they scattered, giggling.

"Oh, they're very real. They are living biological creatures similar to some of the mobs. Most have been engineered by the Borant Corporation, and therefore are owned by the Borant Corporation. This is the only world they know and have ever known."

"That's really fucked-up. Do they know what they are?"

"Their minds are altered every time they are regenerated. The next time this floor is formed on some distant planet, these NPCs will wake up like it is just another day. But they will have also been changed, planted with false memories. Inconvenient memories—like some crawler sitting them down and explaining to them that they're props on an intergalactic television series—will be erased. Take those goblins you told me about, for instance. They were addicted to meth. They were fighting the llamas over it. That storyline didn't exist in the previous season. That was added for this world and this world only. Next time they'll be addicted to solar berry extract or something like that. Or they'll be fanatics of some god. Or something else."

"What the hell?" I asked. That was just as bad as, and in some ways worse than, what they were doing to me and my fellow humans. "But these are still living creatures? How is that legal?"

"Borant created them, so they own them. One can't alter the memories of naturals. People who were born in a natural biological process. Not unless they sign away their rights."

"And people are okay with this?"

"Most are. The galaxy, as a whole, has plenty of other things to worry about. The rules regarding this stuff are pretty strict, almost as strict as those regarding AIs. These biologically printed mobs and NPCs are not allowed to exist outside of a Syndicate-monitored production. Using them for any purpose other than sanctioned entertainment is highly illegal. It's basically considered a war crime."

"So, there are no intergalactic brothels filled with genetically engineered women?"

Mordecai grimaced. "Not legal ones. But there is one place where such things do exist legally." He pointed down.

"But you said . . ." The realization struck me. "Oh, so the deeper floors?"

"That's right," Mordecai said. "This third floor won't have any tourists on it. Most of them are on the 18th floor. It's like a billionaire's luxury retreat. The galaxy's rich and elite congregate on the 18th floor to party and gamble and satiate their most base desires."

"I don't understand," I said. "I assumed the 18th floor would be hell on Earth filled with dragons and lightning giants and shit. What would happen if a crawler managed to get there?"

"Nobody ever has," Mordecai said. "So, I don't know. The same with the 15th floor. Borant and the system AI are required to have a plan in place, but nobody has ever gotten that deep, so nobody knows. That sort of thing is way above my pay grade."

As we walked, we passed multiple shops and guildhalls and inns. The inns were listed as safe rooms on my minimap.

Mordecai spent some time explaining class and skill guildhalls. Donut and I both could train at Rogue guildhalls. Donut also had

access to Bard halls, and I would have access to Fighter halls. Sometimes there would be special halls for certain races, too. He said he'd
never seen a Primal hall, but it was possible it existed. Quadrupeds
generally didn't have halls.

We reached the end of the street, where a small fence had been
erected. A pair of the well-armored guards stood by a small gate
about as high as my waist. The two guards were decked head to toe
in plate mail, and I couldn't tell what sort of creatures they were,
only that they were bulky and tall. Each was armed with a long steel
blade. I examined one.

> Village Guard Swordsman—Level 75.
> Everyone likes the strong, silent type. In order to find out
> what's underneath that helmet, you'll have to first kill the guard.
> Go ahead and give it a try. I double-dog dare you.
> Village Guards are tasked with protecting the population
> centers of the third floor from the creatures who roam the Over
> City Ruins. They are only on duty when the sun is up, so don't
> go whining to them for help when it's dark.

The guard was unmoving. He stood there like a statue.

"He's kind of scary," Donut said as we paused at the gate.

"Don't mess with the guards," Mordecai said. "Don't attack the
NPCs. Don't try to rob the stores. Don't get drunk and pass out in
the streets. There is no jail here. Only the death penalty. If you run
afoul of the guards, don't try to fight them. They are slow, but there
are a lot of them. Run from them and into the ruins. They won't
follow you there. You will never be able to return to that particular
village."

Beyond the gate were more buildings, but they were decrepit and
abandoned, made of crumbling, moss-covered bricks slumping in on
themselves. A rolling fog obscured the distance, but even in the
shadows of the fog, I could see faint buildings of all shapes and sizes.

"Okay," Mordecai said, indicating the area beyond the gate. "The ruins. It's the same as the dungeon, but it's all old, rotting buildings, abandoned and overgrown parks, and so forth. There's this whole storyline about the existence of the city. It's all based on a children's story that never made it into your Earth's culture. Basically, there's this massive dormant volcano, and a magical world existed solely inside of the volcano. That world consisted of six layers. The very top layer is where we are now, the Over City. It is where most of the people lived. A great monster lived at the bottom of the volcano and breathed out poison gas one day and killed or transformed 90% of the volcano world. The descendants of the survivors live in these villages. The resulting monsters live in the ruins."

"That's quite morbid," Donut said.

"So, we're on top of a volcano right now? In the game's story, I mean?" I asked.

"Yes. This floor is supposed to span the length of the volcano's crater."

"What's the next level down?" I asked.

"For you, the fourth level is just a random dungeon level. Same with the fifth. But the sixth floor is also part of this volcano city storyline. For the NPCs here, it is the next level down. It is called the Hunting Grounds. It's another urban level with similar villages, though the villages are much bigger, and the original residents were much wealthier. The ruins are junglelike and filled with vines. And it's the first level where brave and insane tourists can go to hunt crawlers. Not too many do it because it's both expensive and dangerous. There are no protections for the hunters. They're in real danger from both the mobs and the crawlers, and every season a handful of rich dumbasses get themselves killed."

"What about gods?"

"That's a whole different thing, and those don't appear until the fourth floor. I'll explain that later. For now you need to get to work."

"Okay," I said, turning back to the village. "There are shops here. Should we go shopping now? And should we open our boxes now?"

"Yes, shopping," Donut said. "Definitely shopping."

"Not here," Mordecai said. "This is a small village. These shops are overpriced and will gouge you and won't buy any of your items. You need to get yourself to a larger settlement, and there's very little time." He pointed east. "See that wider road there? Follow it for about a half day, and you'll come across a bigger village. It will have better, richer shops."

"How do you know?" I asked.

Mordecai pointed at a discolored rock on the ground just outside the gate. "Focus on that, and select the tooltip that pops up."

I did as he asked. "Holy shit," I said a minute later.

A holographic sign popped up, growing out of the ground like a tree. It showed arrows with signs and distances in kilometers. Pointing north along the main road it read, **MEDIUM-SIZED SKYFOWL SETTLEMENT. 34 KILOMETERS.** There were other signs, too, pointing to safe rooms, restrooms, and most importantly, stairs. The closest set of stairs was six kilometers away.

"There are safe rooms in the ruins? We don't have to rely on the villages? And do the villages have names?"

"Yes. The safe rooms and restrooms will be scattered the same as before. There will *not* be tutorial guilds in the ruins. Only in the villages. Not that it matters, as I'll teleport to the safe rooms anyway. Also, the villages don't have names. The system designates them as tiny, small, medium, large, and extra large. Not very exciting. This one is small. You can actually name them yourself if you manage to kill the mayor. Don't bother, at least on this floor. You'll likely end up dead, and it doesn't come with any real benefits when the timer is only eight days."

"Okay," I said. "So, I guess we'll grind our way to that other village."

He nodded. "Make sure you check out the signs every once in a while to make sure you're still on the correct track. All medium villages on this floor will have a tutorial guild. Meet me there. When you get there, we'll hit some shops together."

"Will the monsters be a lot harder on this floor?"

"Oh yeah," Mordecai said, grinning sheepishly. "I should probably tell you this part. It's hard to remember without my checklist. There is night and there is day on this floor. There will always be monsters in the ruins. They are more dangerous at night. The daytime ones should be cake for you two, but you might want to keep Mongo back at first. Don't go out at night until I say you're ready. The villages will always be safe during the day. At night, only the village main roads are safe. Usually. The alleys will be very dangerous. In some cases, more dangerous than the ruins." He flapped his incubus wings a few times and looked directly at me. "Stay away from girls with horns on their heads. Your charisma is a lot higher than it was before, and they are attracted to that. They will be coming out of the woodwork at you. Work on your punching skills, and use that new *Fear* spell every single fight. Remember to stop at a safe room to open your boxes and so Donut can get her next spell book from the Book of the Floor Club."

"I forgot about that!" Donut said.

Mordecai turned and started walking back into the village. He was making a beeline straight for a pub. He called over his shoulder, "Don't stop at the first safe room you find, though. Give it at least two hours. Maybe four. And, Donut, keep working on that *Magic Missile* spell. You're almost at skill level 10. I'll be on chat if you need me."

"If I had known he was going to be so bossy, I wouldn't have picked that manager benefit," Donut muttered.

"Shut up, Donut," I said under my breath as I lifted the latch to the small gate that led out into the ruins. It opened with a noisy screech. The two guards didn't move a muscle. We wandered out into the streets, leaving the safety of the village behind.

4

Views: 371.5 Trillion
Followers: 7.8 Trillion
Favorites: 1.1 Trillion

DONUT WORKED ON MONGO'S TRAINING WHILE WE WALKED ALONG the road. I pulled a stick from my inventory and tossed it. She was working on getting him to stay put until she told him to go fetch it. He was about 80% of the way there already. The problem was, when he got too excited, he absolutely refused to listen to orders.

Donut stopped at the first restroom we found. She went inside, and the little dinosaur went berserk at the door, attacking and scratching at it and screaming at the top of his lungs until Donut came out.

"You need to learn patience, Mongo!" Donut said. "Follow Mommy's example."

"Yeah, because you're known for your patience," I said.

I marveled at the ceiling as we walked. It was much, much higher here than it'd been in the hallway. Some of these buildings were four stories tall. In the smoky distance, some were even taller than that. But I could still tell the sky was but an illusion. Lights reflected off it oddly, revealing the façade.

ZEV: Hello, hello.

DONUT: HI, ZEV!

ZEV: Hi, Donut! Good news, you two. Odette's show was another hit. But more importantly, the majority of viewers are giving thumbs-up to your choices for class and race. A few people have expressed confusion as to why Donut chose Artist Alley as this floor's selection, but generally people like the idea of the Former Child Actor class. A couple people are grumbling that it doesn't allow for growth, but most seem to believe it's offset by Carl picking something that requires such rigorous training. Also, so far both of you have picked unique classes. Nobody else out there has chosen them. That's always a plus. There are a few other Primals out there, but not many. No straight cats, though someone chose a were-cat race. And there are a few cat girls walking around. It's still early. A lot of crawlers haven't picked yet.

Donut looked absolutely scandalized. I laughed.

CARL: Good to know, Zev. Question. Can people see Mordecai now?

ZEV: No, not generally. They know you have a manager, and they got to see him when he introduced you into the world. But from now on, it's how it was before. By the way, I checked, and no VIP crawlers are nearby as far as I can tell. I'd avoid adding any of the close-by locals to your party. They're all too boring.

DONUT: WHAT IS THE NEXT SHOW WE ARE GOING ON?

ZEV: So, this floor is eight days. I'm still in negotiations with a few programs. It'll likely be during the fourth night, but I haven't locked in an interview yet. I've had to take in a few extra people just to field all the interview requests.

CARL: Okay, thank you, Zev.

ZEV: Ta-ta for now.

DONUT: BYE, ZEV!

"What is a cat girl?" Donut asked. "I don't like that. And a were-cat? Whoever that is needs to just learn to commit."

"Watch out," I cried, jumping back. A knife bounced off my

chest, clattering harmlessly to the ground. I looked up at the creature who'd thrown the blade, a monkey wearing a painted human skull as a mask.

Former Circus Lemur—Level 8.

Grimaldi's Traveling Circus was one of the Over City's favorite attractions before that fateful day so long ago. Hundreds of years later, the feral and transformed descendants of that circus still stalk the ruins, seeking out adults and children alike to dazzle and entertain.

And by "dazzle and entertain," we mean "devour the flesh from their bones and use their remains as armor."

Grimaldi's Amazing Juggling Lemurs were one of the circus's key attractions. Children from all over the realm would laugh and clap as they watched these funny little creatures juggle all manner of items, from balls to pins to knives.

You can probably guess where this is going.

The red-furred monkey thing—apparently a lemur—was wearing a black-and-red-painted human skull as a mask. It'd appeared in the second-floor window of a dilapidated building. It was just sitting on the window ledge, little legs dangling off. He hadn't appeared as a dot on my minimap until after he'd thrown the knife, which he'd tossed directly at my head. Luckily the knife flew low and hit me in the chest, bouncing off my jacket thanks to my cloak's anti-piercing benefit.

"Oh fuck," I cried as four more lemurs appeared in the window. Donut and I jumped into an alley as more knives sliced through the air. Two of them embedded in the wooden floorboards.

Mongo screeched in rage, and Donut yelled for the dinosaur not to rush out into the street.

I prepared a smoke bomb as I examined the map, figuring out the best way to get to them. There were no windows facing the alley, but they'd figure out where we were in a minute. An unsettling throaty roar filled the streets, followed by an answering call from several blocks down. There was a lot more than just five of them. I put the smoke bomb away and pulled out one of my boom jugs.

Admin Notice. A new tab is available in your interface. Quests.

"The hell?" I said.

A musical chime, like trumpets blaring, filled the air. It only lasted a second. Sparkles and illusionary streamers danced at the edges of my vision.

New Quest. The Show Must Go On.

The words appeared spinning in the air, slamming into place in front of me, like the title of an old-school television special. Sparkles cascaded off the word "Quest."

You've discovered the remnants of an ancient circus. Hundreds of years after the toxic cloud that devastated the Over City, this traveling circus endures. But instead of joy and laughter and cotton candy, it now delivers devastation and pain. Their cotton candy is probably really gross by now, too. Find out why this circus still exists and put an end to its reign of terror.

Reward: You will receive a Gold Quest Box.

"What the fuck is this?" I said. "A quest?" Mordecai had mentioned quests once or twice, but we'd never talked about them.

CARL: Mordecai. We just walked into a quest. Should we stay
    here and try to figure it out?
MORDECAI: You should try to figure out your face.
CARL: What?

MORDECAI: Mom loved him more. Well, who's the dead one
    now? I'm glad that cat used her ashes as a bathroom.

"What's wrong with Mordecai?" Donut asked.

CARL: Are you drunk? It's been like 15 minutes!
MORDECAI: Did you know incubi have a very low tolerance
    for . . .
CARL: Mordecai?

He didn't answer.

"Shit. It looks like we're doing this on our own," I said. We
couldn't stay here. I pointed across the street to the next alley down.
There was a safe room about three blocks over. "Get ready to run."

I jumped from around the corner. My plan was to try to toss the
boom jug through the window, but I now saw multiple lemurs on
the building's roof. I added a bit of extra *oompf* to the toss, arcing it
high. I pulled myself back into the alley and crouched low as more
knives slammed into the ground. The jug detonated, and the building against my back shuddered. High-pitched, frenzied screams rose,
and I could feel the heat from the building.

A flaming lemur leaped from above and landed in the alley. I
punted it, and it flew across the street, flying way farther than I expected. It cracked into the stone wall of a building. Behind us, more
flaming lemurs started to fall from the roof.

"Run," I cried.

We rushed from the alley, crossing the street. Multiple red dots
appeared behind us. The entire top of the now-engulfed building
was filled with the X's of dead lemurs.

"Goddamnit, Mongo," I cried at the little dinosaur as he broke
away and headed right for the now-dead lemur I'd punted. He
screeched, jumping through the air legs first, and executed a perfect
pounce onto the corpse. The dinosaur growled with glee as scorched
lemur fur went flying. I altered course to grab him.

The dino chicken howled in rage as I scooped him up. A knife bounced off the bricks inches from my head. I hazarded a look over my shoulder, and I stopped dead at the sight.

A giraffe. A goddamned giraffe ran down the street at us.

The giant animal was covered in lemurs who clung onto its neck like it was a tree trunk. The giraffe was about a block away. It bent its neck, then swung it, flinging a dozen of the lemurs into the air in our direction. One of the little monkey things was flung too high, and he bounced off the rocky ceiling with a crunch. He plummeted to the ground, smashing into the wooden street.

The remaining lemurs screamed as they flew, brandishing shining knives as more knives flew at us from the windows of the now-burning building. I ducked, but most of the blades clattered onto the street, flung from too far away. The giraffe-riding lemurs landed and pulled more knives from bandoliers draped across their shoulders. They bounded sideways toward us, howling in a deep, guttural screech.

"Control your damn chicken!" I cried, dropping Mongo to the ground as I pulled a smoke bomb. I lit it and dropped it as we turned down the alley and fled. We rushed to the next street over and crossed, then entered another alleyway, this one much tighter than the last.

"Mongo, follow!" Donut cried as she leaped to my shoulder. She landed backward and fired a pair of magic missiles. Mongo screeched and flapped his little arms, but he kept up with us, running along at my left side.

This next street, the last one before the safe room, held a single red dot in the center. I pulled another smoke bomb and tossed it ahead of me.

"Hit it with a missile as we cross!"

Smoke filled the street ahead of us, but it caught on a breeze, blowing in the wrong direction. *Shit. These things suck.* At the last moment, I remembered Mordecai's advice that I use my *Fear* spell as much as possible.

We rushed into the street, and I cast *Fear* just as Donut shot a full-powered magic missile. My breath caught in my throat at the sight of the creature.

Warning: Scary-ass mobs are immune to *Fear* effects.

My first impression was *Slender Man*. Slender Man dressed as a clown. Holy shit.

Donut's missile flew low, but I realized that was on purpose. She hit it in the leg, and it toppled over. As the clown creature fell, its description popped up.

Terror the Clown—Level 10.
It's okay if you just pissed yourself. You wouldn't be the first.
Standing just over 11 feet tall, the clown-on-stilts was always a favorite amongst the snot-nosed kiddos visiting Grimaldi's three-ring circus. Now, ravaged by time and the curse of the Over City, the once-affable stilt-clowns have been transformed into tall, bloodthirsty monstrosities who want nothing more than to make balloon animals out of your intestines.

The monster was humanoid, but with splotchy bone white skin, no eyes or nose, and a red tooth-filled mouth that was much too large. It wore tattered and bloody clown clothes over its emaciated frame. Its extra-long arms hung almost to the ground. It held a giant butcher knife in each hand. It wore a red curly-haired wig and a little hat with a flower.

Donut had shot it directly below the knee. It flew onto its back, throwing a massive red shoe into the air. Blood gushed from the wound. The place she'd hit should have been a stilt, but it appeared the monster's legs actually were that long.

A health bar appeared, but the magic missile had only taken about 20% of its health.

After a quick glance at the minimap—the lemurs were still a

block away—I sprinted toward the monster as Donut pumped it with two more missiles.

"Watch its arms!" I cried as I formed a fist. Donut leaped from my shoulder.

"Sic 'em!" she yelled as she skidded to the ground.

Mongo and I both leaped into the air. I landed on the clown's chest as Mongo screamed and started tearing at the prone clown's ankle just above the shoe.

The clown's chest caved in with a *crack* as I landed. It felt as if I'd just crunched into a wooden pallet that had splintered under my weight. I fell to a knee and pulled my hand back to punch.

Another missile crashed into the clown's rising arm as I punched it in the face as hard as I could. Its neck snapped back. A long forked tongue lolled out. The little hat went flying, and the red wig fell off. I pounded again and again until its head caved in.

A mass of red dots was getting closer, and they'd be here in fifteen seconds. I pulled up the clown's inventory:

Clown Meat.
    Big Top Ticket.
    35 Gold.

I looted it all, plus both of the oversized butcher knives, the red wig, and the little hat. Mongo remained at the clown's ankle, tearing at the skin and growling like a dog with a bone. I bent to pick him up, and I realized he'd gotten noticeably larger. I picked him up anyway, and he squealed in rage. I put him back down a foot away.

"Tell him to follow us," I said as I turned toward the next alley. "Hurry."

"Mongo, come!" Donut cried.

This alley curved into a small labyrinth dotted with doors and stone walls. The safe room appeared to be a tavern about fifty meters down a dead-end alley. A sign hung in front of the tavern, naming it THE BELLY-RUBBED PUG. A pug in a top hat and a suit appeared on the sign. I worriedly watched the wave of red dots swarm into the main street as I pushed open the door and ran inside.

———

UNLIKE THE SAFE ROOMS FROM THE PREVIOUS TWO FLOORS, THIS appeared to actually be some sort of Renaissance-fair-style pub. The three television screens remained, and the general layout was similar to the manned safe rooms. A Bopca Protector stood behind the counter, looking at us with curiosity as we entered.

The first thing I noticed was that the sleeping rooms—there were only five available—now cost money to rent. Ten gold a night, which was nothing. Between Donut and me, we now had almost ten grand in gold. The food cost money as well, but it appeared to be equally inexpensive.

I kept my eye on the red dots to see if they would follow us into the alley. If they knew we were in here, we'd have a problem. They didn't appear to have seen where we'd gone.

I moved to the counter to order a drink. I needed one bad.

Thwum.

Mordecai teleported into the room, standing just to the side of the main bar. He stood with his pants down to his knees, eyes closed. "Now, ladies," he said, his voice slurring heavily. "One at a time. Granny first. There's plenty of Mordecai to . . ." He trailed off. He opened an eye, looking upon us.

"My good sir, I must ask you to sheath your sword immediately!" the Bopca cried. "This is a family establishment!"

I glanced over at the gnome. His name was Gordo.

Mordecai quickly pulled up his pants. He was still in his tuxedo, but the tie and jacket were gone. His barbed tail got caught on the edge of his belt, and he couldn't pull his pants up all the way. He awkwardly fed the tail through the pants and fastened himself. He stood there swaying. I could smell the alcohol wafting off of him.

It'd been twenty minutes since we left him. Twenty minutes.

"You weren't supposed to go to a safe room for a couple more hours," Mordecai said. He wagged his finger. "If this is going to work, you need to listen to your manager."

Mordecai stumbled and held out his hands, balancing like he was standing on a surfboard. "Where did those two girls and their grandma go?"

Then he vomited on the floor, sat in it, and passed out.

Gordo leaned over the counter and made a face. "This is your manager?"

"Yep," I said.

He shook his head sadly. "You two are so dead."

"Yep," I said.

5

MONGO HAD RISEN TO LEVEL THREE AND ALMOST DOUBLED IN SIZE.
He was going to be a very bright and colorful monster when he was
done growing. His pink-hued feathers grew longer and thicker along
his little arms, mixing in with a line of deep red feathers. His tail
also grew longer, making him appear more dinosaur-like and less
like poultry. The skin around his eyes took on a bluish tone. His
beak had widened and grown larger, too. A nose chomp from him
now could do serious damage.

"They grow up so fast," Donut said sadly. "He's too big to sit on
my back now."

"Pretty soon you're going to be able to sit on *his* back," I said. I
knew the real version of these things on Earth wasn't as big as they
were in the movies, but I could tell already that the game was growing Mongo toward a more cinematic, crowd-pleasing size.

While Mordecai snored loudly in a pile of his own vomit, Donut
and I opened our boxes. We each had a Silver Earth Box. We also both
received a couple random achievements. I had no additional loot boxes,
but Donut had a Gold Pet Box she hadn't yet opened. The most nota-
ble new achievement was for stumbling upon our first quest.

New achievement! It's Elementary, My Dear Crawler!
    And you thought all you had to do was bonk monsters on the
head.
    You've received a quest! Puzzles and intrigue and mysteries,
oh my! If you want to survive in this world, you're going to need

to be more than just a pretty, sword-swinging barbarian. Some quests require brute strength, yes, but sometimes you also gotta use your noggin.

Reward: We don't want you getting bored. That's your prize.

That was interesting. If there was some sort of mystery involved, I wondered if it required us to actually talk to people. If that was the case, Donut's astronomical charisma was going to be valuable.

Donut opened up her Earth box and gasped.

She'd received three items. Two were unopened boxes that appeared to be from Amazon.com: a scented candle and a large-sized cat tree with multiple scratching posts and platforms and a round cat hammock. It was larger and fancier than the one she'd had in our apartment. I would have to put it together myself. The candle was labeled "Sea Breeze" but smelled nothing like the sea.

The third item was a potion. An **Earth Hobby Potion**. I read the description.

Earth Hobby Potion.

Per subsection 1256-C of the Indigenous Planetary Species Protection Act, this particular reward is required by the Syndicate Government to be awarded to all crawlers who have chosen a domestic class.

Taking this potion is optional. However, it may not be sold or transferred to other crawlers or entities.

Upon drinking this, you will immediately obtain a level three skill ability in a unique Earth-based hobby. The benefit is chosen at random. However, you will not receive a skill that you currently have.

Gods, I hate it when the lawyers make me put their crap into the descriptions. Don't you? Anyway, this could be something useful like Parkour or Jiujitsu, or you could get fucked and receive some useless crap like Stamp Collecting or Kombucha Brewing. Don't get your hopes up. The fact that your planet was

filled with so many boring assholes with inane, ridiculous hobbies tips the scales way out of your favor.

I laughed. Why would something like this be required? What would be the purpose? Was it some bureaucratic attempt at preserving Earth culture? It didn't make sense, yet at the same time, it reminded me of some bullshit the military would enact.

In the Gold Pet Box, Donut received a black magical collar for Mongo that placed his orange dot on the map wherever he was. He screamed and tried to rip it off, but after a few admonishments from Donut, he relented and stopped scratching at it.

In a dark corner of the safe room stood a mailbox, and Donut went to retrieve her spell book. She pulled it out. "This sounds positively delicious," she said. She glowed as she applied the book to herself.

"I swear to god, Donut," I said. "You better have read the description first."

"Oh, relax, Carl. Watch." She waved her paw, and Mongo, who was currently running in circles around the prone form of Mordecai, suddenly split into three. Now there were three of them running in circles. One of the forms squeaked in concern, jumped up on the counter, and started growling at the other two forms. A moment later, the other two also jumped on the table. The first one cried out in fear and ran, running to hide behind Donut. The other two looked at one another, then jumped down and resumed circling Mordecai like a pair of sharks.

"Please tell me that's an illusion," I said. The two new Mongos were physically mirror images, but they weren't moving like exact duplicates. Each one seemed to have a mind of its own.

"They're real!" Donut said. "Isn't it great? They only last for a minute! It's an expensive spell, too. It costs 26 points."

Sure enough, the two little dinosaurs stopped running after a moment. They looked at each other, and then they fell apart, revealing little gears and servos and electric parts. The clockwork pieces disappeared in a puff of smoke a moment later.

"It's called *Clockwork Triplicate*. Isn't it great? I can only cast it on pets and minions, though. So no clockwork Carl."

The real Mongo squeaked with concern at the two little black piles of ash on the floor.

"That is a good spell. You'll want to practice with that one. You've grown a decent catalog," I said, looking over her spell list.

Donut's spells currently were:

Heal—Level 1 (Max).
   Torch—Level 10.
   Magic Missile—Level 9.
   Puddle Jumper—Level 3.
   Second Chance—Level 5.
   Heal Critter—Level 1.
   Clockwork Triplicate—Level 1.

I hadn't realized her *Torch* spell had risen to level 10. She usually turned it on as soon as we left a safe room, and it followed just above us for most of the day. She'd been adjusting the brightness on the fly when we were attempting to be stealthy, but I hadn't thought about it. Most of the halls on the second floor had come with ambient lighting anyway.

"Will you put my tree together?" Donut asked. "And maybe light my candle? Miss Beatrice used to light candles."

"Just a minute," I said. I had a quick memory of Donut walking too close to a line of candles, and of Bea flipping out. She was always paranoid about the cat catching on fire, yet she had a million candles all over the apartment.

I still had my own Earth box to open, which I did now. Like Donut's, mine contained two random items and a Hobby potion.

The first item was a small cactus plant in a clay pot. The short, squat cactus was only about three inches tall and was covered in yellow spikes. The pot still had a price tag on it. $3.99. It'd come from a Home Depot.

The second item was a shrink-wrapped set of small paperback books.

"Oh wow," I said, turning the pack over in my hands. It was a collection of Louis L'Amour books. Westerns. My dad had had an entire shelf of them. As a kid, I'd sneak one here and there and read the entire book in one night, hiding under the covers with a flashlight. This was a pack of 18 books, all from the same series. The Sackett Family Saga. I hadn't read any of these. I put the books into my inventory. My hands were shaking, I realized, and I wasn't sure why.

I examined the cactus, wondering what to do with it, and why they'd chosen this to give to me. Both of Donut's gifts had been deliberate. A candle to remind her of home and a cat tree for comfort.

I sighed, putting the plant into my inventory.

"So, you want to get a new hobby?" I asked. I didn't have high hopes it would be anything good.

"Okay," Donut said. Her entire body glowed for a moment. She made a face.

"Scutelliphily," she said a moment later, pronouncing it slowly. "I don't . . . I don't even know what that means. I'm a scutelliphile. That sounds obscene. How can I have a skill in something and not know what it is? This makes no sense. What a waste."

I chuckled. "I don't know what to tell you, Donut. It warned us the skill would be something stupid."

I put the potion in my hotlist and clicked it. A warmth spread through me.

You have gained a skill!
　You are now Level 3 in the Cesta Punta skill.

That was it. There was no other explanation.

"Cesta Punta?" I said. Was that a martial art? I looked at my hands. I didn't feel any different.

"Was your potion worthless, too?" Donut asked.

"I don't know," I said. "Maybe." Donut was right. It was stupid and pointless if we didn't know what it was.

"It's likely the art of cracking nuts with your toes," Donut said. She turned to the Bopca. "Gordo, darling. Get me some walnuts. We need to experiment." She laughed.

"Of course. Right away, Your Majesty," he said. He scurried into the back kitchen.

This guy was even more subservient than they usually were. Her charisma had rocketed up to 70. Mordecai had said while that number seemed crazy high on the lower floors, we were going to see and need much higher numbers than that just to keep our heads above water. With only three points per level, we needed to fight for potions and items and bonuses and everything we could to make those stats soar.

Since it was one of the few spells that worked inside of a safe room, I made Donut cast her new *Clockwork Triplicate* spell over and over. It currently took Donut about 20 seconds to regenerate a single mana point. Mongo quickly got used to having two clockwork friends suddenly emerging out of nowhere. He now squeaked with joy when they appeared, and he ran up to them. The other two also jumped up and down with excitement, and the three would tussle, rolling over each other, knocking over chairs, and pouncing and jumping on tables. The tooltips over their heads didn't indicate which one was the real deal. I'd quickly lose track of the real Mongo until the two eventually fell apart. Mongo would peep sadly when this happened and would run up to Donut and start screaming, hopping up and down, demanding that she bring them back.

"I don't think I'm gaining experience in the spell," Donut eventually said. "It should've gone up to level two by now."

"Hmm. Maybe it doesn't count in safe rooms." I looked over at the snoring form of Mordecai. "It'd be nice if we had someone to ask," I said loudly. I'd tried to wake him earlier, but he was out cold.

"Should we move him so he's not in a pile of his own vomit?" Donut asked.

"Probably," I said. "But I don't want to touch him again." When I had tried waking him the first time, his tail had risen ominously, like a cobra. "The last thing we need is some weird incubus spell activating and your manager getting put in a time-out. Besides, something tells me this isn't his first rodeo."

I really didn't feel like putting together Donut's cat tree just yet, and I told her I would do it later tonight. So instead, while Donut played with Mongo and his clones, I spent some time fiddling with explosives.

I needed to be doing this at a sapper's table, which would stop the dynamite from degrading and would supposedly offer more ways to work with the stuff. I had an idea, but I quickly gave up on it for now. I had that new Bomb Surgeon skill, and even though it was only level one, I could sense how useful it would be. I could feel the depth of the blasting cap in my dynamite sticks. I could feel how close a piece of dynamite was to prematurely going off without having to consult the description.

Instead of dynamite, I moved my examination to my stash of goblin smoke bombs. The apple-sized bombs were just a bit too big for my slingshot, and their design didn't really allow me to break them down. I wondered if I should switch to a sling. Frustrated, I put it all away.

I had a lot of random chemicals and a load of black powder, but with my limited knowledge of chemistry, I didn't have the correct combination of items to make what was in my head. I needed to seek out a store that sold explosive supplies or, better yet, find a village of hobgoblins and raid their stash. It seemed they had higher-quality stuff than the goblins.

We were supposed to make our way to that larger settlement before it got dark, but I made the executive decision to stay in the area and explore. I wasn't certain when night would descend, but we still had several hours before the next recap episode.

The plan was to go out there and sneak around the edges of this supposed circus. We would try not to poke too hard. Not until we knew exactly what we were dealing with.

"Come on, Donut," I said. "Let's go clown hunting."

———

THE FIRST THING WE NOTICED WHEN WE EDGED OUR WAY OUTSIDE was the group of three X's on the map. These were crawlers, and they'd fallen not too far from where we had encountered the lemurs.

"Ah, damnit," I said. I remembered what Zev had said about not joining up with any of the other crawlers in the area, and I suddenly felt guilty for not going to seek them out. I'd been so overwhelmed with all the newness of this floor, I hadn't really thought about it. I regretted that now.

We carefully approached the area, walking through the thin alley. Mongo stopped and sniffed the air. He let out a low growl.

"Stop," I whispered. I searched the minimap, but I didn't see any mobs.

Mongo was looking straight up. I followed the path of his gaze, and I finally saw it. A skull-headed lemur lounged on the edge of the roof. It hadn't noticed us yet.

The moment I saw him, his dot appeared on my map. These things had some sort of stealth ability. He was overlooking the street with the dead crawlers, his back to us. A trap. I could only see one lemur, but I had no doubt there were more.

"Back," I said. "Let's go in this building and sneak up on him."

These buildings were nothing but the bare shells of old houses. None had doors or windows, just the holes where they used to be. We backtracked and peered inside.

We crouched by the entrance. Mongo was being good and remained silent. The second floor and the roof both were made of nothing but beams of rotting wood, all surrounded by the stone bricks of the house. We could see the lemur from here, sitting idly on the edge of the roof. There were no stairs or easy way for me to get up there.

"Want me to take him out?" Donut asked.

"We need to do it silently," I said. My slingshot would only piss it off. Donut's magic missile could be a little loud.

"Be quiet, Mongo, and watch how Mommy does this."

"Wait. Goddamnit, Donut," I hissed.

But before I could protest further, Donut leaped into the air and landed on a second-floor beam. She crossed the roof, walking low. *Huh,* I thought. She'd managed to be a lot quieter than I thought she could be considering her . . .

She jumped to the center ceiling beam, landing right behind the lemur.

Even from here I could hear the little charm on her collar jingle as she landed on the roof. In this silence, it was as loud as a damn church bell. Her backside armor also clinked loudly onto the beam.

Mongo, deciding he wanted in on the fun, screeched loudly.

The lemur turned, looking over his shoulder just as Donut pounced.

She somehow managed not to fall off the edge and into the street below. She slashed savagely at the creature, and he crumpled over, falling into the building, bouncing off one of the second-floor beams and cracking into the ground. Mongo rushed forward and pounced, landing hard on the not-yet-dead lemur. He ripped savagely at the furry monster's stomach, unzipping him like he'd been trained. Mongo squeaked and shoved his head into the lemur's now-open belly.

Holy shit, I thought, rushing forward.

Donut jumped down and sat next to her kill, looking triumphant.

"We're gonna need to do something about that bell of yours if you want to be stealthy," I said. "You're too fragile to do stuff like that without planning it out."

"I need to make a good example for my child, Carl."

"He's not your child, Donut. He's a pet. We don't put our lives in danger for our pets."

I regretted it the moment the words came out of my mouth. Donut looked as if I'd slapped her. I suddenly felt like an enormous asshole.

Mongo ripped off the painted skull, revealing the dead lemur's own skull.

"Ew," Donut said, looking horrified. The look of hurt had disappeared just as quickly as it had come. "Carl, do you see that? It's disgusting!"

"Yeah, that's really gross," I said, happy for the quick change of subject.

The human-skull hat covered a secondary skull with a pair of bulbous bloodshot eyes. The thing had no fur or skin on its head at all. It looked even more scary without the skull hat than it did with it.

The lemur held a poor lemur skin and a small bandolier containing six throwing knives. Donut took all of them. The knives were each about the size of my hand with little black handles.

"Donut, you should go back up there," I said. "Slowly and quietly, and look over the street. See if you can spy any more lemurs on the roofs. Also see if you can tell where the main part of the circus is."

"No need," Donut said. "I already looked. There's one more lemur across the street, but he's asleep. I can probably take him out with a missile and nobody will notice. And a few streets over, you can see the large circus tents. There's a park, I think. It's the same direction from where the giraffe came. I could see at least three of the giraffes walking around over there. I didn't see any of the scary clowns, though. Also, if you're really quiet, you can hear the music from the circus."

I just looked at Donut. She really was growing, getting more efficient. Again, I felt bad for the pet comment. But at the same time, it was true, wasn't it? Donut was different. She was more than a pet.

Donut gazed down lovingly at Mongo, who'd eaten his fill.

"You did good," she said. "You're almost at level four already!"

The little dinosaur hopped up and down, waving his bloody arms and splattering gore everywhere.

"Okay," I said. "Let's kill the guy across the street, examine the bodies of those crawlers out there, and then check out the circus. Sound like a plan, partner?"

Donut paused and then nodded slowly. "Okay," she said. "Partner."

6

DONUT TOOK OUT THE SLEEPING LEMUR WITH A MAGIC MISSILE. WE waited five minutes to see if anything would react, but only silence followed. In those moments as we waited, I could hear it, the distant whisper of a calliope playing slow and haunting circus music. Once I was relatively certain the watchers were gone, we approached the three dead crawlers.

As we came closer, it was apparent there were enough blood and guts to comprise five or six crawlers. Like with the brindle grubs, the X's disappeared if the bodies were significantly destroyed. It seemed there'd been a large-scale battle here, and I suspected they'd taken out several of the lemurs, too, but their bodies had already been removed. As I suspected, the three crawlers had been left as a trap.

Of the three I could easily examine, two were human and one was a large treelike creature. I'd had that on my list, but I couldn't remember the name. When I examined the corpse, it didn't tell us their new races. All three were women.

Corpse of Crawler Grace Bautista 3. Level 8. Killed by Former Circus Lemur.

All of them appeared Asian, maybe Filipino. All had the same last name. All were level 8. All killed by lemurs. Grace, Nica, and Lea. None of them had any inventory, meaning some of their group were probably still alive.

"That one, the tree lady is wearing an anklet," Donut said. "And this one has two rings."

Sure enough, as I examined the corpses more closely, I could tell they'd been looted hastily. Their inventory was gone, and their weapons and armor appeared to have been removed, leaving them in regular street clothes—all except the tree woman, who was naked save for the anklet. Whatever had transpired here had happened quickly. These three were sisters or close family members, and all three had died at the same time. I shook my head. Fuck this game.

The tree creature was humanoid but with a badly misshapen body. She was closer to an Ent from *Lord of the Rings* than Groot from *Guardians of the Galaxy*. But even that comparison wasn't correct. Her facial features remained human, but she'd been bent over and hunchbacked with an extra set of limbs erupting from her back.

It took a few minutes to pry the anklet from her ankle, which was likely why they'd abandoned it. I also pulled the two rings off the fingers of the second one, the human named Nica.

Both of the rings were +2 to strength. Since Donut couldn't wear them, I rubbed the blood off and put them on myself, giving me a total of four rings. And just like that, my strength was back to an acceptable level. I didn't take any joy from looting the corpses of fellow crawlers, but I now realized how much of an advantage it was to be in an area where other crawlers existed. I could see the allure of being a player killer. This game gave a lot of loot.

I examined the simple anklet. It appeared to be made of wood. It had three little beads attached to it that clicked when I shook it, like seedpods. It wasn't nearly as loud as Donut's charm, but anything that made noise was a distraction.

Enchanted Anklet of the Fallen Oak.

Imbues wearer with +1 Dexterity, +1 Constitution, and gives +3 to the skill Double Tap. It's also an anklet. One would think

anklets enhance the beauty of feet like toe rings do, but they are excessive, jangly distractions that make you look too garish.

"Let's see if it'll let you wear this," I said. I suspected it would. She already had one bracelet wrapped around her forward leg. I could barely see it through all the fur.

Donut looked at the anklet with distaste. "Wood?" she said. "What is this, the 70s? Anklets are for the foot model, not me."

The AI clearly didn't want me wearing this thing, but I wasn't going to say that out loud. "It has a constitution buff. You need it."

She sighed and pulled it into her inventory. "I'll put it on my back leg so nobody will see it."

It appeared in a blink, forming around her rear-left ankle. It was a fourth the size as it was before, and it remained hidden in the tufts of fur. She shook her leg a few times with distaste. Thankfully the little beads barely made any noise. If we kept her hairbrush buff active, her constitution was now seven. It was still much too low for my tastes.

"Read the description of that Double Tap skill and tell me what it does," I said.

She shrugged. "It says if I hit the monster twice in a row with the same attack, there's a chance the second hit does critical damage."

"Okay, good," I said. "Now let's get out of the street."

The closer we came to the edge of the circus, the louder the calliope music grew. The music didn't change. It was a slow, haunting *oom-pah-pah, oom-pah-pah* of a polka played at half speed. I looked worriedly at the sun, which edged close to the distant rooftops. I hadn't seen any safe rooms since the last one.

We hid inside of a building that overlooked the massive circus tents. We'd killed five sentinel lemurs on our way here. While the lazy lemurs were hard to spot, they also seemed easy to sneak up on as long as we moved slowly. Donut had killed most of them, usually allowing Mongo to finish them off. The little dinosaur hit level four, and now he was about the same size as the cat. The dinosaur quivered with anger and potential energy every time we approached a lemur, and sometimes the excitement was too much for him. He'd let out a quick screech and then clamp his beak shut, as if he knew he'd messed up.

We came across a sleeping lemur sprawled out on the floor of one building, and it was just too much temptation for Mongo. The dinosaur squealed and pounced, landing on the stomach of the lemur, who awakened and managed to croak before I could also jump and smash his skull with my foot. A lemur-laden giraffe walked down the street soon thereafter while we hid against the inside wall of the building. But it passed by, not pausing.

Through the hole of a missing window, we now observed the circus. It consisted of three massive tents, multiple wagons, several cages filled with shadowy forms we couldn't see, and at least a dozen other smaller tents. In addition to the lemurs, giraffes, and stilt clowns, we saw a few other types of mobs, including a group of short, fat clowns and a large ogre-like creature wearing a leopard-skin leotard. The ogre had a tentacle sprouting from the side of his neck.

One of the tents was flanked by a massive faded sign that read GRIMALDI'S WORLD O' FREAKS, ADMISSION ONE GOLD COIN. NO CHILDREN OR THOSE WITH WEAK CONSTITUTIONS ALLOWED. A line of illustrated ten-foot-tall images stood on either side of the sign, showing the freaks and other attractions within the tent. One of them was the ogre creature with THE OVER CITY'S STRONGEST CITIZEN written over it.

The other illustrations were a faded mix of sideshow characters and attractions like THE OVER CITY'S FATTEST WOMAN and GARTH, THE TWO-HEADED TROGLODYTE and TINY, THE AMAZING, FIRE-BREATHING GNOLL.

There was one peculiarity amongst the signs. The last of the tall illustrations held an image of a horned, elf-like woman covered head to toe in tattoos. The sign read TSARINA SIGNET AND HER AMAZING BATTLE SQUAD. But someone had painted a large circle around the poster, crossing out the image. "Wanted. Traitor" was written above the sign. As we watched, one of the round clowns walked by, pushing a wheelbarrow that appeared to be filled with animal skins. He paused at the sign, zipped down his pants, and urinated on the poster.

"My word, they don't seem to like that lady," Donut said.

"No. No, they don't," I said.

We watched for a few more minutes. The clowns and lemurs appeared to be hard at work, but what were they doing? The entire circus was surrounded by a well-worn five-foot-high battlement made of rocks, wood, and bones. The clowns started draping animal skins over the barriers. A pair of stilt clowns pulled a wagon out into the street and started erecting what looked like trench warfare defenses. They dumped jack-like wooden structures connected to one another by circling barbed lengths of wire.

"They're getting ready for a battle," I said.

MORDECAI: It's getting late. Are you guys close to the other town yet?

CARL: Hello, Mordecai. How's your head?

MORDECAI: I've had no . . . Wait, what do you mean?

CARL: Where are you?

MORDECAI: I'm in my room. Are you two near the town or not?

Huh. He must've teleported back to his base the moment we left the safe room.

CARL: Do you remember anything from today?

DONUT: YOU WERE DRUNK AND YOU MOLESTED SOMEONE'S GRANDMA.

Mordecai didn't answer for several moments.

MORDECAI: Where are you right now?

I went on to explain everything that had happened. He didn't ask any questions and waited for me to finish. It didn't take long to explain.

> MORDECAI: Okay. Back the hell out of there and get your butts to that safe room. You are in way over your head. Do it now. It will be dark soon. I will explain just how stupid you two are once you get there.
>
> CARL: Maybe we wouldn't have been stupid if you hadn't been passed out in a pile of your own vomit. We were just about to head back. See you there.
>
> MORDECAI: Night comes on quickly. You'll want to hurry.

Mongo growled.

"Down," I hissed.

Outside, dozens of the lemurs and stilt clowns appeared. They came from all directions, heading back toward the circus. These were the sentries, I realized. They were headed back to home base before it got dark.

We had to remain low and press ourselves against the interior wall of the decrepit building, or we'd be seen by the passing mobs. We huddled as the *clomp, clomp, clomp* of a giraffe walked by on the wooden slats. Donut jumped to my shoulders and peered over the windowsill while Mongo crawled into my lap. I found myself making *shhh* noises while I rubbed the rough, half-feathered back of the little dinosaur's head.

"They just keep coming and coming," Donut said. "We shouldn't have come here, Carl. It's getting darker, too."

"Okay," I said. "If they're retreating back to their base, they probably won't follow us. Let's give it a minute and run."

Donut nodded.

We waited until the steady progression of lemurs and clowns started to abate. There had to be a thousand of them. The sun still hadn't fully sunk below the artificial horizon. Outside, the stilt clowns had finished erecting the barbed wire defenses and were now starting to line up behind the wall. Another group of monsters I hadn't yet seen circled around a group of cauldrons, like witches stirring a magical soup. These monsters were tall and thin with emaciated arms and fabric robes and masks that hung in tatters, like undead executioners. Except the fabric was bright purple and yellow. On this side of the park, there were four cauldrons set up, and each cauldron had four of the brightly colored robed figures surrounding the bubbling and hissing pot.

A group of the round clowns pushed the large red-and-yellow-painted animal cages to the edges of the walls, the doors facing outward. Roars and trills shook the massive pens. Whatever was in there, I guessed they would unleash the monsters on the attackers. I caught glimpse of tentacles and claws reaching outward from one of the cages. I was reminded of the Krakaren boss we'd fought earlier, though these tentacles seemed less octopus-like and more—I don't know—wormlike. I felt a visceral revulsion at the sight.

"Yeah, fuck this. We're out of here," I said. "Let's go."

A pair of lemurs and a clown remained on the street as we emerged. Donut hit them with three quick magic missiles as I rushed up at them. I punted the first lemur directly at the clown, who'd fallen backward. The squealing, on-fire lemur ricocheted off the struggling clown's head, who stumbled again, hitting the ground. While Donut and Mongo quickly dispatched the third lemur, I leaped up on the clown like I'd done before, crushing in his chest and pummeling him in his face, smashing it in. I could feel the extra strength I'd gained from the rings with each punch.

More strength. I needed more strength, and I could kill these things with a single hit.

I looted a second big top ticket and a hunk of clown meat.

I eyed a group of ten lemurs one street over. They howled and pointed at us, but they didn't move to pursue.

"Run," I said. We turned and bolted down the street, not bothering with the alleys. The safe room was only four blocks over.

"Did you see!" Donut shouted as we ran. A whistling noise filled the air as she breathlessly talked. "My magic missile can set things on fire now! My spell hit level—"

Wham! Half the street where we'd just been standing exploded, sending us both flying forward. I hit the ground and rolled, coming to a stop. My ears throbbed. Rocks and debris showered over us. Mongo squealed in pain. He glowed a moment later as Donut cast *Heal Critter.* She rushed to the small blood-splattered dinosaur, clucking over him worriedly.

"What the hell was that?" I yelled, pulling myself to my feet. "Come on!"

A purple-and-yellow comet rose into the air from the direction of the circus. It whistled as it bounced off the ceiling and hurtled at us. The brightly colored projectile was a mortar round, I realized in that fraction of a moment. It'd been fired from the cauldrons. They were firing goddamned magical mortars at us.

"Shit," I cried. "There!" I pointed at a nearby entranceway, and all three of us dove inside. I covered Donut and Mongo as another, louder detonation echoed. My health plummeted as darkness descended.

Rocks bounced off me as the building collapsed around us. I slammed a healing potion as my health continued its downward arc. The ground cracked, and we fell again. *Shit. The ground is made of wood,* I thought. *We're falling through.* We crashed to another stop, rock and wood falling around us, tumbling and rolling. I couldn't hear anything for several moments. Underneath me, Donut and Mongo squirmed to get out.

I rolled over, freeing them. Debris and dust cascaded, and I couldn't stop coughing. My health remained about halfway full, and I cast *Heal* to bring it all the way back up. We were in murky darkness. Mongo let out a cry of fear.

Light filled the room as Donut cast *Torch.*

We waited for another mortar round to drop, but it never came. They'd probably assumed they'd gotten us. After the rocks finally settled, I could still hear the distant, haunting calliope music.

"That was most unpleasant," Donut said. She started rubbing dust off Mongo's feathers.

We'd fallen into what appeared to be a basement of some sort. I looked about. Above, a dim light shone through where we'd fallen, about twelve feet up. I looked uneasily at the ground, but I couldn't see it. It was nothing but rubble and wood. This room had been built below the main level of the Over City. I didn't know that was a thing. Smoke rose lazily through a gap in the wreckage.

The room wasn't large. It appeared to be about twice the size of Mordecai's base with walls made of rough stone. There'd once been a staircase leading up, but it had collapsed in on itself. Rotted remnants of barrels lined one wall. The only way out was through the hole we'd fallen in.

"Can you use your *Puddle Jumper* spell to get us out?" I asked. I could also build a ladder, but it'd take a few minutes. We were almost out of time.

"I don't know," she said. She backed up, peering up at the ceiling. "The hole is too small. I need line of sight, and all I can see is the sky. If I make the hole bigger, it should work. One moment."

She leaped up through the hole. Mongo cried out. He started furiously leaping in the air, trying to jump as high as Donut. "She'll be right back," I said. "Calm down, little dude."

Mongo screeched in rage and jumped again, leaping astonishingly high. He'd jumped almost ten feet in the air, just shy of the hole.

"Wow, that was great," I said.

He squeaked sadly, looking at the hole.

A moment later, a larger chunk of floor fell in, and Donut jumped down. Her hair was all poofed out. Mongo started squeaking and bouncing around her like she'd been gone for hours.

Donut ignored her pet. "She's out there, right on the street," she said breathlessly. "She's just standing there like she's waiting for us. There's only one way out of the building, and she's right there. I think she knows we're here!"

"Who?" I said.

"The elf lady from the poster. Tsarina Signet!"

"Oh shit. Did she see you just now? Was her dot on the minimap red? What level is she?" I didn't see anything on my map.

Donut paused. "She looked right at me, but she didn't move! The dot is white! But she is really scary-looking. I didn't have time to examine her properties. I got too scared! She's glowing. She's completely naked except for this quite lovely thong that Miss Beatrice would just adore. But this lady is swirling with tattoos that are moving and swimming about like a fishbowl. I don't like tattoos, Carl."

I sighed, looking up at the hole, calming slightly. If her dot was white, then we weren't in immediate danger. "You have a tattoo," I said absently. "Remember? And I have two now. And you know Bea had a tattoo, too. That awful tramp stamp."

"Miss Beatrice's tattoo is a masterpiece and an exception to the rule," Donut said. "And *our* tattoos were placed upon us against our wills."

Bea's tattoo was a faded Persian cat on her lower back surrounded by weird, uneven wisps. The cat it was based on was Princess Chonkalot, Donut's long-dead grandmother and Bea's childhood cat. The awful tattoo looked like a stoned Ewok. I never understood why she'd gotten a tattoo in a place where the only ones who'd see it were people smashing her from behind. I'd made the error of jokingly mentioning that once. And the Ewok part. Yeah, that'd been a mistake.

"Her dot is white, which means we can talk to her," I said. "Let's ask her what the hell is going on, then get to the safe room. Can you teleport us up there?"

"Okay," Donut said, sounding uneasy.

I scooped up Mongo. The last thing we needed was the little monster attacking her. "Beam us up, Donut."

Ten seconds later, and we crouched at the crumbled-in entranceway to the now-destroyed building. Darkness had fully descended on the area. My heart thrashed as I remembered Mordecai's warning.

Light glowed from the street, and I squeezed through the rubble of the collapsed doorway to go outside. In the distance, about a block and a half down, the circus was lit like a holiday display. The three big top tents glowed, and multiple fires surrounded the encampment. Spotlights shot into the air, waving about.

A line of clowns and lemurs and giraffes stood nearby. They could clearly see us here. Why weren't they firing their mortars?

I examined the almost-naked elf creature who stood quietly by herself in the now-darkened streets. She stood about five and a half feet tall, and she reminded me of Lexis, Odette's production assistant. She was an extra-thin humanoid creature with long, pointed elf ears, short horns jutting from her forehead, and sharpened fangs. She had a malevolent, horrifying look about her.

Her skin gave off a mild luminescence, and in this glow, I could see the tattoos. From her toes to her face, she was covered in thick-lined old-school tattoos of monsters. Most of the creatures were Asian themed or nautical themed, like Japanese oni and small Chinese dragons and dozens of other monstrosities like sharks and octopuses. Like Donut said, these tattoos were alive. They moved about her body, twirling around each other, rippling her skin.

Tsarina Signet—Half-Naiad, Half–High Elf Summoner. Level 60.
     This is an Elite.
     The High Elf King Finian, leader of the Liana Sector of the Hunting Grounds, was such a horny bastard, it was said he'd bedded women from over 5,000 different races during his rule. Most scholars agree this has to be an exaggeration considering King Finian's harelip and obsession with knitting, but

nonetheless, at least one of these trysts did take place, resulting in the unique combination of half-Naiad, half–High Elf. Considering the Naiad Confederacy's tendency to drown outsiders and the High Elves' inclination to hunt down and murder any mongrel child of the late king, Signet here has probably had a tough life. Maybe that's why she ran away and joined the circus.

WARNING: This is a fairy-class NPC. Creatures of this class inflict 20% more damage against you due to your goblin pass.

The moment the description ended, a new notification popped up.

New Achievement! Meet an Elite.

Sometimes they're NPCs, sometimes they're mobs, but usually they're just assholes. Elites are powerful one-of-a-kind entities. These are the non-boss, non-divine hero class of *Dungeon Crawler World*. If you come across one of these egomaniacs, they will either want to fuck you or kill you. Either way, they will *always* want to use you. They tend to think this whole production is all about them. Be careful. Where there's one elite, there's usually more.

Reward: Elites will now show on your map as white or red dots with a black cross.

I swallowed. The woman was decidedly terrifying to look upon, yet I found myself attracted to her. The effect was sudden and almost overwhelming. With horror, I felt myself getting physically excited. I pictured myself pulling the woman into my arms, kissing her on the mouth. I took a step toward her. *It's a spell,* I realized. What had Mordecai said? *Stay away from girls with horns on their heads.*

CARL: I think I'm being charmed by an NPC with horns. What do I do?

MORDECAI: It's not a real *Charm* spell because if it was,
you wouldn't be asking me about it. Is it happening to
Donut, too?

DONUT: HE HAS AN ERECTION, MORDECAI. IT'S VERY
INAPPROPRIATE. MONGO IS APPALLED.

MORDECAI: Okay, Carl. She likely has 100-plus charisma, which
gives some inherent buffs. One of those is something
called Puppy Dog, which can make men mad with desire.
It's a weak effect at first, but the longer you're in her
presence, the worse it'll get. There's only one surefire way
to break it. You need to fracture your own finger. Do it fast.
It will negate the effect. Uh, make sure you don't rip your
finger off.

Shit. I still clutched onto Mongo. I reached over, grasped my left
pinkie, and I bent it back so it snapped loudly. Pain exploded. I cried
out. *Holy crap. That just happened.* I looked stupidly at my bent-back
finger.

It worked. I felt the spell rush away. The effect was similar to
having a bucket of cold water dumped on my head. I just sat there
and breathed heavily.

The woman looked down with amusement at my finger.

"My, my," she said. "It's been a while since I've seen that trick in
action."

She had a seductive voice. It did not match her face. I drank a
health potion.

DONUT: IT WORKED. YOU ARE A GENIUS, MORDECAI.

MORDECAI: Gods, Donut. Do you have to type in all caps? That
trick works for most charm-based spells. But you have to
do it to yourself. The problem is that by the time you're
truly charmed, you don't know you're charmed. This is a
succubus. Get away from her and get back to the base.

DONUT: SHE IS NOT A SUCCUBUS. IT SAYS SHE'S A HALF-
      NAIAD AND ELF. IT ALSO SAYS SHE'S AN ELITE.
MORDECAI: Holy fuck. Get the hell out of there. Do not get
      involved in whatever she's trying to rope you into.

"We're sorry to have bothered you," I said while Donut and Mordecai talked in the chat. "We need to head back now."

Signet took a tentative, almost shy step toward me. In my menu, I prepared to click *Protective Shell* if I had to. It wouldn't have an effect on her if her dot remained white, so if I needed it, I had to time it properly. "I came here to see if you were okay. I watched you get attacked by my former family. They can be quite . . . unwelcoming . . . to strangers these days."

I watched a sea dragon pulse across her small breasts. The black tattoo paused to look at me and silently hiss before wrapping itself around her back. On Signet's arms, the monsters danced about one another. I caught a glimpse of a giant three-headed ogre who held a curved sword, which he sharpened on a wheel.

I realized Mongo had gone slack in my arm. I looked down, and the little dinosaur was staring at the woman, little eyes wide. She reached out and patted him on the head. He made a happy little squeak. This was what happened with the goblins and the laminak fairies, I realized. Only this time we were the ones getting seduced by the ultrahigh charm.

"We're okay," I said as Donut leaped up on my shoulder. "Thank you for your concern. We really need to get going."

The woman reached forward to pet Donut, but the cat pulled back and let out a growl. Mongo looked between Donut and Signet, confused. I felt the small dinosaur tense, the spell broken. He also let out a little growl. *Good boy,* I thought.

"We're not getting involved with this weird little quarrel, sweetheart," said Donut. "Carl and I want nothing to do with you and your circus freak friends. We will be leaving now," Donut said.

"I'm afraid it's too late for that," Signet said as she took a step back and spread out her arms. The tattoos on her body began to swirl, moving faster and faster until they blurred. She nodded toward the circus, and I reluctantly turned my head.

At this distance, I could barely see what she was indicating. A cheer rose from the line of clowns and circus animals. A moment passed, and I realized, with dread, that I *could* see what had changed.

The cages of the beasts were all open. I glanced at my minimap, and the red dots appeared one by one. In front of us, behind us, and to our sides.

We were surrounded, and they were moving in fast.

7

"WHAT WAS YOUR NAME AGAIN?" SIGNET ASKED ME. SHE DIDN'T move from her arms-out Jesus pose.

"Uh, Carl," I said as I frantically searched the map for the best way to flee. We had nowhere to go. I regretted making Donut use her *Puddle Jumper* spell already. The spell had a five-hour countdown, and we really could've used it about now.

"Carl. What a strong name. Be a dear, Sir Carl. You seem like a strapping lad," Signet said. "Please keep those mold lions off of me while I organize my battle squad. I usually have this part done before I have to face them. Your presence distracted me, so it's only fair. Besides, if you run, they will take you down."·

"Carl, I don't like this," Donut whispered as I put Mongo down. "I think we're in real trouble."

"Get ready," I said. I formed a fist and faced the closest red dot. It was right there, fifty feet away, across the street and down the alley from the house with the basement. But I couldn't see it. I watched the dot move toward us. The mob moved *through* the building.

No, not through the building. *Over* the building. It was on the roof. I looked up and tried not to gasp.

Mold Lion—Level 15.

    Mean, green, and it gonna eat yo spleen!

    Madam Kiki's Dancing Lions were an integral part of Grimaldi's Traveling Circus. Crowds would roar in approval as the diminutive lion trainer stood in the middle of the ring, cracked her whip, and the dozen male lions took to their hind legs and twirled like ballerinas. What a sight it was!

On the day of the great cataclysm, the gentle and tame lions were some of the first to transform. The spores of Scolopendra took quick root within the lions, turning them into the fiends you see today. Further transformations occurred as a result of the vine.

As with all early victims of the cataclysm, these creatures are filled with rage. They will stop at nothing until your innards wet the floorboards of the Over City.

"That was needlessly gruesome," Donut muttered as I gawked up at the lion.

The monster was a regular-sized male lion with a mane. Half of his body was covered with a green, lumpy, glowing fungus that pulsated like he was being eaten. The green mold covered his legs and chest, and splattered tendrils of the stuff covered the lion's face, like a pair of hands caressing it from behind. The lion's right eye glowed like an emerald. Erupting from his mane were tentacles. Dozens of long, pink-and-green fingerlike worms waved in the air, making the creature appear to be some sort of fucked-up cat Medusa.

The monster roared. Behind me, an answering roar followed. Then a third. The lions appeared all around us, all of them on the roofs of the buildings. They were going to pounce at any moment.

"Holy shit, lady, how long is this going to take?" I called to Signet. We now had six lions circling us.

The half-naiad's eyes glowed. The tattoos swirled faster and faster along her skin. She did not answer.

For the past day, I'd been trying to organize scenarios such as this in my mind. We needed to come up with contingencies, ways to respond to certain threats. If Donut and I trained, we could call out the play and each of us would know how to respond. I had one such contingency already worked out in my head, something for this exact scenario—surrounded by powerful monsters. The problem was, I hadn't explained this yet to Donut.

I looked about for the strongest-looking wall. *There.* Just on the other side of Signet.

"Okay, Donut," I said as I slowly circled behind the half-naiad. I had to mentally gauge the distance. "Save your magic until I tell you. Can you take another potion yet?"

"*Yes,*" she said, voice full of fear. Mongo stayed under my feet. "What're we doing?"

"Got a plan. When I say, cast that last scroll of *Confusing Fog.* Okay? Get it re . . . Oh shit, now, now!"

All six lions pounced at once, and their terrifying roar filled the dark street.

I slammed down on *Protective Shell.*

Earlier, I'd tossed a goblin smoke bomb, and it'd caught in the wind, resulting in the bomb being rendered ineffective. The *Confusing Fog* didn't have that problem. The lions bounced off the shell like fireflies off a bug zapper. Each of the six lions ricocheted in a different direction, all of them howling in outrage as the billowing eddies of fog spread out around us.

Signet, as I'd hoped, was not affected by my shield. She remained within the spell's area of effect. The magical shell would only last twenty seconds. The translucent-only-to-the-good-guys fog, however, would stick around for a good two and a half minutes thanks to Donut's high intelligence.

One of the lions bounced off the shell and flew into the sturdy wall of the building. I'd judged the distance correctly, and the lion was momentarily caught between the wall and the dome shape of the spell. The spell pushed the lion against the wall as it blindly scrambled for purchase with its claws, but it had nowhere to go, and it hung just a couple feet off the ground, wedged in good. The lion was on its side, back against the wall and belly facing us, angled downward. Blind and confused, it howled and scrambled, unable to push off the shell. In a second it'd figure out that rotating would save it. I had to act fast.

Its body sparked where it came into contact with the shield. A damage bar appeared and slowly started to descend. Behind me, another lion roared in pain as one of his friends instinctively slashed at him. I bolted forward, pulled my fist back, and punched the trapped lion in the mold-covered chest just as he started to rotate.

He howled in pain and tried to slash at me but couldn't angle his claws—which were inches from my face—past the invisible shell. I punched again and again. I felt something give. My next punch went in deeper than I expected.

Mongo screamed and flew through the air, attaching himself to the lion's unprotected belly, ripping at it as I pulled out my dripping gauntlet and punched again. My hand entered the chest cavity, and I opened my fist, grasped, and pulled.

I fell back onto my ass as the entire lion plummeted to the ground and rolled toward me. Surely it hadn't been twenty seconds yet? The green mold turned black before my eyes, and the worm tentacles all dropped, mixing in with the matted and dirty hair of the mold lion.

It was dead.

Mongo shrieked with glee. The dinosaur grew before my eyes. I wasted a precious second staring stupidly at the mold-covered lion heart in my hand. *Holy shit. I pulled his fucking heart out. I pulled out the heart of a fucking lion.*

"Second Chance!" I cried, scrambling to my feet as I put the heart into my inventory.

Donut's spell only cost ten of her 29 magic points.

The protective shell fizzled out just as the reanimated lion rose to its feet. It stood, both eyes dead, guts trailing from where Mongo had eviscerated it. Signet still hadn't moved or changed.

Undead Minion of Crawler Princess Donut—Mold Lion—Level 5.

The zombies were a third as powerful as their former selves, but they weren't blind.

"Kill!" Donut yelled, pointing at the closest lion. The zombie growled and pounced, landing on the back of a lion whose health was already cut in half. It was over in a second, the zombie having ripped open the throat of his confused friend.

I shouted instructions at Donut as I formed a fist. At any moment the four remaining lions would realize we were unprotected.

Donut raised the second lion from the dead and downed a mana potion. She then spent 26 points to cast *Clockwork Triplicate* on the new zombie with the ripped-out throat.

"Kill the others!" Donut cried. Two of the lions jumped forward to attack. A moment later, the other two followed, wading into the fray. The two automatons fell into pieces before the final lion was dead. The two zombies also fell to the last lion, whose health was down to nothing. It growled, looking about just as the fog started to clear.

Mongo squealed and charged.

Donut hit the lion with a magic missile just as it swiped at the dinosaur. It dropped dead. Mongo, oblivious that Donut had just saved the idiot's life, pounced, landing on the lion's back, and started ripping. He'd gone up to level six. He was now a hand taller than Donut, about the size of an actual turkey. His tail was longer, too. A set of long feathers sprouted from the back of the tail.

Donut and I were both now level 14. A notification popped up telling me I couldn't assign my points until I reached a safe room.

"Well, that was unexpected," Signet said.

I turned to look at the woman. Nothing had happened. Her tattoos stopped swirling around her body, though they continued to move as they had before. Her eyes no longer glowed. I'd been expecting her tattoos to turn into the monsters. Her description had stated she was a summoner, and she'd said she was summoning her "battle squad."

"What's going on?" I said. "Did your spell not work?"

"No, it didn't," she said. She had a sour look on her face. "My spells are Blood Magic. They require a proper sacrifice to work. I choose the sacrifice and cast the spell, and my lovelies take the blood and form."

I indicated the six dead lions. "You have blood right here." Down the street, the group of circus creatures cried in outrage once they realized the lions were all dead. We needed to get out of here. The mortars were going to start firing again at any moment.

"I can't use them," she said. As I watched, one of the lions twitched. I jumped back and formed a fist. Donut screeched and leaped onto my shoulder. A green line of mold oozed off the lion and hit the ground. It started creeping back toward the circus.

Donut fired a magic missile at the ground. The mold shriveled and died.

"Don't bother," Signet said. "The mold isn't dangerous, not directly, and you won't get it all no matter how hard you try. Believe me. You can incinerate the bodies, and you'll still miss some. All it takes is a single microscopic spore to get back to the vine, and tomorrow this lion will be regrown and ready to attack again." She sighed. "Let's back up a block before those acrobats start shooting at us. This night's attack is canceled. What a disappointment. My boys were really looking forward to it."

We walked away from the circus to the jeers of the clowns. A few mortars did fire, though we were clearly out of range.

"You can only cast that summoning once a night?" I asked.

Signet gave me a half smile. Her ghoulish face looked downright sinister. "That is correct, Carl."

DONUT: CARL, I DO NOT LIKE THIS LADY EVEN IF HER DOT IS WHITE. WE NEED TO DITCH HER.

CARL: We will. She's even crazier than you think. Let me do the talking. Get ready to run just in case, but I don't think we'll have to. I want to get some info from her first. I don't think she's dangerous, not anymore, not as long as we don't provoke her.

"So," I said, trying to sound casual, "which one of us was supposed to be the sacrifice, me or the cat?"

"You, of course," Signet said, seeming not a bit surprised I'd figured it out. "The moment one of those lions cut you open, all of your blood would've flown into me and animated my squad. We've never used Primal blood before, but I can sense how powerful it is. But you received nary a scratch."

"Wait," I said. "All my blood would've flowed out of me even if I'd just received a single cut?"

I'd already deduced the real reason why her spell hadn't worked. She didn't really want us to protect her. She'd wanted to charm me and then have me die while defending her. She hadn't been casting her spell while all those tattoos were swirling about. She'd already cast it, and they were just waiting for my blood. This NPC was crazy and dangerous, but she was also clearly part of the quest, and I intended on getting the full story.

"Just a single cut wouldn't do it. It has to be a life-ending cut. I must say, it can be a hassle."

"What sort of creature do you usually use?" I asked.

She shrugged. "I usually catch something, the bigger the better. I'm not allowed to bleed the sacrifice myself. Otherwise I would've just killed you. I have to capture something and then capture a second, different something, put them together so they fight, guess which one is going to lose, and then cast my spell on the loser before they receive their first injury. The moment they're dead, my battle squad arises. How powerful they are depends wholly on the quality of the blood."

DONUT: SHE IS GOING TO TRY TO CAPTURE US, CARL. WE
     NEED TO GET OUT OF HERE.

Donut was right. It was stupid to keep following her. I paused in the street. We were only two blocks over now from the safe room.

But before we left, I had to ask one last question. The all-important question.

"Why are you attacking them?" I asked.

She indicated a tall white building. "My home is over there. I moved in because it is close to the vine, and the circus can no longer move from their spot. I have refreshments. If you'd like to join me for an evening drink, I will regale you with the sad tale of Signet the Bastard and Grimaldi, the man she loved."

"Bastards can be girls?" Donut asked, speaking for the first time.

"Yes," Signet said. "I learned quite early the term does not discriminate between male or female."

"We have to get going," I said. "But I would love to talk more about this with you later. But only if you promise not to try to sacrifice us."

She smiled. "After seeing how well you two fight, you needn't worry about that. If you promise to help me with my assault, I will tell you the full story."

"We will come back tomorrow night," I said. "But if you don't mind, we'll meet up after you've already summoned your squad."

She smiled at that. She tapped the ground with her foot. "I'll meet you right here an hour after sundown tomorrow night."

———

"WHAT'S THE POINT OF HAVING ME AS A MANAGER IF YOU TWO suicidal idiots don't listen to my advice?" Mordecai raged after we arrived back at the Belly-Rubbed Pug safe room.

We'd had to dodge a single mob on our way to the inn. It was a spider thing, but its body was an eyeball the size of a beach ball. It'd woven a web across the street, and we'd had to take the long way to the room.

The recap episode was about to air when we arrived. We approached the room, and I sent a quick message to Mordecai that we were going in as a courtesy. If I'd known he was going to be such an ass, I wouldn't have warned him.

"Within minutes of us going out there, we got that quest," I said. "I asked you if it was important or if we should ignore it. Well, guess what. You didn't answer because you were shit-faced."

Mordecai took a deep breath. "I apologize. I have not had the pleasure of drinking in an Over City pub in a very long time, and I took advantage of the opportunity. I did not take into account the incubus's weakness, which is alcohol. But if I had been of sound mind, I would have told you that quests are great for experience and loot, but only if you are comfortably ahead of the difficulty curve for the level. Since we only have eight days, and you are currently playing catch-up, I would've said to skip it and *do what I originally told you to do.*"

"And we probably would've taken that advice had you actually given it," I said.

"Furthermore," Mordecai continued, "after I was cognizant of my surroundings, I told you to stay away from the goddamned elite, but did you listen? No. You made a date with her for tomorrow night. A date, should you decide to attend, that will surely result in all of the blood seeping from your veins and into her minions."

"I don't like that lady," Donut said as she munched a freshly prepared tuna steak. Mongo devoured a plate of something that looked like raw hamburger meat on the floor next to her. He looked up and squeaked agreement.

"She's an elite," Mordecai said. "Never trust an elite."

"So what, exactly, are elites? How are they different than other NPCs? Is it just because they're more powerful?"

Mordecai sighed. "Okay, so, elites. There are thousands of them spread throughout the urban levels of the dungeon. Unlike most mobs and dungeon NPCs, they can—and do—freely travel between the urban floors. In addition to the crawl, there is also a more scripted aspect to the dungeon. Think of it as a soap opera or a serial. All of these stories activated with the opening of the third floor. Every season they have multiple storylines pop up at once, like in September when all the new shows come out on television. There are also a few running stories that have been spanning multiple seasons, but that's all on the ninth floor. That's too complicated to explain right now."

"Wait," I said. "So, they're like actors?"

He shook his head. "Do you remember what we discussed earlier about how Borant owns and alters the minds of some mobs and NPCs? Elites are never naturals. They are designed, printed, and then imprinted with the memories needed for them to act out their drama. As far as they're concerned, this is their real world."

"But that's how it is with most of the other mobs," I said.

Mordecai shook his head again, this time more adamantly. "No. Regular mobs are autonomous. Once they're set loose in the dungeon, what they do is up to chance. Here is the thing with elites, and this is extremely important, so pay careful attention. Your quest with this circus and this Signet woman is a storyline, a drama created for the viewers by a team of writers. It will play itself out whether or not you get involved. It will have its own show and team of people working on that show who have been working on it for a very long time and who will be very protective of it. Some of these dramas and storylines become quite popular in their own right. While elites aren't directly controlled by the AI and the writers, they are constantly being nudged and manipulated. If the writers don't like where a storyline is going, they will hot-patch new instructions right into the elites' minds. There are AI-controlled rules to keep the dungeon 'fair' for the crawlers, but those rules are much looser when it comes to elites. If it comes down to saving the life of a single crawler or blowing an entire drama that's been building for weeks, what do you think is going to happen? I've seen it a dozen times. A hot-shit crawler comes across an elite, and instead of trying to solve the quest, he decides to go all murder hobo and kill the NPC. Something always happens. Something bad. Most of these elites have very thick plot armor, and in those stories, *you're* the extra. The red shirt. The guest star. Not every quest will involve elites, but if it does, then I will always suggest that you stay the hell away. Especially when that storyline just launched, because there's a whole team of writers and producers out there who don't want their precious little series to get canceled after the first day. And if they can write in the death of a popular crawler, all the better. It will guarantee their show gets more viewers."

"So when we talk to that Signet woman, we're on another show?" Donut asked.

Mordecai just looked at the cat. "Out of all of what I just said, that's what you take away?"

"Wait," I said. A notion came at me. Something Signet had said. "But if this level is only eight days, what happens when the floor collapses?"

"The important elites will go down to the sixth floor, and the story will continue. While you crawlers are dicking around on the fourth and fifth floors, these dramas will continue to play out. That is, until you guys get there to mess it all up. That's part of the fun for the viewers, seeing how crawlers crap all over the producers' hard work. It's like taking Jason from a *Friday the Thirteenth* movie and tossing him into a late-season episode of *Jane the Virgin* just to see what happens. But, like I said, the producers and writers aren't going to allow you to just come and do it this early. They will fight back."

"But only if we're going against their planned storyline," I said. "If we're aiding the narrative, they might actually do the opposite. They might help us."

Mordecai scoffed. "You can also just sit here in this pub and play with yourselves for the next seven days. It might be fun, but it's also a one-way ticket to getting left behind. Forget this quest and go to the city."

The center television screen snapped on, and the opening music for the recap episode played.

"Special edition! See what your favorite crawlers chose as their race!" the announcer cried.

I sat back and thought about everything that had happened today while we watched a shortened version of the bloody first part of
the show. Some large group of crawlers fought against a demon-like
city boss with crab pincers. The boss ripped through them in seconds, killing about forty crawlers with horrifying alacrity. The demon cackled with glee as it killed them all.

The first crawler they showed getting her upgrade was Hekla of
Brynhild's Daughters, the woman from Iceland who'd gathered a
large group of female crawlers around her. It showed her entering the
safe room alone.

"Where's the rest of her group?" I asked.

"They didn't get together until later," Mordecai said, "so they had
different game guides. They'll come out scattered to the wind."

"Yikes," I said. "That sucks." I patted Donut on the head. I was
about to say something about how it would suck if Donut and I got
separated, but I thought better of saying that out loud.

Hekla emerged from the guild, and the program showed a spinning 3D version of her new character. Her new race was Amazonian.
She looked mostly the same, but she was a good foot taller than before and much wider. The pretty blond woman had been in good
shape before. Now she looked like a professional bodybuilder. It
didn't show her stats, but I could tell it was clearly a strength build
with a good amount of dexterity, too.

A scrolling paragraph of text appeared, much too fast for me to
read, that explained her new class. She'd been allowed to pick an
Earth class, and she went with the obvious choice. Shieldmaiden.

"I couldn't read what it said," I groused.

"You're being forced to watch on a flat display," Mordecai said. "If
you were using a standard view screen, you'd be able to grab that
paragraph and pull it up. You'll be able to buy such a display for your
private base later, but they're likely prohibitively expensive."

The next few groups were crawlers I didn't recognize, but who
had picked odd races or classes, including a man who turned himself
into a massive slug and a woman who turned herself into a

four-armed, blue-skinned replica of the Hindu goddess Kali. The same woman picked an odd class called Kabaddi Raider.

"A few groups aren't done with their selection," the announcer said. "But it appears just about 80% of the crawlers have opted to remain human."

"That's way more than I thought it would be," I said. "I'm surprised."

"Not me," Donut said. "You humans were always a cocky bunch."

"You didn't change, either," I said.

"Of course not, Carl. Why would I stop being a cat?"

"It's usually around that percentage," Mordecai said. "Sometimes higher."

"Really?" I asked.

He nodded. "Whenever there's a poll of Syndicate citizens, the vast majority of them always say they'd change into something else if they were put in that situation. But the truth is, when people are *really* given the opportunity to be something else, and that change is real and permanent, most opt to stay the same. They get scared. Even if there's an obviously better choice, it's terrifying to take that leap. And if that something else is a *major* change, there's always a learning curve. Sometimes it's better to stay in familiar skin. Believe me, it can be a real mind bender to suddenly find yourself two feet taller or shorter. Or if you lose limbs or, worse, gain them."

"We're on!" Donut cried as we appeared on the screen. I was shown first. "Look, Mongo. Uncle Carl is on television." She pointed up at the screen. Mongo looked and started bouncing up and down, waving his arms.

They played a brief history of the Primal race. They showed another human from many seasons ago who'd chosen the same race. They showed him flying through the air with white wispy angel wings, wielding a massive sword made of lightning as he charged at a humanoid demon the size of a goddamned football stadium standing knee-deep in a lake of fire.

"What the hell is that?" I said, watching the brief scene unfold. It faded away before the actual battle could start. The paragraph that explained what a Compensated Anarchist was appeared and disappeared.

"That, my boy, is a divine guardian, one of the behemoths of the 12th floor. A country boss. He is guarding a fire gate, an entrance to the 13th floor."

"Holy fuck," I said.

"Yeah," Mordecai said.

"Is that the guy who made it to the 13th floor?"

"No," Mordecai said. "But he was a famous crawler. He's from before my time. He died a minute later. The next time you're with your friend Odette, you should ask her about him."

"Shush," Donut said. "Talk after they show me!"

As they revealed Donut's selection process, I couldn't get the image of that Godzilla-sized monster out of my head. It was a literal kaiju. Sure, it was a country boss, second only to a level boss, but it was still only the 12th level. That was the floor Donut and I needed to get to if we wanted any sort of freedom. There were six levels after that. What sort of bosses would be down there? I thought of the rage elemental. They were regular mobs from the 13th floor. The thought of scaling up our power to that level in such a short amount of time seemed impossible.

The show ended with Lucia Mar's transformation. Her two rottweilers, as non-sapient pets, did not get the opportunity to change, so they remained dogs.

Lucia had chosen one of the oddest, most fucked-up races I'd seen so far.

"What the hell, kid?" I said, watching the show, completely aghast at her choice. "Why?"

A Lajabless, it was called.

She'd grown from her young street-kid appearance to a full-grown adult woman. As the 3D image spun, her face altered from that of a great beauty to a skull-faced monstrosity. The announcer explained that she would spend half the day as a beautiful woman and the other half as lady Skeletor. While she was in her woman form, her magic ability was doubled. Spells cost half as much, but her strength was cut in half. While she was sporting her *día-de*-holy-shit face, it was the opposite. Spells cost more, but she was twice as strong.

She also now walked with a limp. No more running on walls for her. Her right leg, and just her right leg, had transformed from a human limb to that of a hairy goat, complete with a cloven hoof.

As she emerged from the guildhall, clomping on her new leg, even her two dogs looked freaked out by the transformation.

"She looks like she smells really bad," Donut said.

"That race seems like a terrible idea," I said.

"Maybe," said Mordecai. "But she's likely the most powerful crawler in this game. There's probably a slew of hidden benefits in that racial choice that makes it worth it."

And then there was her class choice. Again, I couldn't see what the details were. Just the name.

It was a triple class. A cleric–magic user–warrior combo called a Black Inquisitor General.

"Wow," I said. "And I thought that kid was a scary mofo before."

The show ended, and a moment later the announcement came.

Welcome again, Crawlers, to the third floor!

There are still a few stragglers working on their class and race choices, and that's okay. The vast majority of you are out and about and just starting to learn about the wonders of the Over City. We welcome you to a *Dungeon Crawler World* tradition.

You all have made some wondrous and unique choices. Of the just under 700,000 crawlers who've made a decision, we have seen almost 40,000 different class choices. Can you believe that? That is a record, and we are very proud to see such diversity.

A couple announcements regarding this third floor. While the bathroom penalties have been removed, we want to remind the crawlers that restrooms still populate this floor. In the villages you may find restrooms in any pub and in some shops. In the ruins, the toilets are just as prevalent as they were on the higher floors. Please do not force us to backtrack.

We are already seeing much interest in the sponsorship program. And while the program doesn't officially get underway until the fourth floor, potential sponsors now have the ability to put in early bids. Therefore, remember to be as entertaining as possible!

Finally, many of you are discovering new abilities and spells and wish to try them out. We urge you to do so. But this is just a general warning that any attempts of violence against non-combatant NPCs should be avoided. While this practice is technically not against the rules, the Borant Corporation wishes to keep the citizenry as safe as possible. As a result, we have adjusted the experience counter for citizens down to zero. In addition, city guards have been given a slight boost in stats.

That's all for now. Get out there and kill, kill, kill!

"What's with the warning about the NPCs?" I asked.

"Who knows?" Mordecai said.

We spent some time talking about the day and some of the things Signet had said. She'd mentioned that Grimaldi had turned into something called a "Vinev," which led to a long, yawn-inducing conversation about plants and parasites and mind control. Mordecai counted on his fingers, giving me and Donut a long list of ways to deal with each kind of plant-based monster. This, apparently, was a subject of great interest to Mordecai.

"Now go rent a room and get some sleep," he eventually said as he handed back the pile of potions. He'd been showing us how to combine certain potions to make them more potent and work more quickly. "I want you two up early. Tomorrow is going to be a big day."

"What're we doing?" Donut asked.

"Oh, it's going to be amazing," Mordecai said. "It's going to be a day for the history books. It'll be the first time you two do exactly what I tell you to do."

8

TIME TO LEVEL COLLAPSE: 6 DAYS, 23 HOURS.

Views: 998.3 Trillion
Followers: 16.5 Trillion
Favorites: 3 Trillion

I AWAKENED TO FIND A LONG MESSAGE FROM BRANDON JUST HOV-ering in my field of vision. I put it aside for the moment while I let myself wake up. As usual, Donut had insisted we share a room. But instead of sleeping on my neck, she'd slept upon her newly erected cat tree, which barely fit in the room. It'd taken me the better part of an hour to put it together, using the paper instructions and provided Allen wrench. It seemed so surreal, so ridiculous to be completing such a mundane task in the middle of all this. But the tree was light, and we'd be able to store it and bring it out each night. While Donut slept on the top platform, Mongo curled up at the bottom. I also lit the cheap candle for her. It filled the small rented room with the scent of home.

I watched Donut for a bit, and I could tell what she was doing. She wasn't really asleep. She was just closing her eyes and pretending that she was back home in her favorite spot. After some time, I blew out the candle and went to sleep myself. When I woke up, Donut was back in her usual place on my neck, and Mongo had jumped onto my legs, sinking the whole bed in.

We'd also purchased a room for Mordecai, though when I wandered out to get breakfast, he was passed out at a round table with a still-full glass of something that smelled like mead. Gordo the Bopca was also passed out at the table, snoring so loud, it sounded like a chain saw.

"Gordo, wake up! Wake up immediately!" Donut cried as we entered the main room. "I need my breakfast, and you need to brush me!"

"Hold yer horses, ye blowhard," Gordo said, sitting up. He wiped the drool off his face. He shook his head and mumbled something under his breath. "I need to freshen up a bit, and I'll get you fed. Don't you worry. And you can brush yourself, Princess."

"Well, I never," Donut said, looking appalled. She looked up at me expectantly. "Carl, do something."

"Mordecai teach you the finger-breaking trick?" I asked, sliding into a chair next to the still-asleep incubus.

"Finger breaking? No. He made me a potion," Gordo said. The short gnome stood and wiped himself off. "I told him I didn't quite feel myself since you two arrived, and he offered to mix me a draft using a few things behind my bar. Something that'll allow me to regain my dignity." He glared at Donut. "It's not right, taking advantage of me kind nature like that."

"This is an outrage!" Donut said as Gordo disappeared into the back. "Mordecai, I wish to speak with you. Wake up!"

"Where am I?" Mordecai said, sitting up. He looked about wildly. He settled when his eyes met mine. "Oh," he said. The incubus smelled like the floor of a biker bar. I got up to change seats, but Mordecai grabbed my arm, preventing me from moving.

"Do you always drink this much?" I said. "Why is it we're just seeing this now?"

"You're *my* manager, Mordecai," Donut said. "Why are you turning the help against me? Now who's going to brush my hair?"

MORDECAI: Listen up both of you. Don't say anything out loud. I
    had to make him a potion that would knock him out so I
    could go into his kitchens and find the newsletter.

CARL: Newsletter?

MORDECAI: Yes. Bopcas and shopkeepers don't have access to the feed, so they get a physical newsletter delivered after each recap episode. Once he passed out, I went into the back so I could read the brief. I also stole a few items for potions. I don't have an inventory like you do, so take this.

He pulled several items from his pockets and handed them to me under the table. I pulled them into my inventory without looking. Almost all of them were loose herbs.

CARL: Holy shit, Mordecai. Is that cheating?

MORDECAI: Managers only have one rule. We can't engage in direct battle with mobs. Everything else is fair game.

DONUT: YOU ARE LIKE A SPY. I KNEW YOU WOULDN'T BETRAY ME.

CARL: So, did you learn anything?

MORDECAI: Yes. The brief is regional, and it warned of a potential major battle event happening in this area today or tonight. If they're taking the time to warn the Bopcas about it, then it's a big deal. It's likely related to your elite friend. So you two need to eat your breakfast and hightail it to that town, and never come back this way. No dawdling.

CARL: Okay.

"Don't forget to assign your stat points," Mordecai said as Gordo returned with what looked like a bowl of lumpy oatmeal. He plopped two bowls on the table.

"I did last night," I said. "I put all three points into strength."

Donut's magical brush appeared on the table in front of me. "You're going to have to do it," she said. I sighed and picked it up. I still needed to do my foot routine. While I brushed her, I pulled up the note from Brandon.

BRANDON: Carl. You there, buddy? We were really happy to see
    you two on the recap tonight. I wanted to let you know
    we're still dealing with selection. It's slow going. None of
    the residents can choose human, lest they remain in their
    current condition, and there is a lot of pushback. The ones
    with cognitive issues have to pick some really weird races
    in order to remain viable. I'll tell you all about it later. I
    stayed human. Chris and Imani did not. Most of the
    residents are still level one, but you would not believe the
    loot boxes they got for hitting the third floor without killing
    anything or dealing any damage. They all are getting
    Legendary Pacifist Boxes along with a ton of other ones.
    It's ridiculous how much magical gear we now have. Some
    of these bastards are going to be more powerful than Imani
    pretty soon. Anyway, Mistress Tiatha says we're likely
    pretty far from you now. I wanted to thank you again for
    your help. I hope we see each other again.

I sent him back a quick reply, asking him to stay safe. I contemplated telling him about Agatha, but I decided against it. I didn't want anything to do with that, and I feared putting it in writing would be a mistake. I also asked if he knew what Donut's new talent, Scutelliphily, was. Or if he knew what Cesta Punta was.

I also gave him a piece of advice, the same advice Odette had given us. If they weren't done yet, and somebody had that manager ability, he needed to talk them into choosing it. Despite Mordecai's raging alcoholism, I could already tell that benefit was the best chance we had at survival.

A half hour later, Donut, Mongo, and I headed back out into the Over City ruins. The artificial sun had just risen, leaving long shadows throughout the wooden streets. Lazy wisps of smoke rose from random places throughout the city. The world smelled of sulfur and something else, something acrid, like an outboard motor that was burning too much oil. The air was cooler in the morning, though still warmer than the previous level. I took a deep breath of the smoky air. Mongo squeaked a few times, and Donut leaped to my shoulder.

I pulled up the first dungeon locator we came across to make sure I hadn't gotten myself turned around, and we turned toward the skyfowl settlement. We had a good 30 kilometers to go.

"Look, the blood is all gone," Donut said as we passed a place where we'd killed a lemur the day before. Mongo had made a real mess of the body, splattering blood everywhere.

"Remember what Mordecai said? Every floor has a janitor mob. The rats, then the brindle grubs. We haven't seen the ones for this floor yet. They might only come out at night."

"Are we really going to do everything Mordecai says?" Donut said.

"Today we are," I said. "He may have some issues, but he knows what he's doing. He was right, and I was wrong yesterday. We should never have kicked up that hornet's nest. Especially now that we know how those elites work. We need to stay as far away from those assholes as—"

You have been stunned!
    You have been paralyzed!
    You have been rendered unconscious!
    Why do you got to get killed? You ain't so little as mice.
    I didn't bounce you hard.

———

MY HEAD FELT AS IF A PICKUP TRUCK HAD ROLLED OVER IT. I groaned. Multiple increasingly frantic messages from Mordecai appeared in my vision. I mentally waved them away. I sat up, looking around frantically. I was in a darkened room. I'd been placed on a ratty old couch that stank of mildew. I still had all of my equipment. My health was full.

Donut? Where's Donut?

My chest pulled with fear. *No, I don't want to be alone.*
"Donut?" I called. "Where are you?"
No answer.

CARL: Donut? Fuck, please answer me.

There was no answer. I pulled up my minimap, but I didn't see her at all. I couldn't see anything. But she was still there in the party menu, which meant she was alive. Only slightly relieved, I called for her again, this time louder.

I heard something. A screech. It was distant, but it came from another room. The moment I heard it, an orange dot appeared on my map. Mongo. Mongo was still alive.

Calm down. Take a deep breath. Think about this for a moment.

What had happened? I tried to remember. We'd been walking and talking. We'd barely just hit the main road. I hadn't seen anything. Mongo hadn't warned us of the attack. I'd been stunned, then paralyzed, then knocked out.

The AI seemed to think I was about to die. It'd read a quote from *Of Mice and Men*. As a kid, I'd had to read that damn book three times in school, as a result of constantly moving around. Later, as an adult, I'd kept a copy with me in my bunk. I'd read it over and over. It was one of my favorite books, not because I liked the story but because it felt so familiar to me, like comfort food. It was kind of a fucked-up scene for the AI to quote, but it almost felt like it was supposed to be soothing.

CARL: Mordecai, I just woke up. I don't know what happened. I
    don't know where Donut is. I don't know where I am.
MORDECAI: Oh thank the gods. Are you tied up? In a cage? In
    a web?
CARL: I'm on a couch. I'm not tied up, and I still have all my
    stuff. It's dark in here, though. I can't see anything.

MORDECAI: Okay. I can see Donut is alive. I can't see where she
is. If you just awakened now, she'll probably wake soon.
You'll see her on your map when she does as long as she's
not too far. Spend a few minutes looking around, gather all
the info you can, and tell me what you see.

The level countdown had gone down significantly. I calculated in
my head. I'd been unconscious for fifteen hours. Holy shit. It was a
kick in the teeth. Even if I somehow got out of this, whatever the
hell this was, I'd lost fifteen fucking hours. When every second
counted, that was a serious setback.

I checked my notifications to see if there were any clues. I'd received three achievements. One for getting stunned, a second for
getting paralyzed, and a third:

New achievement! Lazarus!
You have been hit with—and survived—an offensive spell
that was higher than level 15. The fact you are not a quivering
stain of meat on the dungeon floor right now is testament to
your sheer luck. It's either that or you're banging the producer.
Reward: You've received a Platinum Lucky Bastard Box!

It didn't tell me what the spell was, but the moment I read it, I
was certain I knew who had cast it.

"Signet," I said. "Are you here?"

"You hurt my feelings," she said, whispering in my ear. I felt a
warm hand on my upper leg, between my boxers and kneepads.

"Fuck," I said, practically jumping out of my skin. Her firm,
strong hand held me in place. Had she been next to me the whole
time? Goose bumps crawled across my skin.

"You called me an asshole," she continued. She practically bit at
my ear. Her breath was hot on my neck. I tried not to shiver. She was
level 60. If she wanted me dead, there would be nothing I could do

about it. "You were leaving. You had promised me you would come back."

"Where is Donut?" I said.

"She is safe. Don't you worry. I even saved that little dinosaur of hers. Your friend is still asleep and will remain asleep."

"I want to see her," I said.

"Of course, of course," Signet said. "We shall see her on the way out."

"I'm not going anywhere without Donut," I said.

"You will do exactly as I say," Signet said. "I followed you and your pet this morning. I wanted to see if you would abide by your promise. You lied to me, Carl. I was tempted to just melt the both of you right then. But I can be forgiving. I have a forgiving nature. My mother was a naiad, and she taught me that grace should always be observed, even in the face of betrayal."

"Your mother sounds very smart," I said. "But I will be grabbing my cat, and we will be leaving now."

Her hand remained on my knee in the dark room. I felt her palm rustle unnaturally as something moved by just under her skin. "Like I said, your cat is asleep. My mother taught me more than just grace. She taught me magic. Heirloom magic, which is the strongest. The spell is called *Water Lily*. Isn't it a beautiful name? She was a princess once. My mother, I mean. Before the confederacy usurped the crown. I would be tsarina were I full-blooded. I told this to Grimaldi once. He changed my name to Tsarina Signet after that."

Holy shit, this bitch is crazy. "What does the *Water Lily* spell do?"

"It puts you to sleep, of course," she said. "And you don't wake up until I cancel the spell. If I die, she dies, too."

A new wave of fear swept over me. "What do you want me to do?"

She smiled. "Just fulfill your promise. That is all."

"I promised you we would help you assault the circus. I can't do that without Donut."

"You're going to have to try. This is my deal. My grace. This is how you win back your life."

Shit.

THE BOTTOM FLOOR OF SIGNET'S BUILDING WAS AN EMPTY SHELL with broken walls on three of the four sides. Outside, the sun had made a full journey across the sky. It sank now behind the distant buildings. Donut lay asleep in the middle of the room, placed upon a rotting cushioned chair. It was the only thing in the room other than a large cage containing Mongo, who hopped up and down and screeched at my approach.

"Donut!" I cried, rushing up to the cat. I went to a knee and stroked her soft fur. I remembered brushing it earlier. It was hard to look at her like this. *She's so small, so vulnerable.* She had **Unconscious** hovering over her body.

I reached over and opened up Mongo's cage. The dinosaur jumped onto the chair and pushed his head questioningly against the cat, who did not wake up. He let out a worried screech.

Signet stood nearby, her hands clasped in front of her. Her small, bare breasts would've been a distraction at any other time, even with her ghastly face. Her tattoos seemed to congregate on her body, facing whatever direction I was in, all of them staring at me intently.

"We can't leave Donut here," I said, looking about the room. We were practically outside. Any wandering mob would find her. I worried about the janitor mob, whatever it might be.

"She will remain," Signet said.

"No. Fuck you," I said. I reached to pick her up. A health bar appeared the moment I lifted her. It started quickly falling.

"Carl, I would return her immediately to her place. A water lily must not be removed, lest it die."

I quickly put her limp body back in the chair. The bar stopped moving down. A moment later, and it began to ease its way up.

"Come, Carl. It is almost time for me to cast my summoning. We have much to prepare before the assault."

"Just a minute," I said. "Watch out, Mongo." I started pulling the last of the redoubt pieces from my inventory. I had multiple pieces of wood and metal in my pack. I erected an ugly, quick, and dirty shelter around the cat, like a pyramid. I worked as quickly as I could.

"Carl," Signet said. "Now."

"Jesus, you're worse than Bea," I said as I put the last piece in place. The obstacle wouldn't protect Donut from a determined mob, but this was better than nothing. Mongo jumped to the top of the neck-high, haphazard pyramid. He looked down through the jagged hole in the top and then back at me.

I put my hand against the side of the dinosaur's head. He was still small, but at level six, he was now bigger than Donut. "I don't know if you understand me, but you have to stay here, and you have to protect her. It's the most important thing you've ever had to do. I gotta go now, but I will be back. Do you understand?"

Mongo screeched, looked down at Donut through the hole in the top of the pile of crap, and screeched again.

I turned and followed Signet out the door. I was giving Mordecai a running commentary of everything that was happening. I had a plan. A loose plan I'd formulated on the fly. But I couldn't do it on my own. I asked him what he thought, and he told me I was batshit crazy. I took that as a good sign.

CARL: Zev, are you there?
ZEV: Hi, Carl. I'm watching. The whole universe is watching.
    We're all rooting for you.
CARL: That's what I'm hoping for. I need your help.
ZEV: You know I can't interfere.
CARL: No, not like that.

I explained what I wanted her to do. She told me it was impossible. I told her to try anyway.

"I'm sorry it came to this, Carl," Signet was saying as we walked. "You surprised me yesterday when you survived. I won't make that mistake today."

"Why are we doing this, Signet? Why do you attack the circus every day?"

"Of the entire crew, I was the only one who made it through the attack without being altered by the poisonous cloud. And the one who got the worst of it was Grimaldi."

"Grimaldi? So the guy who owns the circus? Last night you said you loved him."

"I do love him. He is the love of my life. He saved me when I was a child. He took me in when nobody else would. He protected me from the high elves, took me from the Hunting Grounds, gave me a life. But most importantly, he gave me a family. As I became an adult, I grew to love him as more than just a father. We were going to share our lives together."

"So, what happened?"

"You have to understand how horrible it was, the cataclysm. Scolopendra's poison cloud was a nine-tier attack. It attacked you in nine different ways. The lucky ones simply died. The others were transformed, all in different ways."

This was the second time I'd heard that name, Scolopendra. It sounded like this was the monster at the bottom of the volcano. I filed that information away.

She continued. "Grimaldi was more than just the owner. He was also the circus's ringleader. We were nearing the end of a show when the cataclysm came. He stood in the middle of the center ring. The others were all out there taking their bow." Signet took a deep breath. "He transformed into the vine. All the others in the tent, no matter how they transformed, were soon infected with the mold-covered parasites. This put them under Grimaldi's control. The lemurs, the clowns, almost everyone. They do as he says. And if they die, the spores return to the vine, and they are reborn the next day."

"And that's why you attack the circus every day? Why did you survive and the others did not?"

She didn't answer my question. "Last night I cast my spell,

expecting you to perish. Tonight, I am putting my faith in you. You will have to be the one to defeat the sacrifice. I have captured Heather multiple times, but always for the purpose of killing the sacrifice. I have yet to use her blood to summon my team. I am trusting you tonight to kill Heather. While her blood won't be as powerful as yours, it'll be some of the most potent blood I've used."

We rounded a corner and stopped. Lying asleep in the middle of the road was an unconscious . . . *something*. She was under the same *Water Lily* spell as Donut.

"That's Heather?" I asked, feeling sick.

"Yes."

"And you want me to kill her so you can take her blood and summon your people?"

"Yes again."

I stepped forward. "Okay. Cast your spell before she wakes up. I'll kill her now."

"It doesn't work that way, Carl. I can't influence the battle, or the spell doesn't work."

"That's the stupidest shit I've ever heard."

"If it wasn't like that, I would've just killed you last night."

I swallowed. I examined "Heather."

It—she—appeared to have once been a black bear. She wore a tattered pink clown hat and a pleated clown ruff around her neck, both of which appeared to be physically attached to her body. Like the lemurs, she had no skin on her face. Above her neck was nothing but exposed skull and a pair of round red eyes.

The horrors didn't stop there. Her two front paws had been transformed to white worms, like her claws had been replaced with mops. These were different than the worms that made up the lions' manes. Even in sleep, they moved and undulated. I felt my gorge rise at the sight.

But most absurd of all were the bear's two back legs, which had a pair of roller skates attached to them. She also wore a pink tutu.

Signet took a step back. "Okay, Carl. She's going to wake up, and I will cast my summoning spell. Then you go kill her."

Admin Note: Boss Battles that arise concurrently with secondary productions or as parts of a Quest may present themselves differently. You will still receive awards commensurate with the boss's proper rank. If you survive, of course.

"Oh fuck," I said.

9

THE USUAL MUSIC AND BOMBASTIC OVER-THE-LOUDSPEAKER AN-
nouncement never came. The system was treating this just like a
regular mob. But this clearly wasn't just any old monster.

> Heather the Bear!
> Level 19 Neighborhood Boss!
> Performing since she was a cub, Heather the Roller-Skating
> Bear was one of the longest-running attractions at Grimaldi's
> Traveling Circus. Her retirement had been only weeks away
> when the cataclysm hit. Now the tired old bear has been trans-
> formed into a monstrosity, barely recognizable from her former
> self. She lives out her days as a hunter for the circus, seeking
> out juicy mobs and unsuspecting crawlers. She finds and inca-
> pacitates her prey using her overwhelming speed and strength.
> Then she drags her quarry back to the circus so the clowns may
> feed.
> Somewhere in there, deep, deep down, there is a spark of
> the old Heather. The beloved bear has moments of lucidity as
> she runs down her terrified prey. In those brief moments, she
> thinks: *Good. I've always hated all you assholes anyway.*

Unlike most boss battles, it didn't appear that I was locked into
the area. But I couldn't run, could I? I looked wildly about. Behind
me was a large intersection. A two-story building sat at each corner.
It was already too dark for me to see inside.

CARL: Mordecai. Boss battle. Level 19 black bear with worms
     for claws and roller skates for feet. Tips?
MORDECAI: Roller skates? Like those little shoes with wheels
     on them? Are you serious?
CARL: Yes, I'm fucking serious!
MORDECAI: Male or female?
CARL: Female.
MORDECAI: Shit. Okay. What about your *Protective Shell*? Has
     that reset yet?
CARL: Yes. It did about 15 minutes ago.
MORDECAI: Black bears are the smallest of the bears, but they
     are faster and stronger than they look. Female bears are
     much smarter than the male ones. I don't know what the
     worm claws mean. Don't let her hug you. Use your shell.

Heather roared and stood to her full height, balancing on her two
legs as she spread her two upper arms out.

"Fuck me," I said, scrambling back. I'd seen plenty of black bears
in my life, and they usually weren't that big, most no larger than big
dogs. Heather was an exception. She was *huge*. On her roller skates,
she stood about eight feet tall. The pink clown hat sat cockeyed on
her skull head. I could see where the cone of the hat was fused directly to the bone, like she was some sort of fucked-up bearicorn.

The worm claws came to life, dozens of little appendages wriggling and undulating.

. . . And growing longer and longer. The bone white worms appeared to glow in the fading light as they spread to the ground, like
pasta being made directly from the bear's hands. As the swirling
worms fell, I caught glints of actual bear claws at the ends of the
paws.

Holy shit, I thought. *That's really fucking gross.*

Where the hell was Signet? I looked about for the elite. My eyes
caught movement, and I spied her through a hole in a building across
the intersection. She was on the second floor, and her arms were

raised like they'd been yesterday. Her strange tattoos twirled about her body the same as before.

I sensed the movement before I saw it. I'd only looked over my shoulder for a second, but the bear had halved the distance between us. She sailed across the wooden slats on her roller skates, gliding at me. The well-oiled skates made a *whisk, whisk, whisk* noise across the ground. She whipped her arm back as I twisted, pulling a pair of smoke bombs from my inventory and tossing them at my feet. I pulled two more as I started to run. I'd learned my lesson the other day not to use just one of these things.

Too slow. Heather swiped from fifteen feet away. The worms swept at me like a whip before I'd even realized what the hell was happening. Dozens of worms rushed at me, slapping into me, and wrapping around me three quick times like a damn tetherball. The wet, cold ends of the worms hit the exposed skin of my upper legs, and I felt them start to burrow into my body. *I need pants. I really fucking need pants.* It felt like knives going into my skin.

Yes, yes, this is new flesh. Primal flesh. Delicious flesh.

Strong he is. Do we taste this? He will feed our clowns well.

The clowns hunger, Primal. They are ravenous. And now they know of your flavor.

I smashed down on *Protective Shell* as the smoke started to billow from the smoke bombs. The worms severed off the bear, cutting them in half and killing them. The ends half-burrowed into my skin dropped away. The bear, which had been almost on top of me, rocketed back, hitting the ground and rolling away. I'd blown it a good fifty feet back.

What the hell was that?

The worm things had entered my skin and immediately started talking in my mind. The words had come all at once, piling on top of one another. I couldn't tell if it was one voice or a thousand voices. Male or female. It'd felt as if someone had taken their dirty fingers, sunk them directly into the meat of my brain, and dragged.

Fuck no. Fuck that. I would die before I let that happen again. I jumped into action.

I rushed at the fallen bear, leaving the protection of the shield behind. I pulled nuts and bolts and dumbbells from my inventory as I ran, scattering them on the ground.

I was too close for a boom jar or a stick of dynamite. Instead, I pulled a regular jug of moonshine and tossed it at the bear as hard as I could. The jug shattered against the bear's head. I'd thrown it significantly harder than I'd expected or anticipated. *Wow.* Even with my enhanced strength, I hadn't been expecting the sheer violence of the toss. I skidded to a stop.

A health bar finally appeared as Heather screamed in rage. Moonshine splashed over the bear, who remained on her back, struggling. The pungent stench filled the intersection. The puddle highlighted itself in my vision, and the words **Flammable Liquid** appeared floating over it. *That's new,* I thought as I pulled out a torch, lit it, and tossed it at the bear.

I didn't wait to see what happened next. I turned and ran toward the still-billowing smoke plume. Like last time, it was an irritatingly narrow cone of smoke despite the multiple bombs. It'd caught in the wind, swelling away from the bear. But the smoke cone was just wide enough to hide within.

Whoosh.

I felt the heat of the moonshine igniting. I ran into the smoke and turned in time to see the bear pulling herself to her feet, her entire body aflame. The red-and-blue flames rose into the night air. The billowing fire partially obscured Heather's health bar. It moved down, but at a crawl. It wasn't even in the red yet.

The on-fire bear shrieked and started roller-skating at me. *Whisk, whisk, whisk.*

Now, if you've never had a flaming, skull-faced bear on roller skates barreling at you at full speed, you don't know what you're missing.

She stumbled and fell, tripping over a dumbbell. When she rose again, half of her skin and fur remained on the ground, revealing an exposed rib cage filled completely with worms, like a knot of ramen noodles. The worms burst forth from the flames, reaching every which way.

For fuck's sake.

I'd been saving it for a dire situation, and I pulled it out now. The scratcher lottery ticket I'd received from that lucky bastard box. Fireball or Custard. I had a fifty-fifty chance. It would either fire a level 15 fireball, which would probably kill it immediately. Or it would splatter the thing with strawberry custard, which would heal it.

I awkwardly held the paper ticket in my left hand as I scratched off one of the five spots, revealing a little spinning circle. The tiny icon flashed back and forth from a red fireball to a pink glob. The skating boss was nothing but a skeleton now. Only the hat and the roller skates remained on fire. Even the round, bulbous eyes were gone. A mass of worms covered the skeleton, as if it were wrapped in yarn.

The health bar was only half gone.

Hiding in the smoke seemed to do nothing. The arm whipped back once again.

The spinning icon on the ticket stopped.

Custard. Yummy!

The voice said it out loud, deep and bass heavy, like it was the announcer dude from that goddamned *Candy Crush* game. I had a sudden, inexplicable memory of Bea playing that game on her phone with the volume turned all the way up while I was trying to watch TV.

"Mother fuck!" I cried, jumping back as the beach-ball-sized custard ball burst forth and splattered against the bear, who staggered and—once again—fell on its back.

The skeletal bear roared in pain as custard boiled against her skin. Her skin and fur reformed over her body, spreading across her frame in odd, jerky clumps, like a stop-motion film. The bear struggled upward again. The damn thing was like the Terminator. Her health bar started to ease back up.

But something had changed. The roller skates fell off the bear's feet as she struggled. So did the hat. Both dissipated into dust. The skin on the bear's face formed. She did not stand as she had before, but remained on all fours like a normal bear. Her tattered black fur held a silver sheen especially evident around her muzzle.

By healing it, I'd killed the worms. The bear let out a howl, mournful and afraid. She sat down and lowered herself painfully to the ground. The last of the boiling custard sizzled away. The bear looked at me, all of the fight out of her. This was Heather, the real Heather, free of the parasites that'd been controlling her. She looked at me with her newly formed eyes.

End it, those bitter eyes said. *I should never have lived this long.* She made a quick, pained whimper, and her eyes closed.

I approached the bear. I kept a wary eye on her claws, looking for any sign of a trick. The bear sighed heavily as I approached. Her health bar, which had moved to the top, was now falling again on its own. Without the worms and mold or whatever the hell magic was keeping this thing alive, her body was breaking down fast. This elderly bear, Heather, was not who I'd just fought. Not really. She was just the shell.

I was tempted to just let her die on her own. But only for a moment. I formed a fist, and I smashed her head in with two quick punches. Then I stood, and I finished her off by pressing my foot against her skull and crushing. Her skull caved in easily.

Winner! appeared in my interface. That was the only indication I'd just finished a boss battle. A few achievements came and went into the folder. I'd gone up to level 15. I was pushing 16 already. Donut was going to be pissed.

The bear's body shuddered. A line of red rose from the corpse, even through the flames. The blood flew through the air, angling upward toward Signet's now-glowing body.

MORDECAI: Congrats. You just won your first solo boss battle.

A black crackling shell of smoke surrounded the building where Signet cast her spell. Mordecai said he knew exactly what spell this was, and it'd likely take a good ten minutes for it to finish. In the meantime, I figured I'd better stay the hell away and just let it happen.

CARL: Not gonna lie. I'm surprised. I thought for sure she wanted me to die and that she'd cast that sacrifice spell on me again.

MORDECAI: She probably did. Like I said, the system lets them fudge with reality when you're dealing with elites. Which is why we stay away from them. Have you heard back from Zev yet?

CARL: No. Donut is still okay?

MORDECAI: Yes. I get a warning when her health is down to 20 percent, but that's all I have. Her status hasn't changed.

CARL: Did you learn anything for me?

MORDECAI: I visited my old friend Eklund. He's the only game guide in this town I know. He's too smart for his own good, unfortunately. I couldn't get him to look up the cure for the *Water Lily* curse, but I am headed to the town alchemist now to see if he has a clue. Eklund did, however, tell me the name of the program.

CARL: And?

MORDECAI: I think your hunch is correct. It's called *Vengeance of the Daughter.*

CARL: Oh, thank god. Okay. Thanks, Mordecai. Keep looking.

I looted the remains of the dead, bloodless bear. Like with any other neighborhood boss, I received a map upgrade. I grabbed it, and the neighborhood came alive with dots. At this distance, I couldn't see Mongo and Donut, but I could see the entirety of the circus a few streets over. Hundreds of red dots surrounded the edges of the circus like before, waiting. In addition, dozens of other red dots spread around the map, some of them moving, some sitting still. These were the night denizens of the ruins, and I needed to stay away from them all.

A group of white dots centered around Signet. As I watched, another appeared. Then another.

I felt a stab of concern. While it was a lot—there had to be at least thirty of them—it wasn't nearly enough to take on the sheer numbers of that circus.

The smoke cleared, and just as it faded, Signet appeared, followed by her summoned minions.

"Wow," I said, taking in the sight. I took a step back, almost tripping over the splattered remains of the dead bear. I didn't know whether to be in awe, to laugh, or to cry. *I am so fucked.*

The smallest of the monsters, a floating head thing, was about ten feet tall. The largest, a twisting, undulating sea serpent, was as tall as a three-story building. The three-headed ogre was the second largest of the motley collection, wielding an enormous saber. He stood behind Signet as she approached me. The ogre crossed his arms, and his saber caught the wind, flapping.

The others crowded into the intersection and flowed into the streets around us. A hammerhead shark floated in the air above me.

"Can these things actually fight?" I asked as Signet came to stand before me.

The tattoos were all gone from her skin. Her white flesh glowed, her nakedness starker now that her only adornment was the thong. I detected a very slight blue shimmer to her skin, almost as if she were covered with very fine scales, too small to see with the naked eye. Her face, without the constant, swirling lines, was easier to discern.

While still strange-looking, Signet wasn't nearly as repugnant as usual. Now I could see the half–sea creature that she was. But I only had a moment to ruminate over her appearance. My attention was focused on the "army" that towered behind her.

While all the tattoo monsters were huge and fearsome, they were not what I expected. Not at all. They were still . . . tattoos. Drawings. While absolutely huge, the monsters were barely three-dimensional. Reverse Shrinky Dinks. Each one was like a paper cutout of a monster blown up to massive proportions and then cut out with scissors and left to flap in the wind.

Every one of them was a deep red outline, with a white translucent substance between the lines, like wax paper or maybe onionskin. The back sides of the paper monsters were blank. I had the sense I could easily punch through each one. If I looked upon them at any direction other than straight on, I could see them for what they were. A paper army. The monsters moved and blinked and roared, but all of it was confined to the plane on which they had been drawn.

I examined the three-headed ogre:

Blood-and-Ink Elemental—Summoned Minion of Tsarina Signet— Level 50.

    Created by a combination of sacrificial Blood Magic and an artist's imagination, these short-lived elementals vary wildly in their strength and abilities. Their potential relies heavily on too many factors to list here. Kind of like humans. If you have to guess, odds are good the one you're looking at right now is probably hot garbage.

"Of course, they can fight," Signet said. "Do you think Grimaldi would prepare such a defense each night for something other than a real threat? Now we must hurry. Heather's blood was powerful indeed. I have summoned my entire retinue, but I decreased their longevity in exchange for more strength. We have but a short amount of time."

How can paper fight? I wanted to demand, but Signet strode forward before I could ask. As she walked away, I caught sight of one last tattoo on her shoulder blade. It was of a tiny figure, too small for me to see clearly. It was a fish of some kind. The tattoo faded away, like a sea creature diving under the waves.

The monsters rustled past me, marching and floating toward the circus. The long sea-serpent monsters floated sideways, so they always faced the circus. I remained gawking up at the menagerie. The three-headed ogre turned, his entire body folding over as he glared down at me. "Follow or you get the smash," the middle head said in a deep, rumbly voice.

"You can talk!" I exclaimed.

"I can smash, too," he said.

I followed. I ran to catch up to Signet, who strolled toward the circus as if she didn't have a care in the world.

"I honestly don't know what the hell you want me to do here," I said. "I've never participated in anything like this. I have shitty armor and all I do is punch stuff."

"You are more than that. I believe you actually freed Heather tonight. For two centuries, she's been caught in that loop, and you freed her. She was a grumpy old bear, and I told Grimaldi more than once that she was going to snap and try to eat a spectator if we didn't retire her soon. But she was family, and you freed her. Thank you."

"Yeah, thanks for the warning, by the way," I said. "That was a one-on-one fight. I won't be able to pull any fancy tricks in a giant battle."

"Just don't die," she said. "We usually push through the defenders, and this is the strongest we've been in a while. It's the final defense I need help with."

"There's, like, a thousand of them!" I said.

I pinged Mordecai, and told him everything. I told him I didn't think these elemental things were a real threat.

MORDECAI: Don't worry about that. If they're as big and as
   numerous as you describe, it means her skill in that spell is
   likely over 15. They can fight. They're gonna put on a hell of
   a show.

CARL: What is that spell anyway?

MORDECAI: *Ink Marauder.* You draw something on paper, cast
   the blood sacrifice, and it animates the drawings. Certain
   classes can tattoo the monsters upon themselves. By
   doing it that way, her own blood powers the minions,
   keeping them alive on her flesh. They can leave her body
   when she casts the sacrifice spell. They take on a 2D
   appearance, but it's been long rumored that certain
   sacrifices can lead to the minions being complete, fully
   realized renditions of the monsters they depict. Assuming
   that is her most powerful spell, I don't see the producers
   allowing her to blow that wad this early in the story.

A distant cry filled the night, followed by the *thwump* of a magical mortar. The projectile sailed into the night sky, bouncing off the
ceiling into a neighborhood one street over. More mortars started
raining down. I tried to stick as close to Miss Plot Armor as possible.

The floating head and several dragons circled around us, moving
ahead. One of the elementals—an octopus—caught a mortar round
directly in the chest and burst into flames. If Signet was controlling
these things, she wasn't doing it out loud. Dark shadows filled the
air. *Lemurs,* I realized, seeing the dots on the minimap. They were
being flung by the artillery giraffes. I could hear the distinctive roar
of mold lions as well. They moved fast, streaking down one street
over as paper monsters moved to intercept them.

We were only one block from the circus now. The haunting calliope music rose into the night, mixing in with the roar of the lemurs
and clowns. More lemurs burst into the air, this time aimed directly
at us.

The ogre leaped forward, sailing over the top of me and Signet, and landing on the ground. All I could now see was the back of the flat elemental. He swung his paper saber in the air at the line of lemurs.

Dozens of the skull-headed monsters screamed as they were flung away, but a moment later, I heard the *thwap, thwap, thwap* of knives embedding themselves into the giant ogre. Despite the paper appearance, the knives slammed into the elemental like he was made of plywood. He took no heed of the damage. He swung again. And by "swung," I mean his paper arm folded over on its own and kind of waved at the mobs.

There was something I was missing about the ogre's attacks. He'd swing, clearly miss, and yet dozens of lemurs would fly away. He had some sort of area attack I couldn't see from behind.

I did, however, see the eel's lightning attack. A pair of long moray eel–like creatures swept down and shot lightning from their mouths, turning the red dots of mold lions into X's.

Next to me, Signet fired a yellow bolt into the air from the palm of her hand. It arced over the shoulder of the ogre and hit something distant. Dozens of voices cried out in pain. Behind me, an entire building exploded as the mortar fire resumed.

"Jesus Christ, lady," I said, ducking. "You do this shit every night?"

She fired two more of the arcing yellow bolts. "This is what you do for family," she said.

MORDECAI: I know the recipe now. It's just satch toad extract mixed with a standard healing potion. I should have known. Negates all naiad sleep effects and curses. Simple.
CARL: Do you have any of that stuff?
MORDECAI: Not in this town. But it's common enough. I can buy it at the alchemical market in a medium or large town.

Fuck. That wasn't going to help us now.

CARL: Okay. Plan B it is.

I dove to the ground as another building exploded. We were only fifty meters from the picket, and the clowns were starting to throw rocks at us. The largest of the serpents swept down and exhaled a stream of water, blasting hundreds of clowns and lemurs in all directions. I dove behind a low wall as more mortar fire sailed overhead. A shark twisted through the air above me, howling as it burned.

CARL: Zev, you talked to them yet?

ZEV: I messaged the producer, but he didn't want to speak with me. He's waiting to see how this plays out, I think. My boss made me run your request by the Syndicate AI referee, and it said they'll only allow this under very strict circumstances. I can't, and they can't, give you any help whatsoever. Believe it or not, though, this isn't the first time this sort of thing has happened. In fact—

CARL: Later, Zev. Stay tuned. I'll need you in a bit.

Despite my earlier reservations, the clowns and circus creatures were no match for the tattoo monsters. The defenders soon fled, falling back to the massive triple tent. The ogre elemental swiped his saber and the defensive wall shattered. Hundreds of lemurs and clowns and thin mortar acrobats lay dead. It'd happened so fast. My entire map was awash in X's.

There were still hundreds of the monsters left, but they were all now inside the main tent. The paper army flapped their way onto the circus ground, pushing through the barbed wire fortifications like they were nothing, surrounding the massive pavilions. All of the secondary tents, including the freak show tent, soon fell. I noted the elementals were simply pushing the small tents over, as if they were being careful not to tear the fabric. All that remained was the big top. Only a few of the elementals had been destroyed. An octopus tattoo had returned to Signet's skin, along with a few of the sharks. They swished about angrily.

The music was coming from a large, coach-sized contraption

sitting just outside the big top. Steam rose from the humming, spitting instrument. The long brass tubes hissed out the slow-motion
music. The ogre moved to smash the machine, but Signet raised her
hand.

"This music hurts my heads," the knife-riddled monster groused.

"I know," Signet said. "We go over this every time." She stepped
forward and turned a dial on the machine. It wheezed once and the
music stopped, plunging the night into silence. She lovingly stroked
the fire-scorched wood.

Signet then pointed up at the giant sea serpent, which floated in
the sky above the brightly lit tent. The circus's spotlights remained
lit, and they arced back and forth, adding to the surreal vision. The
behemoth was almost as large as the center big top. The tattoo monster folded back on itself and then fired a blue waterspout. I cringed
in anticipation, but the water dissipated before it could touch the
colorful top. The world around me filled with a fine mist, and I suddenly found myself soaked.

Signet hung her head low. "Damn," she said. "Damn, damn,
damn. I'd hoped, with the power of Heather's blood, that we could
overcome the protection this time."

"Why didn't that work?" I asked. In the distance, something
howled in the night.

"This is where our fight usually ends," Signet said, indicating the
tent. "There is magic here protecting the exterior. Ancient magic. I
have been banished, so I can't go inside. My minions can't go inside.
The outside is impenetrable, but not the interior. If we break down the
tents, the spell will disperse, and we can finish this." She pointed at the
piles of dead bodies. "Some of these clowns will carry big top tickets.
Find one and brandish it. It will allow you to go inside. The tickets are
magical. They will promise you safe passage within the tent as long as
you don't enter one of the three rings. You need to go in there and collapse the tent. There are three poles. You must break each one in turn."

I looked at the tent dubiously. "I take it these three poles are in
the middle of the rings?"

"That's right," she said.

"What about the vine thing?" I asked.

"Also in the ring. The center ring."

This setup was designed to be completed by a group of at least three crawlers, not a solo player. There was no feasible way I could do this. Not with a straight-up fight.

I pulled one of the tickets I already had from my inventory. I'd already examined it, but I looked at it again.

Big Top Ticket.

Lucky you! This ticket admits one adult into the Grimaldi's Traveling Circus Big Top Show.

The holder of this ticket is guaranteed Safe Passage through the public areas only. *Grimaldi reserves the right to rescind this safe passage guarantee to drunks and purveyors of violence.*

Guaranteed good time or your money back!

Something told me I wasn't going to be having a good time.

10

I HELD THE CIRCUS TICKET TIGHTLY IN MY HAND AS I APPROACHED the main entrance. This close to the big top tent, I could see the effects of time on the fabric and the rest of the circus. The red carpet below my feet was threadbare and stained with blood. The tent sidewalls were also stained and filled with tiny holes. Another few years, and Signet wouldn't need a magical army to knock this place down.

"You must hurry," Signet said. "We only have thirty minutes before the battle squad fades."

"If I die, you need to promise to let Donut free," I said.

"It will be done," she said.

The entranceway was shaped like a giant clown face, and I had to walk straight into the clown's mouth. Time had faded the clown's pupils, making the eyes completely white. *I hate clowns,* I thought. *I really hate clowns. Whoever invented these things needs to be punched in the face.*

I had to proceed through a short, curving tunnel. Music once again rose, coming from deep within the tent. This song was faster and happier, more in the style of traditional circus music. My minimap was a sea of red dots, including one right around the corner. *Oh fuck, oh fuck, oh fuck,* I kept thinking as I inched my way forward. I held the ticket out in front of me.

I turned the corner, and I stood face-to-face with one of the round clowns. The thing was shorter than me, but almost three times as wide. He wore a brightly colored but filthy pink-and-blue gown with a dirty white ruffle around his neck. The gown cascaded over his lumpy, misshapen body. Unlike the stilt clowns, which only had sharklike mouths, this thing had a much more human face, but with pointed teeth. The white, red, and blue greasepaint seemed overly thick, like the frosting on a cake. The clown's stomach made a rumbling noise, and his entire belly shifted, like his flesh was alive.

The stilt clowns were armed with butcher knives. These guys just had long, yellowed fingernails, like the claws of a badger.

Clammy the Clown—Level 9.

With a face not even a mother could love, the circus was the perfect escape for the young, portly boy who would grow to become Clammy the Clown. An expert at tumbling and with a solid work ethic, Clammy was a perfect addition to Grimaldi's family.

Kids always love the fat clowns. They're jolly. They're happy. They make you laugh. The resurrected Clammy clones still exhibit all of these qualities. Except, perhaps, the making-you-laugh part. They sure are happy and jolly when they're eating you, though.

The clown hissed at me, but I held up the ticket, brandishing it like a shield. The enormously fat clown leaned in and sniffed the ticket, like I was holding a treat up to a dog. He hissed again, blasting me with the stench of raw meat. But he stepped aside and allowed me to pass.

And thus I entered the main arena of Grimaldi's big top.

As a kid, one of my earliest memories was going to the circus with my mom on my fourth birthday. She'd temporarily left my dad and run away to her parents' house all the way down in the middle-of-nowhere southern Texas, dragging me along.

It was during that time she'd taken me to the circus. It hadn't been one of the major traveling circuses, like Ringling Brothers, but a small, ghetto one. Anyone who has ever lived in the American Southwest knows exactly what I'm talking about. Even little kid me had registered that this was a low-rent version of the real deal.

They'd had clowns and acrobats, plus a bunch of other weird attractions, like guys on motorcycles riding around the inside of a sphere and women juggling chain saws. They'd also had animals. I remembered camels and dancing poodles, and a clown who walked around with a small monkey on his shoulder. They hadn't had elephants or giraffes, but the main attraction had been a crusty old tiger who'd sat in the middle of the ring while a woman in a leotard twirled fire sticks around it.

Most of these memories came back to me, years later, from photos. I'd found the shoebox with those pictures more than a decade later, hidden under my parents' bed. This was after another birthday of mine, the one when I was left alone in the world. The box had been my mother's. Her secret, filled to the brim with photographs and ticket stubs and a deflated balloon. The items were only of that time, the few weeks of our lives when she'd run away.

But of all my patchy, incomplete recollections of the circus, there was one characteristic of that day I will never forget.

The smell.

It was unlike anything I'd ever experienced. It was the scent of peanuts and cotton candy and roasting corn and hay and animal musk and cheap plastic toys all rolled into one. But it was more than that. My four-year-old mind couldn't possibly register it at the time, but it was the scent of happiness, of joy, of being a kid, of not being afraid. Over the years I'd catch similar scents in places such as the county fair, or carnivals, or whenever I visited a place with livestock. But this was a different, oddly specific aroma that had been indelibly imprinted on me as a four-year-old, a scent I'd sometimes remember as the path I could've taken, the world I could've lived had my dad not found us and taken us back. It was a scent I'd been chasing all of my adult life.

It's funny how that happens sometimes. We associate smells with memories, and when that memory is triggered, we are momentarily pulled away, no matter the current circumstances. That's exactly what happened here, as I stepped into the most fucked-up circus in

the history of the universe. I was surrounded by bedlam, by unorga-
nized chaos and clutter, by one *what the fuck?* after another, and that
smell just came out of nowhere, smacking me like a goddamned
baseball bat, and making me think of my fourth-birthday party,
when I'd been with my mom and visited the circus, and I'd laughed
and clapped and dropped my hot dog onto the dirty bleacher before
picking it up and eating it even though it tasted like dirt. My mom
had cried, had been crying, and up until that very moment when the
smell hit me for the second time in my life, I'd always thought she'd
been crying about the damn hot dog.

And it made me mad, so fucking mad. I had so little of my mom,
so little memory I could call my own. It was one of the few things this
fucking place couldn't possibly take from me, yet that was exactly what
had just happened, and it was so unexpected, so violent, so final that I
no longer cared about the stupid plan, or about trying to save my life.

I just wanted to tear it all down.

But you don't want to hear about any of this shit, do you? It's not
important. Not when we were weeks past the Earth's expiration date.
Not when I was standing there like an idiot as I watched a unicy-
cling woman clown roll past me while greedily devouring what
looked like a goblin leg. The colorful yet demonic acrobats who,
moments before, had been firing magical mortars at monsters the
size of buildings were now sailing back and forth above me. The
lemurs juggled. The clowns sang.

I thought of Donut, passed out and exposed, only protected by
Mongo. I took a deep breath and tried to calm myself. *You will not
break me. You will not break me.*

It was as if the battle outside hadn't occurred. These were still the
fucked-up, transformed versions of the circus workers, but each and
every one of them was feverishly performing a parody of their original acts, all of them shoved tight against one another. As I watched,
two of the acrobats collided in midair and fell, crunching to the
ground. Nobody took any heed.

A weathered wooden sign stood in my path: a cutout of a figure with a speech bubble. It was of a dwarf wearing the red-and-black coattails and top hat of a ringmaster. On the wooden sign it read, I AM RINGMASTER GRIMALDI! WELCOME TO MY CIRCUS! WITHIN THIS TENT, ALL YOUR WORRIES AND FEARS ARE LEFT BEHIND. ALL WE ASK IS FOR YOU TO SIT DOWN, RELAX, AND ENJOY. LET US TAKE THOSE BURDENS FROM YOU, EVEN IF FOR JUST A SHORT AMOUNT OF TIME.

I returned my gaze to the performers. What the hell was going on? Did they forget? Was there a spell? Did they just assume they were safe? Furthermore, none of them—despite having red dots on the map—were even glancing at me. It was as if I were invisible.

I shook my head. This fucking game. I still clutched onto my ticket, and I didn't dare let it go. They were leaving me alone now, but I feared if I dropped this thing, I'd be toast.

And then I saw it. The vine. The thing was so huge, my mind hadn't properly registered its presence. I'd thought it was part of the tent or the show, a stage prop. Even after my extensive conversation with Mordecai regarding this thing, I'd been expecting, well, a vine. Like a dude with a bunch of brambles coming out of himself, reaching every which way, maybe curling up the center pole.

This was more of a giant-ass bush or shrub than a vine. It took up the entirety of the center ring, and it reached the ceiling of the tent, swallowing the pole. It was a pale green color, less haphazard-looking than I'd expected. Along the ground, multiple python-like roots spread. Unable to find purchase in the floor of the Over City, the roots spread aboveground, reaching all corners of the tent.

As I gawked, a new achievement popped up, one of the special ones I couldn't minimize. The moment I read it, I felt all of the blood rush out of my face.

New Achievement! You Can't Fight City Hall!
But you can sure die trying.
You have discovered a city boss!
That's right. Let me say that again for the assholes in the back!

A.

CITY.

FUCKING.

BOSS.

Welp. If you gonna go, you might as well do it with style.

Just an FYI. As of this moment in the current season of *Dungeon Crawler World*, not a single crawler has faced a city boss and survived. And for good reason. Only a complete moron would voluntarily put themselves in a situation where they had to fight one of the most powerful monsters on the level.

Reward: A lot of people are probably going to watch you die. That's a better prize than most of us get.

A few additional achievements appeared, but I waved them away. A city boss. Holy fuck. Like with the bear, I didn't appear to be locked into the tent. I took a step back and looked over my shoulder. The Clammy Clown remained at his post, arms crossed, blocking my exit. But I could get out. I could easily get out right now.

No. You can do this. You have a plan. I swallowed and examined the massive plant thing in the center of the arena.

Ringmaster Grimaldi—Pestiferous Vine.

This is an Elite.

Level 85 City Boss!

Before the cataclysm, if you asked any child of the sprawling Over City what their favorite activity was, a good number of them would happily tell you of the great and wonderful Grimaldi's Traveling Circus. Children dreamed of walking outside and seeing the long line of circus carts rumbling through the streets, of the tents being erected in their local park. Circus night was a holiday. A time of joy.

To Redstone Grimaldi, nothing was more important than his family. He loved each and every one of them. When the cataclysm came, and the poison cloud swept over the circus, he was center stage. He remains there to this day.

Transformed from a simple dwarf to a hulking Pestiferous Vine, Grimaldi uses his special powers to keep his family safe and alive. No matter how many times they die, no matter how many crawlers the clowns devour, he brings them back, memories intact. Well, mostly intact. Somewhere in there Grimaldi may be aware that this may not be the most moral of choices. But that's what we do when it comes to family. We protect them at all costs.

And besides, you know what they say.

The show must go on.

After the description ended, nothing changed. Nobody moved to attack. The vine didn't move at all. My eyes caught the largest of the roots. It snaked up into the empty bleachers. I walked toward it, slipping past clowns and lemurs and other oddities. I passed the strongman ogre with the appendage coming out of his neck. I realized with a start that the single-headed ogre's countenance bore a striking resemblance to the center head of the three-headed ogre tattoo monster. He held the same jagged scar across the side of his head.

This creature was also an elite. His name was Apollon the Mighty. He stood behind a small stand with a faded sign that read, ICED CREAM. A FROZEN TREAT FROM ANOTHER WORLD! NO CHEWING NECESSARY! GLIDES RIGHT IN LIKE A WINTER DREAM!

"Cone?" the ogre asked as I approached. He held up what appeared to be a petrified ice-cream cone. He dipped it into a bucket attached to the stand, and when he pulled it up, the cone was filled with writhing bone white worms similar to the ones who'd infested Heather the Bear.

"No, thank you," I said, swallowing hard so I wouldn't be sick.

The creature watched me pass, a strange look of confusion on his

face. His dot was red with a cross on my map. The strange appendage, a thick vine branch, I now realized, twitched oddly. I kept moving, clomping onto the bleachers.

> CARL: It's an elite and a city boss. You didn't tell me they could
>   be both! Holy shit. A city boss. Is this still going to work?
> MORDECAI: Uh. I was right, though, correct? It's a Pestiferous
>   Vine?
> CARL: Yes. It's fucking huge, though. It's as tall as the tent!
> MORDECAI: It should still work. The core will be the same size. I
>   think.
> CARL: You *think*? Holy shit, Mordecai!

"There are a few different kinds of collective mind-control vine
monsters, but the combination of spores and parasitic worms means
it's likely something called a Pestiferous Vine," Mordecai had said
last night. This was after the recap show, but before we'd gone to
sleep. Signet had mentioned "the vine" a few times, and I'd asked
Mordecai if he knew what that was. "It's a sign of lazy writing, if you
ask me," he'd said. "It's like on Earth television shows. Every time
there's a cop show, the cop's marriage always sucks. There's always a
storyline with a serial killer. There's always that asshole lieutenant.
These vine things on the third floor, they're . . . What is the word?
A trope. That's it. Pestiferous Vines are a trope for these shows. It's
because of the volcano story. The girl finds her grandma had turned
into one of those things."

At this point, we'd already agreed that Donut and I would be
idiots to have anything to do with the circus quest. But Mordecai
had insisted on turning the subject into a lecture regarding collective
mind-plant monsters, which were common in the dungeon, as they
were common in the universe.

"Every season," he'd said, "crawlers fall by the hundreds to these
things, especially on the sixth floor. But plants are always easy to
kill. *Very* easy to kill, as long as you know the trick. The problem is,

the trick is different for each one. Take that Pestiferous Vine, for example. It's a plant that infects other mobs. It's called a vine and it looks like a plant, all right, but it's really a hybrid fungus combined with a type of plant you don't have on Earth. Don't get me started. Anyway, it excretes these mold spores that infect parasitic worms, who in turn infect other mobs. What happens next depends on a variety of factors, depending on the mob and the type of worms. It's fascinating stuff because there are literally billions of combinations. And these vines are real, too. This isn't made up for the dungeon. Anyway, once the worms infect the mobs, this tri-symbiont—well, maybe tri-parasitic depending on how you want to look at it—relationship forms."

"So how do you kill one?" I asked. My head had started to hurt from the conversation. Donut had lost interest and was running around with Mongo in the restaurant.

"For the Pestiferous Vine, it's kind of a good-news-bad-news thing. The good news is they're one of the easiest ones to kill. The bad news is it's not instantaneous. The vine loves moisture, and it loves blood. You drip a few drops of blood directly onto one of the vines, and it'll slurp it right up. But"—Mordecai leaned in closely, his eyes sparkling as if this were the most interesting subject in the world—"if that blood is from something that has been poisoned, it breaks the link with all of its symbionts. It takes about fifteen to twenty minutes to work, unfortunately. But one moment the vine is alive and well, the next, it's mulch. It doesn't feel it. It doesn't know it's been poisoned. But it's still dead."

"Does it kill all the other mobs?"

"Depends. Some immediately go insane. Some drop dead. Some don't realize anything has changed."

"So, you poison yourself, dribble some blood on it, and it's dead?"

"That's right. It won't know, but if it suspects, you need to be careful or it can save itself."

"How? Is there a cure?"

"Yes. If you've given yourself an antidote, and you give the plant an equal amount of the same blood, it will cure it. You can't just pour an antidote potion on there. It has to be the same blood. So be careful. If it knows you poisoned it, it'll try to get its monsters to bleed you."

Assuming Mordecai's information was correct and still valid, then I could kill Grimaldi right now from my spot in the bleachers. Still, I was nervous. Mordecai had warned me multiple times that when it came to elites, the rules didn't mean shit.

I sat down on the cold bleacher next to the vine. I tried to act casual, but I knew I had to be fast. If these producer guys had been watching my feed last night, it was possible they had already deduced what I was about to do. Everyone in the arena continued to ignore my presence. I took a deep breath. *Okay. Here we go.* I pulled my nightgaunt cloak off and put it over my legs, like anyone settling in would do. My constitution lowered by four points when I removed the cloak, but it also removed my poison resistance.

Poisoning myself was easy. I had a ton of potions. I pulled a health potion and held it in my hand. I drank one by clicking it in my hotlist, and then I quickly drank the one in my hand before the potion cooldown. I'd done this once before when Donut had been injured during the fight with the Juicer.

You have been poisoned!

"Oof." It felt as if I'd been kicked in the stomach by a damn horse. It took everything I had not to double over and cry out. Before, I hadn't felt this part. My health started to plummet. I kept one of the lemurs' juggling knives in my belt, and I pulled the palm of my hand across it, cutting deep enough to create a long gash. I squeezed my hand together as blood rained down on the vine.

I cast *Heal* on myself, which didn't stop the poisoning. I waited the next few seconds before my potions opened back up, and I took one of my few poison antidote potions. I'd received those way back in the very beginning, from a Silver Adventurer Box.

I gave myself a second to just breathe. I pulled the cloak back over my shoulder and looked about to see if anything had changed. Nothing. I hazarded a look down, and the blood was almost all gone. All that remained were a few drops that'd landed on either side of the thick root.

I had no idea if it worked or not.

11

I WAITED A FEW MOMENTS TO SEE IF THERE WAS ANY SORT OF SIGN that the city boss was sick. There was nothing. It was time for the next part of the plan.

CARL: Zev. I did it. But the plan has changed. I want you to message them right now and tell them exactly what I say.

ZEV: Oh my gods, Carl. The net is going *crazy*. Only a few people understand what you just did. But word is getting out. Your numbers are just going up and up. It's amazing. Both of these dramas playing out at the same time.

CARL: Zev. Are you listening? This is important.

ZEV: Yes, yes. I'm sorry. Go ahead.

CARL: To the producers of the program *Vengeance of the Daughter*. I just poisoned Grimaldi. Even though he's an elite, I suspect you're going to let him die. I know this is all part of your plan. This is Signet's story, not his. The title of the program says it all. This is just the first act, the origin story. This is really about her getting down to the Hunting Grounds and fucking up those High Elves and maybe the Naiads, too.

    I also suspect that as soon as Mr. Grimaldi here dies, all hell is going to break loose. And when that happens, I will probably die. That's also part of your plan, isn't it? I'm looking at the three poles right now, and I can see how you've set this shit up. That center pole isn't going anywhere. But that third pole looks like it's made out of Popsicle sticks. Just a little push, and it's timbeeerrr. Hell, that thing will probably break on its own when Grimaldi dies.

You don't really need all three poles broken, do you? One will be enough for whatever plan you and your writers have. I'm spitballing here, but maybe a rip in the tent that'll allow Signet access? Of course, this would be after I'm dead. That's all you're expecting out of me, isn't it? You're serving your viewers something amazing either way. If I do it, awesome. If I fail, tragic. And no matter what, your program is drowning in viewers.

I have an offer for you. If you want these ratings to continue, I suggest you listen carefully.

This is what I'm proposing. I know you can't help me in any way. That's against the rules, and the last thing we want is to draw the ire of the system AI. But I want to be on your show. As a regular. If Donut and I both happen to survive past tonight, and I make it to the sixth floor, I will sign an exclusive agreement to only complete elite-themed quests on the sixth floor that are directly associated with *Vengeance of the Daughter*.

Look at the ratings you're experiencing right now. I am told that new programs such as yours rarely receive anything like this. Most fail right out of the gate. You probably went out of your way to place this circus near me and Donut in the hopes we'd stumble upon it. Now imagine the ratings if we continue to participate in this storyline.

You have thirty seconds after the end of this message to agree. If you *do not* agree, I am going to cut my hand again, and I am going to give Grimaldi here some of my healthy blood. And you know what that means. And after I've un-poisoned the vine, I am going to sit here for the rest of the night and enjoy the show. Nothing will happen,

though I might spout some of these theories out loud.
Signet won't get inside. Your special guest star's
appearance will be a dud. After all this buildup, people will
be *pissed*. It'll be Geraldo and Al Capone's vault all over
again. You probably don't know what that means.
Translation. Nobody will watch this shitty-ass show ever
again.

But if you agree, I have a plan. A good fucking plan that
people won't stop talking about. But I'm not going to
attempt it without a deal.

ZEV: This is not what we discussed.

CARL: Send it now. Quick, before he dies.

ZEV: They already heard it. My boss patched them in. We're
waiting for their response now.

Out in the arena, nothing changed. Down at the bottom of the
bleachers, Apollon the ice-cream-selling strongman looked up at me,
and we met eyes.

ZEV: Okay, they're no longer listening. It's a deal. They say, and
I quote, "Let's see what you got for us, Crawler. If your
stupid ass can get out of this, we look forward to working
with you in the future."

CARL: You're our agent, Zev. I want this to be official. On paper.
Or whatever you guys do.

ZEV: Don't worry about that. It's official. I have the power to
sign on your behalf.

CARL: That's terrifying, Zev. Okay, they're about to be pissed
off. If they ask, tell them I know what I'm doing.

ZEV: Do you?

CARL: Fuck no. I'm making this shit up as I go along.

With that, I once again cut open my hand, and I dripped the
blood on the root, healing the boss monster. Again, nothing changed.

I had no idea if it would've worked or not, but at least for now, I wasn't going to find out. I stood and walked down the bleachers, approaching the strongman.

As I walked down the stairs, I pulled up my inventory and found the *Wisp Armor* spell book. I'd been holding on to it because it appeared to be super valuable, and I wanted to sell it. Donut asked me about once a day if she could have it, and I'd almost relented a few times. It was a magic protection spell, and it would have been useful to her. But at the same time, *I* was supposed to be our party's tank. I needed protection, too. I wanted to wait until I saw what sorts of spells were available at the magic shop first before I decided what to do.

But I no longer had the luxury of waiting. I read the book's description again.

Wisp Armor.

    Cost: 5 Mana.

    Target: Self Only.

    Duration: 5 minutes + 1 minute per level of spell. Requires 5-minute cooldown.

    Surrounds your body with tendrils of light. While ineffective against physical attacks, this spell negates 75% of incoming damage from magic-based attacks. Provides temporary immunity to mind-control effects. Higher skill levels increase both effectiveness and duration. It also makes you look all wispy and ethereal and druid-like. A great spell to have if you're a club kid or trying to bang a vegan.

I activated the book and added the spell to my hotlist. Because of that *Heal* spell I'd cast earlier, I had to take a mana regen potion to bring my available magic points back up to five. My mana regenerated faster than it had before, but it was still maddeningly slow.

I approached Apollon.

"Hey there, buddy," I said. "You got any of them there ice-cream cones left?"

"Yes," Apollon said. The large, muscular ogre moved slowly but with deliberate ease. I wondered how strong he really was. I hoped I wouldn't have to find out. He pulled out the mass of worms on a rotten cone, and he handed it to me. "Compliments of Grimaldi," he said.

I looked at the wriggling mass of worms on the rock-hard cone. I cast *Wisp Armor* on myself. A six-minute timer appeared as sparkling lights started to twirl around me like a swarm of comets. I opened my mouth.

Like the sign said, no chewing was necessary. The worms glided right in, entering my mouth and sliding down my throat.

I met eyes with the ogre, who just looked at me. Even he seemed shocked I'd just done that.

You have been infested with a parasite!

"Delicious," I squeaked as I tried not to vomit.

DO NOT WORRY. YOU ARE ONE OF US NOW.

Yes, love. We will not feed you to the clowns. We don't feed family to the clowns.

One of us, Carl. One of us. Gooble Gobble, Gooble Gobble.

We see your memories.

We are you. You are us.

The words spoke in my mind as I stumbled toward the exit. I felt them in my gut, writhing, expanding, growing. The Clammy Clown moved aside as I pushed through the exit.

No, Carl. We have use of you, and it is not safe for you out there. Papa Grimaldi cannot regenerate you like the others. She will kill us. She will kill you. You are special. No. Why do you not stop?

Something shifted in my gut. The worms stiffened, grew more rigid.

Carl.

This was a new voice. It wasn't the all-voices-at-once of the parasites. This was Grimaldi.

Carl. No.

"Can you hear me?" I gasped. When I spoke, I felt the still-growing infestation enter my throat, like I'd swallowed a string that wouldn't go away. I gagged. I felt the ends of the worms growing up into my mouth.

Carl, I can hear you. Our minds are one. I know what you are doing. Come back. Please, come back.

I felt the mental tug that attempted to get me to stop, but thanks to my *Wisp Armor*'s ability to negate mind-control effects, I still had autonomy over myself, but only for the next five minutes.

Despite the protection of the spell, my brain felt odd, disconnected from the rest of my body, like I was in a room with a constantly dimming light.

This is what it's like to go crazy, I thought. *To lose control.*

No, Grimaldi answered. *No, son. This is nothing like that.*

I ran back out into the night. Signet stood right there at the exit. She was polishing a spot on the massive calliope. The tattoos had all returned to her flesh. Had I really been in there that long?

"Carl!" she said, surprised. "I thought . . ." She examined me, her eyes narrowing. The flashing lights continued to swirl about me. She raised her hands, and they started to glow yellow.

"Wait," I said.

"This is who you send, Redstone?" Signet called, raising her voice. She spoke with an odd mix of anger. "He's not even in the family."

"Wait," I said again. "I'm not Grimaldi, but he can hear you. I've been infected, but this spell is keeping them from taking full control."

Signet lowered her hands. "You didn't knock the poles down," she finally said.

"No," I said. "It wasn't going to work."

"I'm going to have to kill you, Carl. You won't be able to keep the infestation at bay for much longer."

"Listen. We only have a few minutes. When was the last time you two talked? It's clear you love this goddamned circus. That's why you attack it every night. You're trying to free them from this. And you, Grimaldi. I know your brain is a jumble. If it's anything like mine is right now, I can only imagine what you were going through when this thing happened. But somehow, of all of your family, the only one who escaped was Signet. You did that, didn't you? You protected her somehow. Because you love her. And now, hundreds of years later, you two assholes are trying to murder each other even though you want the same thing. You want to protect your family."

The worms in my throat surged into my mouth. The sensation was like I was suddenly vomiting. "She hurts the family. She has turned her back," I croaked.

Fucking hell. They'd physically forced me to say it. I felt blood start to drool down the side of my mouth. My throat felt as if I'd swallowed razors.

"Don't do that," I gasped. "Holy shit. Just think it, and I'll say it out loud."

"My brothers and sisters are suffering," Signet said. "The clowns have been transformed into these things. They kill those who they used to entertain. And you facilitate it, Redstone. You have a kind heart. You're protecting them because they're family. But they wouldn't want this. They would want it to end, and you know it."

"Please," I said. "Please, Grimaldi. Listen to her. Look, if you truly know my memories, then you know why I'm here. I went into that fucked-up circus tent because I was trying to protect *my* family. When I killed that bear and freed her from this, I saw it in her eyes. She was *grateful*. And you know it. Every time those clowns eat someone, their soul is dying just a little bit more. This entire world is nothing but death and hopelessness, and I am starting to lose it, man. Signet says you used to be kind. I need—we all need—some of that kindness right now. I get the sense this Over City was a pretty bleak place even before the cataclysm. You were the joy that the people needed. But now you're killing them. And worst of all, you are killing the one you tried to protect the most. Signet shouldn't be here in this place. She has business down below in the Hunting Grounds, and you are keeping her from it. You are her family, and she will not leave until this is done. You can change that."

A moment passed. My timer was at less than a minute. I prepared the double healing potion, the one Mordecai had mixed last night. He insisted it would cure me of a parasitic infestation.

Come on, you assholes, I thought. Surely the producers of this ridiculous drama could see the bone I just threw them. Hopefully they had enough control of Grimaldi to take the bait.

No, no, no, I thought as I felt the worms surge back into my mouth.

"I have un-banished you, my love," I growled.

I slammed the potion, and then I fell to my knees and started vomiting a never-ending stream of dead and dying worms onto the ground.

Signet started to walk toward the entrance.

"Wait," I called, still coughing. "Wait. You need to free Donut."

"Your friend will awaken when the sun rises. Do not worry." She paused. "Thank you, Carl. I do not know if we will cross paths again." She turned and entered the tent.

As the flap opened, and she stepped into the mouth of the giant clown, I smelled it one last time. The scent of the big top. It was but a fleeting hint of that scent, and the moment it was gone, I knew I would never smell it again. I'd lost something today, but if this story with the circus had a relatively happy ending, I knew I'd gained something as well.

I suddenly remembered something else about that day at the circus with my mom. One of the items we'd taken home from the show had been a pair of little sapling trees with the roots wrapped in nets. That was something this circus always did. They gave little trees to all the kids. My mom and I had planted those trees in my grandparents' backyard. Years later, long after my grandparents had died, I'd looked up that house on the internet, and I found the satellite images of the backyard. The trees were still there. They'd grown huge.

All it takes is a little seed, my mom had said that day as we planted the trees. *Just little seeds here and there, and soon enough you have a forest.*

While Signet's story was only just beginning, I knew my part in this particular chapter of *Vengeance of the Daughter* was now done. Whatever was about to go down in there, it no longer concerned me.

I felt a slight pang that I'd missed out on my chance to solo-kill a city boss, but I was also certain I wouldn't have survived the experience. Besides, I'd done something much more productive.

The seeds were planted. The roots were already beginning to dig. *You will not break me. Fuck you all.*

Quest Completed. The Show Must Go On.

A half dozen achievements passed by, landing in my inbox. I'd jumped from level 15 to 18. Another wave of nausea swept over me, and I resumed heaving piles of dead worms onto the ground.

Something Zev had said had been bothering me for several minutes, and now that my mind was finally starting to clear, it made me jump to my feet.

It's amazing. Both of these dramas playing out at the same time.

Both of these dramas? What was the second one?

MORDECAI: Carl. Donut's health just dropped below 20%. Go. Go now.

12

I HURTLED THROUGH THE ABANDONED CITY.

I started about a mile and a half away from the old building where Signet lived. The neighborhood map's view of the local mobs ended just one street before. I avoided the scattered monsters. There weren't many in this area, but a few of them appeared to be large and fast.

> **MORDECAI:** Donut's Cockroach skill just activated. She went down to zero, but it kept her alive. She's now at 5%.

I rushed into the street, turning and running straight for the building's entrance. Several dots populated the map. In her unconscious state, I couldn't see Donut's dot, but I was relieved to see the orange dot of Mongo in the center of the room. He was surrounded by about 10 red dots and a metric shitload of X's.

As I approached, two more monsters appeared, coming from around a far corner as they rolled toward the open building. They were squat and black and covered in spikes, each about as tall as my knee. They moved like tumbleweeds. A mighty roar emanated from the building, deep and loud. A moment later, two of the round monsters flew out the door and bounced off the street. I formed a fist and pushed into the darkened chaos. I couldn't see shit. I pulled a torch into my left hand, lit it, and tossed it into the room.

"Mongo, I'm here!"

It took my brain several moments to register the scene before me.

Mongo had once again doubled in size. That roar had come from him. But more importantly, his health was deep in the red. He stood on the ground before the pile of garbage I'd erected around Donut, screeching in fury. Half of the defense was gone, scattered about the room, exposing the chair and Donut to the roomful of monsters. Mongo stood defiantly in front of the hole, like a hockey goalie protecting the net.

Both Donut and Mongo had been transformed into pincushions. Each of them was riddled with long black spikes. As I watched in horror, one of the rolling black mobs threw itself at Mongo, who leaped painfully into the air and slashed at the creature with his feet. The monster spun away, trailing gore. Mongo hit the ground, but stumbled and fell onto his side, crying. Several new spikes erupted from the dinosaur's feet. The sleek black spikes were about 15 inches long, and some of them had completely pierced the bottom of the pet's foot and spewed from the top.

I examined the properties of the mobs as I rushed toward Donut.

Street Urchin—Level 8.

These pokey little puppies only come out at night. Long, long ago, some of the richest citizens of the Over City kept these things as pets. Their name—Street Urchin—was a source of great amusement to the privileged. They would often joke about keeping a street urchin chained up in their homes, only letting the nocturnal creatures out to feed. The small, mindless creatures could clean an entire living space in a matter of minutes. When the cataclysm came, the Street Urchins were transformed into what you see today. Larger, deadlier, and a lot spikier. And after they cleaned the corpses of their former owners, they moved into the ruins and resumed their duties as the janitor mobs of the Over City.

The ruins' version of a Roomba, these things only have one purpose: to remove dead bodies and any other refuse left behind by inconsiderate crawlers. They won't bother you if you don't bother them. But you best not get in their way.

They can be very tenacious when it comes to taking out the trash.

Holy shit. These little assholes were here because of me. They were attacking Mongo and Donut not because they were aggressive mobs, but because of the defenses I'd erected around the cat. They were trying to get to the wood and metal hunks I'd stacked. And because Mongo was putting up such a ferocious fight, they were attacking back. And Donut was getting skewered in the process.

I read the *Heal* scroll, one of the ones I'd gotten from the survivor's box, focusing on Donut. She glowed. The spikes squeezed out of her body and scattered onto the floor like pine needles. Then I tried a second *Heal* scroll on Mongo, but it didn't work. *Damnit*. I couldn't use a potion on the pet, either.

"Hang in there, buddy," I said. I started throwing the hunks of wood and metal into my inventory. And when one of the street urchins approached, I'd throw a piece of metal at it. It'd make a chittering noise but stop approaching us. Instead, it'd roll over the refuse and start to devour it. As I worked, more and more of the mobs appeared, cleaning up the bodies of their fellows.

After I pulled the last of my makeshift defense into my inventory, I cleaned up the needles at my feet by picking them up and tossing them into my inventory. After that, the small, round monsters lost interest and wandered back into the street.

Donut remained asleep on the chair, but her health had been restored. Mongo lay on the ground, whimpering. His health was deep in the red. Dozens of the black needles jutted from his body in various places. I didn't dare pull any out.

CARL: Quick. How can I heal Mongo? The scroll and the potion didn't work.

MORDECAI: Take out a Heal potion. You should have a cinnamon
stick in your inventory. I also gave you a couple branches
of thistle rot. Put the entire cinnamon stick in the potion.
Wait five seconds and add the thistle rot. Put the cork back
on and shake it. Then pour it down Mongo's throat and try
not to get your hand bitten off.

I did exactly as he instructed. Both the cinnamon and the thistle
thing had come from the stuff Mordecai had stolen from the Belly-
Rubbed Pug's kitchens.

A new recipe has been added to your crafting menu.

A pair of achievements appeared. Then another as I forced open
the sharp mouth of the dinosaur and poured the now-brown potion
into the pet's mouth. The needles dropped to the ground. Mongo
groaned and shook his head. He sat up, nudged Donut with his
head, and then he shrieked loud enough that my ears hurt. Then he
started bouncing up and down, waving his arms and circling around
me, hitting me with his head in joy, as if he'd just realized I'd returned.

"You did it, Mongo," I said, petting the dinosaur, who made a
purring noise when I patted him. "You saved Donut."

Mongo had risen from level six to ten. Before, he'd been about
the size of a turkey. Now he was almost as tall as my waist. Colorful
feathers covered the creature. Donut could probably ride on the back
of him now.

We still couldn't move Donut from her spot, so I sat down and
leaned against the chair, settling in. We still had several hours of
night left. Signet had said Donut would awaken in the morning. I
hoped she'd told the truth. Mongo, despite being much too large for
this, curled himself onto my lap, hanging over both sides.

I found myself thinking about my mother, my father, and Bea.
Of my few friends from before, like Billy Maloney and Sam. Of my

coworkers at the boatyard. They were all gone. All I had left in this world was right here.

Mongo soon started to snore. I could feel Donut's warmth against the back of my neck. She breathed softly, oblivious of all that had occurred tonight.

This, I thought, *this is my family.*

———

JUST BEFORE DAWN, A BRILLIANT LIGHT SHONE INTO THE AIR FROM the direction of the circus. The world rumbled. The map was too far off my screen for me to see what had changed.

Signet never returned, but she was true to her word, and Donut awakened with dawn.

"Where are we?" Donut asked, stretching and looking around. Her eyes flashed, which meant she was looking through her menus. "What did you do to Mongo! How did you finish the circus . . . ?"

Mongo bowled her over, squeaking with absolute delight, bouncing around.

Donut, despite having done nothing, had risen to level 15. The system had leeched enough of my experience from the evening into her. I suspected most of it came from completing the quest since she'd participated in quite a bit of the early part. She'd also received a loot box for it.

"Come on," I said. "We're getting out of here."

"I am so confused," Donut said, stepping onto the floor. "Did I do something? I don't remember anything. But I had the oddest dream. Ferdinand came and visited me, and I ran to him, but he turned into a porcupine, and I kept getting his quills in me. It was quite unpleasant."

I laughed and laughed.

———

I TOLD DONUT THE STORY OF THE PREVIOUS EVENING AS WE quickly, but cautiously, set out for the skyfowl settlement. She was oddly quiet about the whole thing. She still seemed out of sorts.

As we passed the circus, I wasn't surprised to see that the tents were gone. The X's of all the corpses were gone, too, unfortunately. I kicked myself for not looting the coins from all the dead. Even though I hadn't killed the city boss, I'd hoped to return and loot whatever the city boss dropped, but there was nothing. I wondered if that meant he wasn't dead.

Something new did emerge from the wreckage. A staircase to the fourth floor, right in the middle of the park. It'd been hidden before. Usually these things appeared on my map, even if we couldn't get to them, like the one guarded by the Ball of Swine. This one had not been there before. I asked Mordecai about it, and he said many of the stairwells from now on would only become visible to us after we completed quests. This one had probably been there the whole time, right underneath Grimaldi.

I wondered if Signet had gone down the stairs. For her, she'd move directly to the sixth floor. Whatever story she had going on now would continue, undisturbed by us crawlers until we made it down there. *If* we made it down there.

"Why didn't you just kill that boss?" Donut asked. "You still would've won the quest, and think of all the experience we would've gotten!"

"It was a trap. If I'd killed it, we'd both be dead right now."

"Well, if I had been there, we would've done things differently."

CARL: Also, I don't want to add this part out loud. This is a
    good thing. We now have yet another group looking out for
    us. It's in that production studio's best interest to keep us
    alive. I doubt they can help us much, but the more
    advocates we have, the better.
DONUT: Until we get to the sixth floor and they have written
    out some story designed to get us killed. Or worse, they
    realize more people are talking about you than they are
    about Signet, and they try to get us killed before we even

get that deep. We are guest stars, Carl. It's too dangerous for a show to have guest stars that are more interesting than the main character. That's why they killed Barb on *Stranger Things*.

CARL: That . . . that does make sense. Except the Barb part. You're better with this television stuff than I am. When we get there, we'll need to think of every possible scenario.

DONUT: GUESSING THE PLOTLINES OF TELEVISION SHOWS IS MY SUPERPOWER.

The second she said that, I realized she hadn't posted the earlier, longer chat message in all caps. I decided not to say anything about it. It gave the impression Donut was maturing. Slowly. Very slowly.

But there was more to it, something that had been bothering me for a while now. Donut made a lot of seemingly rash decisions and comments, yet they were almost always *good* decisions, even though they oftentimes didn't look like it at the time. And while I knew her intelligence being higher than mine didn't really mean she was smarter than me, I'd been suspecting for a while now that so much of her camera-facing self was an act designed to hide her true cunning nature from the world. The problem was, now we were *always* camera-facing.

As outgoing, as brash as she was, she was still new to this world, new to having real, sapient thoughts. She was still coming into her own. The adult she would become was in there somewhere just starting to emerge, but Odette was right about her. She was still a child, and she held many childlike attitudes and beliefs. It'd be a long time before she fully matured. But it was clear if she did manage to grow up, she'd develop into a fiercely intelligent person.

At the same time, she seemed to hold the belief that outward cleverness and quiet efficiency were things she needed to hide or, worse, suppress. Part of it was the nature of the beast. After all, we needed to be popular to survive, but I was starting to really worry about her development, and I had no idea how to talk to her about it without sounding like an ass.

I had a quick memory of Bea's mom. It was just this past Thanksgiving, and we'd driven over to spend the weekend at her parents' house. I'd been asleep on the couch, but I awakened to hear Bea and her mom whispering as they drank their vodka, the ice cubes clinking in the glasses. We'd brought Donut, and she'd been asleep on my neck on the couch. They had like ten other Persians around the house, and Donut was always freaked out by the other cats, so she always stuck by me or Bea when we visited. I'd woken up, and I had to pee, but Donut snored, and I hadn't wanted to wake her. So I remained glued to the couch, eavesdropping on Bea and her mom.

Bea's mom had said, "You have to make them think you're dumber than you are. That's the only way to catch a good man. You can't control the ones who are smarter than you. And you don't want the dumb ones to know they're the dumb ones. Once a man realizes he's stupider than his mate, he gets mean. You're lucky to have found Carl. I just wish he was a doctor or a lawyer."

That Bea's mom thought I was a dumbass was nothing new, so this didn't surprise me. I didn't particularly care what she thought about me.

Bea had sighed. "Yeah," she said. "He's not complicated, that's for sure. It doesn't take much to make him happy. He says what he means. He won't fight me, even if I try to fight. He's not a doctor, but he makes good money, and he doesn't spend it on anything. Plus I love him, Mom. I know I screw it up a lot. But I do love him. I really do."

That attitude—that we had to wear a mask, even toward our family—it was one I could never understand. A lot of people, men and women, thought like that, and I didn't get it. And now I was afraid Donut had inherited that same attitude directly from Bea and her mom.

A few minutes later, Bea and her mom had a different conversation, one about Donut. It was something I was glad now that the cat hadn't overheard.

I was reminded of something else I wanted to talk about. I sent a message to Zev asking if she was available to talk.

ZEV: Hello, you two. You sure know how to make a splash. I just heard back, and we have you both booked for a new show the day after tomorrow. It's called *Danger Zone with Ripper Wonton*. It's a roundtable. A real roundtable. There will be other crawlers there and a few other intergalactic celebrities, maybe a politician. The show covers a few different hot topics of the day.

DONUT: OHH, THAT SOUNDS DELICIOUS.

ZEV: It has an audience-participation segment, too. People will call in and ask questions. This is uncensored, so be ready for anything.

CARL: I can't wait. Hey, Zev, I have a question. The real reason I messaged is, I was wondering if you could tell me who the production company behind *Vengeance of the Daughter* is? Is it a kua-tin company?

ZEV: No. Nobody in our system is allowed to run serials while we run the game. These are done by private groups, just like with the talk shows. We're not well-known for our dramas anyway. I'm afraid the nuances of compelling scripted drama are lost on the average kua-tin.

CARL: Okay, so who runs the one we just contracted with?

ZEV: It's an entity called Sensation Entertainment, Incorporated. They're from one of the center systems, which tend to be more integrated. The gentleman I was dealing with was a Sac.

CARL: What the hell is a Sac?

ZEV: It's a race of people. They're pretty common. Since you don't know, I can't tell you, I'm afraid. It's not that

important. Good luck today. I'll keep in touch and will let
you know when it's time to go to your interview.
DONUT: BYE, ZEV!

WE FOUGHT SEVERAL RANDOM MOBS AS WE TREKKED. MOST OF
them averaged around levels 9 to 11. Each of us practiced with our
spells, casting over and over, trying to get them to level up. Mordecai
explained that spells did eventually level up when you just randomly
cast them, but the system was smart enough to distinguish between
practicing and actual combat usage.

Donut managed to level her *Clockwork Triplicate* spell up to level
three, much to Mongo's delight.

I practiced my *Fear* spell on every mob we saw. All of the circus
creatures had been immune to it, but the other Over City mobs were
not. The problem was the spell tended to make them run away, and
if we didn't kill them, we didn't get any experience.

To solve the issue, Donut and I came up with the first move of
what I would call our "playbook." I gave a name to each play, and as
soon as it was called, we'd follow a set of predetermined reactions.
While it was good to be adaptive and fluid, the fight with the mold
lions taught me that having a set of canned reactions to certain situ-
ations could be beneficial. Either of us was allowed to call plays, and
once someone did, we needed to follow the play without question.
That way we'd work together and know what the other was doing.
This first one I called "Panic." I'd cast *Fear*, and Donut would hit it
with a missile. Simple. It wasn't complicated, and it was pretty much
what would naturally happen anyway. But I figured it would be a
good start. As time went on, we'd have more and more complicated
sets of reactions, including ones that integrated Mongo.

We practiced the Panic play, and I managed to raise my *Fear* spell
up to level three. The spell was simple. If I successfully cast it, the
mob either ran away, or it stood its ground, but its dexterity was
lowered by an increasing amount each level. At level five, it would

work on groups of mobs, so I needed to work on it as much as possible.

And speaking of Mongo . . . that little dude wasn't so little anymore. Now that he was level 10, he was starting to look scary as fuck. I was glad he was on our team, and I was extra glad Donut had spent so much effort on training him to follow orders. He still had a tendency to scream at the sight of monsters, but he was much, much better at not turning into a death chicken berserker until we unleashed him. His experience with protecting Donut had bonded the two even further.

He had a jump attack that was just amazing. He could now leap twenty feet from a complete standstill. He'd fly through the air, feet-first, and his claws could disembowel an enemy before it even realized what was happening. I knew these things were pack hunters. The idea of facing a group of fully grown Mongos was goddamned terrifying. I didn't know what floor these things normally lived on, but I hoped we'd never have to face them.

WE STILL HAD PLENTY OF LIGHT LEFT BY THE TIME WE REACHED THE medium-sized settlement.

From a distance, the town looked similar to the last one. But the closer we came, I saw a few distinct differences. The town was easily four times the size. And the buildings were much bigger.

And then there were the NPCs. A little more than half of them were skyfowl. Eagle-headed humanoids who could fly. This was the same type of creature Mordecai had been before he'd turned into a shapeshifter. I'd seen the photograph of his brother in his apartment, and there had been a few of them in Odette's audience. But this was the first time I'd really gotten the chance to look at them.

They were smaller than I'd expected. The average male was about five and a half feet tall, so just below the average human in height. But, oddly, they didn't have separate arms. They had large wings with little finger bones protruding from the center joint. It appeared they mostly used their large talons as hands. The eagles swooped about, flying just under the ceiling, circling around, going about their day, and doing whatever medieval-style eagle people did.

Other NPCs, including humans and orcs, also wandered through the town. The town guards were the same walking suits of armor. I pulled up the map, found the closest tutorial guild, and we headed straight for it.

As we walked, I caught sight of multiple crawlers. Most of them saw us and froze. A few waved and called out. Donut preened at the attention. I was currently level 18 and Donut was 15. Most of these guys hovered around levels 10 to 12, and most didn't have any stars by their names. I wondered how the hell they were still alive. Donut wanted to stop and talk to them. I did, too, but we had so much to do.

"Look, look!" Donut said just before we entered the tutorial guild. Mordecai's door was attached to a small nondescript building a street over from a bustling market. A few players were coming and going out of the room, though I knew when they entered, they were transported to a different instance of the guild.

I followed Donut's pointing paw. She indicated a tower rising into the air from a street we hadn't yet ventured to. At the tip of the tower was a familiar rotating symbol of a knife. The large art-deco-style sign was out of place in the primitive fashion of this town. Under the knife in tall, thin letters, the spinning sign read, **THE DESPERADO CLUB**. And under that, in smaller letters, it read, **SO FUN IT HURTS**. And then, **MEMBERS-ONLY SECTION + PUBLIC PUB**.

"I've always wanted to go clubbing," Donut said. She looked at Mongo. "Do you want to go dancing with Mommy?"

The not-so-little dinosaur squealed.

"Something tells me they won't let Mongo in there," I said as I pushed at the door to the tutorial guild.

I paused before going in. I spent the moment looking out at the world, marveling at the sights and sounds of this large town. Everything was happening so fast. I had a sudden, inexplicable feeling of longing wash over me. I wished this were all over. *It doesn't take much to make him happy,* Bea had said to her mom. It was true. I wondered what level we had to get to before they'd allow us to settle in a town like this.

"What kind of nightclub doesn't let your children in?" Donut grumbled, oblivious to my sudden reverie. "We'll just see about that."

13

Views: 1.4 Quadrillion
Followers: 30 Trillion
Favorites: 6.2 Trillion

THE FIRST THING I DID AS I SETTLED INTO MORDECAI'S CHAMBER was collapse into one of the classroom chairs. I'd been awake all night, and I really needed to get some sleep. The weight of the past 24 hours suddenly crashed down on me. I watched Mongo, equally exhausted, walk straight to the fireplace and sit in front of it. I could tell he wasn't yet used to his larger size, and it took him several moments to get comfortable. He eventually settled on his side, like a dog.

Mordecai transferred back to his own room a minute after we arrived. He arrived with a loud *pop*, and the drink in his hand sloshed onto the floor. The incubus cursed loudly at the sudden, unexpected teleportation. I'd forgotten to warn him. Whoops. Even though he was drinking, I could tell he wasn't nearly as trashed as last time.

"Oh thank the gods," Mordecai said, putting down the drink. "You're at the medium settlement? I was getting sick of that small town. They only had three bars, and I'd been kicked out of two."

"So, when you go out there without us, it's going to be that skyfowl town now?" I asked.

"That's right," Mordecai said. "Since I'm now a manager, for me, it'll match up with the last place Donut entered. If I was still a standard guide, I'd be able to dial it wherever I wanted." He sighed wistfully. "There's a guide-only town you buggers can't get to. I was really looking forward to it. Don't forget, I've been on this planet for decades. During the preparation stage, we can't mingle so much. So it's only when a dungeon is active do I get to see some of my friends."

I felt a short wave of guilt for making Donut pick the manager benefit. But then I remembered we'd probably be dead already if we hadn't picked it.

"Why aren't you puking drunk?" Donut asked. She jumped up on Mordecai's shelf and sniffed the drink. The flagon had "The Boll Weevil and the Chowder Pub" written on it. She crinkled her nose. "I thought your kind can't drink."

Mordecai shrugged. "I had to make a potion that negates the effects of alcohol on demon spawn. It's simple stuff. Then I dilute it at 43%, and it makes it so the alcohol works as intended. Almost." He frowned. "I think I need to add a bit more dilution next time."

"You're really into potions, aren't you?" I asked.

"Yes. While I focused on fire magic, I also spent a lot of time working on my alchemy. I was a mycologist on my world. I studied fungus. It was something that held great interest for me, and the two go hand in hand. The sixth floor, even though it's considered an urban level, is very thick with vegetation. Odette made me spend a lot of time learning about that stuff when we made it to that floor."

"Huh," I said. Donut looked at me sharply the moment he said that. She'd understood the significance of that last sentence the same moment I did. Neither of us said anything.

"I have a shitload of achievements and boxes to open," I said. "I also have 12 stat points to assign."

"Do the stat points last," Mordecai said. "See what sort of gear you've gotten. It's getting too late to hit the stores today, but we'll do that in the morning."

"The first thing I'm going to do tomorrow is buy pants," I said.

"I may not be able to wear shoes, but if we're eventually going to go to a jungle level, I'm gonna want my legs covered."

"Also, we want to go to the club," Donut said. "Is it only open at night?"

"The Desperado Club will always be open," Mordecai said. "It won't be too hopping on this floor. On the sixth and ninth floors is where it gets really interesting. I'll tell you guys about it tomorrow. Don't go tonight. Carl needs rest. For now, open your boxes, and then you need to find a pub with open rooms. You can't sleep here. You'll want to watch the recap episode. You missed the one last night."

"Were we on it?" Donut asked.

"You were, and I reckon you'll be on it again tonight after what you two just pulled."

"Was there an announcement?" I asked. "I don't remember hearing it."

Mordecai nodded. "It happened while you were still conked out in that elite's lair. You didn't miss much. There were a lot of patch notes, but I don't think you have to worry about any of them. There's a *Golem* spell that's not working properly, so if you come across it, don't use it. Oh, and they introduced something called collective bidding for sponsorships, but she didn't explain it very well."

Mordecai had said the number of achievements we'd receive would start to wane when we got to this floor, but I had over 20 of them, the most I'd ever received at one time. Many of them were related to fighting the boss while solo and completing the quest. A few of the achievements of note were:

New Achievement! One Quadrillion!
   You are one of the first ten crawlers to have achieved one quadrillion views! That means one of two things. You're either one of the best crawlers in the game, or you're such a hot mess people can't wait to see you fail.
   Reward: You have received a Gold Fan Box!

Admin Note: You have received your first Fan Box. Fan Boxes contain items that are voted for by those who follow your progress. Once a box is received, you may not open it for thirty hours while the fans vote for the contents.

Donut also received the same achievement. She was literally hopping up and down with excitement over it. Mordecai was telling her not to get her hopes up while I moved on to my next achievements:

New Achievement! Yellow-Bellied Chickenshit!

You initiated a boss battle, and it somehow ended with neither of you dead. What a disappointment you are. What a goddamned smear.

Reward: Pussies don't get prizes.

New Achievement! Johnny Quest!

Not only have you been given a quest, but you actually completed it without dying. We like it when you do what you're told. It means you're a good dungeon citizen and not a traitor to your people at all.

Reward: In addition to the Gold Quest Box you've received for completing the quest, new quest locations will *sometimes* appear on your map. Notice how I italicized "sometimes"?

The next one was even more interesting.

New Achievement! Hadji!

You have completed a quest, but you completed it in a way unusual enough to trigger the Hadji Achievement! And like the oft-exploited street children of Kolkata, where there's one, there's usually more. This is one of the rare achievements that can be rewarded more than once.

Reward: Your Gold Quest Box has been upgraded to a Platinum Quest Box!

"There's another level past that, too," Mordecai said after I described the Hadji achievement. "I don't know what they call it this season, but it'll double-upgrade your prize."

Donut also received the Hadji upgrade. I watched as she opened her boxes. She'd received a bunch of the usual items from the lower-tier boxes along with a few random objects like colorful bows and collar charms not as good as her butterfly charm. The system said she could only have one. The hair bows also couldn't be worn unless she took off her crown, which we couldn't allow her to do.

She opened the Platinum Quest Box, and it held 5,000 gold along with two items. A skill potion and a pair of "fang caps."

"Both are great items," Mordecai said, nodding. "Those teeth caps don't go well with Donut's fighting style, however. You should either sell them, or you might want to consider giving them to Mongo. Most gear can't be swapped with your pets, but some items can. This is one of them. Also, teeth caps come in pairs, and your dinosaur can wear up to six pairs of these things. It's something unique to his type."

While Mongo's face was mostly the beak of an overgrown chicken, when he opened the beak, a row of sharp, ripping teeth circled the interior.

The skill potion gave her level three in something called Acute Ears, which didn't just improve her hearing; it vastly increased the information that appeared on her minimap regarding not-yet-identified mobs. Basically, if she saw a red dot on her map, it now told her how large the mob was, and if it was a type of mob we'd already run across, it would tell us with "somewhat-reliable" accuracy.

Donut immediately drank it down. She pulled the twin metallic metal caps from her inventory and allowed me to inspect them. They looked like a pair of loose vampire teeth.

Enchanted Fang Caps of the Expectorating Tizheruk.
    This is a Fleeting item!
    Fun fact. There is not a single dentist from your world left in

the dungeon. A few made it to the first floor, but every single one of those fuckers is now tits up. There're a few hygienists left, but I wouldn't want to rely on those chuckleheads. What I'm getting at is that you need to install these yourself. Make sure they're facing the right direction. You can always take them off, but this is a fleeting item. That means they disappear once they're off. So don't fuck it up.

Turns two of your incisors into ripping, tearing, deadly chompers that would impress even the most self-hating goth.

Increases melee bite damage by 50%.

Each bite attack has a 25% chance to inflict a level 5 Poisoned status.

Each bite attack has a 10% chance to inflict a level 5 Paralyzed status.

"I'm totally giving this to Mongo when he wakes up. Carl, you'll have to put them on him."

"Are we sure that's a good idea?" I said. I eyed the still-sleeping Mongo uneasily. He hadn't chomped down on Donut or me in a couple days, but he snapped at the both of us. A lot. Both Donut and I were immune to poison, but not paralysis, as we'd both learned the hard way when Signet had captured us before.

Mongo chomped at the air in his sleep. It sounded like an ax splitting wood.

I sighed and moved to my boxes. I had several more than Donut did. She harrumphed at that. I could tell she was pissed that I was now three levels above her, but she hadn't actually said anything out loud. In fact, I had received a lucky bastard box for surviving Signet's initial attack on us, but Donut hadn't. She received the same Lazarus achievement, but instead of the box, her reward status said, "You're lucky to be alive. That's your reward." None of us were sure why. Mordecai suspected it was because Donut's health had zeroed out while Mongo was defending her, and she'd been saved by her Cockroach skill. But that didn't make sense to me.

"It's just one of those things," Mordecai said. "Get used to it."

I started sifting through my rewards. I received multiple sticks of goblin dynamite and smoke bombs. I also received a whole box of hobgoblin dynamite along with three globs of hobgoblin pus—the remote-controlled explosive detonators—in the Bronze Boss Box from my fight with Heather. I'd never seen hobgoblin dynamite before. The sticks were white instead of red. They had a larger yield and were much more stable.

I'd also been receiving a lot of random odds and ends lately that were simply labeled "Trap Supplies." They all went into my inventory. Mordecai warned me not to mess with that stuff until I had my sapper's table set up. "I don't know too much about trap making, but I do know it's just as dangerous as handling explosives," he said.

I'd been expecting another lottery ticket in my lucky bastard box, but instead I received a single casino chip.

"Holy cow," Mordecai said, snatching it up before it could get sucked into my inventory. He held it up to the light. "I've never even seen one of these before." He continued gawking at it as my Platinum Quest Box opened up.

In addition to 5,000 gold coins, I received a single scroll. A scroll of Upgrade. I immediately read the description. A 20-minute timer appeared over the scroll the moment I picked it up.

Scroll of Upgrade!

Warning: This item has a short shelf life.

Maybe it's not as good as getting something new, but sometimes it's better to just take something you're already comfortable with and improve upon it. Kind of like buying your girl new tits.

Once you read this scroll, one random, currently equipped item will receive an upgrade. That upgrade could be small. It could be huge. But since this item has a short shelf life, you gotta do it now or forever hold your peace.

"I hate these short-shelf-life items," I said.

Mordecai was still peering at the casino chip. "They do that because if they didn't, you could hold on to it and save it for a really deep level, making it more valuable than they intended."

"Can I just take everything off except one item?" I asked. "If I wanted them to upgrade my ring, can I remove everything but that?"

"Yes, but I wouldn't," Mordecai said. "I've seen people try that several times, and the upgrade is never very good when they do that."

"Okay, I'm just going to do it now, then," I said. I pulled the scroll into my hotlist and activated it.

My Enchanted BigBoi Boxers glowed. I read the description. And then I read the description of the new benefit I'd just received.

I looked up at the ceiling. "You motherfucker," I said. "Well played, asshole."

Mordecai barked with laughter. "Those things are probably now your most valuable item."

The upgrade was actually pretty awesome. But it came with a terrible catch.

Enchanted BigBoi Boxers.

   This item has been Upgraded once.

   All right, you already know the description of this item. Something something Incredible Hulk, blah, blah, blah. Now you want to know how this item has been upgraded. Right? So here are the original benefits of these naughty little undies:

   +2 to Constitution.

   Wearer may cast a level 15 *Protective Shell* once every 30 hours.

   That's some good shit right there. But we can do better than that. Here's a few additional benefits.

   +5 to Dexterity.

   +5 to Intelligence.

+3 more (for a total of +5) to Constitution.

\+ The Freeballing Benefit.

The benefit's description was:

Freeballing.

And I'm freeeeee! Freeee Ballling!

Usually reserved for monk classes and those too soused to reliably dress themselves, recipients of this benefit receive an additional 100% damage bonus to all attacks that originate below the waist. In addition, all skills that originate from below the waist train 20% faster. But as the name implies, this benefit allows only a single layer of armor or clothing to cover your crotch area. And since you're already wearing these, it looks like you won't be getting trousers anytime soon.

Mordecai was still laughing. "You shouldn't have said you really wanted those pants."

"What? What?" Donut asked. Mordecai explained it to her, and she, too, started laughing. They both laughed so hard, Mongo woke up and started bouncing around the room excitedly.

"Oh, this is delicious. Positively delicious!" Donut said. "Don't worry, Carl. Maybe the next box will contain leather chaps. You can still wear those. Those would really frame out your feet." She looked up at the ceiling. "Can you imagine how sexy Carl would be in chaps?"

"Goddamnit, Donut," I said.

I took a deep breath and waited for both of them to stop howling. For the first time in days, I really craved a cigarette. I tried changing the subject. "These benefits are way better than the ones we received on the previous level."

"Yeah," Mordecai said, finally calming down. He handed me back the casino chip. "You're eventually going to start seeing items that increase your stats not by numbers, but by percentages. That's why it's crucial to build your stats now. And you'll see weapon damage modifiers that are a lot higher, too. It gets a little crazy on the lower floors."

> MORDECAI: Also, I don't want to risk saying this out loud, but as you've just seen, once your brand gets established, they start to shift the type of gear you get. They like it when you get new equipment and, believe me, you'll be getting all sorts of new stuff, but they don't want you completely changing your look overnight. Usually you don't start seeing these scrolls until deeper, but you two already have a name for yourselves. You'll be receiving a lot more of these Upgrade scrolls. That was a really good one. Most won't be that potent.

"So, what is this thing?" I asked, examining the poker chip. It was black with pink, then purple, then pink splotches staggered along the edges. A familiar dagger logo adorned the center. The chip felt as if it weighed 15 pounds.

"Oh yeah," Mordecai said. "So, you're rich. Maybe."

> 100,000 Gold Coin Casino Chip.
> This is a comp chip, and it may not be sold or transferred. You may not redeem this chip directly for gold. This chip must be played at the High Roller's Roulette Table or the Wheel of Fortune game at the Desperado Club Casino.
> Good luck.

"Roulette?" Bea always loved roulette. I would sometimes play blackjack, but I was one of those guys who got pissed off after I lost just a few bucks, and if I won, I would quit immediately. I wasn't much of a gambler.

"It's not roulette like you know it. Go get some sleep. Tomorrow night I'll take you both to the club and show you how that place works."

"Can you get in?" Donut asked.

"Don't you worry about that," Mordecai said, grinning. "They know me there."

14

THE MOMENT WE STEPPED OUTSIDE OF MORDECAI'S GUILD ROOM, I
pulled up the town's map. I looked for the smallest pub I could find.
I found one a few blocks away that didn't appear to be along any
main roads, so we headed toward it. I had been so desperate to find
other people when we first arrived in the dungeon, but for now I just
wanted to sleep. The way the other crawlers pointed and gasped
when they saw us, it wasn't something I could deal with. Not tonight.

Mongo kept biting at the air. Getting the two chompers on him
had been easier than I had expected. The way the system had described it, I thought it would be a difficult procedure, but both of
the golden fangs had resized themselves and snapped easily into his
mouth, clicking into place like they were Legos. He'd patiently allowed me to do it, whimpering like a dog getting his nails clipped.
It'd only taken about five seconds. Now when he snapped his teeth,
little tendrils of electricity exploded from his mouth. It'd scared him
so much at first he'd actually peed himself, which had caused Mordecai to devolve into a torrent of arm-waving shouts and swears. But
once Mongo realized the electric bites didn't hurt him, he spent every
moment afterward chomping the air and grunting with excitement
at the little sparks.

It wasn't quite dark yet, but we stuck to the center of the street.
Skyfowl continued to sweep through the air above us. Most of the
buildings in town were at least two levels, and many featured large
open windows so the fliers could come and go as they pleased. In

fact, some buildings appeared to be completely empty on the first floor while businesses and restaurants filled the higher levels, all catering to the eagle folk.

Most of the shops were now closed, curtains tight, so we couldn't even window-shop. Before we left, Mordecai reiterated his warning to stay out of the alleys when it was dark. The guards remained on patrol, but I knew they would soon disappear. The city became a free-for-all at night. I wanted to be settled well before then. I could only handle so much drama and violence per day.

The pub was called the One-Eyed Narwhal, but the logo was of a fat, bald human unzipping his pants, grinning lewdly.

"Carl, this place looks disgusting," said Donut. Most of the buildings on this street were in various stages of disrepair. I didn't see any eagles here, either. It was mostly orcs, ogres, and humans. "There was a place back there called the Hot Schnitzel. It looked much more inviting. It had flowers out front."

"This place will be fine," I said as I opened the door, looking about. The pub was almost empty. A single orc NPC sat in one corner drinking. The place was set up similarly to the last pub. There was a bar and the three televisions. It smelled of beer and grease. My eyes caught the player countdown and I sighed.

649,433.

That was tens of thousands of people dead since the last I'd looked, but at the same time, that number had slowed profoundly. *The people who've made it this far mostly know what they're doing now.*

The pub only had four rooms available, and they cost 20 gold each, much more expensive than the last place. But we had plenty to spare, and I still had no idea whether or not we were being ripped off. To my surprise, the proprietor wasn't a Bopca, but a human. He was a large, bald level 30 man named Fitz. He was the person depicted on the exterior sign, though the real-life version was twice as fat.

"Your Majesty," Fitz said as we approached the counter. "What a pleasure. What an absolute pleasure. I've never had royalty in the Narwhal. Not once. Are you just dining tonight, or will you require a room as well?"

"Why, hello, Fitz," Donut said, jumping on the counter. She rubbed her paw along the wood and then looked at it, a sour expression on her face. "We require two rooms. One for Carl and myself, and one for . . ." Mordecai popped into the room, right on cue. The incubus said nothing and immediately moved to the bar. He leaned over to gaze at the line of bottles. "And one for this gentleman. What are your fish selections this evening?"

As Donut and the human discussed our dinner, I sat down at a table. I watched Mordecai as he waited to order his drink. We couldn't get away from him, and he couldn't get away from us. I hadn't really thought too much on the implications of the manager benefit from that angle. That was going to get really old really fast.

I'd thrown ten of my stat points into strength and two into constitution. My strength without the gauntlet was now 30. I was literally as strong as six regular humans, and that had a way of messing with your mind. I grasped the edge of the thick wooden table. It felt solid, like any normal hunk of aged wood. I squeezed, and I felt the possibility there. I could rip a hunk of wood off the edge if I wanted. I felt the potential of my power. The whole thing was just so surreal.

"Now don't be giving this guy any of your potions," Donut said as they sat at the table. Mongo ran across the room and started sniffing at the orc in the corner, but the large creature—a woman orc, actually—ignored the dinosaur. He grunted indignantly and returned to us.

The recap show came on just as our food was delivered. Donut received some sort of halibut thing, Mordecai a bowl of soup, Mongo a plate filled with raw meat, and I got a hamburger that tasted suspiciously like it came from Burger King.

The recap didn't show anything too interesting, though they were now focusing on a few crawlers I hadn't before seen. One was a guy with an alligator head and what looked like a Mossberg mag-fed shotgun. He never seemed to run out of shells, and I wondered what the story was there.

"I'm more concerned with how he gets that T-shirt on and off with such a giant head," Donut said.

They also showed the goat lady that Mordecai had told us about a while back. She'd entered the dungeon with 15 goats and managed to keep them all alive for a while. Now it appeared she only had five left. She remained human, and she'd clearly chosen some sort of mage class. Three of the burly brown-and-white goats remained unchanged. In my late teens, before I'd joined the military, the home had made us all get jobs, and I'd spent the summer working on a small farm that had multiple types of goats, including these guys. Boer goats. They were bred for meat, not dairy, I remembered. The bucks were heavy fuckers, heavier than they looked. It had taken three of us to lift one of them.

The other two remaining goats had changed.

"It looks like she got two of those enhanced pet biscuits," I said. I remembered the description had said that eating the biscuit could have varied results.

"Three, actually," Mordecai said. "They showed what happened last night. The third biscuit didn't go so well for her. Or several of her goats."

One of the goats was decked out in armor and walked on two legs alongside her. It appeared the goat had undergone a similar transformation as Donut, though I wasn't sure if it talked or not. It wielded a double-headed ax and occasionally screamed for no reason.

The last goat had transformed into a satanic monstrosity straight from the depths of a nightmare.

"My word," Donut said. "I could've turned into one of those?"

Mordecai grunted. "That's a hellspawn familiar. Carl probably would've been better off if you had."

I laughed and Donut made an indignant cat sound.

The thing was a horse-sized, multibreasted, pitch-black goat monster that looked like it belonged on the cover of one of those 1980s heavy metal album covers, one where if you played it backward, the words would tell you to murder your grandma. The face still had the distinctive shape and horns of a male Boer goat. It continued to walk on all four legs, but the thing was huge, and a group of six human-like breasts grew down the front of the creature. The entire thing had turned black, except the eyes, which glowed red. A constant wave of steam rose from it.

We watched as the hellspawn charged at a group of hyena-faced creatures and trampled them to death.

"Hellspawn are some of the best, most powerful pets in the game," Mordecai said. He looked down at Mongo. "No offense. But if she can keep that thing alive, she's gotten it early enough that it'll level pretty high. It'll eventually grow wings and will be the size of a damn dragon."

"Holy shit," I said. "Is it too late to get another one of those biscuits and give it to Donut?"

Mordecai laughed.

I watched in awe as the show aired a quick fifteen-second montage of Mongo defending Donut. The dinosaur had killed dozens of the street urchin things.

"Good boy. Look, Mongo! You're on TV!" Donut said. The pet jumped up and down. He no longer squeaked. Now he grunted. The amount of enthusiasm he showed was the same, but it no longer had the same effect as before. Having a kitten-sized dinosaur bouncing around you with enthusiasm was cute. Having a mastiff-sized one do the same was not.

I was shown, but only for a few seconds. The show didn't really explain how I'd escaped.

"Don't worry about that, lad," Mordecai said. "Based on your numbers, everyone knows. The actual scene is the property of the *Vengeance of the Daughter* production, which is why they didn't show much."

"I was asleep the whole time." Donut pouted. "They barely showed me at all."

"Sometimes even the side characters need their own episodes," I said. That seemed to mollify her.

While Donut still had many more followers than me, my view count had actually caught up with hers. I wasn't sure which one of us hit one quadrillion first. I didn't know if she'd noticed this or not. I hoped not.

The announcement wasn't too exciting. Just more of the same old stuff. There seemed to be as many bugs on this floor as they had when the dungeon first opened.

"Just wait until you get to the themed floors," Mordecai said. "It's the equivalent of opening an entire theme park filled with rides and roller coasters without ever having tested a single one of them. Last Borant season, the entire fourth floor was inside of some unseen living creature, so the crawlers were moving around intestines and whatnot. The floor was open for 20 days, and the creature they created for the level ended up with a fast-moving bacterial infection that spread over the entire dungeon. The walls started caving in on themselves and filling with gore, all unintentional. That didn't play so well with the viewers, so they probably won't do that again."

The woman orc who'd been drinking alone approached our table. She was an older woman, and she swayed on her feet. She instantly reminded me of an orcish, well-muscled version of Agatha. Her medieval-style shirt was stained red with blood, making her look like a butcher who'd forgotten to wear her apron to work. She wasn't the same skin tone as the Maestro. The tooltip simply called her a level 5 orc NPC. Her name was GumGum.

"I see you're adventurers," GumGum said, leaning in. "I really need your help."

"No. Fuck off," Mordecai said. "Not tonight."

"You don't have to be rude about it," the woman said, and she turned away. She staggered back toward her table.

"What was that?" I asked.

"A quest," he said. "Pubs like these will always be filled with people giving garbage quests. And we're not doing any more quests on this floor. If you look on your minimap, there's probably a little star on top of her icon."

"There's not," I said. "It's just a white dot."

"Well, not all quests show up on the map. Now we're all going to go to bed."

"Fine," I said, watching the woman settle back into her chair. The orc hung her head low, put her face into her hands, and she began to weep.

———

AT THIS POINT, ONE MIGHT EXPECT THAT I WAITED FOR MORDECAI TO go to bed, and then I sneaked out of my room, went to GumGum the orc, and asked her what she needed help with.

One would be right. Almost.

The moment we went to our room, I couldn't stop thinking about her. It was stupid, especially after Mordecai had explicitly told us to just leave it, but I couldn't get the sight of the woman crying out of my mind. I told Donut I needed to use the restroom, and I went back out there.

Mordecai sat at the bar, drinking and chatting with Fitz the barkeep. GumGum was gone.

"She left already," Mordecai said after I returned from the restroom, having pretended I used it. "Look, kid. Let me give you some advice. I want this to sink deep into your thick skull. You can't save them all. The people running this, they know who you are. They will always be baiting you. Worry about yourself first. If you truly want to help others, your best bet is to get as strong and as deep as possible."

I didn't respond. I returned to the room. Donut peered down at me from the top of the cat tree.

"Did you get the quest?" she asked.

"Holy shit, am I that predictable?" I asked.

"Sometimes," she said. And we went to sleep.

———

THE FIRST THING WE DID THE NEXT DAY WAS—FINALLY—START TO
check out some of the town's shops.

"Here's today's plan," Mordecai said. "You shop. Then you spend
the day grinding. You find a neighborhood boss. You kill it. You get
back here before dark. Afterward, if you're not too tired, then we go
to the club. You do *not* go to the Desperado Club without an escort."

"Yay!" Donut said. "Today is going to be the best day ever. Shopping and clubbing! And then tomorrow we go on another interview."

"One thing at a time, Donut," I said as we opened the door of the
shop. This place was called Lucky's General Goods. A bell tinkled
as I pushed the door. Dust swirled, and I sneezed.

Entering Shop.

Mostly empty shelves spread along the walls. Behind the counter
stood a skyfowl. The level 30's name was Edge Dancer. He clicked
his beak at us, blinking rapidly.

"Okay," Mordecai said. "This is a general store and it's the most
common kind of shop you'll find. The more specialized-type shops,
like the armorers and potion shops, are usually only found in settlements. You will find random shops such as this one scattered around
the dungeons from now on. Carl, your charisma is pretty good, and
you will usually get a good price. But you are no Donut. Always
leave the negotiations to her. She will get you the best prices, and she
will sell your items for the most."

"That is because I am a master shopper," Donut said, strolling
into the shop. She looked about with disdain. "This place doesn't
have the greatest selection, does it?"

"You've never been in a store before in your life," I said. I picked
up a familiar item off the shelf. It was a coconut. A tooltip popped
up, though it was shaped differently than usual.

Coconut.

21 Gold.

This is food. I think. Humans do something with it. Dunno, really.

"This is important," Mordecai said. "As you can see, the descriptions of the items in the shops are *not* provided by the system AI. The shopkeepers are responsible for labeling everything. The rules state that they can't lie, so they can't sell you something labeled as a health potion when it's really poison. But they are allowed to exaggerate. And they will. Luckily for you, Donut, you will usually be able to get an accurate description out of the shopkeeper as long as your charisma is higher than their level. You'll want to practice your haggling and negotiation skills each time you enter a shop. Once you train it enough, most items will give you a warning if the description is too overstated."

"I take offense, demon," Edge Dancer said. The eagle glared at Mordecai. "If you knew the skyfowl people, you would know we never cheat our customers."

Mordecai laughed. "Skyfowl merchants will *always* try to cheat those without wings," he said. "My people can be a bit xenophobic. And they'll act indignant when you call them out on it."

Edge Dancer started to say something, but he abruptly snapped his beak shut when Donut jumped on the counter. "You are a handsome fellow," Donut said. "I don't think I've ever seen a bird as strong-looking as you."

The eagle stood straighter. "Thank you, Your Majesty. Is there anything I can help you with today?"

From there, we proceeded to sell a handful of the non-magical, useless crap from our inventory. These guys didn't have unlimited money like some merchants did in games. We had to move to five different general stores to get rid of most of our stuff. Mordecai told us to hold on to the jugs of moonshine, but our extra weapons and random items went to the merchants. Donut was, indeed, a master negotiator. While she ordered the pub owners around like indentured servants, she treated the shopkeepers with pure sweetness and sugar, and they loved her for it.

"Is that the best we can do today, sweetie?" she asked yet another skyfowl proprietor. This one's name was Talon Strong. He looked thoughtful as he considered buying a pile of spears we'd looted on the first floor from the raccoon-headed scat thugs.

When Donut had used her Character Actor skill to choose the Artist Alley Mogul class as the one to emulate on this floor, it had come with multiple skills and benefits, including a huge discount for buying items. Unfortunately, because of the way the Character Actor skill worked, she hadn't received the extra discount. She did, however, receive the extra 15% one received from selling items. And she flexed that skill to the best of her ability. She was in her element.

"I can give you an extra five for the lot," Talon Strong said.

"You're the best!" Donut said, and the eagle preened.

"I'm starting to think you actually had this all planned out when you picked that class," I whispered as we walked from the store.

"Of course, I did," Donut said. "I knew we'd be selling everything on this floor, so I picked that merchant class. Miss Beatrice didn't call me Princess Money Bags for nothing."

"I'm pretty sure it was 'Princess Money Pit.' She called you that because we spent more on you than we did for our rent."

"Well, obviously that investment paid off, didn't it, Carl?"

"Think of general stores like 7-Elevens," Mordecai said, interrupting. We now had a pool of about 50,000 gold, which apparently was pretty good. "They're convenience stores. You buy from them as a last resort. They're fine to sell stuff to because they'll take almost anything, but even with your discounts, you'll pay three times as much for the basics. So, if you want potions, go to a potion store. You want spells, go to a spell store. If you can find one. Also, some guilds will sell stuff, too."

This particular town didn't have a spell store. There were dozens and dozens of places, but most of it was useless to us. We needed magical gear and items to increase Donut's constitution, but there just wasn't any of that here. There *were* several potion stores, however, and Mordecai made me purchase 10K gold worth of alchemical supplies.

We bought one additional item. We spent 15,000 gold on a magical pet carrier for Mongo. Neither Donut nor Mongo was too hot on the idea, but Mordecai pointed out that her pet wasn't properly resting at night. It appeared the dinosaur now felt obligated to protect us in our sleep, despite being in a safe room, and it was negatively affecting his stats. The carrier would allow him to rest. Plus, Mordecai added, no pets were allowed in the Desperado Club. They had a "playroom" for familiars, but their safety wasn't guaranteed. Donut finally relented.

The device was actually kind of cool. It was a square brown box the size of a Rubik's Cube. It had a symbol etched on the outside that looked like a fire hydrant. When Donut pulled it from her inventory, she could activate it, and Mongo would get zapped in there. He'd sleep and regain his strength while he was in the cube. She could call him back out with the press of a button.

"Later, you may get a mount that works in a similar fashion," Mordecai said. "When merchants sell mounts, they usually come with a rudimentary pet carrier."

"What's the difference between a mount and a pet?" I asked.

"Some pets can be both, but plain mounts tend to have low life points and little to no personality," Mordecai said. "You can have as many mounts as you want, though they're usually expensive. And you have to feed them. Mounts don't level or grow stronger."

After we shopped, Mordecai walked us to the edge of town. "No quests. No elites. Kill mobs. When you find a boss, make sure it's a neighborhood boss and nothing bigger. Keep in touch. Get back here before dark."

"Easy," Donut said.

AND BELIEVE IT OR NOT, THE NEXT SEVERAL HOURS WERE RELA-
tively uneventful. We found a cluster of these creatures that looked
like a cross between floating squids and umbrellas. They had a
psionic attack, but because of our high charisma, we weren't affected.
They were called Brain Boilers, and they were upgraded versions of
the Mind Horrors we'd briefly faced on the second floor. They moved
slowly and were easy to kill. A few of them dropped ink pouches as
loot, which Mordecai got pretty excited about.

I alternated between punching and kicking attacks. Mostly
punching with these guys. Mongo easily ripped them to shreds, and
we had to hold him back, as he'd become a serious experience hog.

Donut alternated between her *Magic Missile* attacks, *Second Chance*,
and *Clockwork Triplicate*. I would also cast *Fear*, but the spell wasn't
too effective against them.

I did manage to level my Iron Punch skill up to ten with the
gauntlet bonus. The tenth level of the skill added something called
the Breadbasket effect. Basically, if I landed a solid blow to the mob,
there was a 10% chance to stun it for several seconds.

The neighborhood boss fight could've gone south pretty quickly,
but thanks to Donut's new Acute Ears skill, we knew it was lurking
around the corner when we approached. The monster was called the
Dispenser, and it looked like a giant manta ray thing. It blended in
with the entire side of a building and tried to drop on us as we
passed. We'd been ready, and Donut attacked with two reanimated
Brain Boilers. Once it'd peeled itself off the wall, we had a clockwork
Mongo run at it with a stick of dynamite in each hand. The whole
fight lasted less than a minute.

The real Mongo screamed in dismay at the suicide attack, but
Donut managed to keep the pet under control. We added that move
to our playbook. We called it the "Boomy Boy." As long as I could
keep my supply of dynamite healthy, it was a supereffective anti-boss
attack.

By the end of the fight, Donut had leveled up to 16. I was still at 18, but teetering on 19. Mongo hit level 11. We'd all nudged a few of our skills up as well.

As we turned back toward the town, I spied a single white dot of an NPC and a large group of X's on the map one block over. This was just outside of town, right past the wall. As I watched, the white dot disappeared into town and then returned a few moments later. A new X appeared next to the NPC. Just on the other side of the fence, within the city limits, stood a pair of guards. So whatever this was, it couldn't be something too untoward.

"Let's go check that out," I said.

"It smells really bad," said Donut. Mongo grunted in agreement. We turned down the street and edged our way toward the NPC.

"Oh, Carl," Donut said as we got closer. "Did you know she would be here?"

"No," I said. "But the system knew we'd be coming this way."

It was GumGum the orc. I watched as the large woman easily tossed a dead body onto a pile of other bodies in the middle of the street. It was a mix of humans, orcs, elves, and dwarves. There were about 15 of them, all piled on top of one another.

I attempted to examine one of the dead NPCs, but the system helpfully grouped them all together for me.

Pile of Dead Hookers.
   Well, isn't this awkward?

Sure enough, all of the corpses appeared to be female. All of them wore provocative clothing. They were all contorted and bent in odd ways, as if the manner of death had been by a giant picking them up and twisting them like dishrags. One of them, a dwarf, didn't appear to have a head at all. The whole pile oozed with mud-like gore.

"So," I said, stepping forward. GumGum startled and whirled on me. "This isn't something you see every day."

"Adventurer," she said. She wiped her hand on her shirt. It left a smear of brown. "I was hoping to catch you on your return today. I spied your party leaving this morning."

"And you thought to greet us with a mountain of rotting prostitutes?" Donut asked. "I'm not sure where you're from, but the cultured amongst us no longer use corpses as icebreakers. Next time maybe just bring Carl a milkshake. He likes milkshakes."

"These are the women I've found today," GumGum said. "Something is killing them, and we don't know what it is. And we don't know who these women are, either. They're not from this town. We find them in the alleys, scattered throughout every morning. Most of their blood is removed from their bodies." She wiped her hand on her pants. "But not all the blood. We pile them up outside the gates, and the street urchins take care of them. But we find new ones every day. Sometimes it's just one or two, but sometimes, like last night, it's a lot." GumGum took a deep breath, and I realized she was holding back tears. "It's not right. The skyfowl don't care as long as we move the bodies out. The guards don't work at night. But these were people, and they're just dead. And I don't know why. Can you help me?"

"Uh-oh," Donut said just before the notification came.

New Quest. The Sex Workers Who Fell from the Heavens.
  Prostitutes. Escorts. Street Walkers. Ladies of the Night.
  It doesn't matter how you describe them because these chicks are dead. Very dead. And every morning, several more of them appear scattered throughout the village. Nobody knows who they are or where they come from. Find out why.
  Reward: You will receive a Silver Quest Box.

"Silver?" Donut said. "The last quest was a gold box."

"The last one involved a couple elites and a city boss. This one must be easier," I said. I leaned in and examined one of the dead women. This one was a human. She had distinctive wounds on her shoulders. I'd almost missed it because her entire body had been twisted so her pelvis faced the wrong way. The orc next to her held the same injuries. All the pale bodies seemed to glow in the dying light of the day.

"Well, Mordecai is going to be upset," Donut said.

"We'll see what we can do," I said to GumGum before we turned back into town. After we passed through the gates, I thought of what Mordecai had said the previous evening. *You can't save them all.*

"Don't worry," I said to Donut once GumGum was out of earshot. "We had a good day today. I'm not going to let it get derailed by a quest."

"That's what you said last time," said Donut.

15

ENTERING THE DESPERADO CLUB.

THE FIRST ROOM OF THE LOUD, GARISH DESPERADO CLUB WAS OPEN to the general public. It was packed.

The exterior of the building looked straight out of 1920s New York City. It was all square, concrete columns with a semicircular relief punctuated by triangular sunlike rays, similar to the construction style of the top of the Empire State Building. The club took up an entire street and rose a good six stories into the air. The glowing neon-knife logo spun above that.

"This place seems much too big for this town," I said as we stepped past a bored-looking rock monster bouncer and into the main room.

"There are two main clubs in the Over City," Mordecai said. "The Desperado Club and Club Vanquisher. Generally, once you have access to one, you're not allowed in the other. This one is easier to get into. Club Vanquisher is more like a country club where old clerics sit on leather chairs and smoke pipes and occasionally tell racist jokes. This place is like your Las Vegas Strip mixed in with Mardi Gras and the discos of the 1970s."

"This sounds much better," Donut said. She did that little neck bob before she jumped up on my shoulder, and I knew she was overly excited.

"Oh, believe me, it is," Mordecai said.

"I want to try one of Miss Beatrice's favorite drinks. Either a Sex on the Beach or a Long Island Iced Tea. Or that one. What is it, Carl? She always says it's her Kryptonite."

"A Dirty Shirley," I said.

"Yeah, I want to try that one."

"Cats don't drink cocktails," I said.

"Cats don't shoot lasers from their eyes, either, but here we are, Carl. Mama needs a night off."

We followed Mordecai as we walked through the busy pub. Multiple NPCs and actual crawlers littered the room. It felt as if all eyes were on us. The crawlers watched us. The NPCs stared at Mordecai.

"Mongo would love this place," Donut said wistfully from her perch on my shoulder. The dinosaur had screamed furiously when Donut had pulled out the pet carrier.

"He probably would," I said. I eyed one of the burly, rock-skinned bouncers standing in the corner. "But we aren't going to find out."

"This first room is exclusive to this town," Mordecai said. "Any local can come here. You do not need a pass. Crawlers who've yet to obtain access can come here and pick up quests to win themselves a tattoo."

We approached a red, glittering door at the back of the room. We pushed our way through and found ourselves in a small vestibule leading to another door. Sitting in a chair in front of this second door was a lizard-faced monster. This was the same race of creature as that crawler we'd seen on the recap show, the one with the shotgun.

Clarabelle—Crocodilian. Level 40.
    Employee of the Desperado Club.
    This is a Non-Combatant NPC.
    Crocodilians are an intelligent, thick-skinned, semiaquatic race. They tend not to be the sharpest tools in the shed, but they're certainly more intelligent than their smaller cousins, the Troglodytes. They are inclined to work as muscle or enforcers for both legitimate and not-so-legitimate organizations throughout the universe.

"Hello, Mordecai," Clarabelle said. "You know that disguise can't fool me."

"It's not a disguise when I have no control over it," Mordecai said drily. Then a huge smile spread across his face. He leaned forward and kissed the bouncer on both cheeks. "What's it like in there?"

"Dead. But there's more people than there were last night." The bouncer looked at me and then Donut in turn. "I've seen you two on the recap show. Where's your pet?"

"Mongo?" Donut asked. "You know about Mongo? He'd be so excited to meet a fan! He's in a pet carrier. Do you want me to take him out?"

"No. Do *not* let him out. I'm glad you have a carrier. The pet room is currently out of order. We don't want another incident like last night. I see you two both have a pass. The bar and dance floor are open. The casino isn't ready yet, but you can probably find a card game if you look hard enough. We'll open it up in a few days."

"Thanks, Clarabelle," Mordecai said, patting her on the shoulder. He tossed her a gold coin. We went through the door.

"Holy shit," I said a moment later, gazing upon the room. I had to shout to be heard. "This is considered 'dead'?"

There had to be 200 people of all shapes and sizes in the first room. Pounding dubstep filled the nightclub. Seizure-inducing lights flashed. The floor shook. Smoke rose from all corners.

Mordecai made a circle in the air with his finger, drawing a halo over himself. A translucent bubble formed over his head, making him look like he was wearing Zev's space suit helmet. He motioned for me to do the same. I twirled my finger in the air, and a circle formed, covering my head. Donut also repeated the gesture, waving her paw in the air.

The moment the bubble formed, about 95% of the pounding music filtered out. I could still hear it, but it was now background noise. A new sound emerged. I looked about, and a small portion of the people in the club had the bubbles on their heads. I could hear them talking amongst themselves, as if we were in a moderately busy café.

"There are a few types of privacy bubbles," Mordecai said. "This is the most basic. You can talk to anyone in the room without having to shout. Most clubs give access to this or similar spells."

"Weird," I said. I poked at the bubble with my finger, and it popped. The pounding music returned, startling me. I quickly re-formed it.

"This is the main room of the Desperado Club," Mordecai said. Several rooms led off to different areas. Most of the rooms were labeled with floating neon signs, all in that same 1920s-speakeasy-style font. The whole place gave off a retro-futuristic *Blade Runner* vibe. Of the 200 people filling the dance floor, almost all of them were NPCs. I did see a few bewildered-looking crawlers wandering about. My map also showed the distinctive white dot with a cross, indicating a few elites that trawled the dance floor.

"This room," Mordecai continued, "exists on a different plane than the outside of the club. It's the same thing as my guildhall. The moment you come into the members-only area, you are in the same room as everyone in all the club locations throughout the entire level. So these crawlers you see come from all corners of the Over City. But when you leave, you'll come out where you came in. You cannot use the club as a fast-travel location. Usually." We approached a booth. The four elven NPCs sitting at the table jumped up. They popped their bubbles and moved to the dance floor, allowing us to sit down.

"Most of these NPCs are bots," Mordecai said. "The club will always appear as if it's full of people, but that's just an illusion. If it's a young, buff, or beautiful half-naked creature, it's likely a bot. They're not even real NPCs. You can dance with them. You can even bang them if you have the gold. But they can't hold more than a rudimentary conversation, and they don't exist outside the club. The moment a real NPC or crawler enters through the door, one of the bots disappears, and vice versa."

"Weird," I repeated, looking about. I counted about ten crawlers and three elites. Each of the three elites was engaged in conversation with crawlers. I felt my hackles rise at that.

Donut jumped to stand on the table. "How did you get in here so easily?" she asked. "Do you also have a tattoo?"

Mordecai nodded. "I had a pass early on. They know me here now."

A blue-skinned woman NPC in a privacy bubble came to stand over the table. She didn't have a name or level floating over her. It just said **Waitress**. "Drinks tonight?"

"I want a Dirty Shirley," Donut said. "And you have to put it in a bowl."

"Certainly, Your Majesty," the waitress said.

"Do you have Earth alcohol?" I asked.

"Absolutely, hun. What can I get you?"

"Bring me a bottle of bourbon."

The woman raised an eyebrow. "That can either be a 10-gold request or a 1,000-gold one. That ain't covered by your drink coupons."

"Let's keep it around 50."

She nodded. My eyes caught the haze of smoke filling the large room. It flashed in the light. It didn't smell right, but I felt a familiar tug in my chest. "Wait, do you sell cigarettes here?"

"Absolutely not," Donut said. "He's not allowed to have cigarettes."

The waitress shook her head. "I'm sorry, hun. We don't have Earth tobacco. We have blitz sticks, however. Would you like me to send a pharmacist over?"

I had no idea what a blitz stick was, and the last thing I needed was a new addiction.

"No, that's okay," I said, sighing.

"Actually, who's the pharmacist on duty?" Mordecai asked. "Is it Quint?"

"Quint is working, yes."

"Send him over," Mordecai said. "And I'll take a flagon of Empress's Mead."

"Very well," she said, wandering off.

"What the hell is a pharmacist?" I asked. "And what's a blitz stick?"

"Oh, he's just a drug dealer," Mordecai said. "And stay away from blitz sticks. They're hallucinogens, and they're highly addictive. *Magically* addictive. You don't want that."

"Then why are we summoning a pharmacist?"

"He's an old friend," Mordecai said.

"Are we safe here?" I asked as we waited.

"This place isn't a safe room, though the security here is pretty good. But only in this room. This place has a lot of nooks and crannies. The bouncers aren't in the other areas, except the casino."

I looked up at the neon signs leading off to other areas. Three signs were unlit, but I could still read them. One read **Casino**, one read **The Hunting Grounds**, and the third was **Guild-O-Rama**. Of the lit signs, they were **Bitches**, **Penis Parade**, **Jobs**, **The Silk Road**, and **Restrooms**.

There was a ninth door, but there was no sign over it. A rock monster guarded the entrance. I watched as a waitress emerged, and I realized it was the room to the back.

I'd noticed the Bitches and Penis Parade signs first, and I'd assumed they led to the restrooms until I saw the actual restroom sign. "So, what are these places?" I asked.

"Bitches is the female strip club and brothel. Penis Parade is the same thing, but for those who prefer dudes. Don't go in either of those places, especially not on this floor. You'll get shanked. Plus viewers tend to ridicule the crawlers who go in there."

I immediately thought of that new quest with the prostitutes. Mordecai had just shaken his head when we told him about it, and then he'd told us to ignore it. The quest would go away the moment we left the floor.

". . . Jobs is a place to get quests," Mordecai continued. "These tend to be NPC assassinations and theft-themed gigs. The Silk Road is a marketplace. We'll go in there in a bit. Guild-O-Rama holds several Rogue-themed guild rooms, including an explosives guild. There *are* guilds available on this third floor, but the more specialized ones don't become available until later, so that section isn't open yet."

"Wait, will the Desperado Club be available on the lower levels? Like four and five? And are those really stairs to the Hunting Grounds?"

"Yes, and yes," Mordecai said. "But the club will be harder to find on the fourth and fifth floors. When you go in, you'll find yourself back here in this room, just like my guildhall. Those stairs to the Hunting Grounds open up once you hit the sixth floor. You can only come back up to this floor once you get to the sixth floor. That Hunting Grounds level is much bigger than this one. Something else interesting happens once the crawlers hit that floor. I'll explain that later."

I watched as a group of three human crawlers was led away into the Bitches room by an elephant-headed elite who stood about seven feet tall. I had the urge to get up and tell them to stay the fuck away when the waitress returned, pharmacist in tow.

The waitress placed our drinks in front of us. I received a glass and a bottle that was suspiciously missing a label. Donut received a bowl with a bright red vodka drink. A trio of maraschino cherries floated within. She sniffed at it and made a face.

I barely noticed our drinks. Instead, I stared at the small, floating drug dealer, Quint.

The top half of Quint was that of a sharp-toothed, beady-eyed opossum. The bottom half of the creature was a whirling dervish, like he was halfway being swallowed by a miniature tornado. It twisted and turned on the floor, and I could feel the wind blowing off the small cyclone. Unlike the waitress, this guy had a description.

Quint—Level 75 Half-Djinn, Half–Garbage Scowl.
    Desperado Club Pharmacist.
    This is a non-combatant NPC.

Half-Djinns are common amongst the Hunting Grounds and other forested levels of *Dungeon Crawler World*. Nobody knows for certain why there are so many hybrid Djinns out there, but one theory suggests that a rather ill-timed expletive is the cause of the population explosion. It is posited that a person in control of a Djinn's lamp and the resulting three wishes once exclaimed, "Fuck this forest" or "Fuck this level" or "Fuck you all" or some iteration thereof, and the enslaved genie took that as a challenge. As a result, thousands of half-Djinn, half–forest creatures roam the dungeon. Only a few are intelligent. Only a few are sane. They are all dangerous little fuckers.

If you kill too many of them, rumor has it their daddy may come looking for you.

"I have lost count of the years, old friend," Quint said, looking Mordecai up and down. He had an unexpectedly deep and growly voice, like he was a British street kid trying too hard to sound like Batman. "I thought you were supposed to be free several seasons ago. I was a little sad you hadn't come to say goodbye."

"Hello, Quint," Mordecai said. "I'm on manager duty. This is Princess Donut, and she is my ward. This other fellow is Carl, who is in Donut's party."

"Pleased to meetcha both," Quint said. "Mordecai here used to be one of my best customers in the early days. So, a manager, huh? That's pretty lucky. I'm jealous. It'd be nice to be immortal for once." He stopped, looking up into the air. "Oh shuddup, I ain't telling 'em nothing they don't already know."

"Quint here is a former crawler like myself," Mordecai said. "He actually chose this as a race. He's from a . . . an orcish world, right? I don't remember. Wait, don't answer. I don't want you to get in any more trouble from the AI."

The drug dealer shook his opossum head. "Being a manager is a sweet gig, I gotta tell you. No AI breathing down your back." He looked up in the air. "Because that nanny can be a right bitch

sometimes." He pointed a clawed finger at my chest. "You two don't
bother trying to make a deal on the tenth floor, you hear me? If I
could do it again, I'd push my way through to floor eleven. But you,
pretty girl," he said to Donut, "you got yourself the most knowledge-
able manager in this game. You listen to what he says, okay?"

Donut looked at Quint through half-slitted eyes. "Who are you
again? And why are you floating?" She looked at me. "Carl, is that a
talking anteater?"

Ah shit.

"You've taken like two licks of that drink, and you're drunk already?" I asked, examining her properties.

"I didn't like it. I just ate the cherries. Vodka is gross." She
reached down and lapped up some more of the drink. "I am absolutely not drinking this bile." She took yet another sip.

"Don't worry. Quint here has a potion to snap her out of it," Mordecai said. "Don't you?"

"I sure do, mate," Quint said. "Need anything else? My menu is
mostly the same. I'm more expensive than those gits over in the Silk
Road market, but my stuff is better."

"Your stuff is definitely better," Mordecai agreed. "But Donut's
charisma is 76, and she has a merchant class, which means we'll be
buying it at a quarter of the price you sell it for." Mordecai, ever the
teacher, turned to me and said, "Charisma bonuses don't work on
half-genies."

"It's Djinn. Not genie, mate," Quint said. "You know how I feel
about that."

"I'll tell you what," Mordecai said. "You still offer the starter kit?
And you up for a trade?"

Quint's beady eyes grew even smaller. "I do indeed. But I wasn't
expecting anyone to be able to afford one until the fifth or sixth floor.
What can you possibly have to trade this early?"

Mordecai sent me a quick private note. A moment later two bottles of Rev-Up Moonshine appeared on the table. I'd been using
them quite a bit in battle, but I had a stash set aside to sell. I still

had 23 bottles left, not including the two on the table. I also had
another ten boom jugs left in my inventory.

"No way," Quint said, sniffing the bottle. "That Krakaren bitch
said no more of the stuff was being made this season."

"They *were* making it," Mordecai said. "And Carl and Donut here
are the reason why it was shut down. They have the last of it."

That wasn't exactly true. At least one other crawler out there had
gotten their hands on some. I hadn't received any royalties since the
first few coins, but it meant someone had come across a few bottles
and had made boom jugs.

"Make it four bottles, and we have a deal," Quint said.

"We'll give you three, and you also give me the potion to stop the
world from being wavy," Donut said sleepily. I hadn't even realized
she'd been paying attention. "Oh, my word. Carl, I think I might
vomit. You didn't warn me about this." She took another drink and
then started growling at the bowl.

"Deal," Quint said.

"Wait, what the hell are we buying?" I asked.

"A starter kit," Quint said. "It's a suitcase filled with everything
you need to start your own pharmaceutical empire. You'll be the
dungeon's next kingpin, mate. Just don't be selling in my territory."
He shot at me with a pair of finger guns.

"Trust me," Mordecai said. "I ain't buying all this stuff for gig-
gles. I'm putting together a library for you."

"You need a table?" Quint asked as we made the trade. He had a
merchant-style inventory, similar to my own. The suitcase was actually a large chest. I had to move my bottle out of the way for it to fit
on the table. It was filled to the brim with chemicals and herbs.
Mordecai opened it up and started sifting through it.

"An alchemy table?" I asked. "We already have one."

"Suit yourself. You need anything else? Word on the street is
you're looking for Earth tobacco. I don't have any right now, but I'll
keep an eye out for you."

"Hey," I said to the opossum as Mordecai rummaged through the box. "What happened last night? The bouncer said there was an in-cident with a pet or something?"

"Oh yeah," Quint said. "It was crazy. This woman came in here. A crawler like you. I can't remember what her race was called. It was something I'd never seen before. She was human, a real looker but with one goat leg. Anyway, she had two pet dogs. She put them in the playroom, and they went bonkers. The monsters killed two at-tendants plus another pet, and then they broke out onto the dance floor, snapping and biting and snarling. The bouncers moved in, but their owner cast a spell that froze the whole room. I've never seen anything like it. A crawler from the third floor casting magic that powerful. Anyway, while the room was frozen, she stole a couple bottles of tequila from behind the counter while her dogs made a chew toy of a few dancers. Then she took out a mace from her inven-tory and splattered the brains in of an elite gnoll who'd been talking to her. Luckily she didn't kill any of the real bouncers. You should've seen this place afterwards. The playroom ain't gonna open back up for a week. She got away, but she ain't coming back. Her member-ship has been revoked, thank the gods."

"Holy shit," I said. "That's Lucia Mar."

"Those dogs sound just awful," Donut said, her voice slurring. "Bitch-ass rottweilers. Almost as bad as cocker spaniels. Think they're so smart."

Goddamnit, Donut. "Don't be saying that stuff," I said.

"I don't see any brin root," Mordecai said, his head still stuffed in the chest.

"Yeah, it's hard to come by," said Quint. "I gave you two vials of bujold sap instead. It's more stable anyway."

Mordecai grunted and shut the case. He nodded, and I pulled out a third bottle of moonshine. They quickly disappeared as I pulled in the large case. An anti-alcohol Hair of the Dog potion appeared, along with three licorice sticks.

"On the house," Quint said, grinning, indicating the three sticks. "It's not your Earth tobacco, but you might want to give it a try."

Blitz Stick.

It's like candy, but for your mind. If you eat this, your Intelligence temporarily rises by five points. If you smoke it, there's a 15% chance your Intelligence will permanently rise by 1.

There might be a side effect or two. Or three.

Before Mordecai could object, I pulled the sticks into my inventory. I had no intention of using one, but you never knew what might be useful. Donut took the Hair of the Dog. She immediately sobered up. She looked down thoughtfully at the still-half-full bowl of her alcoholic Shirley Temple. I pulled it out of her reach.

She looked as if she might object, but then she sat up straight. "Carl, Carl, I just got a notification. It says I can now open my fan box!"

"Okay, we'll do it when we're done here," I said. A moment later, I received the same notice.

Mordecai and Quint chatted some more, but I could tell Mordecai was done with the conversation. The real reason he'd wanted to come here was obvious. He was collecting a war chest of potion-making supplies, all in preparation for the fourth floor, where we would be able to set him up with an alchemy table.

I skipped the glass and drank from my bottle of cheap bourbon while Donut popped her noise bubble and moved to the dance floor. The bot NPCs laughed and clapped as the small cat leaped around the floor. A large ogre NPC hopped around her, and she jumped to his shoulder, and they twirled about the floor for several minutes, both of them laughing hysterically.

Mordecai and I watched for a moment, neither of us saying anything.

"Why were you so upset when Donut chose you as a manager?" I asked Mordecai. "Are we really that awful?"

Mordecai didn't answer at first. He looked down into his drink. "It's not you," he finally said. "It's complicated. When I'm done being your manager, I'll still be free. I will get my stipend, and I will make my way across the universe."

I felt relieved. I hadn't even realized it until he'd said it, but I'd been thinking perhaps we'd inadvertently sabotaged his efforts at getting free.

"But that's what you said would happen anyway," I said.

"I know," Mordecai said. He looked up and gave me a grim smile. "Like I said, it's complicated and it has nothing to do with you."

"That dude said you're immortal now. Is that true?"

"Sort of," Mordecai said. "You know how Zev wears that ridiculous armor when she visits? It's because there is no protection for staff on the first three floors. Nobody knows why. It's likely a cost thing. But starting on the fourth floor, the system-based protection kicks on. Not for you, of course. For the employees. And the tourists. Plus a few select NPCs, including the managers."

"So, it's like being in a safe room but everywhere?"

"No," Mordecai said. "In the safe rooms, you're protected from attacks, and those who attack you are punished. You are kept from being injured. This system-wide protection is something different. It's both better and worse. It's worse because you can still be wounded, and you can still feel pain, and you can still die. It's better, though, because when you do die under system protection, you don't really perish. You're just kicked from the game. Your body is transferred out of the dungeon. Before, as just a guildmaster, I wouldn't be offered any sort of security. It's just part of the deal. Nor am I protected right now, not for the remainder of this level. But starting on the fourth floor, managers such as myself are given a protection package. It's the same thing the tourists playing Faction Wars will have on the ninth level. I can still be killed, but I won't really be dead. I'll just be kicked from the game. So as far as you and Donut are concerned, my immortality is irrelevant."

"But why are managers protected when guildmasters aren't? That doesn't make any sense," I said. "I would think it'd be the opposite."

He shrugged. "In the early days, managers were allowed to fight alongside their wards. And when they died, they'd become available again on the next floor. That only lasted a season or two. Now, if I die as a manager, I'll be done for the season. And as long as Donut makes it to the fourth floor, my obligation will also be done. I'll be free to go. They don't protect the other NPCs, like the guildmasters or the merchants. Again, it's a cost thing. There's a whole lot of us. Of them. I think some bosses might be protected, because sometimes you have to face bigger versions later on. But that's it."

Oh shit. "So, you can step in front of a murder dozer on the next floor and be done with all this?"

"Yep," he said. "Don't worry, though. They incentivize us not to do that. The longer Donut survives, the more money I earn as a bonus. It's written into the rules. The stipend I receive as a guildmaster is next to nothing. The money I get as a manager is significantly higher. The better you do, the more money I receive when I'm free. Every level past nine is just an obscene amount of credits." He sighed, watching Donut. Her purple tiara glittered in the flashing lights of the dance floor.

I kept coming back to my first question. Why was he upset about being chosen as a manager, then? And why did Odette know he was going to be pissed? I was missing something, something important, but I could tell he would broach no more discussion on the matter. Not now.

"Let's go check out the Silk Road market," he said abruptly. "The recap show is about to start, and they'll stop the music for that. We'll want to be out of here before the second half of the show. If they show you two on the program, the bots will swarm us, asking us for autographs and to dance. If that happens, we'll never get Princess Donut out of here."

16

THE SILK ROAD WAS SET UP LIKE A FARMERS MARKET. IT WAS A long, mostly empty room with a single row of stalls. An eclectic mix of items filled the tables, but there was room for five or six more rows of booths.

"This room is mirrored down on the next floor," Mordecai said as we entered. Donut sat on my shoulder, bouncing her head to the music that still pulsed through the wall. "Eventually both this market and the next one down will be packed with merchants. Not too many are out yet."

We walked past shops selling black bubbling potions and round magical items called "Spider Shields" that cost 200,000 gold. An eclectic mix of races manned the booths, from short goblins to tall, robed figures with four sets of pincers.

A single booth sat in the back of the room surrounded by five or six empty spaces. I knew exactly what the booth sold as we approached. Multiple notifications floated in the air over the items on the merchant's tables.

"There's a double-sized booth normally set up next door to that one, but it won't appear until the fourth floor. Those guys sell trap supplies. In the meantime, I wanted to make sure you were aware this was here," Mordecai said. "The proprietor is a little odd, but she's harmless. Now give me 500 gold so I can check out that alchemist over there while you browse." He paused. "You two need to make a good impression on this woman because you'll be seeing a lot of each other."

This store was called **Hobgobs and Boom Sticks**. I examined the proprietor.

Pustule. Hobgoblin—Level 30.

She was the first living hobgoblin I'd seen face-to-face. She stood about six feet tall, and she looked mostly like the hobgoblin sample I'd seen during race selection: a large, muscular goblin that got clobbered by the ugly stick. She had an open sore on her cheek that bubbled with black-and-green ooze. The pus ran off her face, down her shoulder, and stained her shirt, which was a threadbare pink graphic tee featuring a unicorn wearing sunglasses. She smelled of rot and sickness. I swallowed. I still held the bottle of cheap bourbon in my hand. I took a drink to get the smell out of my sinuses.

"Carl," Donut whispered. "She's ugly. Like, really ugly."

"She also has excellent hearing," the hobgoblin said, her voice surprisingly feminine. I winced. "Are you in the market for explosives tonight?"

Her tables held multiple boxes of both goblin dynamite and hobgoblin dynamite, along with smoke bombs, detonators, and several odds and ends I'd never before seen, like flat, pancake-like explosives that were basically claymore mines. The yield and stability of the mines were impressive, though they cost 5,000 gold each.

She also sold barrels of gunpowder and a few other chemicals, most of which I already had plenty of. A case of goblin dynamite held 25 sticks and cost 500 gold. The hobgoblin sticks were 20 for 2,000, which was highway robbery.

"Two questions," I said. "Do you sell smaller explosives? Preferably ball-shaped? Also, do you have smoke bombs that don't suck?"

She laughed. "Yes to both questions, though I don't have it all in stock today. Goblin smoke bombs are crap. They don't understand the chemistry, so what you get is a lot of smoke in a small cone for a short amount of time. They're good in enclosed spaces, but if there's any ventilation, you might as well just pull your dick out and point at it." She laughed at her own nonsensical joke. There was an edge of crazy to that laugh, and I suddenly felt uneasy. "A hobgoblin smoke curtain works much better and is inexpensive, but I don't have any right now. I normally carry round bombs. Hob-lobbers. Both impact-enchanted and fused. I only have a case of the fused ones in tonight. Yield is one-eighth a hobgoblin stick, or half of a goblin stick. It packs a punch, if you're interested. I once watched my mother bite the head off of a vorpal muskrat. She said she did it to teach the warlord a lesson, but I'm pretty sure there was another reason."

She'd added that last part without pausing, as if it was just a natural part of the conversation.

DONUT: CARL, THIS LADY IS CRAZY.

I decided it was for the best to just ignore that last part. "Okay, so, does impact-enchanted mean what it sounds like?" I asked.

"That's right. Dangerous to use, but Hob-Lobbing Lobbers use them almost exclusively. Don't drop 'em. Otherwise they're pretty stable. The fused ones work like hobgoblin dynamite. Impact resistant, extra stable. You gotta light the fuse, then toss them. Like I said, I have a case of those. 25 for 500 gold."

I sent a quick message to Donut via chat.

"What's your best price on a case of the hob-lobbers and two cases of regular goblin dynamite?" Donut asked. She jumped down from my shoulder and landed on the table. "Also, we'll be back in a day or so if you promise to bring in some of those smoke curtains."

"Well, two cases of goblin dynamite and the last of the hob-lobbers would be 1,500 gold," Pustule said pleasantly. "I'm sorry if that price is too *ugly* for you."

"Oh sweetie," Donut said. "I think we got off on the wrong foot. Let's start over."

"Yeah, okay," Pustule said. "We wouldn't want anybody getting off on any feet."

Donut gave me a sidelong glance. "Well, it might be a little late for that. But we do want to buy stuff from you. And I think we'll be buying a lot of stuff from you, so I would really like it if we could be friends?"

"Friends?" Pustule asked. "I was friends with Tiff. The muskrat."

"Yes, friends," Donut said. "Hopefully your mom won't bite my head off, though."

"Oh, she died. It was a vorpal muskrat. You can't bite the head off a vorpal muskrat without doing a little dying in the process."

From there, they went back and forth for a few minutes. Donut did not have the extra discount that automatically came with the Artist Alley Mogul class, but she still had that insane charisma, and she managed to talk the hobgoblin down to 1,000 gold for the lot.

After that transaction was completed, I pulled one of my boom jugs from my inventory and placed it on the table. "Out of curiosity, how much would you give me for this?"

She picked it up, examining it carefully. "Nice design," she said. She rubbed the side of the bottle and made a whimpering noise, one I could not decode. Then she pulled the bottle close to her face and licked it. I looked at Donut and mouthed, *What the fuck?*

She snapped back to seriousness a moment later. "Your material cost is much too high. If you used a different accelerant, the effect wouldn't be nearly so hot, but your build cost would be 90% cheaper. If you went out there and sold just the plain bottles of moonshine, it'd be worth much more."

"So how much is it worth as it is?"

"I'd probably sell these for about 7,500 gold. I'll give you half that. You looking to sell?"

"Not right now," I said, taking the boom jug back. It was good to have a value reference in my inventory. I resisted the urge to wipe off the wet streak. "Thanks, though. It was good meeting you."

"I'll have more for you tomorrow," she said as we walked toward the exit. "Beware of meteors!" she called.

"She wasn't so bad," Donut said as we left. "She just needs both a dermatologist and a psychiatrist. I can't tell you how relieved I am you didn't pick that race."

"*Excellent* hearing," Pustule called from her booth, about 50 paces away.

"Wow," Donut said, looking over her shoulder. "You'd think someone who blew things up for a living would be deaf."

I pulled a hob-lobber out of my inventory. It was a hair smaller than a baseball, but it was dense and heavy.

"Damn," I said. "Too big for my slingshot."

"Nobody likes your stupid slingshot, Carl," Donut said.

"At your current strength, you can probably just throw this farther than a slingshot anyway," Mordecai said, coming to walk beside us. He handed me a pile of herbs and vials. "That's what the Hob-Lobbing Lobbers do. They're the hobgoblin equivalent of a bomb bard."

We exited the market and hurried through the dance arena, which was now showing the recap episode. All of the dancers sat on the floor, watching the screen. They'd all gone eerily silent, and the scene was disconcerting. The next room with the locals was also displaying the show. A handful of crawlers watched while the other NPCs went about their business, pretending like there was nothing on the screen.

"You two go ahead," Mordecai said, eyeing the bar. "I'll catch up in a bit."

"You'll catch up whether you want to or not as soon as we get back to the inn," I said.

"I know," he said. "I just don't like missing any of the show. Sometimes they hide important stuff in there. I'll see you back at the inn. Go straight there."

———

WE STEPPED OUT INTO THE NIGHT. DARKNESS HAD DESCENDED ON the city, and the city guards had all disappeared. Still, it wasn't too late, and the streets were still busy. A street vendor selling the cockroach-like scatterers on a stick remained open. It made me think of that first boss, the Hoarder. It seemed like a lifetime ago. Eagles soared above us, filling the sky. Music drifted from the open doors of several pubs.

Still, the alleyways were now dark. Occasionally I'd see a flicker of a red dot. Donut said most of them were small, maybe rats. We stuck to the center of the street.

The One-Eyed Narwhal was only a few blocks over. We didn't really have to spend the night there again, but I liked that the place was much less busy than most of the other inns. We'd easily catch the end of the episode if we hurried. I hoped they'd show Lucia Mar and her dogs going apeshit in the nightclub. I really wanted to see that.

"There you go, Mongy," Donut said, releasing her pet back out onto the street. He formed right in front of us with a *pop*, like when Zev teleported into the room. "Did you miss your mommy? Mommy missed you!" The pet screeched in outrage and hopped up and down a few times, circling around us, waving his arms.

"Oh, get over it," I said. I pulled a pet biscuit from my inventory and tossed it at him. He snatched it in midair. He made a growling noise as he chewed, but I could tell he was placated. He then moved to my right side to walk next to me as Donut leaped to my shoulder.

"He really is well trained," I said. "You've done a good job."

"Of course I have, Carl," Donut said. "I am a product of the pageant circuit, after all. I've had plenty of experience watching what does and doesn't work when it comes to teaching obedience. Maybe when this is all over, I can dictate a book on the subject. You can type it all out for me. That reminds me, Zev and I have been talking about writing a new episode of *Gossip Girl* since—"

And that's when Mongo screamed in rage and rushed straight into the dark alley.

———

"GODDAMNIT, MONGO!" I BELLOWED AS I TURNED TO CHASE THE DI-
nosaur. "And you stay put!" I yelled up at Donut as we rushed into
the alley. "Don't run ahead."

"Mongo! Mongo!" Donut cried as we ran. She cast her *Torch* spell,
and the blazing light rose into the air, illuminating the squalid alleyway. This was more a substreet than a real alley, but multiple
tributaries sectioned off of it, and Mongo turned down one such
street. A group of red dots appeared along with the X of a corpse.

Shit, shit.

I also smelled fire. Like burning meat.

We passed a pair of stinking rubbish bins. Ahead of us, a group of
four figures loomed. Three of them were flying, hovering off the
ground. The fourth was humanoid, tall and lean. This one held his
hand in the air, and it burned, smoke pouring off it. It was the source
of the smell. Mongo squealed and headed straight for the tall creature.

I could also see the corpse. It was GumGum the orc. Her chest
had been rent open.

The flying creatures were floating, disembodied female heads.
Their long hair flapped about them like sea creatures. What appeared to be the rest of the creatures' organs hung loosely from the
holes in the bottoms of their necks, all connected with wet, limp
tendrils of nerve, artery, and other viscera. Blood dripped freely. The
three horrifying monsters screamed at the presence of Donut's light,
and they twisted and twirled up into the evening sky, corkscrewing
and howling like banshees, their loose intestines and lungs swinging
underneath them.

They disappeared into the darkness, but not before their description popped up.

Krasue. Level 16.

Holy crap! These things are terrifying! Who comes up with
this shit?

Said to be the undead shell of a woman who lived a life of sin, Krasue roam the dark places, hiding their hideous true form. They are ravenous, and they devour the blood of the unsuspecting. In other words, these things are flying heads who are also vampires. *And* they bring their organs along because . . . Well, nobody knows why. Probably just because it's really gross.

You may kill the head and trailing organs to fend her off, but this mob doesn't truly die until you find and destroy the rest of her corpse. You will not earn experience for killing this mob until it is dead-dead. Not just dead.

Warning: This is a ghost-class mob. They are only injured with magic or magical items.

Mongo squealed and leaped at the remaining figure, the one with the burning hand, but the mob disappeared in a blink . . .

. . . and appeared right in front of us.

"The final battle is here!" the creature—an elf—squealed, his voice cracking. He cackled with laughter. His hand stopped trailing smoke. "You may have scared off the krasue, but you will not do the same to me! I have trained my entire life for this moment! I have used dark magic to lure your familiar into my trap! Carl and Donut, blasphemers! Prepare to taste the ultimate death!" His hands started to glow red. "Now watch as I—"

I kicked him in the nuts at the same moment Donut's magic missile slammed into his neck. The elf's head ripped off as he was raised bodily off the ground. I felt my foot shatter his testicles and fracture his pelvis. The dead, now-headless elf rose into the air like a rocket. He splattered onto the ground in a heap, blood showering over us. His head tumbled like a poorly inflated soccer ball, coming to a stop in front of Mongo, who picked it up and started shaking it back and forth like a squeaky toy.

For a long moment, neither Donut nor I said anything. I slowly turned to look at the cat.

"Who the hell was that?" I asked.

17

I EXAMINED THE CORPSE OF THE ELF. I REALLY WISHED I'D DONE IT before, as the amount of information given was much less once they were dead.

> Lootable Corpse. Vicente. City Elf. Level 16. Killed by Crawler
> Grand Champion Best in Dungeon Princess Donut with an assist
> by Crawler Royal Bodyguard Carl.

"Ha," Donut said. "I got credit for the kill."

"Well, you did blow his head off. All I did was kick him in the nuts."

"Yeah, that wasn't very manly of you, Carl. I thought nut kicking was a big no-no amongst guys."

"It's not something I want to make a habit of doing," I said. "But if it works, it works."

> ZEV: Yes, Carl. Try to avoid that if you can. A few viewers have
> made some snide comments.
> CARL: For fuck's sake. I can really do without the random
> peanut gallery comments.
> DONUT: I BET THE SYSTEM AI LIKED IT.

Vicente the city elf had almost 1,500 gold in his inventory. He only held one other item. A scroll, which Donut took. It was for a spell called *Meat Hooks*. It was the spell he'd been casting that had caused Mongo to rush into the alley.

"I knew he was a good boy," Donut said. "He'd been summoned. He couldn't help it!" Mongo, still chewing on the elf's head, grunted in agreement. The spell summoned all nearby carnivorous pet-class monsters away from their owners and to the source of the burning stench.

"You'll want to hold on to that one," I said. "You never know when it might be useful."

"He knew our names," Donut said, looking down at the corpse. "And did you see those gross floating things?"

"Your light scared them away," I said, looking up into the night. "Keep it going."

The elf didn't have anything else in his inventory, but he did wear an oddly familiar shirt. This was a military uniform, and it looked out of place here in this town. It was a black button up, and had it been blue, I would've sworn it was a US Coast Guard ODU, the same type of shirt I'd worn every day on active duty.

"Carl, look," Donut said. "There's a patch on his arm." She peered closely at it. "There's two patches. A sew on and a heat transfer. The arm one is handsewn with a chain stitch. It's good work, but it clearly wasn't made on a schiffli like the nameplate on the breast."

"What?" I said, looking down at the two patches. "What are you talking about? What the hell is a schiffli?"

"Huh," Donut said. "I don't know how I know. A schiffli is a type of embroidery machine. I must've watched a show about it or something."

The patch on the shoulder was in the shape of a shield, and it held a crossed lightning bolt and a magic wand being grasped by a talon with a tree in the background. It looked very much like a typical US military unit patch, but with the text in Syndicate Standard. It read **201st Security Group—Magical Ops**. The second patch was a nameplate. It read **Vicente**. That was it. There was no grade insignia or anything else on the shirt, including any sort of indicator of what army this 201st Security Group was a part of. That particular missed detail made the shirt look fake, like it was more of a movie prop than a real uniform.

I pulled the entire black shirt off the headless elf and tossed it into my inventory. I'd show Mordecai when we got back.

We moved to examine the corpse of GumGum the orc. We'd seen her just a few hours before, piling the bodies of the prostitutes out of town. Her eyes stared straight up, almost accusing. I'd told her we'd help, but I hadn't meant it.

Lootable Corpse. GumGum. Orc. Level 5.

It didn't say what had killed her, but based on the injuries—a ripped-open chest, and no blood—I suspected she'd been killed by those three krasue things. I shuddered.

"Why did that weird guy say he'd been training his whole life to fight us? We've only been on this floor for a couple days," Donut asked, mirroring my own thoughts.

"It's obviously a clue in that quest. All of this is some sort of ham-fisted setup to get us to investigate further."

Sure enough, GumGum's inventory held four gold coins and two pieces of paper. One was entitled **Gate Pass** and the other was **Mysterious Letter**. I sighed and took them both.

"She was a nice lady, for an orc," Donut said. "She was doing the right thing. We have to finish the quest now."

"Why?" I asked.

"Because they killed her. And they probably killed her because we got that quest," Donut said. "If we hadn't, she'd probably be in the bar right now waiting to ask someone else to help her."

Goddamnit, Donut. She was right. Of course she was right. The orc's lifeless eyes shone in the reflection of Donut's *Torch* spell. *She's not real,* I thought. *She's a prop, an extra in a high-stakes game show.*

But that wasn't true, was it? She was a real biological creature. What she believed to be real was fake, an illusion. But she was still flesh and blood, an innocent. And she was dead simply because it was part of the story. Just like with all those prostitutes.

You're not going to break me. Fuck you all.

"I think I liked you better when you didn't make so much sense," I said.

"I've always made sense, Carl," Donut said.

WE MADE OUR WAY BACK TO THE INN. I DIDN'T WANT TO SPEND ANY more time in the alley. We'd missed the end of the show, and the announcement boomed over the city loudspeaker as we walked. It wasn't anything new or interesting. Another day, another few bugs. Some druid spell was causing the supposedly indestructible wooden floorboards to evaporate, creating sinkholes and sucking people away, causing them to fall off the map and disappear.

The inn was the same as the previous night. Where GumGum had sat the previous evening was now occupied by a pair of human NPCs, an older couple who quietly ate and talked amongst themselves. Fitz the barkeep grinned at us. "Returning customers!" he exclaimed. "Your Majesty. It's always an honor."

Mordecai was plastered by the time he teleported to the inn. He drunkenly instructed me in creating the Hair of the Dog potion. It involved a gooey weed that smelled like okra mixed with a vial of rubbing alcohol. My first attempt failed, but it worked the second time, garnering me a level three in alchemy.

"I went too far the wrong way," Mordecai said, shaking his head after he drank the potion. "But I was only expecting to be there for a few minutes. Did you see that centauress by the bar? She offered to buy me a few shots. Why'd you two take so long?"

I told him what had happened as I made a few additional Hair of the Dog potions. Fitz offered us free room and board for the night in exchange for three of them. I had plenty of supplies. Since it didn't require boiling or any high-difficulty emulsifying, I could make the potions without a table.

"A military uniform?" Mordecai said. "That's odd. Let me see it."

"No," Donut said. "We'll show you in a minute. Carl and I have fan boxes to open. My people have spent a lot of time and effort on voting for and choosing this. I'm opening it now."

I exchanged a look with Mordecai, who'd warned us both a dozen times now that the lower-tier fan boxes were usually crap. While the boxes wouldn't contain anything awful or physically harmful, the system-generated list of possibilities was often filled with random and sometimes nonsensical items. Trolls oftentimes got in on the voting, and the prize was usually the most ridiculous or useless item on the list. Mordecai said he'd received a skyfowl sex toy in his first box. Later, the fan boxes would be more significant with better items. This was a gold box, which meant fans had to have us on their favorites list in order to vote. But even these boxes were often corrupted. Fans had to pay actual credits to vote for the contents of anything higher. That fee to vote was next to nothing, but it was enough to keep people from casually gaming the system.

"Here I go," Donut said. I braced myself. The box opened, and Donut gasped. "Oh my gosh, Carl, Carl, look!" she said excitedly.

I felt my stomach drop. *You assholes,* I thought.

It was a small framed picture. Of Bea. The square photo had been taken directly from her Instagram. It was the same photo that had caused me to break up with her. In the picture, Bea wore a bikini. She was laughing. And she was sitting on her ex-boyfriend's lap, her arm draped around his shoulder while she took the selfie. Brad was the guy's name. He worked construction part-time and modeled part-time. I knew that because that was the only line of information on his profile. His Instagram handle was Brad_the_Chad69, possibly the douchiest name in the history of the world. He always did the male version of a duck face in his photos, and since I'd never met the dude in real life, every picture I'd ever seen of him made him look like he was taking a shit.

"It's great!" Donut said. "Oh my gosh. I love it so much! Zev was saying she wanted to see a picture of her. Look, Mordecai! It's Miss Beatrice and her friend! Look, Mongo! It's your grandmother! Fitz, come here and look at Miss Beatrice. Isn't she pretty?"

Mordecai didn't look at the picture. He stared directly at me, a worried expression upon his face.

I was expecting it to bother me. It didn't, I realized. That felt important, almost monumental. At the time, I'd been upset. I told myself I didn't like drama, and I dumped her. Which was the right thing to do. But I was still upset. Of course I'd been upset, and I lied to myself about how upset I was. But that was gone now. *Really* gone. After all that had happened, how could it possibly *not* be gone? And the realization was like a weight that I didn't even know was there lifting off my shoulders.

Donut's reaction to the gift was more than a little worrying, but at least she seemed to enjoy the prize. It could've been much worse.

I grinned, looking directly up at the ceiling. I gave a very deliberate shrug. "You really think I'd care about that? Nice try."

"Carl, open yours! Maybe it's another picture!"

I sighed, and I selected my box. If it was something awful, something designed to upset Donut, I was prepared to toss it into my inventory before she could see it.

I wasn't expecting the basket.

"What the hell is that?" Mordecai asked the moment it appeared. He examined it, his eyes going wide. "Oh," he said. "You got a good prize. The rabble-rousers must have spent all their effort on Donut's gift."

"What are you talking about?" Donut asked. She looked at the strange wicker basket. It looked like a large banana-shaped scoop. A group of buckles along with an unfamiliar strap was attached to the end of the object. "What is this thing?" Donut asked. She read the description. "I don't get it. What's . . . How is that pronounced? 'High-lie'?"

I didn't need to read the description. The moment I saw the item, I knew exactly what it was. The buckles were unusual, but my brain was already processing how it worked. This was a good prize. In fact, this was a great prize.

"Hey, Fitz," I said. The barkeep had wandered over to look at the picture of Bea. He still clutched it in both hands, and he was rubbing a finger down the glass, stroking the image of Bea's breasts. "Do you have any oranges?"

He appeared startled, as if he had just realized we were still there. He quickly placed the photo down. "I reckon I do," he said.

"Give me four or five of them, please," I said.

While he went to the back, I picked up the large basket. I ran my hand down it. While it appeared to be made of wicker, it was really made of a light metallic substance. My mind raced with the possibilities. It was so strange. This knowledge was from that Earth Hobby potion. It all came rushing to me.

The skill I'd received had been in something called Cesta Punta. I'd thought it was a martial art. It wasn't. It was a sport. A sport more commonly known as jai alai. It was a complicated, fast-paced, squash-like game where people wore scoops on the ends of their hands and threw balls against a wall. It was dangerous as fuck, and even with helmets, those little hard balls bounced and flew fast enough to knock your damn head off.

The gift I'd received in my fan box was called a xistera. It was the scoop a player wore on their hand. Normally there was a leather sleeve along the back of the handle that you could tighten, which would keep the basket from flying away. You used the scoop to catch and toss the ball, and because of the shape of the basket and the weight of the ball, you could throw very hard and fast, especially if you spun and swung your arm in just the correct manner.

I'd never played it in real life, though I'd known a senior chief who had something similar designed to lob tennis balls great distances. The thing was really for dogs, but he'd used it to toss cherry bombs off the side of the cutter out onto the glacial ice of the Arctic Ocean. He'd let me do it once, and I remembered how far it'd flown.

And at that moment, I realized that small memory, of me tossing firecrackers onto the ice in the middle of nowhere, was likely the impetus for the chain of events that led to this prize. Whether the system really knew my memories or not, they had a rather obvious plan for me. I no longer needed the slingshot with this item. This was better. Much, much better.

I strapped the xistera onto my wrist, awkwardly using my teeth and left hand to fasten the first set of buckles. The second set went just before my elbow. The rounded scoop extended about two and a half feet past my right hand, almost like a single massive fingernail. It felt natural on me. I wouldn't be able to punch or summon my gauntlet while it was on me like this, but I could feel the plastic-like slit just above my palm. Anything I summoned into my hand from my inventory could be pushed directly into the scoop. And conversely, I could make a claw and remove the item in the scoop.

The xistera wasn't magical—at least it didn't say it was—but it was mechanical and made with some pretty neat technology. It had a trick. The second strap just below my elbow had a small pull ring. I pulled it, and the entire scoop yanked in on itself, forming and twisting over my right forearm like a metallic bracer. The motion was quick and smooth. Once the scoop was retracted, I formed a fist to make sure my gauntlet would still work. It did. In fact, the gauntlet fit snugly over the end of the bracer as if it'd been made for it. Now the missing right arm of my jacket didn't look so ridiculous.

"Here's your oranges!" Fitz said, piling five of them on the table.

I picked them up and pulled them all into my inventory. I eyed the entrance door to the safe room, which I knew was the most unbreakable thing in here. I extended the scoop.

I pulled an orange into my hand. I was worried it'd be a little too fat for the xistera, but it automatically widened itself. *Hey, that's pretty cool.*

I spun, arcing my arm over my head. The orange rocketed out of the scoop and smashed right into the center of the door. The fruit completely disintegrated.

"Hey!" Fitz said.

"Wow," Donut said. "That's delightful! Do it again! Fitz, get him some apples and plums!"

Fitz stopped complaining and ran to comply. I attempted to hit the exact same spot. My aim was just a hair off, but I could already tell that as my skill in this grew, I'd become more and more accurate. I really needed to get outside and try it for distance. I could now sling projectiles *fast*. I knew with a rock or a metal ball, it would do some serious damage.

I also realized I was going to have to start tossing a few points into dexterity here and there. I'd been planning on a strength-and-constitution build, but if my accuracy became an issue, a dexterity boost would help.

I tried tossing some of the small ammo I had for my clurichaun slingshot. The little rocks weren't uniform enough in size to properly lob. While the scoop tried to make itself thinner, it didn't get nearly thin enough. Their aim was unpredictable because I couldn't control their passage through the scoop as I swung.

CARL: You win, Zev. No more slingshot.
ZEV: Yay! People are pretty excited about this. I'm glad you got it. It was a close vote with something utterly inappropriate.
CARL: What was it?
ZEV: You know I can't tell you that.

"I'm going to need regular ammo and more of those hob-lobbers," I said after I finished. The human couple who'd been sitting in the corner got up and ran out the moment I stopped fruit-ninjaing the door.

"That's just the tip of the iceberg," Mordecai said. "You'll be able to make yourself smoke bombs, and I can fashion tossables like poison bags and pretty much anything else you can think of. I know a recipe for a rubberlike substance that breaks apart when it hits something. We'll need a table for it, though."

I nodded. I pulled one of the hob-lobber bombs out of my inventory. I examined its properties.

Hobgoblin Hob-Lobber—Fused.

   Type: Fragmenting Tossable.

   Effect: It blows shit up.

   Status: 150. Fortified.

   A mainstay of the Hobgoblin Hob-Lobbing Lobbers, the Hob-Lobber is a stable, mostly predictable, more practical and tactical solution to dynamite. All right? But if you toss it, make sure its wick is lit. While not guaranteed to do a premature blast, it's better than nothing, innit?

"Your rhyming scheme is all off," I muttered.

The round bomb was the perfect size for my xistera. This kind of hob-lobber had a fuse that needed to be lit. A minor inconvenience. I could go back to crazy Pustule the hobgoblin and buy the impact-triggered ones. Though, thinking on it, there was a lot I could do with this kind. *A lot.* Especially once Mordecai got his hands on that alchemy table.

I tossed the heavy bomb into the air and caught it. Everyone in the room, even Mongo, looked at me with a horrified expression. The item's stability was still at 150. I could punt the item, and it wouldn't go off. Besides, this was a safe room. Still, they were all looking at me like I'd lost my mind. I had a quick memory of a goblin bomb bard who'd been doing something similar as we'd passed by. I remembered thinking he was crazy at the time. I put the bomb away, smiling sheepishly.

"I worry about you sometimes," said Donut.

"OH, I KNOW WHAT THIS IS," MORDECAI SAID THE MOMENT I HANDED him the shirt. "You said this was on a city elf, right?"

"That's right," I said. "I didn't get a chance to read his description before Donut and I killed him. So what's the deal?"

"You shouldn't see any *real* uniformed military on this floor other than the guards, or maybe some of the mobs. You will definitely see an organized military presence on the ninth and maybe on the sixth. And you never know what's going to happen on the others. But the only jackholes who organize themselves like this are the city elves. They're a gang, and they called themselves the 201st Security Group."

"Ohh," I said. "I thought that was a unit patch."

"They're morons, is what they are," Mordecai said. "You'll find them mostly in the larger cities, but also in the medium-sized ones that are governed by the skyfowl. I should have known they'd be here."

"Are they mercenaries?" I asked, taking the shirt back.

"They're nutjobs," Mordecai said. "There are a lot of types of elves. High elves, like your elite friend's family. Those guys are the forest-dwelling magical beings you're probably most familiar with. There are dark elves, wind elves, goblin elves, and a dozen more. And then there are the city elves."

"He looked like a normal elf to me," Donut said. "But he was a little crazy. He knew our names."

"Yeah, I don't know why he knew you," said Mordecai. "But anyway, on the surface, you had a small segment of society who believed really crazy things. Like aliens walked among the people and that lizard folk had taken over the highest levels of government. You know what I'm talking about, right?"

"I do," I said. "But they don't seem so crazy now, do they? You guys *were* walking around among us."

Mordecai scoffed. "Yeah, but not the reptilians. Those guys run a shadow government? Please. The last reptilian I knew couldn't even properly run a fantasy football league. Anyway, I'm talking about crazy conspiracy nuts. People who believe the government is trying to use mind control on them, secret societies, gay frogs who shoot tracking microchips into you using cellular towers, and so on and so forth. Not your run-of-the-mill conspiracy theorists, but those who go the extra mile. Tin-foil-hat-wearing, silver-drinking nutjobs. The kind of people who cover their vehicles with crazy, schizophrenic texts about radio signals coming from toilets."

"I know exactly what you mean," I said.

"That's a city elf. They are designated as a separate race because their stupidity is so outstanding, the high elves consider it a genetic defect and kick them out. All elves originate with the high elves, who are big on banishing and wholesale genocide. It's what happens when you live forever but still keep having babies. So the city elves gather in the cities. The young and especially stupid ones always find their way to the 201st. It's a big, poorly organized militia that considers itself a proper military outfit, and it has only one goal. To protect the skyfowl from the earthbound."

I laughed. "What? *They're* earthbound. Aren't they?"

"Yeah, so, they believe the skyfowl are angels. They believe all flightless creatures are so jealous of us—of the skyfowl, I mean—that all humans and everybody else without wings want to destroy them. They believe when Scolopendra unleashed that nine-tier attack, one of the tiers was a spell that made the earthbound want to kill the skyfowl. That's absolutely not true. People want to kill skyfowl because skyfowl are assholes. They don't need a spell to make people hate them."

"But why?" I asked. "Why do the elves care?"

Mordecai sighed. "It's kind of a long, complicated story, and we're brushing on a subject I was going to bring up at a later time. We've touched on it before. Gods and goddesses. In-game deities. We'll get to what they really are later. You don't need to worry about that on this floor. Anyway, all you need to know is that elves worship the Oak Mother, the mother of all gods. Her name is Apito. And in one story about Apito, it is said that in order to maintain the path to heaven, her angels must remain free and alive. And in a completely separate story, Apito is said to have called the skyfowl 'bless-ed.' And in a third, apocryphal story, Apito said only the angels are 'blessed.' In that same story she says any violence against angels is to be stopped, and if it continues, she will destroy all the worlds. Ergo, a batshit-crazy, doomsday cult sect of banished elves now dedicates themselves to protecting the skyfowl in anticipation of the day when the tree goddess destroys the universe."

"All righty, then. And what do the skyfowl think about these guys?" I asked.

He paused. "Skyfowl in general are a diverse people, like humans, but the ones on this level are a little different. They're mostly non-religious. They are, as a rule, negatively inclined toward any flightless creature. They think of you as a servant class, that you're beneath them. In the mythology of the volcano levels, the skyfowl were the ruling class of the Over City, and the High Elves were the ruling class of the forested regions of the Hunting Grounds. So when these elves show up in their cities, oftentimes falling to the ground and slobbering all over themselves as they offer obeisance, they're treated as an amusement, a joke. Nobody takes them seriously. They have their stupid uniforms and their playacting, but I've never seen anything come of it in all my time here. This angel thing is their main motivation, but they also have all sorts of weird theories and beliefs. Everybody makes fun of them. I've never known them to actually inflict violence."

"Well, we're going to find out what's going on," Donut declared. She stood stiffly. She'd put the picture of Bea into her inventory. "I've decided that we're going to follow through with this quest, and there's nothing you can do to stop us, Mordecai."

"Is that so?" Mordecai asked.

"GumGum died because of us. And Carl, Mongo, and I have decided to make it right."

Mordecai just looked at her; then he shrugged after a moment. "If that's what you're gonna do. I ain't your dad. I'm your manager. You know how I feel about quests on this floor. But as long as you spend as much time grinding and killing as possible, then so be it."

Donut looked surprised, then triumphant. I could tell by the nonplussed look on Mordecai's face that he'd already decided we were stuck with this quest whether we wanted it or not. We'd already been sucked in, much the way we'd been sucked in when Signet had kidnapped us.

"GumGum is dead? Did I hear that right?" Fitz asked, looking at us with wide eyes. "GumGum the orc?"

"I'm afraid so," I said. "She was killed by a group of krasue."

"Oh, oh no," the barkeep said. "I . . . I gotta sit down. GumGum dead. I can't believe it. She was m'best customer, she was. Krasue. I knew they'd get her one of these days." The man wandered back into his kitchens.

"I'm going to get him blackout drunk tonight," Mordecai said. "Then I can peek at his stores and the newsletter."

"So we're doing this, then?" Donut asked. "We're doing the quest? And this time I will be awake the whole time? Excellent. Let's solve this mystery. What do we gotta do next?"

"Okay," I said. "Let's work through what we already know. We have dead prostitutes from outside the city falling from the sky. These women have corpses that suggest they've been twisted to death. Furthermore, they have wounds on their shoulders that indicate they've been held aloft by something with talons. Possibly a skyfowl. And just a few hours after we said we'd do something about it, the woman who gave us the quest ends up dead. We're attacked by that crazy elf dude from that gang along with three scary ghost ladies with their guts hanging out. What else?"

"You have those two pieces of paper," Donut said.

"Oh yeah," I said, pulling them both from my inventory. The first was **Mysterious Letter**. It was a folded piece of paper stained red with blood. I opened it.

It was a relatively short letter written in a language I didn't understand. The text was all squiggles and triangles. I examined the letter's properties.

> **Mysterious Letter.**
> GumGum the orc had this blood-soaked letter in her possession. It's in an odd language. Is it a clue? Is it a grocery list? You can't fucking read it, so who knows?

I slid it over to Mordecai as I examined the next slip.

> **Gate Pass.**
> When one walks about the streets of any town within the Over City, the mindless Swordsman guards tend to get a bit squirrelly if you're carrying a corpse with you. When it comes to their black-and-white view of justice, the rule of law is absolute.
> Unless you have a Gate Pass.
> This letter gets the city guard off your back as long as you're not being too overt with your current criminal enterprise.
> Pass only works within the township in which it was issued.

The paper itself said, "Gate Pass. The holder of this pass is doing this on my orders. Magistrate Featherfall."

"That is not what I expected," I said, putting it back into my inventory. It was basically a get-out-of-jail-free card.

"I recognize this text," Mordecai said, still looking at the mysterious letter. He sounded nervous. "I can't read it, but I know these squiggles. It's necroscript. It's something an undead magic user would write out. This is probably a type of scroll. But you can only read it if you have proper skill in the language."

"So it has something to do with a necromancer?" I asked.

"Maybe, maybe not. But when I say 'undead magic user,' I mean that literally."

"Those krasue head things were undead," I said. "The system said they were ghosts."

"Krasue are usually henchmen, errr, henchwomen for something else. I'm thinking you two might have a lich problem."

"What is a lich?" Donut asked.

I answered. I knew this from playing *DnD*. "It's usually an undead magic user obsessed with eternal life."

"Sort of," Mordecai said. "They're pretty nasty monsters. They tend to be smart, too."

"Hmm," I said, thinking. "What does a lich have to do with those 201st Security Group assholes?"

"Hey, Fitz, darling. Can you come back here, please?" Donut called.

The pub owner appeared from the back, rubbing his eyes. He'd obviously been crying. "Yes, Your Majesty?"

"You said you were afraid that GumGum would get hurt by one of the krasue. What did you mean by that? How did you know about those things?"

I looked at Donut, impressed. I chose not to say anything.

"She told me," he said. "She was looking out for them fallen women. But she said sometimes she'd hear one, and she'd go into the alleyway even though it was still night. I'd tell her not to go in there. It ain't safe. But she'd go, and she said sometimes she'd see the krasue in the shadows. She was afraid of them. She had nightmares. But she cared about them women. She had nightmares about one of them falling from the sky and not being dead, and just sitting there and dying, and nobody being there to hold her hand and tell her it was going to be okay. GumGum's mom had been one of them ladies, you see. A lady of the night, I mean. And she'd died after getting stabbed.

GumGum had found her the next morning. Just sitting on the stoop to their house. She'd crawled home and died right there. She'd left a red streak a half kilometer long, and nobody had helped. GumGum had to grow up mighty fast after that. That's why she had a soft spot for those ladies. The nicest orc you'd ever meet. She smelled something awful, but I really liked her."

"So krasue are a normal monster for this town?" I asked.

"There's no such thing as a normal monster for this town," he said. "But it's unusual for the undead to rattle about, the magistrate being a black cleric and all. He can control the undead, so I reckon if he knew about them, he'd banish them floating lady heads right quick. GumGum said she'd complained, and all he did was give her permission to move the dead bodies."

I exchanged a look with Donut. "Magistrate, huh?" I said. "Do you know where this guy's office is?"

DONUT INSISTED ON PLACING THE PICTURE OF BEA ON THE SMALL table next to her cat tree as she slept. Mongo didn't appear nearly as thrilled about the framed photograph as Donut did. He actually hissed at it a couple times before Donut admonished him.

"Good boy," I said later, scratching the top of his head. He chomped at the air, electricity sparking from his enchanted fang caps.

I decided not to read. I had those Louis L'Amour books, but we had to get up early. Our interview was earlier than usual, and I wanted to check out this magistrate guy before it was time to go. Still, I pulled out the mysterious letter. I stared at the symbols, trying to memorize them.

Even though I'd set up the cat tree at her insistence, Donut jumped straight onto my neck and settled in.

"Good night, Carl," she said.

"Good night, Donut," I said, patting her head.

"Promise me you won't let me die alone like GumGum's mom,"

she said. "Or GumGum. I guess she died alone, too. She was probably really scared."

"Don't worry, Donut," I said. "We'll find out who's responsible, and we'll make them pay."

Thwump. Something hit the roof of the inn directly over our heads. It slid off the rooftop and crashed loudly onto the street.

In the morning we'd discover the body of a naked, twisted human prostitute sprawled out in the alley next to the inn.

Scrawled onto her back in torn, bloodless flesh were the words *No, you won't.*

18

Views: 1.9 Quadrillion
Followers: 72 Trillion
Favorites: 13.1 Trillion

"WE'D LIKE TO SEE MAGISTRATE FEATHERFALL, PLEASE," DONUT said, using her sweetest voice.

Getting to this office had been a chore. The town's administrative buildings had no first or second floor, and we'd had to utilize Donut's *Puddle Jumper* spell to teleport from the rooftop of a knife shop to the landing entrance of the town hall. She'd recently hit level five with the spell, which had solved the line-of-sight issue. It basically added support for jumping up to a higher elevation when you couldn't see the ground above you. It was a minor addition to the spell, but one that made it much more useful. The casting delay was also much shorter, now only two seconds instead of ten. Still, hitting level five hadn't decreased the five-hour cooldown, which was the worst issue with the spell.

But we did it. We zapped into the building's third-floor entrance only to come face-to-face with two of the village swordsman guards. They stood stoically, ignoring us as we proceeded deeper into the building.

"How did they get up here?" Donut asked.

"I have no idea," I said. "Weird."

Donut had protested, but I talked her into putting Mongo into his carrier for this excursion. We were headed into the legislative chamber of this town, and the last thing we needed was the murder chicken to go a-murdering when all we wanted to do was talk. "We'll keep him in reserve," I'd said. "Our secret weapon in case we have to fight our way out."

That seemed to appease both of them.

Mordecai had said that every one of these towns had a different type of leadership structure. Before the cataclysm, the skyfowl were in charge of the whole Over City. Now their settlements were scattered, but the remaining eagle-controlled villages such as this one still maintained a similar structure as before, but without the previous oversight.

As a result, this Magistrate Featherfall guy was the big boss man of this village. In the old days, he would have answered to a regional governor, who in turn would answer to the royal chancellor, who in turn would answer to some dude in some sprawling capital city that was on the ninth floor.

This third floor was actually a high-end shopping mall of sorts, catering only to skyfowl. The administrative building and home to the magistrate were directly above this floor, but anyone visiting had to first walk through this section. The shops reminded me of the type of stores one would find at the airport, filled with expensive crap, like silken robes and fancy hats and scrolls. And even though the sparse customers were all the eagle folk, the clerks and assistants were all non-eagles, most of them harried-looking young women human and elves, rushing about, being snapped at and verbally abused by the skyfowl shoppers.

We walked down a long, wide hallway flanked by the shops. A red carpet stretched from the landing to a stairwell at the end of the hall. I was relieved to see it was stairs and not another vertical flyway. As I watched, a human carrying a blue folder filled with papers rushed up the stairs.

"They have to have stairs so the help can get up there," I said.

"That still doesn't explain how they get up here in the first place," Donut said.

Paintings of eagles fighting elves and other oddities adorned the walls. This particular building was one of the largest in town, second only to the Desperado Club. From the outside, it was camouflaged well. The exterior walls of each section were shingled in a different manner, making it look like a group of medieval buildings pressed against one another. The higher-end, more opulent interior made the whole façade seem like something one would find at Disneyland.

We passed multiple guards, a couple of eagle shoppers who startled at our appearance, and a handful of other birdlike creatures called chickadees, whom I'd originally mistaken for juvenile skyfowl. These guys only came up to my waist and were like dwarven versions of the larger birds.

We approached the stairs without being stopped or questioned. As we ascended, the human who'd rushed up earlier rushed back down, almost running directly into us.

"Pardon me," she said. I looked at the name over her head. **Burgundy**. The woman had an odd look about her. She was young, dark haired, and pretty. She had one pale blue eye and a brown one, like a Siberian husky.

"No worries," I said.

She paused. "Are you lost? We don't see too many of your kind up here."

"We're on our way to see the magistrate," I said.

She snorted. "Good luck." Then she continued back down the stairs.

We continued up and walked straight into a reception area.

A large desk sat in one corner, pressed against the far wall, which contained another door. On the desk were piles of papers, what appeared to be an oversized bento box filled with sushi, more papers— including the blue folder Burgundy had just dropped off—and a colorful line of small stuffed animals, from bears to goblins to eagles to sharks. Behind the desk was a row of shelves containing more of the colorful collection. These things were the dungeon version of Beanie Babies, I realized. There had to be 300 of them lined up on the shelves. Most if not all of them still had tags. A few from the top shelf were protected by individual glass cases.

Behind the desk, instead of a chair, there was a perch. And upon that perch rested an elderly female skyfowl. Her feathers were tinged gray, and her large beak was cracked and crazed like brittle old pottery. She smelled like Icy Hot. She glared at the intrusion with a who-the-hell-are-you-and-what-the-hell-are-you-doing-here look upon her sour face. I examined the NPC's properties.

> **Miss Quill—Skyfowl. Level 30.**
>   **Assistant to the Magistrate.**
>   **Cerberus. Heimdall. Aniketos and Alexiares. Qin Shubao. Lev Yashin. Some of the greatest gate guardians of both history and mythology. But none of them, not a one, was as dedicated to their work as Miss Quill.**
>   **If she doesn't want you to see the magistrate, you ain't seeing the magistrate.**

"Do you have an appointment?" she asked Donut.

"We don't," Donut said. "But we have a matter of great importance to discuss regarding the safety of this town."

"And what is that matter?" she asked.

Donut leaned in. "Murder. Murder most foul."

Miss Quill did not appear impressed. "Was it a skyfowl?"

"The suspect?" Donut asked. "We don't know yet, but—"

"No, not the suspect. Put that down!" I quickly placed the lemur Beanie Baby back on the desk. The little stuffed creature wore a bandolier of knives, just like the real version. "Were any skyfowl murdered?"

"No," Donut said. "Not that we know of."

"Then he's not going to care," Miss Quill said. "And if he's not going to care, I'm not going to disturb him. Because he *will* care about being disturbed."

DONUT: MY CHARM ISN'T WORKING ON HER.

MORDECAI: There's probably an anti-*Charm* spell working in the area.

CARL: Plan B it is.

"Is that how it is in this town, then?" I asked. "As long as the victims aren't skyfowl, they can just go screw themselves?"

She looked at me as if I were something she'd just regurgitated. "Do you want the short answer or the long answer to that?"

"The long answer," I said.

"Yes," she said. "That's how it is in this town. It was like this when my late husband was the magistrate, and it's like that now with Magistrate Featherfall." She looked down at her bento box and sighed. "But please, feel free to leave a note describing the situation, and if it warrants further investigation, we'll get back to you."

"And what about the evidence we collected? Should we leave that here, too?" I asked.

"If you must."

I pulled the dead hooker from my inventory and splatted her on the eagle's desk. The corpse's legs, still stiff with rigor, upset the line of Beanie Babies, tumbling them off the edge of the desk one by one, like a line of synchronized swimmers diving into the pool.

I'd been afraid the system wouldn't let me pick up and store the corpse, as it wasn't something we'd tried before. I'd been surprised to find it did let us. It had even helpfully labeled the body as **Quest Clues** in my inventory.

The eagle made a strangled noise, leaping from her perch. Her back hit the wall, and it upset the bottom two shelves, cascading more of the beanbag creatures to the floor. For a moment the only sound was the *plop, plop, plop* of the figures as they slid and tumbled.

"Guards," Miss Quill croaked. "Guards!"

The two swordsmen at the base of the stairs clunked their way up toward us. They both unsheathed their swords as they emerged, rising up like metallic beasts. I remembered the announcement from a few days earlier, that their strength had been "slightly" increased. I really hoped this worked.

"Capture these two! Do so immediately," Miss Quill demanded.

The mute suits of armor looked back and forth about the room. Neither of them moved.

"Oh for the sake of the gods," Miss Quill said angrily. "Look at my desk, you fools."

The moment we found the dead prostitute this morning, with that gruesome note scrawled onto her flesh, I'd called one of the swordsmen over. I pointed to the corpse, I pulled the Gate Pass—the get-out-of-jail-free pass from the town magistrate—and showed it to the guard. Then I took the corpse into my inventory. I hadn't known for certain that actually did anything. But I knew if we were going to be waving a dead hooker around, odds were good the town guards would get involved. Mordecai said they had a collective mind. And if they'd already seen me with the body and had, in their odd way, endorsed my ability to have a dead hooker in my possession, then the act of me simply tossing the corpse onto the desk wouldn't be considered a crime.

Hopefully.

Without a word, the guards turned and walked back down the stairs.

"You useless, worthless piles of junk!" Miss Quill called after them. She returned her gaze to us.

"How do they get up here anyway?" I asked. "Also, how do all those workers in the shops get up here? Is there a secret elevator? We looked for, like, an hour for an easy way up and couldn't find one."

"Take that with you right now," Miss Quill said. "What is wrong with you?" She squatted and began gathering up the fallen toys in her wings. But she had nowhere to put them. Not until the shelf was fixed and the dead woman was removed from the desk.

Donut leaped from my shoulder and sniffed at the ground. "This one is getting really dirty," Donut said, looking at a rat-faced Beanie that looked suspiciously like Mordecai's first form. "And I think the label tore on this one. Carl, stop stepping on them!"

"Stop! Stop it right now! Please, just take it away." The elderly eagle appeared to be on the verge of tears.

"Take *her* away," Donut corrected.

"Let us talk to him, and we'll bring the evidence to him directly," I said.

"He's not here, okay?" Miss Quill said, frantically piling the toys in the corner. She picked one up with her talon and frantically rubbed nonexistent dirt off it with her wing. "Look what you've done, look what you've done."

I glanced at the closed door near her desk. The door was large, metal, and foreboding.

"He's really not here?" I asked.

"No," she said. "He only comes out at night nowadays. Oh my gods, what is that liquid?"

"I don't know," I said. "It's not blood. They've all had their blood sucked out of them. But their bodies still leak. And smell. It's really gross."

Her wings were full of Beanies. "Please, please," she said. "Just take it away. Take *her* away. I'll tell him you were here. I promise."

I reached over and picked the dead woman back up, returning her to my inventory. A milky white stain of fluid covered Miss Quill's desk.

"I'm going to be sick," the receptionist said.

"You better get some paper towels or something," I said. "My grandma collected these things, and they sucked in moisture like you wouldn't believe."

"Don't you touch anything," she said. She gently placed the Beanies held in her wings onto the corner pile. She rushed toward the stairs, yelling that she needed a shirt or a towel.

We only had a minute, maybe less. I rushed to the door to Featherfall's chambers. It was locked. The moment I touched the door, a notification popped up.

This door is locked. Magically locked. It's almost like they don't want you going in there.

"Shit," I muttered, looking around.

My eyes focused on the top, undisturbed line of Beanies sitting above her desk.

———

"JUST TELL HIM WE CAME BY," I SAID TO MISS QUILL AS WE WENT back down the stairs. "And you're welcome for fixing your shelf." She ignored us as she frantically cleaned off her table.

"That was disappointing," Donut said. "Do you think he was actually in there?"

"I don't know. Mordecai seems to think he lives in there, but who knows?"

"We don't even know for sure he has anything to do with it," Donut said.

"Nope," I said. "That's why I wanted to talk to him when he was in his office. I figured if he's some evil, crazy boss, he wouldn't go all Freddy Krueger on us in public. And if he's *not* the bad guy, surely he'd be able to point us in the correct direction. But I don't think it's that complicated. This quest is only a silver one. Plus look at the clues. He's a black cleric? He only comes out at night? It has to be him."

"So we're coming back tonight, then?" Donut asked. "Or did you want to find the 201st Security Group headquarters first?" She paused in front of a store selling robes made for skyfowl. "Would you look at how pretty that is?"

"It's magical silk," a young elven woman said. "It allows skyfowl to stay aloft almost indefinitely."

"It's beautiful. I'd love to learn how to fly. Can you imagine that, Carl? Me flying?"

"We'll be back," I said, turning to look over my shoulder. I pulled the rope from my inventory. It'd only cost five gold for a thirty-foot

length. We'd have to use it to get back to the street. "We'll talk to
him one way or another."

––––––––––

WE STILL HAD TWO HOURS BEFORE OUR INTERVIEW. ZEV SAID IF WE
were fighting or in the midst of something, they wouldn't allow us
to get transported, which was why she preferred us to be in a safe
room when it was time. Still, we had two hours, and I decided we
should use the time wisely.

So we left the city and traveled west, searching for mobs to kill.
A few other crawlers were about, but we avoided them. I kept a wary
eye for those with player-killer skulls over their head. I hadn't forgotten about Frank Q and Maggie My. I wondered what race they'd
chosen, or if they were even still alive.

I didn't yet have any proper nonexplosive ammo for my xistera,
but I had two dozen hob-lobbers. The fuses on the bombs were between six and seven seconds, which was perfect when I was tossing
them like they were grenades. But when I was hurling them at 250
mph at a mob, six seconds was a little too long. So instead, I pre-lit
ten of them, which took two and a half seconds off the fuse. Both
Mordecai and Donut were mortified by the idea of me walking
around with lit bombs sitting in my inventory, but it was pretty
much the only way I could properly do this with the equipment
I had.

We walked past a row of especially decrepit buildings. This particular neighborhood appeared as if it might've been slums before
the cataclysm. Donut sat upon my shoulder, and Mongo walked beside us, randomly growling. I'd been alarmed at first, but there didn't
seem to be anything out there. We hadn't seen anything for fifteen
minutes. Then I saw the X on the map, and I realized it was the
corpse of a neighborhood boss. This area had already been cleared by
someone else, probably a few days earlier.

"Damnit," I grumbled. "What a waste of time." I sighed. "Let's
go get the neighborhood map."

The attack came just as I was about to descend into an abandoned, used-to-be indoor swimming pool. This building had been the Over City's version of a YMCA, though half of the structure was gone. The empty swimming pool sat mostly outside, exposed to the air. The rotting corpse of a two-headed sea creature sat within. The thing had the body of a whale, but with two long Loch Ness Monster–like heads. Apparently the street urchins steered clear of boss corpses. The boss was a level 17 monster called **the Divider**, and it had been killed by a crawler named **Daniel Bautista 2**. The boss had multiple manhole-cover-sized holes in it. The monster's body was massively bloated, despite puncture wounds. It looked like a balloon from the Macy's Thanksgiving Day Parade.

Just as I stepped into the shallow end of the empty pool, the world around us went dark. A dozen red dots appeared on the map. The dots were pretty far away, two sets on either side of the street. They started to close in.

We'd left the inn at sunrise, and we hadn't yet hit whatever this world's version of noon was called. The virtual sun had blazed directly above us just moments before. We'd gone from day to night so quickly, I thought I'd been struck blind. I stepped back from the pool and put my back against the wall. The dots remained out there on the street. They crept slowly and cautiously, almost as if they thought they were sneaking up on us.

Donut immediately cast *Torch*, shooting the light high above the street. The bright light was like a star in the sky. The torch blazed, but it didn't fill the darkness like it should, as if the murk was resisting it.

A moment later, a green bolt shot from one of the red dots, and it crashed right into the torch, snuffing it out.

"Well, that was rude," Donut said.

"Shit, they have an anti-magic attack," I said. We needed to come up with a plan, and fast. I pulled two regular torches from my inventory, lit them, and tossed them ahead of me. They skittered out onto the street. The darkness did not budge. It pushed in on the twin torches, surrounding them like the very air was made of ink.

Down the street, something moaned. It sent chills through me. Mongo let out a half growl, half whimper.

Still, the darkness wasn't absolute. I could make out shapes in the gloom. I couldn't see the mobs, which were still a good hundred feet away, but I could sense the outlines of buildings. A wall of rubble blocked our exit through the gym and to the next street, and there was no passage across the other way. We were boxed in.

Even so, the monsters moved slowly. That made me nervous. Slow mobs were usually the type you didn't want anywhere near you.

"Two of them are city elves," Donut quickly said. "The farthest dot on each side. I don't know what the rest are, but they're big. Should we do Slime Time?"

Of all the predetermined plays we'd come up with so far, Slime Time was Donut's favorite. And for good reason. It was fucking awesome. But now wasn't the time. Plus, I wasn't so sure it'd work. Not here.

"Negative," I said. "Wait one second. Let's see if this does anything."

I stepped away from the wall and pulled a lit hob-lobber into my hand as I extended my xistera. I couldn't see the mobs, but I could sense them there. Moaning and shuffling toward us. Were they zombies? Jesus. That was a terrifying thought. I spun and tossed the bomb as hard as I could directly at the far dot of the city elf, the one who had cast the anti-magic spell.

The sizzling bomb flew with satisfying speed, rocketing out of my xistera like a cannonball. It hit something fleshy about twenty feet from the city elf. I'd aimed so it would fly over the slow-moving monsters, but apparently I hadn't aimed high enough.

Bam! The presumed sound of raining gore slapped onto the street.

One of the dots turned into an X. But only one. My bomb seemed to have sunk into the monster. I now had a clear line to the elf. I spun, hurling a second bomb at the fucker.

This one hit home, perfectly timed. I really wished I could see it.

The hob-lobber blew just before it reached the elf, but the fragmenting explosion ripped through him. There wasn't even an X left after that.

The other monsters groaned, now only forty feet away.

The darkness didn't lift.

I could now hear the sound of shuffling, like feet on the floorboards. Holy shit, these *were* zombies. They had to be. Giant zombies.

No more screwing around. I retracted my xistera and pulled two sticks of goblin dynamite from my pack. "Run into the pool," I called as I lit them both and tossed one in each direction.

The moment I tossed the second stick, the line of red dots surged forward, rushing at me. I watched, in horrified slow motion, as the flying stick of dynamite rebounded off a massive shape, at least twelve feet tall. The stick didn't blow, but it bounced, hissing and spitting and rolling toward me, much too close.

"Oh fuck, oh fuck!" I hopped backward into the empty pool, not bothering to gauge exactly where I was standing. I had no time. I just jumped. I prepared to press my *Protective Shell* spell, but I wanted to be closer to Donut and Mongo before I did it.

Unfortunately, I stopped falling much sooner than I anticipated. I landed directly on the spongy, rotting corpse of the Divider.

And that was the last thing I remembered.

What happened next was later relayed to me by Donut, who was the only one of us to stay conscious for the remainder of the fight.

Both sticks blew, killing most of the remaining monsters and the remaining city elf. I'd fallen far enough to be protected from that blast. However, I was not protected from the bloating corpse of the boss monster, which in turn blew like a goddamn potato in the microwave, either from me falling into it, or from the shock wave of the dual explosions.

The moment the second elf died, the lights snapped back on. The first thing Donut saw was me sailing up in the air like I'd been ejected from a catapult, spinning like a pinwheel. I landed upon the roof of the building across the street.

The detonation of the Divider's corpse did no damage to either Donut or Mongo, though it showered both of them with a blizzard of stinking, gooey gore. Donut grabbed the neighborhood map, leaped out of the pool, and she finished off the last three of the monsters, all of whom had barely survived. She hit two with magic missiles, and she set Mongo on the third. The dinosaur went about his task with practiced glee.

Donut then leaped to the roof of the building I'd landed on and used a *Heal* scroll to bring my health back up. I remained unconscious for another three minutes, despite being healed.

I awakened, staring up at the sky. I'd gone up a level to 19. My brain took several moments to reboot. I'd landed on a pile of rocks, and they dug into my back. I groaned, rolling over, and I almost plummeted through a hole in the ceiling to the floor below. I had no idea where I was. What had happened?

I heard the *thwump* of Donut's magic missile, and I abruptly looked up.

"Good morning, Carl. I haven't seen any more of the elves, but the meat bags keep coming," she said. She fired another missile. "They're pretty easy to kill if you hit them in the right place. Mongo is having a field day. He's already gone up to level 12." She leaned over the edge and yelled, "Good boy, Mongo! Mommy is going to kill the next one, and you get the one behind him." She fired once again.

"What is happening? How did I get up here? Whoa, Donut. What the hell happened to you?"

I'd seen Donut covered in gore before, but this was the next goddamned level. After we'd fought the Juicer on the first floor, she'd been caked in blood and guts. I'd thought we'd never get her clean. That was nothing compared to this. She had to have three inches of red stinking viscera attached to her fur. She was covered like a piece of extra-crispy fried chicken.

"Later," she said. "They keep coming from that direction. They're really slow until they get close, but then they get fast. Watch Mongo kill this one."

I was also covered in gore, but mostly on my back. I felt it slide off of me as I sat up. It was as thick as mud.

I peered over the edge and gaped at the sight. I swallowed. I'd never seen anything like it. I'd had porridge for breakfast, and I regretted it now.

In every direction were splattered, sticky blood and body parts. The swimming pool was filled with red, and much of the viscera was currently spilling into it, filling it deeper and deeper. Hunks of flesh, some pretty big, lay strewn about like boulders. The white shock of bone stuck up everywhere, giving the sense I was looking at the zoomed-in view of a wound, and the bones were actually grubs.

And the smell. Oh god, it hit me all at once. It was the stench of a sewer and the contents of a refrigerator at a restaurant that sold 99-cent tilapia, cracked open after an extended period with no power. My head swam.

"Fucking hell," I said. "What the hell happened down there?"

"*You* did it," Donut said. "You really need to be more careful, Carl."

My eyes caught movement, and I finally saw one of the monsters we'd been facing in the dark.

The beast was a 13-foot-tall pile of body parts, all sewn together haphazardly as it shuffled forward. It was as if Doctor Frankenstein had dropped acid before he'd made his creation. I saw legs and arms and torsos, all smushed together. But there were heads, too. Lots of heads, all human. The thing moved and was shaped like a giant slug. Tentacles made of arms and legs twirled above it, waving in the air. The heads all groaned in unison.

The thing was terrifying to behold, and I was glad I was now up here and not on the ground facing it.

Shambling Berserker—Level 12.

If you weren't fortunate enough to face one of these neighborhood boss monsters on the first level of the dungeon, fret not! Now's your chance to get in on the fun!

You know how you sometimes buy something from IKEA, and

after you're done putting it all together, you have a few parts left over? It happens to the best of us. What you see here is a Shambling Berserker, the smallest iteration of this creature. Also known as the Mini Grinder or the Shrilling, this creature consists of extra parts we found after creating the World Dungeon. Waste not, want not.

This undead abomination is oftentimes found in groups, summoned as a slow but very tenacious assassin. Once you're targeted by these guys, they don't stop. The good news is, they're mostly harmless. Unless, of course, you face one in the dark. Their power is quadrupled in the dark. And once they go berserk, there's no putting them down. They ain't so slow after that.

So, yeah, actually, you're probably fucked.

I thought of Mrs. Parsons, my downstairs neighbor before all this started. She'd been beheaded in the collapse. Her head had fallen at my feet, but the rest of her had gone down into the depths with the rest of the building. Had they used her headless body for one of these things?

As I watched, Mongo emerged from a pile of gore where he'd been having a snack, and he squealed, running at full speed toward the monster and leaping, feetfirst. The shambling berserker tumbled back and fell apart, groaning as it died.

"They're really easy to kill," Donut said. "They just fall apart."

"That's because it's not dark anymore," I said. I felt as if I'd been hit by a damn truck. I still didn't know exactly what had happened. "I'm pretty sure our Featherfall friend sent these dudes after us."

"Probably. Also, I think we should have a new rule," Donut said.

"What's that?"

"It's quite evident we shouldn't be throwing explosives when we're blinded."

I laughed. "That sounds like a good rule."

Below, Mongo screeched with victory as he eviscerated the pile of slow-moving body parts.

"I got the neighborhood map," Donut continued. "I can see there's about ten more coming. Let me and Mongo kill them, and we'll head back. This has been a great day for experience. I'll hit 17 before we're done, but we need to hurry. There's a safe room around the corner. I need to take a shower before we go on our interview."

I thought of us zapping into a production trailer looking like we did now, and I suddenly felt myself grin. I couldn't help it. I just started laughing. It even sounded a little crazy to my own ears.

"Okay," I said. I pulled a hob-lobber out, tossing it in the air and catching it. "But let me kill a couple, too. I want to see how far I can really chuck these things."

19

THIS WAS A DIFFERENT PRODUCTION TRAILER THAN THE ONE WE'D
used for the Maestro's show, but it was still a rental, according to the
Frisbee-shaped robot running the thing. The boat was even larger
and more well-appointed than Odette's private production trailer,
and I had the sense this one was normally used for dignitaries and
non-crawlers. Or maybe it was even living quarters, as it had a large
bowl-shaped bed and very nifty shower facilities.

There was a tray set out with food, but it clearly wasn't food from
Earth. It was little, purple, squiggly worm things, still alive. They
smelled like fish. Donut and I decided neither of us was hungry.
Mongo sniffed at the tray and slurped it all up.

They'd likely rented this place at the last minute since I'd told
Zev we didn't have time to get properly cleaned up. She sounded as
if she might cry over the chat when I told her. She started lecturing
us on how we needed to be ready for our "media relations obliga-
tions."

The safe room had been a bare-bones version with no food and
only a single shower facility. We'd soaked Donut, and I had Mordecai
brushing her as I got ready. Still, by the time we needed to go, Donut's fur remained heavily matted. The red mud-like gore clung to
her like paint. She needed to get back in the shower again, but we
didn't have time.

So when we transferred to the production trailer, we'd moved to
a special one that contained a shower that was straight out of the
Jetsons cartoon. The Frisbee robot thing's name was D-0NAH, which

Donut immediately translated to "Donna." Donna told Donut to remove all of her gear—except her tiara, of course—and to proceed to the shower. Mongo and I watched as the cat got on a treadmill thing that appeared to have been especially designed for her. It blasted her with water, air, some blue chemical, more water, more air, a robot arm brushed her, and then she got blasted again.

When she came out the other side, she looked as if she was ready for judging at an international cat show. Her fur glistened. There was no indication that an hour earlier she'd been showered with the exploding gore of a multiton, long-dead sea creature boss. I watched as she reequipped her crupper and the rest of her equipment. Donna ushered her back into the cleaning machine, and this time the mechanism focused on cleaning and polishing her gear. She stepped out, and the metal skirt gleamed. Mongo crept up to her and started sniffing at her suspiciously.

"Carl, Donna tells me that one may purchase one of these all-purpose cleaners for a personal space. She says they're expensive, but I think they're absolutely well worth it. We need to save our money. Quick, you go in there, too. It is luxurious."

"Nah, I'm good," I said.

"Carl, the back of your cloak looks as if it was used as a sanitary napkin. You need to get cleaned."

"Crawler Carl, I have been instructed to inform you that you need to avail yourself of the cleaning facilities," Donna the robot said. "You will be in the presence of royalty on the panel, and not presenting yourself properly is considered an insult."

Uh-oh. "Royalty? It's not that Maestro asshole, is it?"

"Prince Maestro has been stripped of his titles and disowned by his father, so he is no longer considered royalty. But no, it is not anyone of the Skull Empire. You will receive a rundown of your fellow panelists at the preshow briefing, which will occur in ten minutes. Now please step into the cleaner."

"Okay, but I'm not getting naked," I said. "Just clean the stuff people can see."

The robot paused. "Very well," she said.

"And then Mongo," Donut said. "He smells really bad."

"Your pet will be required to be stored during the interview."

"*Excuse* me?" Donut said. I stepped into the machine to avoid listening to the ensuing argument. Donna continued talking to me while the treadmill resized itself, instructing me to lift my arms and turn around, but I could see through the plexiglass-like material that Donut was also arguing with the robot. I couldn't hear what was happening, but I could tell Donut was pissed.

Like with Odette's trailer, this facility also had a porthole window. I stared out at the wide expanse of open sea. Unlike the last two times, it was now light outside, and I could finally see the real world. A pair of silver trailer-like objects floated in the ocean a couple hundred meters away. They looked like shipping containers, though they bobbed up and down like any regular ship. In the blue sky, a trio of shapes zipped through the air astonishingly fast.

I wondered how the other humans were doing, the ones who'd been smart enough not to go into the dungeon. The system had said they'd be left alone if they decided not to participate, but even through this little porthole looking through to some random place in the ocean, I could see that wasn't true. How many spaceships and other vessels had descended on the planet? Were they really leaving the other humans alone? Or were they being exploited, hunted, or enslaved?

"We came to a compromise," Donut announced once I stepped out. "Mongo is to be cleaned, but then he's going into the carrier."

I spent the next five minutes watching Donut attempt to talk the dinosaur into walking onto the treadmill. I'd just watched the pet plunge headfirst into a 13-foot-tall undead zombie frittata, but the idea of getting clean appeared to terrify him. Donut finally succeeded by capturing him with the pet carrier and then zapping him back out directly onto the contraption. The cleaner turned on, and the giant chicken started shrieking like a piglet being fed into a meat grinder. We could hear him even through the soundproofing of the device.

"Don't be a baby," Donut called. "Mommy is right here!"

He came out a moment later poofed up and smelling of lavender. He started running in circles around the trailer while Donna clucked after him nervously.

Finally, Donut zapped him away, and the door at the end of the room opened. We walked into an empty studio with a large round table. There was a section for a studio audience, but it was currently empty. Spotlights blazed over us. There was no desk like with Odette's show, and there was no extra-ornate chair like with the Maestro's stupid program. There was a simple glowing sign against the back wall that read **Danger Zone with Ripper Wonton.**

One of the chairs had **Carl** glowing over it, and the one next to it read **Princess Donut.** We both sat down. Like usual, Donut's chair ascended into the air, allowing her to look over the table.

"This is so exciting," Donut said. "I always love going on new shows."

"Yeah, the last new one really worked out great," I said.

A strange creature appeared, entering the room from a door across the studio. I guessed the creature was a he, but I wasn't certain. He was humanoid in shape, but absurdly thin. He stood about my height and was entirely white and hairless. He had oversized black eyes, like pools of oil. A ridge grew from between his eyes and up over his head like a bony Mohawk. He wore simple white clothes. His entire body glowed. When he walked, he drifted as if his feet didn't touch the ground.

Since we were outside the game, he had no name floating over him. He came to hover beside the table.

"Princess Donut and Carl, welcome to *Danger Zone*," he said. His voice sounded like I would expect. Airy and halting, alien-like. He waved at us in greeting, moving languidly. He only had three fingers on each hand.

"Hello. We are delighted to meet you," Donut said. "Are you Ripper Wonton?"

He chuckled softly. "No, Princess. My name is Evo. I am the program's director. I wanted to greet you two personally before we bring everyone else online. We will be live, not prerecorded. We have one other crawler with us tonight, and she has already been briefed." He indicated an empty chair. "She is sitting there at the moment and can't see you."

"What's the name of your race?" I asked.

"Ahh, I am of a people called the Forsoothed. People generally call us Soothers," Evo said.

"We had a lot of fiction and movies about aliens, and a lot of them looked similar to you," I said.

"Yes, it is interesting," Evo said. "Your culture showed the Null more than us, but we have seen examples of our people in your historical records and media. I do not know how you latched onto our likeness. It is most likely one of my brethren visited your world in the past. Some of my people are oddsmakers, and they likely visited this planet to get a sample of the human stock in order to make predictions for the crawl. Visiting the planet except for official Syndicate business was illegal, of course, but that doesn't mean it didn't happen."

"So alien abductions were really a thing?" I said. "Imagine that."

"What about the probes?" Donut asked. "I remember them talking about the probes on television."

"I assume you're talking about anal probes?" Evo asked. "Yes, we've heard about this as well. If that really happened, it was likely done by the Null. You called them the Grays. They are a nasty, unpleasant race. Perverts, all of them."

Evo pointed at the chair immediately to my left. A static holographic image appeared. It was of a tentacle-faced woman wearing a crown. "We must move on. Sitting in this chair will be Princess D'nadia of the Prism. She is a race called the Saccathians. People call them Sacs. They are a common race, but D'nadia's Prism Kingdom is rather small. Still, she is a powerful force in certain trade circles and is quite outspoken. She is a regular on this program. She is a fan of you two and specifically asked to sit here."

I examined the squid woman. This was just a holographic representation, not the real deal. Her skin appeared gray and covered in bumps. A tangle of squid-like tentacles hung from her cephalopod face, like she was a human-sized Cthulhu. She wore a long, flowing dress, and there was no way to tell what was under it. The whole look kind of freaked me out.

The next chair contained a pudgy, fuzzy brown creature that looked like the result of a wombat/Ewok union. The thing only stood about four feet high, and didn't wear any clothes except a fucking orange scarf around his neck, like Fred from *Scooby-Doo*. He had two huge cheeks and giant eyes. He was disgustingly cute. I vaguely remembered that Miss Quill had a beanbag version of this race sitting on her shelf.

"Oh my," Donut said. "That is positively adorable."

"This is your host, Ripper Wonton," Evo said. "He is of a race called a Setonix. People mostly call them Quokkas, though. He will lead the conversation. He is a good-hearted gentleman, despite his strong opinions. He will treat you fairly, but if he disagrees with your positions on anything, he will take you to task."

In the next chair was another female. She was a silver-and-black cobra-headed creature. The holograph towered over the table. Her hooded head had to be a meter wide.

"This is Manasa. She is a famed singer. She's a Naga, but do not worry," Evo said. He looked at Donut. "She's not of the Blood Sultanate, so you won't have to kill her when you hit the ninth floor. She's not really a Naga, either. The real Manasa perished long ago, but she contracted with the Valtay Corporation to keep her career going once she died."

I remembered what Odette had told me about the Valtay system. Their people were little parasites that took over bodies. "So, she has a worm in her brain driving her body?"

"That is correct," Evo said. "And her career is hotter than ever. Her latest single is currently ranked 8th in the entire universe."

The next chair held a stuffy-looking middle-aged human named Tucker. A stand-up comedian. I disliked him already based solely on the stupid grin on his holographic, punchable face.

Evo revealed the last participant, and I immediately recognized the crawler sitting there. Donut gasped.

It was Hekla, the blond-haired Icelandic woman who was now an Amazonian Shieldmaiden. She ran the team Brynhild's Daughters. I'd last seen her just a few nights earlier on the recap episode. Her people had been scattered upon entering the third floor, but she'd mostly regrouped, and they'd taken out an owlbear borough boss. I remembered she had an automatic magical crossbow that tore everything up. The weapon was like a ranged chain saw. I couldn't tell what her stats were now, but two days ago she'd hit level 25, the second crawler to do so, just hours after Lucia Mar. Hekla's muscles bulged as she leaned forward in her chair and I realized this wasn't a static hologram, but actually her.

"Hi, Hekla!" Donut called across the table. She looked at me. "Carl, look. It's Hekla!"

"I can see, Donut," I said.

"Hello, Donut," she said. She looked at me and nodded.

"Is your team holding up okay?" I asked.

"We are surviving," she said. The woman held very little emotion in her voice. Her eyes were the color of sapphires. "One of the Daughters is near you. She recognized the circus from the episode and knows you're in the vicinity. She wants to come back to the team, but I believe we are too far away. She needs some help leveling. Will you assist her? I will take it as a personal favor."

"Of course!" Donut said before I could respond. "We'd love to help your friend!"

Goddamnit, Donut. I paused. "Tell her to come to the One-Eyed Narwhal tonight," I said. "In the medium skyfowl settlement. But just an FYI, we're in the middle of something dangerous right now, and we won't be able to slow down to help her. We'll do what we can."

"Very well," Hekla said. A slight smile curled her lip. "Just don't blow her up."

———

"AS MUCH AS I DISLIKE THE MUDSKIPPERS," TUCKER, THE POMPOUS asshat, was saying, "I can't help but feel that the Valtay have overstepped in their push to take over the season. The courts have long upheld the rights of those seeking bankruptcy protection, and I don't see why that should change."

"Aren't you supposed to be a comedian?" Donut asked. "When are you going to say something funny?" The audience roared. "See, it's not that hard."

To my left, Princess D'nadia trumpeted with her tentacles, a sound that apparently meant amused agreement. She kept attempting to grasp my hand, though her webbed claws just pushed through my own fingers. Manasa, the cobra-headed pop singer, also laughed, her forked tongue flipping in and out.

Tucker sneered. "Well, then, what is your opinion on the matter, *Princess* Donut?"

Donut scoffed. "How the heck should I know? I'm a cat!" More laughter. "But I do know this, Butler. One, I know that I don't know enough about this subject to voice a proper opinion on it, unlike you, who is obviously talking out of your behind. And two, I know my partner here has a very poor opinion of you. Isn't that right, Carl?"

"Yup," I said. "You're a dipshit."

Hekla laughed for the first time since this started. Even Ripper, who was attempting to maintain some impartial façade throughout the program, put his head down and pounded on the table, trying not to let the emotion boil over.

I had no idea if this Tucker guy's opinion was valid or not, but one of the first things he'd done when the roundtable had started was

make a snotty comment about the show lowering their standards by
letting a pet sit on the panel. I'd thought he was going to turn it into
a lighthearted joke, maybe even turn it around on the host, but the
dude was dead serious. The crowd had booed, and he got this self-
righteous smirk on his face. Donut did not like that, and she immediately started tearing into the guy. She was in rare form. They'd
been going back and forth like this for a half hour now. At first I was
worried about her taking on a comedian, but she had the guy against
the ropes almost immediately, and he was too dumb to realize he'd
already lost.

"You know my name isn't Butler. You're just trying to make me
angry."

Donut looked up at me, her eyes sparkling. "Carl, you told me his
name was Butler."

"It's Tucker," I said.

"Tucker? Are you sure?"

Next to me, I thought Princess D'nadia was having a stroke, she
was laughing so hard. It was clear she also disliked this Tucker guy.

Tucker threw his hands up in the air. "Can we move on, please?
I came on this show because we're supposed to be talking about important matters."

"Oh, darling," Donut said, shaking her head. "Bless your heart."

After the audience's laughter died down, there was a short segment regarding multiple intergalactic affairs that neither I, Donut,
nor Hekla had much input on. For most of it, I had no idea what
they were talking about. Some solar system had been invaded by
another system. A race of people had applied for council membership
in the Syndicate. It was mostly stuff like that. Even the audience
seemed bored with the piece.

The issue Tucker had been opining about regarded the Valtay
Corporation and their attempt to collect their debt from the Borant
system. All three of us crawlers were smart enough not to say anything stupid about either Borant or the Valtay, in case they did end
up taking over the crawl, which appeared to be highly unlikely.

Manasa—for obvious reasons—was on the side of the Valtay. Ripper and Princess D'nadia seemed to think both sides were dicks, but also sided with the Valtay. Tucker was mostly on the side of the kua-tin.

Ripper moved the discussion to the Skull Empire. There was unrest in a few of their home systems, partially because of the whole embarrassment with the Pork Boy Snick. People were comparing the Skull Empire to the hedonistic Orcish Supremacy of the tuskling, and new calls for democratic reform were popping up in their systems. People took issue with the royal family spending so much time and money playing around with the crawl and the Faction War Games, while neglecting their duties back home. King Rust had responded by disowning the Maestro and telling his people to shut the hell up. Ripper looked directly at me and asked me what I thought about it.

I took a moment to formulate my response. I'd been anticipating a question about this subject, and I'd been mentally preparing my answer. *All it takes is a little seed.* I reached over and put my hand on Donut.

"I don't have all the details, of course. All I really know is what you've presented today and how that ass, Prince Maestro—"

"Former Prince Maestro," Donut corrected.

"How *former* Prince Maestro acted. If his dad, this King Rust guy, treats his people like his son treats guests on his show, then they *should* rebel. On Earth, we had this fable. Basically, the story goes if you throw a frog in a pot of boiling water, he'll jump right out. But if you stick that same frog in the water when it's at room temperature, he'll just sit there. He won't move because everything's fine. Then you put the pot on the heat. The temperature goes up, and still the frog doesn't jump because it's only a degree hotter than before. Eventually, the frog dies, boiled alive. When the frog was thrown in the boiling water, he immediately knew he was in danger. But because of the incrementalism of the heat from room temperature, he didn't realize he was in danger until it was too late."

"That's a really stupid metaphor," Tucker began.

"Stop," Ripper said, holding up a furry paw. "Let him finish."

"So, I don't really know what's going on with their systems. I'm just a guy from a planet that thought we might be all alone. We got thrown right in and had the lid slammed on us, so Donut and I, and Hekla, we don't have much of a say in what's happening to us. But I'm guessing it's different for the people who live under the Skull Empire. If it used to be okay, but it's not okay anymore, then maybe you should do something about it. Don't compare your circumstances with how they were yesterday. Look at how they were years ago. We're supposed to be making the world . . . the universe . . . a better place for our children. If it's not better, if you're dealing with cruelty, with neglect, then you should do something about it. So yeah. Fuck 'em. Fuck King Rust and his asshole child. If you're unhappy with your government, then kick them out and set up your own, one that represents the people's best interests. You shouldn't have to put up with some loser who's going to take the people's money and waste it on games, especially when those games entail killing people weaker than him with little or no real danger to himself. What a pussy. That's my opinion."

Nobody said anything for several moments.

"You probably don't know this," Tucker said, a hint of triumph in his voice, "but openly using tunnels to advocate for system sedition against a member state is a crime."

"If that's true," I said, "then you're *all* in that same pot." I turned to look at the audience. "All of you. If a government is afraid of what its people say, then maybe there's a reason for it."

"Besides," I added, "what are they gonna do? Throw me in the dungeon?"

Next to me, Princess D'nadia started clapping and making trumpet noises with her tentacles. Hekla, who'd barely said anything this entire time, was looking directly at me. I couldn't read her expression.

Underneath my hand, Donut trembled as the audience roared their approval.

But it wasn't everyone, I noted. Some of the people—*most* of the people—cheered. But not all. Those who didn't appeared uncomfortable. Some looked annoyed. That was okay. Baby steps. That frog metaphor worked both ways.

"Well," Ripper said, "they told me you two tend to leave a path of scorched earth wherever you—"

In front of me, Manasa the cobra blinked in and out of existence and then she disappeared. The entire studio bucked, and Donut and I both fell back out of our chairs. The lights flickered as Donut cried out. I hit the floor, and my HUD, which had been off since we'd arrived in the production trailer, turned on.

"Carl, Carl, I'm going to be sick."

The trailer continued to rock. The sea, which had been dead calm, now roiled.

The studio was gone, and all that remained were our two chairs and a half table. Donna the robot entered the room. "Please remain calm. The system will be restored in fifteen seconds."

ZEV: Oh my gods, are you two okay?
CARL: What the hell is going on?

The HUD snapped away, and the studio returned as the boat started to settle. Ripper, Princess D'nadia, and Tucker remained in their chairs. Ripper talked animatedly with someone we couldn't see. Hekla stood behind her seat, and I suspected she had also been knocked out of her chair, which meant her trailer was probably floating nearby. She hesitantly sat back down. The cobra-headed Manasa did not return.

"Are you injured?" Princess D'nadia whispered to me.

"We're fine. The trailer started pitching. What happened?"

"They're saying there was an attack on Manasa's trailer. She's vacationing on Earth, and she'd ascended to participate in the interview. They say her trailer got hit with a pulse. That's all I know."

"What about you? Are you okay?" I asked Hekla.

"Yes," she said. "I am fine."

"Yeah, us, too," I said.

"I threw up," Donut said, looking up at me. She had puke all down the front of her face. I used the thick fabric from my night-gaunt cloak to clean off her fur the best I could.

"Are you kidding? Are you kidding me?" Ripper said to his invisible assistant. "Let me see the statement." He turned and looked at me and Donut. The furry host opened his mouth as if he were going to say something, but then he changed his mind.

Instead, he turned to his audience. "Ladies and gentlemen, I'm sorry about that. Something just happened on Earth's surface, and we're still gathering information. Manasa has lost her signal, so I'm afraid we won't have her back. Stay tunneled, and we'll get you information straightaway. In the meantime, let's go straight into the Danger Zone."

Nothing happened for a moment, and then suddenly a female owl creature stood at the end of the table. She'd appeared out of nowhere.

"Hi," the owl said. "I have a question for Hekla. Why did you leave your husband to fend for himself when you both entered the dungeon? And do you regret it?"

Hekla appeared stricken by the question. The abrupt change of subject with everything happening around us seemed so sudden, so out of place that it was almost absurd. Apparently, they called the Q&A section of the program the "Danger Zone." Behind us, Ripper had disappeared. Tucker was turned all the way around in his seat, talking quietly with someone off-screen. Next to me, Princess D'nadia had her head cocked to the side and was also listening to something or someone hidden.

"I," Hekla said, stammering "I . . . He left me. He didn't leave me a choice. He was going to get us both killed. Now he's dead, and I'm not."

"And do you regret it?" the owl repeated.

"Of course I do," she said.

"Thank you," the owl said. She disappeared and was replaced by a male orc.

"I am Rolf," the orc said. "This question is for Carl. What is your most enjoyable way to kill?"

"That's kind of a fucked-up question," I said. "I don't like killing."

"No?" Rolf said. "But you kill good."

"He does, doesn't he?" said Donut.

"I guess I like it when it's simple, clean," I said. "A quick punch, breaking their neck."

Rolf made a fist in the air. "This is good. Thank you."

The next question was about Hekla's crossbow. The one after that was a fish creature that looked like a human-sized kua-tin. I think Odette had called them gleeners. She looked directly at Donut.

"Princess, who is Ferdinand?"

Several people in the audience clapped at the question.

Donut tensed, but then she relaxed. "Oh, darling, I just love that outfit you're wearing. It's so pretty. But you are right to ask. This secret has festered for far too long, and I suppose it's time for the universe to know the truth." She sighed dramatically. "Ferdinand is the love of my life. But we've had a tragic courtship. He visited me often at night. We'd gaze upon each other across the wide expanse, and we both knew it was a love that couldn't be. For we were star-crossed lovers, and he was hunted by the authorities. In royal circles, he was reviled, branded as a 'Moggie,' a non-pedigreed cat. It is why I'd jumped out the window that night. I could sense him out there, calling to me."

"Wait," I said. "Are you talking about that creepy yellow cat that would come to the window when you were in heat?"

"Yes, I am, Carl," Donut said. "I imagine it's time you learned of my secret affair. A princess and a ruffian. It wasn't meant to be, but our love was pure."

I couldn't help it. I laughed. "His name wasn't Ferdinand. His name was Gravy Boat. He belonged to Marjory on the first floor."

The cat had also knocked up every female cat within three square blocks. Bea had called animal control on him twice, but they'd never been able to find or catch him. Bea had gotten into a screaming fight with Marjory over it, though I was never really clear on the reasons why Bea had cared so much. Gravy Boat sitting in that tree outside our window wasn't nearly as annoying as Donut yowling while she was in heat.

"He preferred Ferdinand," sniffed Donut.

The gleener disappeared and was replaced by an elf-like creature wearing a top hat.

"Hello," the elf said. "My name is Chappy. My question is also for Donut. If Bea is alive, and she shows up, are you really going to leave Carl for her?"

A chill washed over me. I looked sharply at Donut, who looked back up at me with a look of confusion on her face.

"When we reunite with Miss Beatrice, we will all work together. It will be like before."

Chappy seemed perplexed by her answer. "Surely you don't think Carl will want to stay with her." He turned his gaze to me. "Carl?"

This was a situation that was never going to manifest itself because the odds of Bea being anything but dead were astronomical. And if she wasn't dead by some miracle, one of these talk shows would've dug her up by now. Nevertheless, it was a conversation I still needed to have with Donut. But I wouldn't be having it on live television. Fuck that. I mumbled, "We'll cross that bridge when—"

"I'm sorry to interrupt, folks," Ripper said, his voice quavering. I could tell he was angry, and he was barely holding it in. "But we have some breaking news to share. As you all saw, our program was interrupted. We now have verification that this was because of a senseless pulse attack on a production asset housing our friend and frequent guest Manasa. I am sorry to say, it appears she has perished in the attack." Gasps and cries of surprise and astonishment filled the audience. Ripper lifted his paw to calm them down. Next to me, Princess D'nadia wept. Black oil cascaded down the front of her cephalopod face. "But there's more. In a tragic twist to this story, it is apparent she was *not* the target of the attack. Simultaneous with the pulse"—Ripper paused, unsuccessfully attempting to compose himself; his anger bubbled over into his voice—"Prince Stalwart of the Skull Empire released the following statement."

A screen appeared. The coarse-haired wild boar creature sat behind a desk. Prince Stalwart, crown prince of the Skull Empire, looked very much like his disgraced younger brother. While the Maestro had been overly muscular, Stalwart was leaner, but he still exuded power and strength. And cruelty. Even before he spoke, I could see it in his pig eyes.

Over the orc's shoulder was a window overlooking a large green field that spread into the far distance. The dots of hundreds of soldiers marching in formation appeared down below. The camera was angled to view the field perfectly.

He's on the ninth floor right now, I thought. *He's setting up the Faction Wars segment of the game.*

"Citizens of the Syndicate. By the time this message hits the tunnel, the Earth creatures Carl and Donut will have been executed by a pulse fired from my personal yacht. The Skull Empire will pay for any damages to any private property destroyed in the attack. We are claiming, under the Syndicate rules regarding independent system sovereignty, that this summary execution is both justified and appropriate given Carl's statements advocating sedition. That is all." The message snapped off.

"That was quick," Donut muttered.

"You can say that again," I said. The attack had come barely two minutes after I'd spoken out.

"They hit the wrong trailer," Tucker said. He looked at us. His earlier snootiness was gone. He sounded in shock. "It was meant for you."

"Manasa had switched trailers," Princess D'nadia said. "They said you needed cleaning facilities, and she offered to trade." The princess could barely speak, she was so upset. "She was my friend. For countless years, she'd been my friend. Even though she was a worm head, we'd been close for so long." She turned to the audience and cleared her voice. She sat up straighter in her chair. "The Prism Kingdom officially condemns this action by the Skull Empire, and we will be filing an immediate grievance with the Syndicate court."

"The Valtay and the Skull Empire are strong allies," Tucker said. "Surely they'll see this as a tragic accident."

"Do you know how much money Manasa brings in for the Valtay each year?" Ripper said. "Those idiots. Stupid, stupid. She was a treasure. People think their technological sector brings in the most, but that's not true. Not even close. It's their entertainment assets. They just murdered her."

I felt a sudden wave of anger wash over me. *Now you're outraged? When it was your friend?* The cognitive dissonance was just overwhelming. I didn't dare say it out loud, but what the hell? They destroyed us, destroyed our *planet.* And one poorly shot missile or whatever the hell it was, and suddenly it's a tragedy. *Fuck you. Fuck you all.*

"Carl," Donut said, concern to her voice. "Carl, if they know they hit the wrong trailer, will they shoot at us again? Maybe we should go."

Ripper looked at us and waved at us to remain seated. "It's okay. You're okay. This just in. I am getting word now. The Valtay are claiming one of their dreadnoughts in Earth orbit has destroyed Prince Stalwart's yacht. Again, the Valtay are claiming to have destroyed a Skull Empire royal vessel. From the message, it is clear Stalwart was not on board at the time, but it is rumored that both Queen Consort Ugloo and former Prince Maestro *were* on board."

"So much for their alliance," Tucker said. "That weakens Valtay's position on the bankruptcy action."

"Shut the fuck up, Tucker," Princess D'nadia said. "By the gods, our friend has been murdered."

"Wait, did he say the Maestro is dead?" said Donut. "Carl, did you hear that?"

"I heard, Donut."

As Ripper continued to breathlessly repeat everything that had happened, I met eyes with Hekla, who continued to sit quietly across the table, a rock in the storm. She studied me curiously.

"Is this how it always is with you two, then?" she asked. "What was it he said? Scorched earth?"

I nodded. I put my hand on Donut.

"With a little bit of chaos thrown in," I said.

20

RIPPER WONTON PLAYED A VIDEO OF MANASA SINGING, HER FINAL performance. The large cobra was in an opulent dining room, singing a cappella in a hauntingly sad soprano voice. The entire studio watched in dead silence. It gave me the chills.

"Wow," Donut whispered as the song ended.

The show ended shortly thereafter, and the virtual studio faded away, leaving me and Donut alone in the room. Hekla and the others disappeared before we could say our goodbyes. We got up and returned to the lounge.

I moved to the small window by the bathroom, and sure enough, one of the two trailers floating out there was gone. It had been replaced by hundreds of floating probes of all sizes, zipping about, scanning the water. Two of them whizzed toward me the moment I stuck my head in the window, but before they could get too close, the glass snapped shut like a camera shutter.

My HUD flickered back on.

ZEV: I'll meet you guys at the safe room. Prepare to be transported in a few moments.
CARL: See you there.

"She was really nice. Manasa, I mean. I liked her," Donut said as we waited. She released Mongo from his pet carrier, and he hopped up and down with excitement. He rushed into the bathroom and stood upon the cleaning treadmill. He grunted angrily when it didn't automatically start up.

"Yeah," I said. "That was too bad."

"Do you really believe all that stuff you just said? About people rising up?" Donut asked.

I shrugged. "It's a little naive. It's a nice fantasy, but I know the universe doesn't really work that way. For all we know, that king guy's people are really happy. Just because people complain about stuff doesn't mean they have it bad. Besides, I'm a nobody. It's not like I have the power to change anything. I wasn't expecting that, though. Jesus."

"Yeah, Mordecai is going to be mad. He said you needed to make fun of him a little. Not kill his wife."

We still didn't know all the details as to why Mordecai had suggested we needle at the king if given the opportunity. He never went into detail with this sort of stuff. He was always spouting off things for us to do and keep an eye out for. Monster types. Herbs. Loot. Ways to act if we came across certain types of NPCs. We'd started calling it the daily BOLO. Be on the lookout. Donut had come up with the term. She'd once watched a marathon of *Law & Order*. I suspected the thing with King Rust was long-term strategy, something to do with the ninth floor if we ever got there. Mordecai wanted us to insult the king so we'd stay on his radar, probably so it'd be easier to bait him later.

I meant what I said to Donut. I knew a random dude from the crawl spouting off about revolution wasn't going to spark some great intergalactic crisis. Still, seeds. Mordecai had his plans. I had my own.

That said, there was something else going on, another, invisible player on the chessboard, so to speak. It'd been bothering me from the moment we listened to Prince Stalwart's message.

CARL: We need to be careful. Never even hint of this out loud. I
     think we were set up.
DONUT: WHAT DO YOU MEAN?

CARL: That Stalwart dude was too prepared with his statement. They had the camera all ready with the army right outside the window. Stalwart was planning on killing us from the start. I don't think they were expecting my little speech there, but it played right into their hands.

DONUT: BUT THEY MISSED.

CARL: Stalwart was being played, too. We were just the pawns, the bait. And so was Manasa. Whoever is orchestrating this knew the orcs planned on killing us. That switcheroo was either on purpose to get them to really kill their ally, or they quickly jumped on the opportunity. It humiliates them and damages their alliance with the Valtay. Who benefits the most from that?

DONUT: MANASA HAD THE VOICE OF AN ANGEL. NOBODY BENEFITS FROM IT.

CARL: No, that's not true. Borant benefits. Big-time. If Valtay loses a powerful ally, maybe even goes to war with the Skull Empire over this, then they won't have time to try to take over the Borant system. But I don't know for sure. We have so little information.

DONUT: OR MAYBE NOBODY ELSE WAS INVOLVED. THE ORCS WERE GOING TO KILL US, YES, BUT WE JUST GOT LUCKY.

CARL: Maybe. If so, that was *really* lucky for both us and Borant.

DONUT: DO YOU THINK ZEV IS MAD AT US FOR WHAT YOU SAID?

CARL: Let's find out.

"OH MY GODS," ZEV SAID AS WE RETURNED TO THE SAFE ROOM. She'd returned us to the same one we'd been in when we'd left, the one near the pool with the exploded boss corpse. She stood there in the middle of the room, wearing her ever-present space suit, having arrived before we did. Our HUD didn't shut off like usual when she was in the room. I didn't know if that was some sort of oversight or a bug because she'd arrived first. "That was *terrifying*. I thought you two were dead for certain."

"What happened?" Mordecai asked, looking between us. Donut began to excitedly tell him the story, Donut-style. She started by explaining the cleaning mechanism in the trailer, going into extreme, unnecessary detail.

"How did they even know what trailer we were in?" I asked Zev as Donut continued to regale Mordecai. "I mean, they were wrong, but only because we switched at the last minute."

"That stuff isn't a secret," Zev said. "Rental trailers throw their booking schedules out there for anybody to see so they can coordinate availability. Before today, there's never been a reason to hide who is using what trailer. Nobody has ever attempted to assassinate a crawler outside the dungeon. What a nightmare."

"Stop," Mordecai said, raising a hand to Donut. "What happened?"

Donut took a deep breath. "Carl called the orc king a pussy, and his son's spaceship lasered the production trailer from orbit. But we'd switched with Manasa, and she got blown up instead."

Mordecai looked at me, horrified. "Manasa the *singer*? She was killed?"

"She was so nice," Donut said. "She said she thought Mongo was adorable."

MORDECAI: I distinctly remember saying you should be subtle.
CARL: I may have gone a little overboard. It gets worse.

"There's more," Zev said. "The Valtay responded by blowing the royal yacht into dust. The queen consort and Maestro were believed to be on board."

"For fuck's sake," Mordecai said.

I shrugged. "Hey, all they asked me for was my opinion. It's not my fault Prince Pig Face overreacted. It sucks the mom got killed, but if she's the one who raised those two, it's probably not a big loss."

Zev's suit made a little bubbling noise. "The good news is that nobody is saying anything negative about Carl and Donut on the net. Prince Stalwart is the villain. Wow. Rust is gonna have to disown him, too. I hadn't thought of that. That only leaves the sister as the heir. Our team is fielding a wave of interview requests, but *Dungeon Crawler After Hours with Odette* has the contract on your next interview."

"That's fine," I said. "I'm not too keen on going on any more interviews right now anyway."

Zev left soon thereafter, leaving us in the empty safe room. Mordecai indicated for us to sit down.

> MORDECAI: Okay, new rule. We are not meddling with, mentioning, or talking about any other entities outside of the dungeon from now on. We're not going to mention King Rust or Prince Stalwart until after the sixth floor, if you two idiots make it that far. When Odette asks you about it, you say you have no opinion. You only talk about stuff happening in the dungeon.
>
> CARL: So no more making fun of King Rust?
>
> DONUT: TALKING SMACK IS MY SPECIAL TALENT. MANASA AND PRINCESS D'NADIA BOTH SAID SO.
>
> MORDECAI: His wife is dead. He's neck-deep in shit. It's not your fault, but he's going to see it that way. I wanted to make sure the Skull Clan targeted the Blood Sultanate once you hit the ninth floor. I don't think that's going to be an issue now. Let's just hope he's not *too* mad at you two.
>
> CARL: Why? What can he do to us here?
>
> MORDECAI: Besides assassinating you while you're on the surface? Nothing yet. That's going to change very soon. We'll deal with it when it happens.

"Well, there's nothing we can do about any of this now, is there?" I said out loud. "We still have daylight, and we have a ton to do. We need to get back into town. We have a militia to break up and a magistrate's office to break into."

———

ONE OF THE MYSTERIES OF THE SEX WORKER QUEST WAS HOW THE city elves of the 201st Security Group figured in all of this. Assuming this Featherfall guy was the lead baddie, then their presence in conjunction with the random undead monsters made sense. The city elves worshiped the skyfowl as living angels, and this town's lead skyfowl was a dark cleric who commanded the undead. The city elves were basically a free source of enthusiastic labor that Featherfall was using to help corral his undead minions.

We still didn't know what the hell was going on with the dead prostitutes. That was okay for now. I didn't need to know exactly what was happening to know the best way to weaken the head dude's plans was to first knock out one of his support networks.

I didn't like the idea of going full murder hobo on a group of mentally ill elves. Still, if this group was targeting innocent NPCs and killing them, then I didn't hold much sympathy. Plus, they'd tried to kill us twice. If we didn't take them on now, it was going to just keep happening.

While we were in the middle of our interview, Mordecai had ventured into town and located their headquarters for us. It wasn't difficult. They had a sign and a trio of city elves out front attempting to talk those passing by to enter and hear "The good news about Apito the Oak Mother."

They were only two blocks away from the magistrate's quarters, situated on a mostly residential street in a poorer section of town.

When we left the safe room, a handful of the shambling berserkers remained in the ruins, hanging out nearby. We rushed to the roof of a building and killed from afar. I didn't want to waste my hoblobbers unless I had to, so instead I tried tossing a stick of hobgoblin dynamite. I'd never used the upgraded dynamite before, and I was glad I hadn't tried it while I was on the ground. The sticks were practically mini nukes. I used my upgraded strength to hurl a stick at a shambler a half block away. The resulting explosion knocked me off my feet. The front façade of a distant building collapsed, caving in on itself and filling the street with debris.

I stood and examined the damage, my ears ringing. I'd obliterated the shambler and killed the one behind it. Smoke swirled, dust filling the air.

Uh-oh, I thought.

The dynamite's power was great, but the sticks were utterly impractical to use in regular fights. Even with my strength, I wasn't so sure I could toss them far enough to be safe when I wasn't two stories up.

"My goodness," Donut said. "You need to be careful with those things, Carl." She returned to my shoulder. In the distance, a third shambler had turned and was now approaching from another road that wasn't blocked with rubble.

I wished I had a method of tossing them farther. With my xistera, I could toss a hob-lobber four times the distance, but the sticks weren't shaped properly for the basket. I pulled another hobgoblin dynamite stick out and looked at it.

"Wait, are those the same ones you used for the thing?" Donut asked.

"Yeah," I said. "Three of them."

"Maybe we should have tested them first," she said.

"That's what they're gonna put on my tombstone."

"Don't be silly, Carl. They don't give us tombstones here."

I laughed.

"You know it tells me I can't touch them," Donut continued, peering down at the white stick. "It says there's a 75% chance it'll explode if I try to."

"Really?" I said. The stick's stability remained at 80% for me, which meant I could bonk myself on the head with it and nothing would happen.

"I don't think you're supposed to touch that stuff unless you have the proper skill. Or you're desperate. And I thought the goblin dynamite was scary. I wonder if there's something even higher on the list," she asked. "What's the next step above hobgoblin?"

"I don't know," I said. "I don't know if there is one." My Explosives Handling and Dangerous Explosives Handling skills had both risen to nine. Both skills increased the yield of the explosions. As it was now, a single stick of hobgoblin dynamite could kill most anything.

No, not everything. I thought of the divine guardian. The country boss from the 12th floor that we'd seen on that brief clip on the recap show. That thing wouldn't even notice if I'd shoved an entire case of the things down its throat.

Thwump. Donut's magic missile took out the third shambling berserker.

In the distance, the sun sank low. We only had a good two hours of sunlight left, and I needed to use them. "Come on," I said. "Let's go talk to the elves."

THE SIGN DIDN'T ANNOUNCE THE BUILDING AS THE HEADQUARTERS of the 201st Security Group, but as we approached, it was clear that Mordecai's intelligence was correct. The simple hand-painted sign over the building held the symbol of a tree with the words APITO EDUCATION CENTER. On my minimap, the building was labeled as a Corrupt Temple. A quick note to Mordecai confirmed that anything labeled "corrupt" meant that mobs could be within.

Three city elves stood out front, each of them holding a stick with an acorn hanging off the end. They were unsuccessfully attempting to hand the sticks to anyone who passed. None wore the uniform shirt. All three wore simple, unadorned brown robes that appeared dirty, as if they spent most of the day gardening.

The building, unfortunately, shared a wall with a residence. About fifteen dwarven kids rushed about the street, laughing and play-fighting. They ranged in age from about five to twelve, and based on the similar manner of their dirty, patched clothing, I guessed they were all siblings, including multiple pairs of twins and triplets. One of the older kids held a stick with a small salamander tied to the end, and he was chasing his brothers and sisters about as they all howled. I think it was supposed to be a mockery of the elves. The stick-wielding kid jabbed the poor hissing salamander toward one of the robed figures. The tiny lizard expelled a single spark of flames at the city elf, who cursed and kicked at the child. Another kid picked up a rock and chucked it at the elf, who in turn raised his hand and cast a spell that reflected the rock back at him. The rock bounced off the kid's head, who started wailing. His siblings surrounded him, and they all piled inside the house next to the temple.

On the corner at the end of the street stood a pair of stoic village swordsmen. They paid no heed to the disturbance. It must be a regular thing. I checked the position of the sun. We still had a good hour before the guards would disappear for the day.

The stick with the small salamander was left in the middle of the street. The poor lizard was trying to drag himself away. I was going to untie the little guy, but Mongo jumped forward and swallowed the salamander whole, taking half the stick with it.

"Mongo, gross," I said. "Stop eating stuff you find on the ground."

The raptor made a face, as if the salamander had tasted foul. He made a retching noise.

"That's what you get," I said.

"You need to chew your food, Mongo," Donut said.

The three city elf NPCs glared at us as we approached. One of them rushed inside.

"Hello, Carl," one of them said. He turned to Donut, sneering. "Disgusting, vile *blasphemer.*"

"Me?" Donut said. "What did I do?"

I examined the elf.

Salvatore. City Elf. Level 16.
Root Druid.

Temple Recruitment Wand Bearer.

The Wand Bearers are the warm and fuzzy faces of the Apito Education Center, which is the outreach department of the 201st Security Group militia. While oftentimes doubling as door guards, the Wand Bearers are some of the most pious, most indoctrinated, and therefore, the most dangerous members of the silly little cult.

This particular group consists of members of the Magical Ops arm of the 201st. Translation: If you're gonna dance with these guys, be prepared to deal with all sorts of magical schools.

The second elf was named Carmine, and his description was almost identical, except instead of a Root Druid, it said he was a Wind Mage.

"How do you know our names?" I asked.

Salvatore spit on the ground. "Eat moss and die, apostate. The master told us the Oak Fell and their rotting assistants would come to the city soon, and the final battle for heaven would commence." He looked down at Donut, snarling. "When you agreed to help that orc, we knew it was you. You even wear the filthy symbol of your blasphemy."

"What the flying fuck are you talking about?" I asked.

CARL: Mordecai. Quick. What the hell is the Oak Fell? Also, once again, our charm isn't working on these guys.
MORDECAI: The Oak Fell is Apito's version of the Antichrist. That's not stuff one usually contends with until the 12th floor. We need to get you two a *Dispel Protections* spell, which'll handle the anti-charm and other security protocols these quest locations usually have. They're annoyingly common in skyfowl settlements.

"We had to torture her to tease your name from her lips," Salvatore was saying.

The third city elf returned, followed by a half dozen more of his friends. These guys weren't wearing the brown robes, but the uniforms of the 201st. They formed a semicircle around the entrance, blocking it. All of them were level 16, but there was a menagerie of magic types, from a fire mage to a summoner to a light healer. Their dots remained white on the map. For now.

"Wait, you had to torture who?" I asked. I'd missed what he said because I was talking to Mordecai.

"GumGum," the city elf said. "She was serving an important purpose, removing the unworthy filth from the streets. But then she started asking questions. Questions, it turns out, that attracted the Oak Fell. Just as the master predicted."

"You tortured GumGum?" Donut asked, her voice incredulous. Next to her, Mongo growled. Actually, I realized it was more of a retching noise. The dinosaur was looking a little green. That salamander wasn't sitting well in his gut. Still, the noise he'd made sounded downright menacing. The city elves all tensed. *Easy, easy.* Not yet.

"Yes," Salvatore said. "Just as we shall torture you. You defeated our champion, Vicente. He trained his entire life for the final battle. Now he blossoms on Her tree. The master had warned us a single champion would not be enough. We are chastened that we did not follow his guidance. We shall not make that mistake again. Now you will face all of us."

"You nine are all of you?" I asked.

"We were twelve, but now we are nine," Salvatore said. "Just as it was in the scriptures during the great fall."

"Vicente? Is that the guy whose head I blew off? And you kicked in the nuts?" Donut asked. She turned to face me. All nine of the city elves hissed in unison and took a step back.

Donut looked back over her shoulder. "What? Are you scared of my butt or something? I'll have you know it is glorious." She waggled it at the elves, jingling the crupper, which hung like a skirt across her backside. "This is an award-winning derriere!"

One of the elves, a type of mage called an "Icer," growled. His dot on the map flickered to red, then back to white. They were all looking down at Donut with scowls and dismay.

DONUT: CARL, THEY ARE GOING TO ATTACK US.
CARL: Don't move. Stay in that position. Shake your left
       rear leg.

Donut lifted her back leg, revealing the small magical anklet with the three little beads. She shook her foot, and the beads made a rattling noise. The elves growled and hissed like a pack of wild animals. One of them, the female light healer, started scratching at her own face, causing rivulets of blood to form.

What the actual fuck was wrong with these assholes?

They were scared of Donut's anklet. We'd found it on a dead crawler who'd been killed by the lemurs. I remembered it only gave a couple of minor stat boosts and a skill called Double Tap. There wasn't anything too remarkable about it except its name, **The Enchanted Anklet of the Fallen Oak.**

The description was all about how I shouldn't wear it, which was why I'd given it to Donut. Apparently, these guys weren't fans of magical items made from oakwood. I guessed that made sense since this Apito lady was called the Oak Mother. I'd be pretty upset too if someone was walking around with jewelry made out of dead babies.

"Let me get this straight," I said, looking at Salvatore, who wouldn't stop spitting on the ground like a damn maniac. The whole group had devolved from a bunch of angry but competent-appearing magic users to this unstable mess of nutjobs who all looked as if they'd just escaped from a mental hospital. The transformation had occurred in seconds. The fire mage had pissed himself. The summoner was sucking his thumb. "You assholes think Donut here is this Oak Fell Antichrist person because she's wearing that anklet?"

"I told you wood jewelry is ugly," Donut grumbled.

"You are the bearer of the forbidden oak," Salvatore said,

speaking directly to Donut. He stood stiffly, formally. He pulled the acorn off the tree branch still in his hand and ate it, crunching loudly. His entire form started to glow blue. **Magical Fervor** appeared over his head. The others all produced acorns and ate them. Soon, the entire group glowed.

CARL: Magical Fervor.

MORDECAI: Triples their mana points and increases their
    strength. It also makes them glow and talk really loud.
    They'll be immune to your *Fear*.

Ahh shit, I thought. The plan had been to goad these guys into attacking us in front of the town guards. As long as they made the first move, Mordecai assured us the guards would fight on our side. But now I was worried the two swordsmen at the end of the street wouldn't be enough for this.

Protective Shell wouldn't protect us from magical attacks. I had my *Wisp Armor*, but that wouldn't help Donut. My mind raced. We had two different plays in our book that might work. We had "Mold Lion," which was named after the first fight we'd used the plan in. The second, newer one was called "Mic Drop." That one would probably work better, but it would likely end with the guards hunting us, which was something I wanted to avoid if possible.

DONUT: Mold Lion again?

CARL: I think so. Get ready.

I prepared to jump forward into their midst. I'd cast *Protective Shell* anyway, which would physically launch them in every which direction. Like with the mold lions, it would hopefully kill a couple. If so, Donut would have a few precious moments to raise them from the dead, which would give us a few meat shields and even out the odds.

Salvatore continued his rant, but under the influence of the

Magical Fervor buff, his voice carried as if over a loudspeaker. I kept my eyes glued to the dots on the minimap, waiting for them to turn red. If I moved a second too soon, we'd be doubly fucked. The shell wouldn't push the elves, and the swordsmen guards would move in on us instead. "The angel, our master, prepares us for the end of days," Salvatore squealed. "He has almost achieved all his tasks. We are prepared to blossom on Her. We, the 201st Security Group, are prepared to make the ultimate sacrifice to protect the angel, who in turn works toward Apito's vision of the Plantation. Apito warns us of the great beast who yearns to unravel the heavens and kill all the gods. And now this great deceiver, this devourer of all that is holy, has a name. She is Donut the Oak Fell. The Death upon Us All. She Who Ends. And with the help of my brothers and sisters, I will—"

Thwap!

Salvatore crumpled to the ground, screaming as he clutched at his head. The enormously pregnant female dwarf hit him again with the rolling pin, yelling. Behind her, the group of young dwarves who'd been playing in the street all returned. The rock thrower from before had a massive bandage around his head. The one who'd been holding the salamander on the stick picked up the broken branch and stared at it.

"Where's Benjamin?" he called.

The dwarf woman, who was apparently the mother of the entire crew, continued to pummel Salvatore with the rolling pin. "Throw a rock at my boy, will ya! I'll teach ya a lesson ye'll never forget, ye crazy lump of reconstituted snail shit! You arseholes waving yer silly branches all about all day long! We is sick of it, we is!"

Thwap! Thwap! Thwap!

Down the street, the two swordsmen guards turned toward the scuffle.

The pregnant dwarf stopped bashing in the head of the elf, who wasn't quite dead, but he wasn't getting up anytime soon, either. I read the name over her head. **Eunice. Level 30. Fathom Dwarf.** She stood up, glaring at the other elves. Silence followed, punctuated only by the sound of her heavy breathing and the blood dripping from the rolling pin. The harsh odor of urine filled the street.

I stared in surprised astonishment at the tableau. The woman had come out of nowhere. The other elves looked at each other, none of them moving, equally frozen with surprise by the unexpected violence. The summoner elf continued to suck his thumb. The healer continued to scratch at her own face. The scene only held this way for but a moment, though it seemed to go on forever.

The stalemate ended when Mongo yakked the salamander back out onto the street.

The small, now-dead lizard was still tied to the end of a broken stick. It landed in a slimy puddle with a *plop*.

"Benjamin?" the young dwarf asked, stepping forward. His name was **Ricky Joe. Level 2. Juvenile Fathom Dwarf.** He looked at the unmoving salamander. *"Benjamin?"*

It all went downhill from there.

The Icer elf, the first to break from his shock, shot a boomerang-shaped pulse at Eunice the dwarf. It hit the pregnant woman square in the chest, and she rocketed back, frozen solid. Her health moved to the red. A second, smaller health bar appeared over her stomach. This one was also in the red, though not as deep. **Frosted** appeared with a sixty-second countdown. The young dwarves all cried out, running to their mother. All except young Ricky Joe, who knelt before Benjamin the dead salamander. His lower lip quivered as he picked up the broken stick. Slime dripped off it.

At this moment, not a single dot on the map was yet red. But the swordsmen guards clomped noisily onto the scene, unsheathing their massive weapons. They moved toward the frozen pregnant dwarf. The remaining children scattered, rushing across the street, all except the one with the bandage on his head, who draped himself over his mother's form.

"Leave me mum alone!"

The guards did not care. They both lifted their swords over their heads.

I was very aware that what I did next would be considered a Very Stupid Thing.

I was also aware that nobody left on the street at this moment was innocent. Nobody except maybe Benjamin, who was already dead, and the baby dwarf in Eunice's belly. The elves were assholes. The rock-throwing dwarf kid was a prick who'd gotten what he deserved. Eunice obviously had some anger—and birth control—issues she needed to work out. And Ricky Joe the salamander torturer was obviously well on the path toward the life of a serial killer.

All of this ran through my head as I attacked the guards.

I formed a fist, stepped forward, and I punched the closest of the two level 75 village swordsmen as hard as I could.

My fist smashed into the side of the armored creature. It was as if I'd punched the side of a Sherman tank. I left an impression in the metal, but the guard did not stagger. A health bar did not appear. He and his companion paused their attack and turned toward me. Both of their dots turned red on the map.

Uh-oh.

Warning: You have been branded as a troublemaker at this settlement. Guards will now attack you on sight.

The same moment as I punched the guard, young Ricky Joe decided to also enter the idiot-of-the-day contest.

The boy, still clutching the half stick of wood with the dead salamander tied onto it punched Mongo the velociraptor in the face.

"You killed my best friend! You—"

The boy moved to punch a second time, but when he pulled his arm back, he found that it was no longer there. Mongo, quick as a snake, had bitten off the dwarf's arm below the elbow, swallowing it along with Benjamin for the second time.

"Mongo, hold!" Donut yelled, saving the idiot boy's life. For now. The dinosaur, once again, looked ill.

I leaped back into the midst of the still-gawking magic users as the swordsman's wide blade smashed into the ground. The blade missed me, instead drilling into Salvatore, who'd just been healed back to consciousness by the face-scratching light healer. He'd been sitting on the ground, shaking his head. He was cleaved in half, cut right down the center like a damn bagel.

Behind the guards, the children swarmed their still-frozen mother and began pulling her back across the street. And standing between the guards was little Ricky Joe, looking at the stump of his arm, which was now shooting blood into the air like one of those summertime sprinklers for kids. I reached forward and picked the heavy dwarf child up, shoving him under my left arm like a football as I pulled a boom jug into my right arm.

"Mic Drop!" I yelled.

"Are we taking the kid?" Donut cried, wasting a precious second. I jumped out of the way of another sword cleave. These things were strong, practically indestructible, but they were also slow as hell.

"Yes, go!" I lit the torch on the boom jug.

"Set!" Donut shouted.

I lightly tossed the lit jug straight up into the air. I watched it rise as I mentally counted down the two seconds. The jug reached its apex and started its descent right toward my head.

All four of us—Me, Donut, Mongo, and Ricky Joe—blinked away, reappearing on the roof of a building across the street thanks to Donut's *Puddle Jumper* spell.

I whirled, facing the scene just in time to see the boom jug hit the ground and fully engulf everyone and everything standing there by the entrance to the temple. The remaining eight city elves were instantly crisped. The two city guards, both of them in the process of swinging their swords at me, recovered and looked at each other. A health bar appeared over both of them, though it barely moved, and they seemed oblivious to the raging fire. They stepped away from the conflagration. They faced the fire and stopped moving. They hadn't seen where we'd gone.

Thankfully Eunice and the other children were far enough away to not be caught in the blast. The door to the building next to the one we were standing upon opened, and a pair of human NPCs rushed out and pulled them inside as other NPCs rushed into the street to see what was happening.

The fire moved to the entrance of the corrupt temple, and soon the entire building, along with the home next door, was engulfed.

I pulled a health potion and shoved it in the mouth of the still-squealing Ricky Joe. The blood stopped flowing and his health bar returned to the green. His arm did not grow back. The boy turned to the ill-looking Mongo and moved to hit the dinosaur again, this time with his left arm, but I held him back.

"Give it back! Give me my arm back!"

Mongo obliged.

21

WE WAITED UNTIL SUNSET BEFORE LEAVING OUR HIDING SPOT ATOP
the building. After the brief, chaotic fight on the street down below,
the two guards remained in their position facing the fire. They did
not move. They did not look up. Multiple NPCs, including skyfowl,
came to inspect the burning building. Nobody paid us any heed.

Nobody, except Mordecai, who spent a solid 10 minutes straight
swearing at us over chat because we'd activated the guards' aggro.

Ricky Joe sat cross-legged on the roof, sullenly clutching onto the
remains of his severed limb and the twice-eaten corpse of his pet
salamander, Benjamin. He'd screamed bloody murder when he
learned we wouldn't be able to reattach the arm, but Donut had
talked him into sitting down and calmly waiting for night to descend. Once the building was fully engulfed, it appeared whatever
spells protected the immediate area also fled, once again allowing
Donut's charm to be effective.

"Hey, kid," I asked as we waited, "you know that wasn't very cool,
right? Tying the little lizard to the end of the stick? It's pretty
fucked-up."

"You shouldn't say bad words to kids," Donut said. "But yes,
Ricky Joe. You shouldn't do that."

"At least I didn't eat him," Ricky Joe said. "And Benjamin liked
it. Fathom dwarves strap them to their hats when they go into mines.
He was in training."

A few moments later, the two guards abruptly turned and walked
away. I watched them clank their way through the town's streets.

They converged with other groups of the swordsmen, and they all entered a building on the same street as the magistrate's head-quarters.

"Hey," I asked the kid, indicating the burned-out husk of the temple. The child's own home, which was attached to the building, had also burned to the ground. "Did you ever see anything unusual coming in and out of there? Or hear anything weird?"

"Weird?" he asked. "They were always weird. One of them would cry for his mama every morning. We could hear it through the walls, we did. There were a lot of weird smells, too. My brother Bubba Lane said he saw something fly from the roof a couple nights ago. He said it was a krasue, but it was probably just that skyfowl lady."

"What lady?" I asked.

"I don't know her name. They all look the same to me. But she visits a lot. She usually comes just before dark and then leaves right away, walking with a bunch of other ladies. She didn't come today, though."

"Wait, what are the other ladies?"

"Women, usually elves and dwarves and humans. They show up all day long. I don't recognize any of them. I think they're trying to join the church. They're usually dressed like they're about to go to the Desperado. Bubba Lane says it's because women are stupid. My mama slaps him around some when he says that and then pinches his ear until he apologizes. Then she makes us all line up and call *him* stupid. He doesn't like that much."

"Do you know where the skyfowl takes the ladies?" Donut asked.

"No," he said. "We're not allowed to go past the street. Mama says it's dangerous out there."

I looked at Donut. So, a bunch of women from out of town were coming to this temple, and then they were led away by a female skyfowl. Interesting. We needed to get moving.

There was no easy way off the roof. Donut's *Puddle Jumper* wouldn't reset for another four hours, and we needed it for the next part of the evening's investigations. I sighed as I pulled out my rope, reflecting on all that had changed since we'd woken up this morning. It had been a crazy long day, and it wasn't over yet. We wouldn't be able to casually walk around town anymore. We'd be fine at night, but while the sun was up, we'd be attacked by the guards, which really sucked. There were other nearby towns, but this was the largest one in the area. And with just about three days left until collapse, it was getting too late to venture far from the only exit we'd discovered so far, which was a half day's walk from here, in the ruins of Grimaldi's circus.

Donut pulled Mongo into the pet carrier and waited for me to climb down the rope. I had to carry the protesting Ricky Joe under my arm. I ended up accidentally dropping him the last ten feet, but he was mostly fine. He belly flopped hard onto the ground, losing his weak grip on the severed arm and salamander corpse. He started wailing. "Oh, you're fine," I called as I climbed the rest of the way down. "Walk it off, kid." His health had barely blipped.

The moment we hit the ground, Donut casually leaped off the building like it was nothing. I grasped the rope and pulled it into my inventory.

"You need to work on your jumping, Carl," Donut said as she released Mongo. "Or figure out how to fly."

An ear-piercing scream from within the next-door building reverberated through the street.

"That's me mom," Ricky Joe said. "She's in labor again. She's going to be really mad if I miss it. I'm in charge of holding her left leg. Bye, Princess Donut! Bye, Mongo!" He rushed toward the door.

I exchanged a look with Donut and shook my head.

ONE-EYED NARWHAL. OUR FUNDS WERE STARTING TO RUN LOW. I'D picked up three more boxes of hob-lobbers, all of them the impact-detonated version. Pustule had also brought a ten pack of the hobgoblin smoke curtains, which were round, fused bombs that would supposedly work much better than the goblin smoke bombs. I purchased all ten.

Mordecai was already in the Narwhal when we arrived, which meant he'd walked there on his own from his guildhall. The recap show was about to begin, and he sat at the table chatting with a strange woman. A crawler, I realized, seeing the blue dot on the map.

"It's Hekla's friend," Donut said. "Yay! She found us!"

Shit. I'd completely forgotten about that. As we approached, the woman turned to look at us and I stopped in my tracks. She was . . . odd-looking. I couldn't tell her age. The blond-haired woman's eyes were too big, too high on her face. Her nose was crooked and sideways, and her chin appeared to be lumpy. Also, I could see that the individual hairs on her head were much too thick. She appeared to be wearing a poorly sewn tracksuit and blocky snow boots. I examined her properties.

Crawler #9,077,265. "Katia Grim."
　　Level 9.
　　Race: Human.
　　Class: Monster Truck Driver.

I blinked a few times, trying to wrap my mind around it. She clearly wasn't human. And what the hell was a Monster Truck Driver class? My eyes focused on that level 9. She was 10 levels below me. She had a pair of stars by her name. A neighborhood and borough boss. Still, level 9. That was going to be a problem.

"Hi, Katia," Donut said, jumping on the table. "Are you Hekla's friend?"

"Hello," she said shyly, nodding her head. "Yes. Thank you so much for meeting me. Hekla said you'd be here."

Mongo approached her hesitantly, sniffing at her. Seeing that she wasn't a threat, he made a few circles and then curled up on the floor.

"Hello," I said.

"Hello, Carl," she replied. "Hekla told me everything that happened during your interview. It's . . . crazy. She wants to talk to you, but in a minute. She and the Daughters are fighting a boss right now. I won't get any experience because I'm too far away."

When she talked, her mouth moved oddly, like her voice was overdubbed. Strange.

I wouldn't be able to talk to Hekla directly. I could talk to other crawlers over chat, like the way I talked to Brandon, but only after we both initiated the chat handshake, which had to be done in person.

"Anyway," she said when I didn't respond, "Mordecai was giving me a few tips." She smiled. "It's much appreciated. My game guide isn't very helpful."

"Hekla is so cool," Donut said. "She's like Xena Warrior Princess, but better."

"Yes, she is," Katia said. "She's amazing. She saved my life."

MORDECAI: If you can train her up, she'd be a good addition to
    the team. Good enough to maybe poach her from this
    Hekla. But she is very, very far behind. Probably too far
    behind.
CARL: Can we trust her?
MORDECAI: I don't know yet. She seems genuine. She's also a
    bit of a train wreck.
CARL: What the hell is she? She's not really a human, is she?
MORDECAI: Let her explain.

"What sort of tips was Mordecai giving you?" I asked out loud.

She sighed heavily. "Bannon—that's my game guide—talked me into picking this race and class, and I don't know what I'm doing."

"What race are you? It says human, but you don't look it."

"Easy," Mordecai said. "She's trying."

I finally sat down at the table. Over the bar, the recap show began.

"What does that mean?"

"I'm a doppelganger," she said. "It says human when you look at me because that's what I'm trying to emulate. Before Mordecai helped me with my ears, it said my race was 'What the f-word?' so we are making progress."

"A doppelganger?" I said. I looked at Mordecai. "Is that the same thing as what you are? A Changeling?"

"They are similar," he said, "But not exactly the same. A doppelganger is a very difficult race to master, and her guide should have talked her out of it. As a Changeling, I can switch to any race that I have physically touched, with a few caveats. At least that's how it works for crawlers. As you know, I lost my ability to choose my shape when I became a guide. Anyway, a doppelganger is different. She is like clay. She once had a regular form, and she is wearing gear. All of that, her body and gear, adds to a certain amount of mass. With that mass, she can shape her body into anything she wants of equal mass." He looked over at her sadly. "She doesn't gain the non-physical abilities of the shape she is forming, unlike a Changeling. She just looks like it. The problem for Miss Katia here is that she can't just say, 'Make me into a human.' She has to shape it herself."

"It hurts, too," she added.

"And it hurts," Mordecai agreed. "She has to mentally chisel her appearance herself. And since she isn't yet a master sculptor . . ." He let it hang, indicating her face. "But I have some experience in this subject, and I am helping her obtain a more natural appearance."

"It's really tricky," she said. "I only return to my regular appearance when I am asleep or in the bathroom. And it doesn't let me shape myself when I'm in the bathroom. I've been using the reflection off a health potion as a mirror." She waved her hand over her face. "With obvious results."

"Wait, this will help," I said, rummaging through my inventory.

I found what I was looking for and placed it on the table. It was a hand-sized chunk of broken mirror. I'd looted it on the first floor from the remains of the gym after our fight with the Juicer. I had enough broken glass in there to form a wall of mirrors.

"Oh wow, thank you," she said, picking it up. She had a timid way of moving. She reminded me of a rabbit. Skittish and furtive, like she would bolt if I raised my voice. *How is this woman still here? How is she alive?*

She tentatively looked into the mirror. "One of those stores had a handheld mirror, but I couldn't afford . . . Oh my gosh, I look like a Juan Gris painting."

I didn't know who Juan Gris was, but I imagined he was someone who sucked at painting faces. As I watched, her face twisted and heaved like something was underneath it moving things about. Her eyes changed shape and moved into a more correct position. It was like watching someone model clay with invisible hands.

"I gotta do clothes, too," she said. "I'm wearing a magical leather jerkin right now, but once it's equipped, it disappears and adds to my mass. The only thing that doesn't disappear is my weapon."

"You'll get better and faster at altering your appearance as you practice. It's a skill, like any other," Mordecai said patiently.

"What's with that Monster Truck Driver class?" I asked.

Mordecai answered for her. "I can't look these up anymore, so I'm not certain on the exact details, but from what I can gather, it's an Earth version of the Staunch Barrier class mixed with a Jouster class. It's a relatively common combined class called a Juggernaut. In other words, she's a straight-up tank that gets an increasingly massive constitution bonus the faster she is moving. And based on her current constitution while she is standing still, she is quite the power-house."

"Wow," I said.

On the screen, the crocodilian guy with the shotgun had teamed up with a human who looked familiar, but I couldn't remember where I'd seen him before. They jumped off a burning building together while being chased by three-legged insect things.

CARL: What's the catch?

MORDECAI: Massive constitution and good dexterity. She sucks at everything else, especially strength, which seems counterintuitive. She is not a fighter. And her level is low, so despite her ability to absorb a lot of physical and magical damage, she's still far behind the curve. I once fought indestructible wombat things on the eighth floor. The monsters could absorb a direct hit to the face with a Celestial Warhammer, but they were small and weak. So instead we just picked them up and dunked them headfirst into buckets of water. They quickly drowned.

CARL: Jesus, Mordecai.

MORDECAI: My point is that the strongest, most indestructible wall in the world isn't that tough if you can pick it up and toss it aside. It's just like with your shelf plan later tonight.

Katia looked up. "Okay, Hekla is done with her fight. She says, 'Hi, Carl and Donut. I am glad you haven't been assassinated. Please help Katia.' That's me. 'I think it'll be best if you let her join your party to get experience. The farther away they are, the less shared experience they get. Please keep her out of too much danger. I really appreciate your help, and I promise to make it up to you.'"

CARL: We letting her join our party? Won't that dilute our experience pool too much?

DONUT: WE HAVE TO. WE PROMISED HEKLA.

CARL: No, YOU promised Hekla.

MORDECAI: As long as you button up this quest tonight, you

can spend the last two days grinding, and you'll be on
track, even with her tagging along. Before you got here, I
talked Fitz into letting me look at his herb stash, and I
managed to steal last night's newsletter. There's
something in there we need to talk about. But get her in the
party first.

"Tell Hekla we said that we'll take it from here and to stay safe,"
I said.

We spent the next few minutes getting her to join our party. I
took a look at her stats.

Strength: 11
    Intelligence: 8
    Constitution: 51
    Dexterity: 30
    Charisma: 8

"How did you manage to get your constitution so high?" I asked.

"I have a ring that adds 15 to constitution. I got it in a loot box
when we first started. Then I got a couple other constitution buffs,
and then when I picked that class, it added even more."

"What else can you do?" I asked, examining her properties.

"I have an ability called Second Fuel Tank, which absorbs damage and reflects some of it back. It triggers randomly, but it's limited
to only one time a fight. There's my Rush ability, which uses my
body as a battering ram. I can only do that once a 30-hour day. I also
have something called Pathfinder, which helps me find stairwells
really easily."

I exchanged a look with Mordecai.

"I don't have any useful spells. Oh, and I'm immune to wind spell
damage. Also, I'm good at fixing engines."

"Were you a mechanic?"

"No. I've never actually fixed an engine before. But I got my

Earth Hobby potion. I am a 'gearhead.' I was an art teacher before all this happened."

"An art teacher?" I asked, looking dubiously at her poorly sculpted face.

She smiled sheepishly. At least I think that's what she was going for. Instead, the smile looked a bit ghoulish. "What is the saying? Those who can't do, teach?"

"Okay, listen up," Mordecai said. "Now that you're in the party, we need to have a discussion about experience and something I just learned."

"Hush, hush!" Donut said, pointing on the screen. "Look! It's me!"

"Oh fuck," I said, looking at the headline.

It was a graphic of Donut, her eyes slit. It was an image from last night when she'd been drinking at the bar. A lightning bolt appeared, and on the other side of the screen, an image of two rottweilers slammed into place. It was purposely reminiscent of the boss battle graphic.

Princess Donut Versus Cici and Gustavo 3!

"It's a feud of epic proportions! Princess Donut has thrown the gauntlet down, directly challenging Cici and Gustavo 3, the two beloved pets of current front-runner, Lucia Mar!" the orange-hued lizard announcer breathlessly intoned.

"I have done no such thing!" Donut said, incredulous. "They're lying!" She turned to me. "Carl, I do not like this. Since when has the news been allowed to lie?"

Donut's image appeared on the screen, her leaning over her cocktail. "Those dogs sound just awful. Bitch-ass rottweilers. Almost as bad as cocker spaniels. Think they're so smart."

"Lucia Mar appeared earlier today on *Knuckle Cracking*, and this is what she had to say."

The screen flickered, changing to a shot of Lucia Mar. She sat on the couch next to a wolf-headed host. Lucia was in the strength-based, skull-faced cycle of her Lajabless form. She and the wolfman laughed cruelly as Gustavo and Cici ripped apart some small, fuzzy animal while the audience howled encouragement.

"What the hell is this bullshit?" I asked.

"It's an arena fight show," Mordecai said. "I already told Zev to never let you on one. The fights aren't real. It's complicated."

The scene cut to Lucia Mar's face, zoomed in super close. Her skull eye sockets teemed with bugs.

"What do you say to the challenge? Will you come back to this show? We could make it a main event. Donut versus one or both of your boys?" the wolfman asked off-screen.

"No," Lucia Mar said. "This show is a waste of time. Every moment spent not gaining experience is a waste of time." Her voice came out raspy with her thick Spanish accent. "I will find this Donut in the dungeon, where her death will be forever. Cici and Gus will tear this *puta* apart. And then I will rip Carl to pieces and take all of his shiny toys."

"She seems nice," I said.

I had to remind myself that this was a little kid. What kind of fucked-up childhood did she have?

"This is an outrage!" Donut said. "That wasn't a challenge! Carl, we need to tell them that it was a mistake. I don't want to fight those two stupid dogs. We'd kill them easy, sure, but I don't want those ugly skulls after my name."

"Goddamnit," Mordecai said, looking up at the screen. "Goddamnit to hell."

"They're going to bring us together somehow, aren't they?" I asked.

"Of course they are," he said. "But not yet. They'll want some buildup first."

"Will it happen on this floor?"

"No way. It won't be until after the third round of sponsorships, so on or after the sixth."

"Does that mean they'll go easy on us until then?"

"Maybe," Mordecai said. "But probably not."

"What ever happened to them trying to kill us off early?"

"They're still trying to end as early as possible. But they need money, so you high performers are going to be treated differently. All of this ties in with what I need to talk to you guys about. Borant is warning the shopkeepers and pub owners to be extra careful not to anger crawlers. It doesn't explicitly say this in the newsletter, but I can read between the lines. Some of you guys are getting much stronger than you should. That kid trashing the Desperado Club two nights ago is proof of that. Most loot boxes are controlled by the system AI, and it appears the system is attempting to compensate for the shorter time limits. Borant controls the mobs and the experience earned, for the most part, but the System AI is still the ultimate arbiter and is using that strength to even out the odds."

"Is that why you didn't have a fit when we decided to take on this quest?"

He shrugged. "You were already snagged in that quest's net. It happens. I could tell this was a good one from the get-go. Usually you have to just bring something from point A to point B, and it's done. Or you just have to kill someone. These more elaborate quests are also a symptom of the shorter floors." He paused as the announcement came on. It was nothing new. "Now, you two get a couple hours of sleep. Once Donut's *Puddle Jumper* resets, you'll go back out there. And since you've pissed off the guards, we need to make sure you finish this before the sun is up. In the meantime, I'm going to help Katia train her face. She's not going out with you tonight. But when you're done with the quest, you'll spend the rest of the time on the floor grinding together."

MORDECAI: Try to keep her alive. But if she does die, make sure
    you get those rings off her finger.
CARL: You are stone-cold, Mordecai.

THIS LATE IN THE EVENING, THE ENTIRE TOWN WAS ASLEEP. THE
pubs were all closed. Nobody walked the main streets. The only
light was from the sign of the Desperado Club a few streets over,
towering over the city. An eerie silence punctuated the night, broken
occasionally by horrific, unearthly screams that seemed to come from
everywhere.

In order to break into the magistrate's home, we first needed to
get into an alleyway, scale the exterior of a small building we'd
scoped out earlier, and then use the *Puddle Jumper* spell to hop over
to the roof of the magistrate's building.

The alley contained a group of level 14 monsters called Shadow
Leaks. They were smokelike ghost-class mobs that swarmed at us as
we approached the side of the building. They utilized a stinging-cold
attack, which I was resistant to thanks to my nightgaunt cloak.
Thankfully my magical gauntlet was able to damage them just as
easily as if they were made of flesh, and Mongo's magical teeth caps
could also hurt them. The ghosts gave off an unusually high amount
of experience and were easy to kill. Mongo hit level 13 and got noticeably larger, rising to the height of my chest. He'd gone from
dog-sized to pony-sized just like that.

Donut leaped from my shoulders to the back of Mongo to see if
she could ride him. But the dinosaur got so excited that he started
jumping up and down, tossing Donut away. She poofed all her hair
out in anger and returned to my shoulder. "We'll work on that later,"
she mumbled.

This residential building was ringed by a series of conveniently
placed trellises on the exterior that made for easy scaling. Mongo went
into the carrier as Donut leaped from window to window, quickly
reaching the third-floor roof. I followed, scaling the trellis, which
creaked ominously. But I quickly made it to the angled, shingle-
covered roof, my heart thrashing.

The long magistrate building spread before us. Earlier, we'd come in from another side, using a different building's roof to enter through the main entrance and into the mall below. This building we stood upon now was a full story higher than the last one, and we were going to jump straight to the magistrate building's roof.

That was assuming if anything was left after I blew the three sticks of dynamite. I had hidden them inside the shelves that held up Miss Quill's Beanie Babies. When I'd reattached the shelves to the wall, I'd found that they were hollow inside. I'd placed three sticks and a glob of hobgoblin pus, the remote detonator, in the second shelf. We wouldn't be able to blow through the magical door that protected the next room over, but just by knocking on the wall, I could tell we could easily breach directly through the wood.

I spent a moment examining our surroundings, searching the air for flying mobs. I didn't see anything. Just one building over from this one, directly across the opposite street, was the large warehouse-like building that held all of the inactive swordsmen guards. I could feel it there, an ominous presence, sandwiching us between the equally imposing magistrate's building. I hoped the guards remained within like they were supposed to. Mordecai insisted they'd remain inactive all night, but I was worried. We were about to cause a very large, very loud ruckus.

We'd originally had a different plan, but after my test earlier with the hobgoblin dynamite, we'd had to rethink how we were going to proceed.

"Here we go," I said to Donut. "Get ready."

"Wait, I have to remember my lines," said Donut. She shook her paw and cleared her throat.

I sighed and pulled the mysterious letter from my inventory.

It was Mordecai who'd figured out what the mysterious letter really was. We'd found it within GumGum's inventory after she'd been killed. We figured it was something she'd pulled off the dead body of a prostitute. It turns out, it was likely planted there on purpose in the hopes it would be picked up by whoever was in charge of investigating the deaths.

Earlier this morning, as we'd stood outside of the Narwhal staring at the dead corpse with the words *No, you won't* carved into her body, which had been in response to me saying we'd hunt down and kill whoever was responsible, I had been horrified.

"Whoever this is, is listening to us talk. He can hear and see us," I'd said to Mordecai.

"That's unlikely. You were in a safe room."

"Yet here we are," I said. "He'd done it fast, too. She'd dropped just a few moments after I'd spoken."

"Tell me exactly what you were doing at the time when they dropped this girl on the building."

It was only then I realized I'd been clutching onto the mysterious letter as I'd told Donut that we'd get revenge for GumGum.

"I should have realized," Mordecai said after thinking on it for a moment. "Don't take it out. It won't work while it's in your inventory. It's a necroscript scroll all right, but it's also covered in blood. I thought that was from the dead body it was found on. But I think it's actually the blood of the caster. The scroll has already been used. Scrolls usually disappear once used, but not always."

"Well, what is it?" I asked.

"*Suppurating Eye,*" he said. "A common lich spell. It's usually not in scroll form, but it's not unheard-of. The caster reads the spell, then leaks a bodily fluid onto a surface. The caster can then see and hear anything happening near the spilled fluid. It's like placing a spy camera. He spilled it directly on the scroll, which he knew would be picked up. As long as it's out of your inventory, he'll know where you are and can hear you talk. You probably won't be able to sell it to anybody, so you should get rid of it."

"Or we can use it!" Donut said. "We can talk to him and tell him what a jerk he is, get him mad enough to come to us."

"That's actually a great idea," I said.

"Of course it's a great idea, Carl. I always come up with great ideas."

I now gingerly placed the scroll on the roof tiles.

"I still don't know what this is," I whispered. "When we're done here, we need to sell it."

"Do you think there'll be more scrolls in there?" Donut asked. She was overacting, but it was too late now. "It looks valuable. We should find one without blood on it."

"After we finish looting that filing cabinet in the reception area, we can look through the office for more scrolls."

I added, "We should probably steal all of those stuffed animals on Miss Quill's desk, too. Especially those ones on the top shelf in the little cases. I bet those are worth something to somebody. And if they're not, we can always use them to light campfires."

"Good idea. Plus, Mongo needs a chew toy."

"Okay, we're going to wait another minute to make sure nothing is flying around above us. Then we'll zap over to the roof, hammer our way through the ceiling, and drop into that office. The key to that door has to be in there somewhere."

"It's a foolproof plan," Donut said.

I put the letter back into my inventory.

⸻

"THERE!" DONUT SAID, POINTING INTO THE SKY. A GROUP OF FOUR krasue emerged, coming from underneath the building. It appeared they'd been on the first, unoccupied floor waiting for us. They emerged now, heading toward our position on the roof.

"Go," I whispered.

Donut zapped Mongo back onto the roof. Before the dinosaur could screech, she hissed, "Quiet!"

The dinosaur grunted angrily, then realized he was on an angled roof and started scrambling. Donut quickly cast *Clockwork Triplicate* on the dinosaur and then pulled the original Mongo back into his carrier. We'd need him again in a minute, but not right now.

The two clockwork Mongos both squeaked with disappointment

as Mongo disappeared. I pulled the lit hobgoblin smoke curtain into my xistera and tossed it onto the opposite roof. I then lit a second one and wedged it into a roof tile at our feet.

Donut gave a quick set of instructions to the two dinosaurs, and they both howled as the heavy smoke started to billow into the night air. I quickly pulled the mysterious letter out.

"We're jumping onto the roof now," I said. I crumpled up the letter and tossed it up in the air. One of the Mongos grabbed it and swallowed it whole. They then turned and leaped from the roof to the top of the magistrate building, soaring up through the air and landing easily. One of them howled, the sound carrying heavily into the night.

"Holy shit," I whispered. They'd leaped across the alley and up an entire full story. "You were right. I didn't think they'd be able to jump that far."

"Mongo has the same pounce ability as I do," Donut said. "And he's a lot bigger."

"Maybe I should ride him instead of letting you have all the fun," I said as the smoke completely filled the night air. Pustule had been correct. These things were much better than the traditional goblin smoke bombs. It was like a heavy fog had filled the entire area. The two pets disappeared from view.

The swarm of red dots indicating the krasue turned back toward the roof of the building. The dinos had jumped before the fog had completely filled the area, and the floating women heads had seen the motion. I hadn't been certain the fog would work on ghosts. Mordecai said it wouldn't on most kinds of non-corporeal ghost entities, but it would on these guys because they had a physical presence. I still didn't know how he kept all these rules in his head.

My attention moved to the map. "Okay, the clockwork Mongos are on the roof right over the magistrate's office." If the guy was listening in, hopefully he'd been fooled into thinking *we* were now on the roof, and his crew had moved to the office to intercept. "Get down." We moved to the back of the roof, crouching down. We should be plenty far away at this distance, but every time I said that, I was proven wrong.

"I feel bad about ruining Miss Quill's collection," Donut said. "She really loves those things."

"Something tells me she's not going to care anymore."

I pulled the hobgoblin pus out and jammed on the detonator. A clockwork Mongo howl filled the air in the moment before night turned to day.

22

"NICE," I SAID, EXAMINING THE GAPING HOLE IN THE BUILDING.

Below, the entire town had been jarred awake by the explosion. Lights turned on throughout the village. Cries and shouts rose. The dark shadows of skyfowl burst into the air all around us, but most stayed back from the destruction. The magistrate's quarters burned. We'd blown up half of the building. But not all of it.

> Admin Notice. A new tab is available in your interface.
> Admin Notice. Your title has changed. This change will revert upon collapse of this floor.

A wall of notifications scrolled by, surprising me. I jumped up two levels to 21. Donut also jumped two levels to 19.

"Well, that was easy," Donut said as she cast her *Torch* spell, filling the rooftop with brilliant light. The smoke bomb sputtered to a stop, and the light reflected off the remnants, pulsing. It reminded me of the dance floor of the Desperado Club.

I had been expecting the krasue to swarm at us, which was why we'd waited until now for Donut to cast her light spell. They should've been immune to the explosion, but I didn't see them anywhere. We'd probably blown them halfway across town. I kept a wary eye out for red dots.

"*Oh shit,*" I said, examining the notifications. We had not received the one I'd hoped for, but I still had several interesting ones.

New achievement! Assassin!

You have killed a ranking NPC town official. *Sniff* It seems like just yesterday you were nothing but a scared level 1 crawler with beautiful feet, pissing yourself as you faced down a rat. Now look at you. You've moved all the way up to political assassinations. What's next? Killing a god?

Reward: You've received a Bronze Assassin's Box!

New achievement! Ultimate Extreme Power!

Easy there, Charlemagne. This is only a medium settlement. It's not like you've conquered most of Europe. But you have killed this town's acting Magistrate.

You know what that means? Welcome to the wonderful world of public administration.

Reward: You've received a Platinum Tyrant's Box! You have also gained control of the Medium Skyfowl Settlement. Good luck, Magistrate.

New achievement! CockBlock!

You have assassinated an NPC whose existence was required to complete another crawler's quest. [*NPC Killed: Miss Quill—Skyfowl. Level 30.*] Who was that other crawler? What was the quest? Who fucking cares? You get the reward they were promised!

Warning: You may only receive this award once. The next time you do it, we tell them who you are. And then they get a new quest to kill you. Nobody likes CockBlocks.

Reward: You've received a Silver Quest Box!

So it appeared we had killed both Miss Quill and Magistrate Featherfall in the blast.

"Are we jumping over there or what?" Donut said. "We're supposed to be jumping!"

"Hang on," I said. Every instinct I had told me to wait. "Something's not right. Let me think for a second."

"Hey," Donut said a moment later. "Why did you get the fancy name change and I didn't? This is an outrage!"

I looked at the menu. My title had changed from **Royal Bodyguard** to **Magistrate Carl of Medium Skyfowl Settlement**.

I didn't laugh. Mordecai had already warned me that one of us would likely win the town if we killed the magistrate. But he'd also said when you killed the quest's head boss dude, you either auto-won the quest or it failed, depending on the situation. Given the mysterious circumstances of this quest, he'd given us a 50/50 chance of winning that quest box. And that was okay with me as long as the quest went away. Either way, we'd get a ton of experience since the guy was also the head of the town. But nothing had happened with the quest. It still sat there in my menu. Did we kill an innocent NPC? We hadn't even met the magistrate, and we'd just blown his house to bits.

"Listen, we have a problem. I think we screwed up. Magistrate Featherfall is dead, but the quest is still there. That means he wasn't the head bad guy. And it looks like Miss Quill wasn't the bad guy, either, like I was suspecting. And to top it off, we fucked over some other crawler's quest."

The plan had been simple. Using the mysterious letter as bait, we were going to make Featherfall think we were about to breach through the ceiling, drawing him to the area to face us. After Ricky Joe had claimed that a female skyfowl was visiting the city elves, I thought perhaps Miss Quill was really the bad guy. That was just the sort of thing the AI would pull, which was why I'd mentioned something about burning the stuffed animals. Either way, whoever was listening in would hopefully be there. Mordecai said a lich would get blown to bits just as easily as a human. The only monster we'd have to worry about post-detonation would be the krasue, which wouldn't be hurt by the explosion.

After the blast, if there was anything left, we'd storm the

magistrate's office and mop up the remaining bad guys and hopefully figure out what the hell was going on over there.

"If Miss Quill was there to get blown up, then she had to be in on it. Why else would she be there this late?" Donut asked.

"Maybe," I said. "She said he only came out at night now. Maybe she altered her schedule to match. Or maybe she lived there."

"Or maybe she was a bloodsucking pawn of the lich. We don't know, Carl. Let's go look. Quit being a wuss."

"Okay," I said after a moment. "But let's be cautious. I have a bad feeling about this one. Turn off your *Torch* for now, but be ready to snap it back on."

"Wait, wait, look," Donut said. "Look at our notifications again. There's a Bronze Boss Box in there. I told you one of them was a bad guy."

I looked, and she was correct. I hadn't noticed it buried there with the others. So, either Featherfall or Quill had been a neighborhood boss. That made me feel a little better. But which one was it? It didn't say.

The dynamite had blown a massive hole in the roof, peeling it up like it had been drilled through from below. Thankfully the building wasn't fully engulfed in flames. Not yet. Smoke continued to rise from the hole, but it was minimal for now. The boom jug from earlier this afternoon had managed to burn a building to the ground in a matter of minutes. The effect of this blast appeared to be much more powerful, but also much less incendiary. If I was going to be blowing shit up more often, I needed to know what to expect. This particular blast, while huge, was not what I'd anticipated. The physics surrounding this stuff was still beyond me, and that was dangerous. I needed to learn, and fast.

Donut used *Puddle Jumper* to get us over to the roof across the way. We went from the angled tiles to the flat beams, but the ground below us suddenly felt unsteady, ready to break.

"You there!" a voice called. I looked up. A pair of skyfowl NPCs had grown brave enough to fly closer to the explosion. They hovered over us now. "What are you doing?"

"I'm the new town magistrate," I called. "I'm on magistrate business."

The two eagles looked at each other. I wasn't certain how this sort of thing worked, if they'd recognize my authority or not. If this were the real world they'd say . . .

"Fuck off, you crazy assholes," the skyfowl called down to me. "Go back to the Desperado or wherever you came from. You shouldn't be up here. There's been an explosion, and that roof you're on is going to cave in. We ain't saving your stupid wingless asses if you fall through."

"Well, fuck you very much," I called back to them.

The other skyfowl turned to his companion. "I don't feel so well. There might be something in the air. Let us flee from here, my brother."

The two circled a few times and then flew off.

I kept an eye out for mobs as we cautiously approached the hole. We looked down into what had once been the magistrate's quarters. The epicenter of the explosion was still another 50 feet ahead. Through the hole in the roof, I could see all the way to the ground far below. Half of the magistrate's home and front office was just gone, along with the entire south end of the building. The floor of the mall level was also a massive hole. And below that was a pile of smoking debris. However, deeper into both the mall and the living quarters above, I could see that the floor was mostly intact.

"No wonder there's not that much fire," I said. "It's like we punched a hole right through the structure, both up and down. Weird."

Donut pointed to the side of the building. Across the street, another structure had half caved in. Thankfully it was a business and not a residence. I was glad we'd chosen a different building to stand upon. "Your explosion went up, down, and to the side. But it didn't blow this way. I wonder if that magic door protected it."

"Maybe," I said. "But either way, that reception office is just gone.

If that's where Miss Quill and Featherfall were standing at the time, they wouldn't have had a chance."

"Those poor stuffed animals," Donut said. "Now let's go down there."

Donut started to wiggle her butt, and then she jumped deftly down into the magistrate's quarters as I tied my rope to a chimney. This was starting to get cumbersome. Donut was right. I needed a better way to go up and down. I descended. I swung my way into the chambers. I left the rope there, hanging all the way past the mall level. The full length of the rope ended about 15 feet off the ground.

A few fires crackled here and there. I gave them a wide berth as we explored deeper into the large building. Donut released Mongo, who immediately moved to a small, empty cage against one wall and started sniffing at it.

The magistrate's office had been just on the other side of the reception area, which meant it was now gone. There was no sign of the magical door. It was probably buried in the debris along with the corpses and all of Miss Quill's Beanie Babies. And past the office were the living quarters, which extended the entire length of the mall below it. There wasn't much here. A few tables and T-shaped roosts. There was an open chest against a wall, but it was empty.

Donut inspected a small cage that interested Mongo. It appeared as if it once held regular-sized mice or rats. The door was open. She said it smelled moldy, like it hadn't been used in a while. All I could smell was smoke. She pulled the cage into her inventory and came to examine the chest, which I poked at with my foot.

"Hey, Donut, look. The clasp is broken. That didn't happen with the explosion."

"So, it was sitting here already looted before we blew it up?"

"That's what it looks like."

"Maybe another crawler broke into here before us," she said.

"Maybe," I said. "We're the ones who killed Featherfall, though. Keep one eye on the map."

I looked around. The entire apartment seemed oddly empty. There were shelves, but nothing was upon them. Nothing hung on the walls. That empty cage had been a food box, but it hadn't been used in a while. There was a heavy door against the far wall leading deeper into the house. I leaned into it, opening it slowly.

The moment I pushed against the door, I saw the X appear on the map. I pushed the door all the way. The moment I did, several dozen additional red dots appeared, along with an equal number of X's. I froze as I formed a fist, ready to defend myself. Nothing happened. Nobody moved.

Holy crap.

"Mongo, shush," I hissed as the feathered dinosaur forced his way into the room. He opened his mouth to howl, and I pressed my left hand down on his beak. "Shush," I repeated.

Donut leaped to my shoulder, putting herself in the firing position. Still, nothing in the room stirred. Donut gasped, her entire body going rigid.

"Carl," Donut whispered, her voice terrified. "You were right, Carl. This was a bad idea. I don't like this. Please, let's go. Let's go now."

I swallowed, examining the horrific sight before me.

We'd stepped into a serial killer's wet dream.

The entire room was filled with naked female corpses hanging upside down from the ceiling as if we'd just walked into a meat locker. There were humans and elves and dwarves, along with a scattering of others, such as orcs and a single ogre. The ones that appeared as X's on my map were all missing their heads. The others, at least thirty of them, still had all their parts, but the heads were detached, hanging a good six inches below the necks, with only the white of bone and straw-like arteries keeping them attached. It appeared as if someone had grabbed their heads, given them good yanks, and then left them there, bobbleheading. Wisps of purple energy swirled around the red-dotted ones, like they were being recharged.

They all appeared to be asleep. Their eyes remained closed.

The horrors didn't stop there. At the center of the room, hanging upside down in a massive dream catcher made of bone, was the na-ked, emaciated corpse of Magistrate Featherfall. His featherless wings were spread all the way out, with nothing but goose-bumped gray skin left, like a pair of uncooked chicken wings with grasping fingers at the first knuckle. His milky white dead eyes stared out at us under a cracked beak. A clear fluid dripped from both his mouth and eyes. At the top of the hoop-shaped construction, his taloned claws were spread out and splayed, facing the ceiling. The whole sight was reminiscent of a fucked-up, inverted parody of da Vinci's *Vitruvian Man*. His body was lashed to the bone structure with old frayed rope. It appeared as if he'd been there for some time. His body was in the process of being mummified. The circle twisted in the air, rocking back and forth, creaking.

Lootable Corpse. Former Magistrate Featherfall. Dark Cleric. Level 32.

"How did we get credit for killing that guy when he was like this?" Donut whispered. "He looks like he's been dead a long time."

"I don't know."

This was a nest of krasue. The original description said to truly kill them, one had to find their bodies and destroy them. The ones without heads were, I assumed, out and about in the town. But if that was the case, then why did they appear as corpses on the map? The descriptions just said they were regular NPC corpses. Were the bodies technically dead until the krasue returned? I supposed it didn't matter as long as we killed the bodies. But could we? I knew we couldn't kill the ghosts without using magic. But what about their bodies?

The entire ground was sticky with gore and lumps of fallen, for-gotten body parts. The smell was almost unbearable.

If we wanted to approach Featherfall, we'd have to brush by

several of the hanging women. The closest one, a blue-skinned elf, was a mere five feet away. She was young and thin, hanging from the ceiling with her ankles in a noose. Her long, dark hair cascaded below her, not quite long enough to reach the ground. I resisted the urge to punt her head.

"We need to get closer to loot his body," I said.

"Yeah, no, I'm not taking another step in there. Those things are going to wake up."

"If that explosion didn't wake them, then maybe they'll stay unconscious."

"Of course they're going to wake up, Carl. Have you *ever* watched a horror movie?"

She was right. And with the blood splattered all over the room, I strongly suspected whoever the head bad guy was, he probably had that *Suppurating Eye* spell going. We couldn't stay here long. I sent a quick query to Mordecai, who said the headless ones were maybe fair game to physical attacks, but the ones with their heads and the purple swirls were likely protected. But he wasn't certain.

"Okay," I whispered. "Let's kill this one here and see what happens. If it works, we'll carve a path. We'll loot and run."

"Okay, let's step back. I'll hit her with a missile," Donut said. "If they all wake up, I'll cast my *Torch*. Maybe it'll scare them away again."

"Hey," she said a moment later. "Not fair. It says the area has been muted. I can't cast spells."

I sent another note to Mordecai.

MORDECAI: Spells in your menu and scrolls won't cast if you're in a muted zone. Everything else—including magical items, potions, and spells you've already cast—will still work.

"Okay, Mongo," I said. "You're up." He had those magical teeth caps, and those should do damage. "Go bite that elf's head off. But you gotta be quick."

Mongo croaked and looked at Donut for confirmation.

"Sic 'em," she said.

The dinosaur rushed forward, weaving at his target snakelike. At the last moment, he turned his head to the side, like he was eating a taco. He chomped down on the dark elf's head.

Crunch.

The barely detached head caved in under Mongo's alarmingly powerful bite. The head slopped to the ground, followed by a rush of organs and blood, as if her neck was a drain that had just been unclogged. The purple swirls of magic blinked off.

Mongo raised his head into the air and howled, blood cascading off his face.

The purple aura around the others blinked out. The hair on the back of my neck stood on end. *Uh-oh.*

Mongo, oblivious, moved deeper into the room, biting a second, then a third. He ignored the ones that were already headless. The dinosaur jump-attacked at a fourth, but he moved through the body as if it wasn't there. He howled in rage and turned to bite, this time latching on the woman's legs, ripping her from the ceiling. She crumpled to the ground.

"Get back here!" I said.

"Mongo, return!" Donut cried.

All around the room, the krasue began waking up. They wailed, loud and high-pitched. The heads all started wiggling at once, working to fully detach themselves from the rest of their bodies.

"Donut, go long," I yelled. This was one of our oldest plays, but it didn't exactly fit the situation. Hopefully she would understand the idea.

"Carl, that's not going to . . . Oh, I get it! With what, though?"

"With light!"

She leaped from my shoulder and ran away, scrambling out into the other room and presumably to the roof. Once she was out of range of the muting, she'd cast her *Torch* spell and then return.

I rolled a smoke curtain into the chaos as I formed a fist, rushing toward Mongo, who was gnawing down on yet another creature. My feet splashed in the gore. I punched at a krasue as I passed, my magical gauntlet connecting with a wet *splat*.

I pulled a regular torch and lit it, tossing it to the ground. The women squealed in rage, dozens of them peeling themselves free. One by one, they righted themselves, floating into the air, trailing organs as their now-empty bodies waved back and forth, turning into X's on my map. They backed away from the sputtering torch, which invaded the smoke-filled room with a pulsing red glow. They didn't flee like last time. The light wasn't as powerful, and they were also blinded by the smoke. They started to swirl through the room like flocking birds, bumping into one another and the hanging bodies and the bone hoop in the center, which started to spin. A krasue whipped past me, smacking me in the face with a still-beating heart. I swung but missed.

"Back out the door," I said to Mongo, pointing behind me. The pet looked up and screeched. He snapped at a krasue, connecting with a hanging lung, ripping it free. The creature squealed and plummeted to the ground, bouncing and rolling with arteries whipping about like a jellyfish.

We pushed through a hanging curtain of headless corpses as I yanked the Fireball or Custard lotto ticket from my inventory. We ran into the living room, which was also now filled with smoke. We stopped at the gaping hole, and I turned back.

This apartment was big, but I didn't know how much more punishment it could take before the whole building collapsed. I wasn't sure how powerful a level 15 fireball was. The last time I'd tried this, the 50/50 chance ticket cast custard.

Where the hell was Donut? I glanced at the map, and it appeared she was just above us, on the roof. There were more red dots now circling the cat, keeping their distance.

"Fire in the hole!" I cried as I scratched the ticket. I was fully expecting it to cast custard again.

Fireball. Spicy!

The egg-shaped ball of fire leaped out of my hand and rocketed toward the doorway to the bedroom. The flaming projectile was the size of an open umbrella. It didn't move as quickly as one of Donut's magic missiles, but that didn't matter. It rolled directly through the open door, shattering the jamb on either side, cleaving through the smoke and detonating as it hit the upside-down corpse of Featherfall.

The entire building rocked again. The floor buckled. Burning heat washed over me, hitting me with a small amount of damage. The room turned to X's before half collapsing down to the next level. Black acrid smoke filled the air, mixing in with the white of the smoke curtain. Above, the red dots harassing Donut all disappeared.

A moment later, Donut leaped down and landed on my shoulder, trailing her ball of light. It glowed brighter than I'd ever seen before. I had to shield my eyes.

"Did we get them all?" she asked. "They all disappeared when you did that."

"I think so. But I think we fried whatever loot Featherfall had."

"Let's go look."

We reentered the bedroom. The entire floor slumped down like a ramp down into the mall level. The fireball spell had crisped everything in the room. The ashes of Featherfall were scattered along the debris.

"He wasn't the boss," I said. "If he was, he'd have a neighborhood map on him, even after we destroyed the body."

"Then it had to have been Miss Quill," Donut said. "She was the boss lady all along. But her body is behind us, probably buried."

The building shuddered again.

"It's going to collapse," I said. "We gotta get out of here."

"But what about the quest? We haven't figured anything out."

I was about to say, *We're out of time*, when I noticed the red dot on the map. One of the corpses, burned to a crisp, had just switched from an X to a red dot. As I turned, forming a fist, the dot blinked again, this time turning white.

It was a woman, one of the headless corpses. She was on the ground, and her head had magically returned to her body. She was a familiar human with long, dark hair. She'd been marked as a krasue that brief moment her dot was red, but now that it was white, the system designated her as a human. The lower half of her body was nothing but darkened char. She looked up at us, blinking in pain. She had one pale blue eye and one brown eye. This was Burgundy, the same woman we'd run into on the stairs when we'd visited earlier. One of the assistants to the magistrate. Her face was oddly unmarred by the damage.

Donut leaped down, sniffing at her. The woman's legs had turned to flaky, obsidian-colored logs of charcoal. "Carl, we have to help her."

I knelt down and pulled a healing potion.

"No," Burgundy said, her voice weak. "If you heal me, it'll heal my body. Then I will turn into one of those things again. It's too late for me. I am cursed. Damned. The kindest thing you can do is kill me while I'm still mortal. Hurry. Please. It hurts."

"So, you're a person during the day, and one of those things at night?" I asked.

"Yes," she gasped. "I was brought here by the elves. I worked in another settlement, but they told me I could get a job at the Desperado Club. There was an entrance in this town. They talked me into coming. Everyone knows if you work in the club, there's a chance you can descend. I could go to the Hunting Grounds. And then maybe even deeper, where it's safe. But it was all a lie."

"You were a prostitute?" I asked.

Her lips quivered. "Yes, and if you don't like it, fuck off. I've stabbed men for less." She coughed.

"We're just trying to figure out what's going on. Lots of your friends have been appearing in the alleys, twisted and dead."

"It's going to be okay, sweetie," Donut added. She reached up and stroked at the woman's hair. "Tell us as much as you can about Featherfall."

"Featherfall?" she asked. Her voice was getting weaker. "Can you make that light brighter? I can feel it keeping the curse away, but it's fading." Donut's torch was like a blazing sun. She couldn't make it brighter. "Featherfall wasn't the one who did this. He's been here the whole time, hanging on that thing. He was dead when I got here. His body was turned into a dark fetish, one to keep our bodies safe at night. Miss Quill's the one who has been running the city the whole time. She's the real magistrate."

I felt an odd amount of relief wash over me. Miss Quill *was* the bad guy. We'd killed the correct person. When the system said I'd killed a public official, it was her, not Featherfall. Also, this was like the hundredth time in the last day that the AI's description of something had been inaccurate. It'd said Quill was the assistant to the magistrate. It'd said Katia was a human, when she was really a doppelganger. It said Burgundy here was also human, when she was really one of those vampire things. The map labeled all these corpses with an X, when they could still turn into monsters. That was important to know, that we couldn't trust anything.

But if Quill was the mastermind, why hadn't the quest ended? I reread what we were supposed to do, focusing on the last line.

Nobody knows who they are or where they come from. Find out why.

The quest didn't tell us to *save* the women. Or to kill who was responsible. We just needed to find out what was going on. We were almost there. We just had to get it out of this woman before the entire building crashed down.

"Okay," I said. "So how did you get like this?"

"The elves had me go to their temple, and once I was there, Miss Quill came and got us. She asked us so many questions. I didn't know why at the time. I thought she was going to take me to the club. Instead, she brought me to him."

"To who?"

Below, something crashed. It reverberated throughout the entire floor. The smoke bomb had cleared, but the black smoke from the fires was now thicker.

"To her husband. He's in another place. It's across the street. It is where the swordsmen guards stay in the evening. He is on the floor above. The guards don't know he's there, or they don't care. They can't look up."

"Her husband?" I asked.

I tried to remember what Miss Quill had said about him. It wasn't much. She'd said he was dead. And that he'd been magistrate before Featherfall. That was it.

"Yes. His name is Remex. He's doing something, casting a big spell. I don't know what. He's not alive, nor is he dead. He's something in between, something monstrous. He's trying to bring himself fully back to life."

Fuck. Another bad guy. I'd been hoping all the bosses were dead.

"But what does that have to do with you guys?" I asked.

"Do you know what I am? What I have become? I am a krasue. A woman who lived a life of sin. One who died in anger and pain, and returned from the dead. During the day we live and work in this building, working as assistants and in the shops below. Collecting. At night, we are his army, doing his bidding, helping the city elves, whom he has also glamoured into his control."

"Collecting what? And what about the women we find in the alleys?"

"Every time a new skyfowl or chickadee comes into one of the shops in the mall, we are to pluck a feather from their plumage. I do not know why. We give them to Miss Quill."

"That doesn't sound good," said Donut. Mongo grunted in agreement.

"As to the women . . . they are those whose sins aren't enough.

They are women who have come to work at the Desperado Club, but when they are brought to Remex, when he twists them, when their heads sometimes fly from their bodies, they do not always turn into krasue. It is not a perfect thing, this transformation. Sometimes they simply die. When this happens, he allows us to feed upon them. Then one of his avatars picks them up and drops them in the alleys. Miss Quill says they have to drop them within a few blocks of his lair. He controls the avatars as if they are his own limbs, but they can't go far. Not yet."

"Avatars?" I asked. "Are they other skyfowl? I don't understand."

Crack! The rest of the room slumped forward farther. Burgundy's body began to slide away.

"Kill me, please!" she cried as the roof above her started to cave in.

Donut hit her with a magic missile in the moments before her body disappeared.

23

I PULLED THE ROPE BACK INTO MY INVENTORY WHILE I STILL HUNG 15 feet off the ground. I was very happy I'd figured out that neat trick early on, before having to invest in multiple lengths of the stuff. Still, Donut was right. I needed a better method of going up and down.

I crashed heavily onto the debris pile, though it didn't hurt like it would've before. I briefly wondered exactly how far I could drop before I would take damage. Above, the entire structure trembled. The whole thing was going to fall in on our heads at any moment. We had to get out of here. The X of Quill's body was there on my map, right under our feet, enticing me. We'd have to dig for an hour to get to her and the neighborhood map, which would be super useful right about now. That wasn't going to happen.

A sparkle of something caught my eye. A single charred box sat half buried in the debris. I picked it up as we fled. It was one of Miss Quill's glass cases. It appeared unbroken despite being less than a foot from the explosion, which meant this thing was likely enchanted. The char rubbed right off. The plush creature within was an armored man atop a black horse. I peered at the tag, which said "Kimaris." I pulled it all into my inventory.

The building rumbled as we cleared the distance. We stopped in the street and turned to watch as the rest of the gigantic building caved in. We'd gotten out of there just in time.

"We know what happened to the prostitutes now. We know why they were falling into the alleys," Donut said, breathing heavily. "How come the quest didn't finish?"

"We know *how* they got there," I said. "We still don't know why. We don't have the whole story." I eyed the dark warehouse across the street. It was a simple, square two-level building. There were no lights with only a large pair of double doors at the entrance. I could sense him there, on the second floor. Remex. "If we want to finish this, we need to go into that building. That's the quest."

A crowd of NPCs watched the municipal building and mall collapse from a short distance away. I looked about in the air, but I didn't see any skyfowl. There had been dozens of them out earlier, but they were all gone. I had the impression they didn't like flying about at night. Still, it was unusual.

A single blue dot of a crawler stood there in the crowd. I met the player's eyes, and he approached us. I focused on the now-familiar name over his head.

"Don't let him see that fallen oak bracelet on your back leg," I whispered.

"Why?" Donut asked. "He's not one of those elves."

"He's related to the dead crawler you took it from. He's also the same guy that killed that boss in the swimming pool. The one that blew up. The Divider."

"Oh, he's disgusting," Donut said as the man got closer. He walked slowly and deliberately. I could see he didn't have shoes, though I suspected for him this was a recent development thanks to his newly clawed feet. "Someone needs to teach him about muted colors. He looks like someone took Jack's hat and made an over-enthusiastic furry costume out of it."

"Be nice," I whispered, trying not to laugh. Jack, the man who had peed on the wall and caused all the chaos on the second floor, had been very fond of his orange Cincinnati Bengals hat.

"No, I'm serious, Carl. This guy could be the second coming of Chuck Norris, but we can't have him in the party. People would laugh at us."

"You know you're a Persian cat, right?" I said.

"What is that supposed to mean, Carl?"

"Don't worry," I muttered. "He doesn't look like he wants to join our party anyway.

"Hey there," I said as he came to a stop before us. The man paused, looking me up and down. I felt my eyebrow rise as he examined me for an extended period.

Crawler #2,165,570. "Daniel Bautista 2."
    Level: 18.
    Race: Tigran.
    Class: Swashbuckler.

He looked like a rejected character from *Thundercats*. He was a well-muscled, shirtless man, about six feet tall. He was furry and orange. *Very* furry. *Very* orange. He had the head of a human–big cat hybrid, with the orange, white, and black markings of a Siberian tiger. But unlike a tiger, his eyes had the vertical slits of a house cat. His nose and mouth were human, though covered with wisps of the orange fur. He also had a long, absurdly shaggy tail. The effect would be comical if the dude didn't look as if he could rip me in half. He held nine neighborhood boss markers. He wore a belt with a curved sword hanging in a scabbard. The sword also glowed orange.

"Were you the ones who killed Miss Quill?" he finally asked. He had an Asian accent. I remembered the three corpses we'd run across several days earlier. Grace, Nica, and Lea. They all had the same last name. I assumed this guy was part of that family. They'd had someone with them who'd looted most of their gear. Donut had picked up that fallen oak anklet, and I'd looted two generic strength rings. If the man knew we had them, would he want the items back? That would be too bad for him if he did. I figured it would be for the best if we didn't broach the subject at all.

"Yes," I said. "I take it you're the guy whose quest we fucked over?"

"I am," he said. "I was supposed to break into her home and kill her. It would get me access to the Desperado Club. But when I went to her home, she rushed off. I tried to follow, but she can fly. She went straight to that building there, and a few minutes later came your explosion and her death."

"Did she have more of the stuffed creatures in her house?" Donut asked.

Bautista grunted. "Yes. Her entire apartment was filled with them. Over a thousand of them. I have taken them all."

I shrugged. "Well, sorry about that. Like I said, we also have a quest that involved her. It's not quite done yet, either."

He nodded slowly. He wanted to say something, but he was hesitating.

"A few nights back, I saw you on the news program," he finally added.

"We're on almost every night," said Donut proudly.

"You fought at that circus. You killed the lemurs. Is there nothing left?"

He was trying to ask about his family, but he was having trouble getting it out. "No. They're all gone. There's a stairwell there now."

He nodded appreciatively. "There is another three kilometers due east from this village. Crawlers have been writing notes with the stairwell locations and leaving them in the bars."

"Good," I said. I paused. "And yes, we saw them. The other Bautistas. We killed the lemurs responsible."

His tail whisked back and forth. "Thank you," he said. "They were my sisters and cousin. All five of them died in seconds. It happened so fast. I was with my other cousin, and we barely got away."

I swallowed. There had only been three bodies, but I remembered thinking at the time that there'd been enough blood for more.

Bautista continued. "He died the next day. My cousin, I mean. He'd given up. I'm all that's left of my entire family. I had four brothers and sisters. Fifteen cousins." He looked off into the distance. "I don't know why I go on. I wish I hadn't chosen this body. I should've remained true to myself. We all die anyway. How can we make it to heaven if god doesn't recognize us?"

I had no answer for that.

An awkward silence followed. I shifted uneasily. "Well, I'm sorry for your loss. And I am sorry about screwing up your quest."

He nodded. "It is no problem. I am happy knowing they have been avenged. I owe you a debt. Call me if you need me, and I will come." He held out his fist, initiating the chat transfer. I hesitated, then reciprocated the gesture. His name appeared on my chat list. Then he turned and disappeared into the night.

"That dude is very intense," I said.

"I would be too if I looked like that," said Donut. "Their game guide let him pick that race. And one of his sisters or cousins had been that weird tree thing, remember? It's like their guide wanted them to look stupid. And Katia's game guide won't help her. And remember that floating brain thing we saw in the recap episode? The one for Frank Q and Maggie My? That thing was talking them into murdering people. I think most of these guides don't like their jobs very much, and they take it out on the crawlers."

"I think you're right," I said. "Let me tell you a secret, Donut. Back before all this happened, it was considered a rare thing for somebody to find a job they truly loved."

"You don't like fixing boats? Or being in the Navy?"

"Not really. And I was in the Coast Guard. Not the Navy. They're different," I said.

"Are you sure? Miss Beatrice always told people you were in the Navy."

"I'm sure, Donut."

"Well, what would you have done if you could do anything?" she asked.

I thought about that for a long moment. I thought of the college applications I started to fill out, but never finished. "I would work for the forestry service as a forester."

"Doing what? Looking at trees all day?"

"Yes," I said. "I've seen enough ocean to last a lifetime. I'd be happy alone in the woods, watching for forest fires. God, I would give anything. That would be beautiful."

Donut grunted. "I know what I would do. I would write TV shows. Zev and I are going to start a television show writing team when we get out of here. We're going to remake *Gossip Girl* but with an intergalactic slant."

I chuckled. "Is that right?"

"Zev says the shows on Earth are better than anything she's ever seen. We could make new ones and bring them to the universe. Maybe if the television shows are good enough, people wouldn't be so interested in watching real-life people kill each other," she said.

I didn't say anything for several moments. "You surprise me every day, Donut."

She didn't give me the snarky response I was expecting.

"So," she said, "we calling it a night or are we going to fight a lich?"

I sighed. We had about three hours until sunrise. "What do you think?"

———

THE MASSIVE DOOR TO THE SWORDSMEN DEPOT WAS NOT LOCKED. It sat ajar, and I kept a wary eye on it as I climbed the ladder up the exterior side of the building. I was ready to bolt at the first sign of movement. I was more worried about the suits of armor than the lich. If those guys in there woke up, we were fucked. Even though I was now the town's magistrate, nobody seemed to acknowledge that fact. Before, Featherfall—or, I guess, Miss Quill—had a *very* small amount of control over the guardians. I remembered when she tried to have them arrest me, and it hadn't worked. Something told me I was going to be chased out of my own town the moment they woke up no matter what I did.

Remex the lich had been quiet this whole time. Donut braved jumping to the roof, and she managed to get a hit on her map. She said it was something regular-sized, like a normal skyfowl. She said it hadn't been moving, and she didn't see anything else in the room. Her map's ability to sense mobs was better than my own, but it was also famously unreliable when it came to hidden mobs, so I was cautious.

Earlier, I'd peered through the open door of the first level to get a quick view of what was going on in there and to gauge the height of the interior ceiling. Even in the dark, I could see them. The inactive swordsmen guards. They stood in silent formation, hundreds of them, reminding me of the Chinese terra-cotta army. They didn't have dots over them on my map at all. I didn't know if that was a good thing or not.

Their metallic bodies swirled with a yellow aura, all of it leading to a point in the ceiling. There would be a soul crystal up there somewhere. Mordecai said that at night the guards were in "stasis" mode, and that they were invulnerable. I'd entertained the quick notion of locking them in their warehouse and just blowing them all to hell, including the lich, over and over again until they died, which would result in an obscene amount of experience. But it looked as if that wasn't going to happen. Not tonight.

And I couldn't just roll a bomb into the lich's chambers, either. He appeared to be the last bad guy standing, so I needed to get the bad guy soliloquy out of him before we killed him. That way we could win the quest.

We had determined that there was no mute spell in the area, or any other protections that we could see. That didn't mean there wasn't a nasty surprise waiting for us, but at least we'd be able to rely on magic.

I placed the tenth and final stick of goblin dynamite on the exterior exposed joist, using the sticky detonator charge to attach it to the structure. Each stick of hobgoblin pus allowed for up to ten simultaneous detonations with one button press. I was going to use all ten tonight if we had to. I hoped we didn't.

Below, half the village stood on the street, watching. They held torches and scythes and other items of medieval weaponry. I hadn't summoned them, but Fitz the tavern keeper had raised the alarm after he overheard Mordecai and Katia discussing the idea of a lich in town. Even though it was the equivalent of 3:30 AM, he'd rushed out, shouting that the "night patrol" needed to defend the city. Since half the town was already wide-awake with the collapse of the municipal building, it didn't take long for a crowd to form.

Before we knew it, we had a group of NPCs gathering around the warehouse. They ranged from orcs to humans to elves to dozens of other, more obscure races. But no skyfowl or the smaller chickadees. It was as if they didn't care about the plight of the city, as long as the damage remained on the ground. Across the street, smoke still rose from the collapsed debris of the mall and municipal building. The night smelled of dust and fire.

After all of our preparations, we now only had about forty minutes left before the armor suits would reanimate. The tops of distant buildings already glowed with the first signs of the faux sunrise. We had to move quickly.

"That's the last of them," I said, stepping my way to the ground. One of the rungs broke off, and I cursed. I spent a quick minute fixing it. I pulled the handmade ladder into my pack. I'd hastily built the thing with crap from my inventory. It was a rickety, slipshod combination of lengths of wood and metal weight bars that would give an OSHA inspector a coronary. It had taken me almost an hour to construct. If we survived past tonight, I was going to build another one of these, but one that would be built properly.

"You ready?" I asked.

"No," Donut said. "I don't like this plan, Carl."

Mongo was in his carrier. He'd proven that we couldn't trust him to stay still when things started to get out of control, and we definitely needed to control the narrative here. And Donut needed to focus.

We were relying on Mordecai's advice to keep ourselves alive.

"Liches come in all shapes and sizes and power levels. You never know what they're going to be," he'd said earlier this evening. "But they all have one thing in common, each and every one of them."

"What's that?" I asked.

He looked up at the ceiling wryly. "They're just like Odette. They never, ever shut the hell up. They are narcissists to a fault. And they are cowards. Now that they have grasped a handful of life, they will do whatever they can not to let it go again. That's why they always have minions. They always have elaborate, grandiose plans. That's why I think you should just blow the building and take a chance at losing the quest."

This was earlier, when we still thought that Featherfall was the lich and that his lair was in that building. But since then, Mordecai had changed his mind. He seemed to think that because we'd killed most of Remex's support system, he would be vulnerable. It was now worth the risk to approach him. Mordecai also said that it made sense that he'd hide above the warehouse of the swordsmen. A magical crystal was used to "recharge" the swordsmen each night, and anyone searching the town using magical means wouldn't see him there.

MORDECAI: Here's another wrinkle. This is obviously another boss. And since that one earlier was a neighborhood boss, I'd bet my left nipple this one is a borough boss. So even if he's been weakened, you need to come to the fight prepared.

So we made the decision. We were going to confront the lich while he was weak. He already knew we were coming. It was likely he'd been watching this whole time. So we would slowly and deliberately ring the exterior of the building with explosives, enough to turn the whole structure into dust.

My original plan was to have Donut stay outside while I went in solo. She absolutely refused.

"You promised me that I wouldn't die alone," she said. "You can't keep that promise if you die before me. We do this together."

I relented, but it required a change to the plans.

Katia now stood in the crowd. Her face was much better, much more natural. She still looked like a burn victim who fell face-first out of the ugly tree, but I wouldn't question she was a human now. I summoned her over.

"Here," I said. "Hold on to this for me." I handed her a pencillike detonator.

"Whoa, whoa," she said, backing up, refusing to take it. "Don't give that to me."

"Keep it in your inventory," I said, shoving it into her hand. "If we die, or if I say so, press the button. No questions. Just do it."

"Why don't *you* hold on to it?" she asked, looking at it like I'd just handed her a live snake. "Carl, the description says it might click on its own."

"Put it in your inventory. It'll be fine," I said.

It disappeared into her pack.

"Why me?" she asked again. She looked ill.

"We don't know if this guy has some sort of mind control. It's a lich thing. We need someone outside the sphere of influence to hold on to the boom switch just in case."

"So, what's your angle here?" she asked. "Mutually assured destruction?"

"That's right," I said. "All we want is information. All he wants is to live. It's a gamble, sure. But it's not like we're not constantly on the precipice of death anyway."

She shook her head. "Hekla warned me that you were crazy."

"Just be sure to be about a block away before you press it. There's enough dynamite in there to blow your weird snow boots back to Iceland." I raised my voice and called to the crowd. "You are all still in the blast zone. You'll want to back up. A lot."

We stepped into the warehouse as the crowd started to scatter. I gave the swordsmen a nervous glance as we quickly moved to the small trapdoor cut into the corner of the room. I pulled my ladder and began to ascend. Donut remained on my shoulder, trembling.

"It's moving. But it's going to the back corner of the room, like it's running away," Donut said.

"Don't kill us," I called as I came into the room. "You kill us, you'll die, too!"

I took a deep inhalation of breath as I examined the monster quivering in the far corner.

CARL: Not a lich, Mordecai. Not a fucking lich!

24

"DO YOU UNDERSTAND ME?" I ASKED.

"Do not approach. No, no. Stay away. Do not blow me up," Remex said. His voice came out in rasps. "Please. Do not get closer."

Confused, I examined the creature's properties. Despite all of our preparations and Mordecai's warnings, he was *not* a boss. Or a lich.

> Remex—Soul Leech Capacitor. Level 1.
>
> This is a Bereft Minion of Miss Quill.
>
> Have you ever played with a Ouija board and realized that speaking with a lost loved one just wasn't doing it for you anymore? Perhaps you wanted to kick it up a notch? Maybe bring them back to life? And then maybe make them get a job? A Soul Leech Capacitor can do that for you.
>
> These fragile but physically strong undead creatures can only be created by a Necromancer or a Dark Cleric. The spell latches onto the most loved soul of the spell's target and yanks that creature back into existence. The resurrected spirit is forever attached to the loved one. But the Soul Leech is like a nick in the plane between life and death, and they exist in neither. A simple scratch from this beast will rip your soul straight from your body. That soul power is stored in the capacitor, allowing the Leech's owner to access huge reserves of mana points.

"You know," I said to Donut, "every time I think these guys reach a new level of fucked-upedness, they surprise me. If he makes one move toward us, *Magic Missile* him."

Remex looked much like Featherfall had, only this guy was alive. Sort of. He appeared to be a zombified, featherless skyfowl. His eyes were black swirling orbs. Hazy black smoke rose from the body. Ethereal wormlike wisps swirled about the creature, like a parody of the full wings he once had.

A thin, threadlike twist of golden light flowed into the creature's chest, tethering him to a golf-ball-sized, amber-hued jewel that floated in the middle of the room. A stalk of light flowed downward through a small hole in the floor. Additional tendrils of golden light whipped about the gem, flying in all directions, as if it was seeking further items to feed. I cringed as the light ripped across me, but I didn't feel anything. It seemed the light was harmless to those who couldn't use it.

The eagle huddled in the corner, gasping. He appeared to be in agony.

CARL: What the hell is a bereft minion?

MORDECAI: It's a minion who is still alive after their controller is dead. It looks like you killed the head bad guy when you blew up Miss Quill. It happens. Quests sometimes look bigger than they really are. I should have known since it was only a silver quest. Sorry about making you waste all that dynamite. Get the information out of him, put him out of his misery, and then get back here before the swordsmen wake up. Otherwise you'll be stuck in that warehouse all day.

I quickly examined the jewel.

Soul Crystal. C-Grade.

Elf technology. It's like a wireless charger. Instead of electricity, it runs on the soul power of everything killed within the area. And instead of charging your iPhone, this particular gem

tops off the town's swordsmen guards each night. Some of that
power is also leeching into something else.

If this crystal is physically touched by living flesh, it will
shatter and cease to work.

Mordecai had already told us a bit about these things. They were
indeed worthless once they were activated. Breaking it would stop the
guards from charging up, but it wouldn't otherwise hurt them.
They'd eventually run out of juice, but it wouldn't happen right away.

"Were you watching? Did you see what I did to the outside of this
building?" I asked.

"I saw. I saw," he said. "You gave your friend the remote. My wife
cast the spell. She has a thousand eyes, all watching at once. Watching, tasting. We see all. She cast the spell through me, and the vision
comes through me and into her. But now she is gone, and it is building, building. There is nowhere to go. Her soul is lost now. With the
sunrise, the release. The release."

He wasn't making any sense.

"So Quill would cast the spells, but she would do it through you?
Is that what it means for you to be a capacitor?"

"Yes. So much power, so much power. With the little ones. With
the antennae. All of it is gathered. Gathering. She has to siphon it
away. She is gone, gone. She is gone. No spell tonight. No siphon
tonight."

"Great, another loon," Donut muttered.

I tried to make my voice soothing. He was still all the way on the
other side of the room, but I didn't want to approach him. "Tell us
about the little ones. The girls. Tell us about Featherfall and Miss
Quill. How you came to be."

The creature blinked, as if seeing us for the first time. The swirls
of light around him lashed about. The cloudiness of his eyes vanished. "Who are you? Where am I?"

I repeated my question, but more slowly. He settled into the corner, wrapping his bare, emaciated wings around himself, like he was a scared child.

"You're here for the story. I understand now. I have waited so long for someone to tell. All I had to do was tell the story, and I would be done."

"Please," I said. "Yes. Tell us, and we won't hurt you."

He nodded slowly. "Please, give me a moment. Don't kill me before it's done. I have practiced this. It's a lot, but I gotta get it out. Here is the story. He . . . Featherfall. He never liked the guards. He only held a small amount of control over them. He wanted more. He asked me, after I retired and handed the perch to him. That's right. He asked me what must be done to control the swordsmen. To control them, I said, one must know what they are. How they are animated, how they came to be. Wait, don't ask about that. That's not important. It's a tangent. We have to avoid tangents. Featherfall was shortsighted. He had no ambition other than power over this small town. His kingdom. Skyfowl ruled this world. Did you know that? Before that demon destroyed it all. I like to think of it as a metaphor. Some say the Primals . . . No. I can't. That's off script. Sorry, sorry. Please. The skyfowl were once on top of the world. In control of the Over City. It's important you know that."

"What happened?" I asked. "How did he get put into that thing?"

"You are like him. You only care about what is in front of you right now. You don't see the larger picture. I think that's what I needed to say."

> DONUT: Carl. Something is happening. Something weird. The counter is being slow as usual, but I think our views are going *really* high. I keep getting achievements for views and followers. You probably are, too. I don't understand why.

I ignored her. "Show me the small picture first. Then zoom it out for me."

Remex shifted, then continued. "Let me finish the story. Don't kill me. I have to start over if you kill me. The orc, he killed me. Years ago."

"I'm going to kill you right here and now if you don't get on with it," Donut said.

He made a half-whimper, half-cheeping noise that sounded utterly pitiful. "I shall finish. After I passed, Featherfall approached my wife. Quill. Miss Quill they say, but I don't know why they added the Miss. He asked her to help him cast the spell. He knew bringing another dark cleric like myself from the dim would make an especially strong capacitor, giving him the additional soul power he needed to subjugate the swordsmen. He put himself into the Night Votive position, with my wife in the room to assist."

I could barely follow his story. "Wait, so Miss Quill knew that you would be ripped from death and turned into what you are now? And she was okay with that?"

"Oh yes," he said. "She's not really . . . No, I can't say that. Remex. Think, think. Oh yes, she also knew Featherfall was making a grave error by casting the spell too close to the Amplifier."

"Amplifier?" I asked.

"Oh yes. You are standing before it. The roof is the antennae, and the soul crystal stores the power. It captures the energy from the lost souls in the area. It is this that keeps the swordsmen animated. High Elf magic. They are the ones who . . . No, another tangent. Wrong path. At night, the swordsmen are recharged. But Featherfall's quarters are right across the way. When he cast the spell, I was manifested and brought into existence. But he was killed by the feedback. My wife, she planned this. She'd been planning it all along, her entire life. It was exactly what was supposed to happen. I was damned the moment I became her husband. I was now a capacitor for her. She pretended as if the magistrate was still alive, and she took up the duties of running the settlement. She was a powerful mage. She had a forgery spell. It fooled everyone."

MORDECAI: You guys are running low on time. Finish this and
    get out of there.
CARL: Almost done.

"And why did you bring the women in? The prostitutes?"

"Don't . . . don't trip me up. You listen. We're getting there. First, she took control of those fool elves. She cast an illusion, a resplendent skyfowl from legend to speak to them, pretend to be an angel, make them believe their tree god is coming for them. I could make them fly, manipulate things. The avatars, I mean. She never liked getting her hands dirty. So she used them. For intimidation. Corpse removal. My avatars. One looked like my son. My boy. Lost in time. But they couldn't move far from here. So my wife instead sent the elves about on her task, to bring the women to us. These women just kept coming, searching for a better life. Over and over. Sometimes, I could see it in their eyes. They were like me. A tenner. 'Don't get undead,' they told us. 'Don't get undead. It's not worth it.' Wait, ignore that."

Getting him to stay on the subject was like trying to steer without a rudder. "Okay, but why did she bring the women to you?"

"For two reasons. My wife had grand plans, plans set forth long ago. But she needed help, help that couldn't be fully accomplished by the city elves. The krasue are easy to control. Easy to make if you have the correct materials. They fly, and they are intact and compliant during the day. Plus the act of generating them creates a powerful spike of soul power, adding to my energy. And since the raw materials come from out of town, nobody would notice she was collecting them."

Donut scoffed. "Somebody *did* notice. GumGum noticed."

"So, you power up every time something dies?" I asked.

"Yes. And my position here allows me to also leech off the souls flowing into the crystal. My wife knew this, but even she couldn't predict the sheer amount of energy. I can feel it. It is so much. Mana points. That feeling when you drink the potion, of the mana points flowing back into you, but it never stops coming."

I felt a chill. I was finally reading between the lines. We needed to hurry this along. "So, your wife was building an army? Why?"

"She was a granddaughter of the royal family. Ambition soared through her. She was going to reclaim it all. But you killed her, and you found me. She dies, but I'm never found. But this time, I have been discovered. There was an orc, once. He found me. He killed me before I finished the story."

"Focus, Remex. Tell me about Quill. When you say 'reclaim it all,' what does that mean?"

"Oh yes, of course. The spell. I need to mention the spell. She was preparing the *Final War*. It is a three-part spell. Heirloom magic. First cast by her grandfather, then her mother. Then she was to complete it. Like Scolopendra's nine-tier attack that ruined our kingdom, she has prepared something that will reclaim the Over City for the skyfowl."

"She was waiting to collect enough power before she could cast this spell, then?" I asked. "And she needed the army to do what? Protect her while she cast it?"

"That is correct. Before, during, and after. And the krasue would be her lieutenants, her eyes and ears for the battle. But she had enough power. More than enough. She'd already started. She did."

"Wait, what would have happened if she'd completed the casting?" I asked.

"Oh, it is a glorious spell. The third and final act of the *Final War* is a long, dangerous spell that takes three nights to cast. She'd done the first. Was going to do the second tonight. Thousands. Thousands of mana points. Once completed, the beasts she unleashed would sweep across the Over City and slaughter all but those whose essence she has protected, those she added to the spell."

"You mean, the feathers?" I asked. "So, the skyfowl and midget skyfowl—whatever they're called—would be safe?"

"Chickadees," Donut said. "I like those guys. They're cute."

"Yes," Remex said. "Them and their entire families. Everyone else would perish."

"Ahh," I said. I looked at Donut. "Everyone would be dead except the fliers. We just stopped a genocide."

"I guess that makes up for you killing all those baby goblins on the first floor," said Donut.

"We're not having this conversation again."

Quest completed. The Sex Workers Who Fell from the Heavens.

"Hey, we didn't even have to kill this guy," said Donut. "And we didn't have to blow up any more buildings tonight, either."

Remex laughed. It was a dry, almost airless croak. "That's it. That's it. I did it. I did it!" The dry laugh turned to sobs.

"What is he talking about, Carl?" Donut asked.

"I'll tell you later." Pity swept over me. *Jesus,* I thought, watching the undead thing cry empty tears. "Remex. It's done. You've told us the story. Do you want us to kill you or to leave you?"

"Kill me, let me live—it doesn't matter now. It doesn't matter. With the sunrise, I will be gone. As you will be, too. Listen, boy. Don't be sad. You didn't know. It's a lucky thing, a mercy to die here." He pointed toward the ground with his wing. "And not make it down there. It is so much better. Wait with me."

"What do you mean?" I asked.

The announcement wasn't just in my head. It came over the loudspeaker, like the daily update.

New Quest. The Fools Who Broke the Glass.
   THIS IS A GROUP QUEST. All crawlers currently within the 45-square-kilometer blast radius will receive this quest.
   Your party has been designated Host of this Group Quest. As hosts, you will not be allowed to opt out from this quest.
   What the hell is going on? Am I glad you asked!
   A while back a certain NPC started casting a very powerful spell, a spell so potent that it had to be completed by a future generation.

Here's the thing with old spells. They're like trees. They grow. They get big. Sometimes huge. Bad shit happens when they get screwed up. The bigger the spell, the badder the shit. And boy was this spell big. Not gonna lie. Your favorite AI was looking forward to it going off.

Oh well. This will be almost as good.

Shit is about to go down. For example, you may have noticed every Skyfowl and Chickadee NPC in the area has fallen ill. Most of them have already plunged into a coma, or death. It's not their fault, but they were tied to the spell, and that's just the way it is.

Just like it's not your fault that you happen to be within 45 kilometers of the fallout from this failed spell. Again, not your fault. (Well, unless you're Crawlers Carl, Princess Donut, or Katia Grim. Then it is your fault.) That's just the way it is. Sucks to be you.

There's going to be an explosion. The epicenter of the blast is marked on your map. Every crawler within the designated blast area is fucked.

The object of this quest is simple. Unfuck yourself. Don't die.

Warning: This is an event quest. If you do not wish to participate in this quest, you will have sixty seconds from the end of this message to get yourselves into a safe room. After that, all access to safe rooms within the quest zone will be shut off until the event quest is concluded. All NPCs who remain indoors, safe room or not, will remain safe. All mobs and neighborhood-level boss monsters within the blast radius subject to both physical and magical explosions will be killed.

Reward: All participants who survive will receive a Platinum Quest Box.

Oh, by the way. The explosion is coming in seven minutes.

Run.

"What the fuck? How is that a quest?" I cried.

MORDECAI: Run. Desperado Club. It's not a safe room, but the
second room is out of the blast radius.

KATIA: I don't have access to the club! I can't go to a safe
room because I'm a quest host!

CARL: *Protective Shell*?

MORDECAI: Won't work. Magical blast. Go.

"Fuck!" I cried. "We have to get to the club. Let's go."

"What about Katia?" Donut said. "That's not fair. We promised
we'd keep her safe. This is our fault."

"It's not," I said. I didn't bother going down the ladder. I just
jumped all the way, hitting the ground heavily. Behind me, the
guards stopped glowing. An entire wall of white dots appeared on
the map. I knew in a moment those dots were going to turn red once
the swordsmen noticed me here. Donut hesitated and leaped to my
shoulder. Her ears were flattened against her head.

Shit, shit, shit! I pulled up my map, looking for the fastest route. The
Desperado Club was three blocks away. We could make it if we ran.

"Look," I said. "This was going to happen one way or another.
That's why they tried to get that Bautista guy to kill Miss Quill, too.
They *wanted* this explosion quest to trigger."

I had a weird chat notification. I pulled it up, and the window
said **Quest Chat**.

This was different than a regular chat. This was like a Discord
chat room, with a whole group of crawler names on the list. There
were about 80 names there.

QUAN CH: Thanks a lot Carl and Donut, you fucking assholes.

That was the only message. *Oh fuck off,* I thought. I clicked it
away. But that list of names, all crawlers who were likely about to
die, stunned me. Eighty people.

I moved to also close the map, but I paused, seeing something unexpected. A tiny round star appeared where the explosion's epicenter would be. I zoomed in tight.

"Carl?" Donut said. "The guards are waking up!"

CARL: Mordecai, the soul gem is the epicenter. Not Remex. If I break the gem, will that cancel the explosion?

MORDECAI: I don't know. I don't think it will stop it. Probably make it blow early. The quest is called the Fools Who Broke the Glass for a reason. They *want* you to do that. Get the hell out of there.

DONUT: WE CAN'T ABANDON KATIA!

KATIA: It's okay. Thank you, Donut. I understand. I'm getting the NPCs back into their homes. Run, guys. Go.

DONUT: WHAT ABOUT YOU, MORDECAI?

MORDECAI: I'm in my room. I'm safe. Hurry the hell up!

"Fuck," I muttered, looking up at the hole in the ceiling.

"Carl?" Donut asked.

"Donut, we have a choice. Save ourselves. Or we try to save Katia and those other 80 people. I have an idea, but it probably won't work. We need to decide. Quick."

"I, uh, I don't know," Donut said, looking about. She seemed to deflate on my shoulder. "We should try to save the others. It's the right thing to do."

I didn't answer. I just reached up and scratched her. And then I ascended the ladder.

We returned to the room. Remex remained in the corner, his eyes closed. He appeared to be fading.

"You returned," he said. He didn't open his eyes. "Welcome to the end of days."

The soul gem hovered in the room. The entire crystal vibrated. The tendrils of light had stopped shooting from it, including the large river down into the room below and the golden strand leading into Remex.

A red timer counted down over the gem. It was at four minutes and thirty seconds.

I pulled Miss Quill's Beanie Baby from my inventory. It wasn't hard to find. Kimaris, the stuffed horse-riding soldier, was the very top item when I sorted my current inventory by value.

The second item on the list was the protective carrier it was stored in. The door to the small glass case wasn't locked. It was a small, hinged flap held closed by a cheap-looking hook and eyebolt. I opened the little door and pulled the stuffed animal back into my inventory.

I gave the glass case a quick examination.

Sheol Glass Reaper Case.

Forged in the fires of Sheol, the mysterious 15th level of the World Dungeon, these protective, expensive artifacts are built and sold by traveling Spider Reaper Minions. They also sell lollipops, which are said to be out of this world.

When you absolutely, positively want to keep something safe, put it in this box. It will protect against *most*—but not all—forms of abuse.

Warning: Every time you open this case, there is a 1.5% chance you will be blasted with the *Sheol Fire* spell. That's not a good thing. The item within the case will remain protected.

I swallowed. I probably should have read that description before I'd opened it to pull the Beanie out. I kept the door open now.

I remembered that moment we'd jumped from the civic building and landed in the debris. There'd been a flash of light. Looking back now, I realized it'd been deliberate. The system had brought my attention to the case. It was just like any regular game. Seemingly random objects were sometimes placed there intentionally, just to keep the game fair. That's what this was.

I held the case in my hand, and I approached the pulsing gem. Careful not to touch it with my hands, I closed the case around the floating gem, like I was catching a firefly with my two hands. I shut the door, and I gingerly hooked it closed.

I tried to pull the whole thing into my inventory, and I received an error.

Yeah. Nice try, asshole.

"Oh, fuck off," I said. I hadn't expected that to work. After taking a deep breath, I let go. I cringed as the case fell a couple inches, clinking to a stop as it fell against the gem floating within. But it remained there, floating. The gem itself was starting to vibrate faster and faster, with little cracks forming along the edge. The glass case's description—that it protected against "most" forms of abuse—did not give me confidence. A magical explosion that was going to flatten 45 square kilometers of dungeon seemed like it would probably be pretty high on the short list of attack types that would break this thing.

We still had two and a half minutes on the countdown. Not even close to the amount of time we'd need to get to safety.

"Oh my god, Carl. Is that going to work?" Donut asked.

"I don't know. I doubt it. But it's worth a try." I paused. "I'm sorry, Donut. I should have told you my idea before forcing you to choose."

She made a grunting noise. "You always pretend like I'm the stubborn one, but once your mind is made up, Carl, it's impossible to change it. There's nothing to be sorry for."

I sat on the ground, exhausted. Donut jumped into my lap, and we stared at the floating glass case.

Remex rocked back and forth in the corner, muttering, "I'm coming, son. Any minute now. I'm coming. I missed you so much. I'm coming."

"What is he talking about?" Donut asked.

"He was a crawler," I said. "He called himself a tenner. I reckon that means someone who got out on the tenth floor. I think he might've been famous once. It explains the views."

"Carl, I don't want to become an NPC," Donut said. "I guess it won't matter if we die."

I reached up and scratched her head. Forty-five seconds. "I'm proud of you—you know that?"

"Why?"

"You've grown. You being worried about Katia? You don't even know her, but you'd promised to keep her safe. My first instinct was to abandon her."

She laughed. "I just don't want Hekla mad at us. We already have that Lucia Mar after us. And Maggie My. And the Maestro's dad."

I chuckled. Fifteen seconds. "Can't say we didn't try—that's for sure."

"Carl?" she asked.

I looked down into her large glowing eyes. "Yeah?"

"I'm not as dumb as I pretend to be. I know she's dead."

"I know." I wrapped myself around her. We both closed our eyes and braced for the end.

25

REMEX SCREAMED. THE SUDDEN, TERRIFYING NOISE JOLTED MY eyes open. I took in the room.

"Fuck," I said, scrambling up. I jumped for the case, which had fallen to the ground.

We hadn't died. Obviously. Light streamed from the container like a miniature caged sun. The explosion had been completely silent. Lancelike rays burst from the glass, one of them streaming directly into Remex's chest, who was now on the floor, screaming and convulsing. Whatever had happened to him, it had bestowed upon him the ability to roar with supernatural volume.

The case itself glowed red-hot. The floor was on fire, the wooden floorboards bubbling and bowing under the extreme heat. I feared the whole thing was about to fall through, taking us with it. The glass case and gem had transformed itself. I didn't have time to read the full description, but my eyes focused on the **Status: Explosion Imminent** in the two seconds before I grabbed it. *Please, please,* I thought. My fingers burned as I pulled it into my inventory. I cried out as the caged explosion disappeared.

"Holy shit," I said as I cast *Heal* on myself. My skin had burned off so thoroughly and quickly it barely even hurt for the initial two seconds. That changed as it started to heal itself. I gasped in pain.

A page of notifications appeared. I waved them away for now. I examined the newest item in my inventory.

Carl's Doomsday Scenario.

Type: Unstable custom explosive.

Effect: An explosion large enough to rattle the teeth of a god.

Status: Explosion Imminent $(3/1 \times 10^7)$

Created by a man who murders babies and steals rare collectibles from his elders, this device is powerful enough to level an entire city and all the suburbs around it. It is created by combining a massively overloaded soul crystal and a Sheol Glass Reaper Case.

Warning: This item can no longer be stabilized.

"The quest hasn't ended," said Donut. "But we're not dead, either."

I just sat there on the floor, breathing heavily. My hand ached, my fingers and palm pulsing despite the healing. I couldn't believe that had worked. I hadn't been able to put it into my inventory until after it had exploded. But what the hell was I going to do with the thing? The moment I removed it from my inventory, it would explode. I would have less than a second.

At least we were alive.

"Uh, Carl," Donut said a moment later. "You don't happen to have any more of those glass cases, do you? Maybe a really big one?"

I looked up to see Remex still convulsing on the ground.

"Oh mother fuck," I said.

"You sure have been swearing a lot lately. I'm not sure I like that, Carl."

Now Remex had a timer over him. Twenty minutes. It hadn't started counting down yet, but the timer blinked red. I cringed as the new notification came.

Quest Update.

You've probably noticed you're not dead. Everybody say, "Thank you, Crawler Carl." I'll give you a second to luxuriate in your victory.

That's the good news. You might want to sit down for this next part.

Remex shrieked, and the world went white for a moment. I suddenly felt heavier, more tired. A massive racket filled the warehouse, like the sound of dozens of pots and pans crashing to the ground.

"What happened?" Donut asked.

"It's like when we're in a production trailer. We just lost all of our equipment stat buffs."

The bad news is there's still an explosion coming. A bigger bang, actually, but the area of effect will be similar. I won't bore you guys with the technical details, but what you just felt is called a precursor burst. It's a foreshock. The first of four before the big show. The one you just felt temporarily removed the magical properties of all your equipped gear. The next one will do something different.

All of this will culminate with a burst of pure, wild magic much more potent than the magically infused chemical explosion from which you guys were just spared. Less physical damage to the environment. More face melting. I prefer this, if we're being honest. Have you ever put a marshmallow in a microwave? Imagine your head as the marshmallow. It'll be kinda like that. Prepare your defenses accordingly.

You now have twenty minutes to save yourselves.

"Come on," I said. "We gotta go." I stood and turned, once again, for the small trapdoor. I gave one last look at Remex, who remained in the corner convulsing. Every instinct told me to put him out of his misery, but I knew that would likely be a Very Bad Idea.

And that's when the floor collapsed.

I cried out, landing in a heap in the midst of a room full of sizzling armor pieces and swords. The EMP-like burst from Remex had deactivated all of the swordsmen guards, causing the armor to fall to the ground like junk. I groaned as I pulled a few random pieces of armor, along with a colossal broadsword, into my inventory. I yanked myself to my feet and downed a healing potion. At least those still worked.

Remex hadn't fallen through. A loud electric hum now emanated from him, still up on the second floor, just beyond the hole in the ceiling. The noise grew louder until it overwhelmed his constant screams.

"Where are we going?" Donut asked. We rushed from the building and turned right, heading due east. I pulled up the quest chat and started furiously typing instructions, giving people their two options for escape.

MORDECAI: Take off every magical item you have and put it in
    your inventory. Stop whatever you're doing and do it now.
    It'll be safe in your inventory, but not on your skin. I don't
    know what the hell you just did, but your current situation
    is only barely better.
CARL: I don't have any clothes that aren't magical except my
    jacket. Even my underwear is magic now.
MORDECAI: Goddamnit, Carl. No time to argue. Nobody is going
    to care about your trunk swinging in the air.
DONUT: WHAT ABOUT MY CROWN?

Thanks to the tiara's *Fleeting* status, it would disappear if she removed it. And then it would be given to another crawler, which would be a very bad thing. Only one of them would be allowed to proceed to the tenth floor. Mordecai paused for an unusually long time.

MORDECAI: Better leave it on. But there's a chance you might
    lose it. It's possible one of those bursts is going to have a
    negative effect on your stats permanently. You might get
    hit with Sepsis, too. The poison effect will be negated, but

> it'll still stagger you. Wild soul magic is unpredictable. It
> turns your own magical items against you. Keep Mongo
> locked up.

Dozens of responses to my group chat post poured in as I pulled my gear off, including my underwear. I also removed my xistera, just to be safe. Removing the stuff was easy, a lot easier than putting it on. I could just transfer it directly to my inventory. *Goddamnit,* I thought, reading the messages in the chat. Three different crawlers had given me the same response. The entrance to the back room at the Desperado Club had disappeared when the safe rooms closed off. They were insulating the club from the impending disaster.

That left us with only one escape.

Katia came jogging up, along with a handful of other crawlers, mostly human. I didn't know any of them. Daniel Bautista was not among them.

"Okay, guys," I said. "If you haven't already, magical gear off. We have sixteen minutes, and we need to run at full speed. We're out of time."

The group just looked at me. Finally, one of them said, "Dude, why are you naked?"

I pointed east. "Go!"

THE NEXT PULSE OCCURRED JUST AS WE LEFT TOWN. A MAN NEAR the back of the group exploded, just like that. His name had been **Conrad E**, and he'd had a Russian accent. He'd been a level 12 Ranger.

"What the hell was that?" I asked as I ran. Ahead, three emu-like mobs appeared, screeching. They were called **Ruin Flockers**. Donut hit two of them with magic missiles as another mage hit the third with a lightning burst. That third ostrich didn't die, but hit the ground. I stomped its neck as we continued running.

"His quiver. All of his arrows blew up, I think," Katia said. "He'd put his bow away, but he'd forgotten about his arrows."

"Donut," I said. "I don't like this. I think you should take it off."

Donut remained on my shoulder, despite being faster than me. Behind, someone shouted about another mob. "Leave it!" I yelled.

"I'll lose five intelligence!" Donut whined. "And my Sepsis debuff. And I really like it."

"These bursts are attacking our magical gear," I said.

"But if I lose it, somebody else will get it and put it on. We'll have to fight them. I don't want to hurt a person."

"I know," I said. I didn't want that, either. I didn't add that only an idiot would actually put the thing on after reading the description. Anybody still around at this point would know better, so I wasn't too worried about that anymore. I leaped over a pile of rubble. We were coming up on ten minutes. A pair of dead crawlers appeared on my map, surrounded by the red dots of street urchins. We didn't have time to investigate.

Before, I'd never been the fastest runner. I had good endurance, more so than a lot of the guys who only trained on weights, but I'd never been a speed guy. I'd always hated jogging, but I played a lot of basketball. Not many team sports trained cardio like basketball, except maybe tennis or soccer. And probably jai alai, too.

Now I ran through the city with ease, moving much, much faster than I'd ever been able to before. My breaths came in ragged gasps, but my body didn't slow down. It was an odd, disconcerting feeling. If we survived this, I really needed to push myself more physically, to test my limits. My brain still thought of myself as a normal human. As a group, even the slowest amongst us moved faster than a squad of Olympians ever could've. I recalled my poor long-lost chopper. It wouldn't have done well on this level, not with all the debris in the streets.

"Well, I'm not taking it off," Donut said.

"That dude blew up, Donut," I said. To our left, a group of four more crawlers appeared. They merged with us.

"Are we sure it's there?" one of them, a shark-headed creature, called.

"It's there!" another yelled back. "I can see it on my map already."

I turned my attention back to Donut. The next burst was due at any moment. They weren't coming at exact five-minute intervals. "What's going to happen if you permanently lose five intelligence, and then you lose the tiara anyway? Then you'll be down ten instead of five."

"But it was my first item," she said.

"It also might catch your damn head on fire. Besides, remember the description? You'll still be an official princess."

"Donut, he's right. You better take it off," Katia said.

"Oh, all right," Donut grumbled.

The Sepsis Crown atop her head crumbled into dust, disappearing like ash.

"Hey!" Donut yelled. To my left, one of the newcomers also cried out. His pants vanished. "It disappeared before I could remove it!"

The second pulse had apparently activated all magical weapons. This third one had destroyed any still-equipped armor.

The fourth pulse ripped through the party just as we pulled up to the small, decrepit building. We'd run the distance in record time.

Chaos tore through the group. A lightning bolt ripped through the party, glancing off a human who tumbled and hit the ground, almost dead. Another person simply teleported away. Katia's whole body glowed, and she leaped forward, clipping me in the process and throwing me down. She ran directly into the wall, and blasted through it like the Kool-Aid Man. I bounced off the floor, crying out. Donut hissed and leaped away. I felt my arm break in that moment Katia slammed into me, but it was healed by the time I finished rolling.

You have been poisoned!

It took me a long moment to figure out what the hell had just happened. Normally, I was immune to poison, but that came from my nightgaunt cloak. Donut had also been poisoned, but she was also now immune thanks to her Former Child Actor class.

The first two items in everyone's hotlist had activated themselves on their own. *So much for items in our inventory being safe.* For both me and Donut, it was a healing potion and then a mana potion. We'd both ingested the second potion before the potion timer ended, inflicting us both with potion sickness. I knew Katia had an active skill called Rush, something she could only do once a day, and that's what'd happened to her.

The poison effect kicked me in the stomach, doubling me over. Once the fifteen seconds passed, I took an antidote potion and surveyed the crowd. We'd all stopped dead in the street outside the building. Katia returned, a dazed look in her eyes. Her nose had been knocked completely sideways and was now just below her ear. She didn't seem to have noticed.

"That really hurt," she said.

Nobody had been killed, but we didn't know what happened to the guy who'd teleported away. I leaned over the human who'd been cooked with the *Lightning* spell. He was unconscious. I poured a healing potion into his mouth. This was one of the newcomers who'd met us as we'd run here. The Asian man's eyes fluttered, then snapped open.

"Please get your dick out of my face," he said. I grinned and backed away.

I looked over my shoulder, and through the hole in the wall Katia had created, I could see it. I glanced at the timers up in the corner of my vision. We had three minutes before the big detonation.

We also had two days and 18 hours left before this floor would collapse.

A familiar face appeared, jogging up with a new group. Daniel Bautista.

"I told you it was here," he said, indicating the stairwell down to the fourth level.

I clapped him on the shoulder. The man nodded and turned toward the stairwell, disappearing down to the fourth floor.

We didn't have a choice. I was going to just send everyone

without Desperado Club access to the stairwell, but with the club closed off, it was either this or death.

"Go," I said. "Everybody down the stairs."

We watched as the procession of people lined up and rushed down the hole.

CARL: Mordecai, are you in your room?

MORDECAI: I'm safe.

CARL: What's going to happen to us when we go down early? Or you?

MORDECAI: I am going to sit here and twiddle my thumbs for three days. You guys won't notice a time difference. I'll see you on the other side. Also, I just peeked out the door. The NPCs are all safe, all that I can see. Nobody is on the street except the guards, who reactivated with that second burst. They all only have a single life point. It's too bad you're not here. Otherwise I'd have you kill as many as you can. It wouldn't be as much experience when you're just finishing them off, but it would still be quite a bit.

I glanced over at Katia, who stood at the entrance to the stairwell, waiting for us.

CARL: Are there any guards still in the warehouse?

MORDECAI: I don't know. Probably a few. They're still moving out to their regular positions. I'm not going over there to look. Now get your asses into that stairwell.

CARL: Okay. Oh, and, Mordecai?

MORDECAI: What?

CARL: Congratulations.

He didn't answer. Donut looked up at me, eyes wide. "That's right," she said. "He's free now, isn't he? We make it to the fourth floor, and he gets to go home once the dungeon is over."

"That's right," I said. I thought of Remex, who was also about to finish his "duty." I wondered how long he'd been stuck here. I remembered what Donut had said when she learned what he really was. *Carl, I don't want to become an NPC.*

And she'd said something else, too. It was heartbreaking, when you thought about it. *I know she's dead.*

I thought of everyone we'd met on this floor, of the crawlers and NPCs we'd come across. We'd been on the floor less than a week, but it felt like a millennium. I thought of Signet the half-naiad. Of Quint the possum-faced pharmacist. Pustule the hobgoblin explosives dealer. I thought of poor GumGum the orc. Of Miss Quill. Of little Ricky Joe, the one-armed child dwarf. I wondered if his mom ever had her baby.

The three of us turned toward the stairwell. Donut pulled Mongo out of his cage, and the dinosaur grunted with annoyance for being stuck so long.

We proceeded down the stairs. I knew from the last time, the floor ended the moment we pulled on the handle. The door at the bottom of the stairs was the same as always, with the oversized kua-tin carving, making them look bigger and more menacing than they really were.

You're not going to break me. Fuck you all.

I examined its properties.

Entrance to the fourth floor.
   This is where the real fun begins.
   Mind the gap.

"What does that mean?" I asked.

We had 100 seconds left.

"Katia," I said. "Pull out that detonator I gave you earlier. It has a ten-second delay. Wait until the timer is at about 15 seconds and push it. Then we'll go in before it goes off."

"Why?" she asked, pulling the pencillike detonator out. The

thing had a range of ten kilometers, so we were more than close enough. "Won't that make the bomb go off faster?"

"Yes, but only by a couple seconds. If people aren't safe by now, they're already dead. I doubt it's going to work, since the detonators are magical. They probably got ruined in that first burst. But if it does, I set the dynamite. I let Donut smush a few of the detonator blobs onto the wall. If we get any experience for it, we'll all share in the spoils."

She shrugged. Just as the timer hit 20 seconds, she pressed the button.

We turned to open the door.

"Hey, Carl," said Donut just as we started to dissolve away. "You probably should have put your pants back on when we still could get into our inventory, don't you think? Aren't we going straight to Odette's show?" She cackled with laughter.

I looked down at the cat, horrified.

"Goddamnit, Donut," I said.

EPILOGUE

"IT LOOKS LIKE WE NOW HAVE DEFINITIVE PROOF THAT SEX TAPE with the late Maestro was indeed a snick," Odette mused. The audience roared. Donut was on her back, howling with laughter as my cheeks burned.

I never considered myself a shy person. I'd been wandering the dungeon wearing nothing but boxers for weeks now. But the sight of myself up on the screen, running full tilt through the Over City with nothing but a one-armed leather jacket and my nuts dangling free filled me with a strange, almost primal sense of vulnerability. I don't know how nudists ever got used to it.

The interview was going well. So far, we'd received nothing but softball questions. I knew that'd soon change. It was still early.

All four of us—Me, Donut, Mongo, and Katia—had gone through the door and immediately appeared in the greenroom. There was a slight, odd *pop* in my brain, similar to the one I'd experienced the very first time I entered the dungeon, but that was it. There was no other sense that two and a half days had passed.

"Whoa," Katia said, spinning in circles at the sight of the greenroom. She stopped, putting her hands out to steady herself. "Are we on a boat?"

I didn't answer her. I only stared. She had changed to a stunning, short-haired woman. Black-haired, probably in her mid-thirties, pale with light wide-set eyes that sat at an odd angle on her face.

"Katia," Donut said, "you're getting really good at the sculpting thing. Plus I like you better with black hair. It gives you more poise."

She reached up and touched her features, then relaxed. "This is the real me, Donut."

As Donut explained to her where we were, I proceeded to the bathroom to build myself a loincloth made of toilet paper. My hands shook as I wrapped the paper around my legs.

Holy shit, I thought. Our last few hours on the third floor had gone by quickly and unexpectedly. And now that I had a moment to breathe, my heart couldn't stop pounding. I found myself sitting on the bathroom floor, my hand to my chest. *How is this real? How is this my life?*

I knew this respite would be short-lived. After we were done here, we'd move onto the fourth floor, and it would start all over again.

"Carl, hurry up. I gotta wee!" Donut said, barging into the bathroom. She stopped short. Her tail drooped at the sight of me there on the floor. A look of concern flashed across her cat face. She didn't say anything for a few seconds. "You better get back out there. Katia and Mongo are eating all the human snacks. Lexis is in there. She said Katia is going to be on the show, too, but only at the end of the interview. She said it's a fourth-floor special, and we're going live just before the floor opens up."

"Come here, Donut," I said.

She immediately jumped onto my lap, butting her head against my chest. "Carl, are you okay?"

"I'll be fine," I said. I gave her head a quick pat. It was strange without her tiara. "What about you? We thought we were going to die, and then we weren't, and it's been nonstop since."

"You need to sleep," she said, also deflecting the question. "Let's do the interview and find a safe room and rest. Okay?"

"Okay," I said, sitting up. I put my arms out, revealing my toilet paper loincloth. "So? What do you think?"

"Are you asking me to lie, Carl?"

"Yes, I am."

Thirty minutes later, I sat on the couch in my ridiculous makeshift loincloth as we watched our last moments on the third floor play out on the screen.

Odette leaned back. "Before I show you what happened next, I want to bring out the newest member of the Royal Court of Princess Donut. Everyone say hello to Katia. And welcome back to the show, Mongo!"

Katia sat next to me on the couch while Mongo padded out and squawked at the virtual crowd, who screamed enthusiastically at the velociraptor. He curled up on the floor in front of Donut. Despite being in his box most of the night, even he seemed exhausted.

After a few initial questions to Katia, which she answered with deer-in-the-headlights, one-word responses, Odette sighed and turned back to me.

"So, guys," she said. "You were only gone for two days, but a lot can happen in two days. Isn't that right?" The audience laughed almost nervously, which made *me* nervous. "So, what do you think happened after you hit that detonator?"

I shrugged. "I was hoping for an explosion at the warehouse, but I know the hobgoblin pus is a magical detonator, so I suspect maybe it was fried and nothing happened."

She clapped, nodding her bug head vigorously. "Smart, smart boy."

The audience had grown dead quiet. An electric feeling of apprehension washed over me. *Uh-oh. What is this?*

"Believe it or not, you're supposed to be dead. You're right. Hobgoblin pus *is* a magical trigger. By all accounts, it *should* have been rendered inert by the initial precursor burst. And if by chance it hadn't, that second burst, which activated all magical weapons, should have set it off, which would've exploded the dynamite, which would have killed Remex the Grand, triggering that final, cataclysmic explosion."

Remex the Grand? "But that didn't happen," I said.

"No," she agreed. "It did not. The Borant Corporation immediately filed an appeal against the AI's decision to rule the detonator exempt from both of those blasts. Just before you came on today, Borant was overruled by a Syndicate court. In addition, and even more importantly, the court ruled the achievements you received as a result of the explosion are also just, and the rewards must be paid."

"Achievements?" Donut asked, perking up. "Rewards?"

"But," Odette continued, "per Syndicate rules, the host is allowed a single veto each season. This is important. It's almost always used to throw an appeal in their favor on the tenth or deeper floors. It has *never* been used this early. And Borant was forced to use their free veto on the prize decision, which reversed the ruling. So, unfortunately for you guys, you won't be receiving what you should. Still, everybody saw what happened. Everybody saw what you were rewarded. Sadly, you won't be getting it."

"What?" Donut said. "I don't understand. What are we not getting?"

"Okay, first, let's watch what really happened after Katia pressed that button."

The screen changed to a view of a news-like program I'd never seen before. It was a news desk setup, similar to the recap show, but with an alien-like Soother host.

The Soother spoke with the practiced ease of a seasoned newscaster. "And while the tragic, controversial tale of Remex the Grand finally comes to an end, a new controversy has erupted in Borant's *Dungeon Crawler World*. A last-minute decision by a trio of trapped crawlers ended in an unexpected result. A result with potentially disastrous, real-life consequences for Borant. Watch this."

I bristled at the newscaster's use of "real-life." The screen showed Katia pressing the button. The scene switched to the view of the warehouse, and of the pus detonating. Multiple swordsmen guards, all with their health in the very deep red, tumbled to the ground. The view switched to the second floor, to the pitiful, curled-up form of Remex hiding in the corner. He'd become nothing but a silhouette of pulsing yellow. In the two seconds before that final explosion, the light disappeared. He cried out in pain just as he was overwhelmed with the blast from the dynamite.

The newscaster continued. "A controlled blast at the last second, which caused a mass soul crystal release from the fallen swordsmen, greatly tempered the resulting wild magic explosion, causing it to be much less destructive than originally intended. In the end, thousands of NPCs and several dozen crawler lives were potentially saved by the action."

I groaned. "Does that mean we didn't have to go down the stairs?"

"Nope," Odette said. She waved her hand, and the screen paused. She looked at us, feigning sympathy. "Do you know how many Celestial prize boxes have been given out in the history of *Dungeon Crawler World*?"

Donut leaped to her feet. Mongo also jumped up, tail waving in excitement.

"Oh my god, shut up, Odette," Donut said, eyes huge. "Are you saying we're getting screwed out of a Celestial box?" She turned to the audience. "This is an outrage!"

Odette nodded. "The answer is 2,145. That's how many Celestial boxes of any kind have been given out. I myself was the recipient of three. The record to a single crawler is four. And before this crawl, the most that have ever been given out in a single season is 18. That was a Naga season long, long ago. You might not be aware of this, but the host company is required to pay taxes to the Syndicate on each and every non-sponsored box given out. They are given a handful of free Celestials each season, but anything above that comes with a pretty hefty bill for the showrunners. And each one is more expensive than the last. That's usually offset by a million other line items that flow into the production. For example, we pay an exorbitant amount to get your butts in that chair."

"As you should," Donut said, her voice still filled with anger. The audience laughed.

"It has been over 250 cycles since the Blood Sultanate of the Naga ran the first crawl to actually lose money, and they are *still* recovering from it. They haven't run a season since then. They only have a place in Faction Wars because they purchased a permanent spot early on."

"For just 18 boxes?" I said. "That seems over the top."

"That season was cursed for multiple reasons, but we don't need to get into that. Anyway, the game is *supposed* to be difficult. Legendary boxes are handed out like candy because they're cheap, but Celestial boxes are an order of magnitude better. The prize in a single box can render an underperforming crawler almost immortal, practically unbeatable until they reach the tenth floor. If they capriciously hand them out, more crawlers will make it to the deeper levels, and the showrunners can drag the season out and earn much more money. So the Syndicate places a heavy premium on such items. And while the AI usually chooses the prizes, the writers running the show are responsible for creating the circumstances in which the boxes are earned. It's a careful balance."

I was trying really hard not to break the golden rule, which was *Thou shalt not talk shit about Borant.* I was finding it very difficult.

"It's just three boxes," Donut grumbled. "I don't see why they had to waste their stupid veto on keeping me, Carl, and Katia from getting an awesome prize."

Odette cocked her head to the side. "Maybe I should show you the rest of that news report." She waved her hand, and the frozen scene resumed. It now showed an Asian half-elf crawler dragging himself into a safe room after obviously surviving the magical blast that had been meant to kill him. He appeared gravely injured, likely from his own equipment turning on him. The show labeled him as the level 15 crawler **Quan Ch**, a class called an **Imperial Security Trooper**. This was the same guy who'd called us assholes in the chat.

"He survived," Donut said. "I'm glad. I felt kind of bad about what I did."

"What do you mean?" I asked.

"Oh, I blocked him from the chat after he called us assholes," said Donut. "You can't let people in your chat rooms get out of control, Carl. You need to rule with an iron paw."

The newscast continued as I looked incredulously at Donut. "As a result of surviving the event quest, all crawlers in the initial blast zone were promised a Platinum Quest Box. But as you're about to see, the survivors received something a little better than that."

We all watched as Quan Ch pulled up his achievements.

> **New achievement! Bandit!**
>
> Screw Hadji. Hadji was a little bitch anyway. You have completed a quest, but it was completed in a way unusual enough to trigger the Bandit Achievement! Unlike the real Bandit, who is usually instrumental in helping Jonny Quest complete his tasks, you didn't actually do anything to deserve this prize. But that's okay because you're still getting it. This is one of the rare achievements that can be rewarded more than once.
>
> *Reward:* Your Platinum Quest box has been upgraded two times to a Celestial Quest Box!

The scene showed him reverently opening the box to receive what looked like a glowing robe. The show didn't give the robe's description, but the moment Quan put it on, he floated off the ground. Magical, wisp-like wings grew from the back of his body. His left hand glowed blue.

The newscaster continued. "An incredible total of 83 Celestial boxes were rewarded as a result of the quest getting a rare double upgrade. Borant immediately appealed, but not before that one box was opened, thus putting Borant on the hook for that one. The Syndicate court has convened an emergency session to determine if the beleaguered company will have to pay for the remaining 82 boxes. If so, it is certain there will be no financial recovery for the once-mighty Borant system."

"So that jerk got a free box for *our* hard work!" Donut cried. "Are you kidding me? And we don't get *anything*? Are we still getting a platinum box?"

"I'm afraid not," Odette said. "Their veto negated all prizes. Nobody is receiving a loot box from that quest except that one crawler.

That same night, they issued a patch that disabled both the Hadji and Bandit upgrade achievements."

I laughed. Everybody turned to look at me.

"It's not funny, Carl," Donut said. She was not acting. The cat trembled with rage.

"Why is that so amusing to you, Carl?" Odette asked.

I shrugged. "It doesn't matter what we do. How hard we work. We keep getting screwed. Losing out sucks, but I've come to expect it. All that matters is getting stronger, getting more experience. We messed that up by getting involved in quests when we should be grinding. We're not going to make that mistake again. From now on, it's all about progression and training."

Odette replied, "You probably didn't miss out on as much experience as you think. That magical burst was muted, but it was still big. You may not have received prizes or experience from the quest, but you still got credit for the actual explosion. Because you technically caused it, your team received a handful of experience for every mob that it killed, including all those swordsmen guards."

She waved her hand, and our stats and levels appeared over our heads. The audience gasped, and then broke out into applause.

Donut had risen seven levels, from 19 to 26. I had risen six, from 21 to 27. The last time I'd set foot in a safe room, I'd been level 19. That meant I had 24 stat points to distribute.

And then there was Katia.

She'd leaped 12 levels. She'd gone from nine to 21.

Odette turned to the audience. "As I promised you guys at the start of the show, I have exclusive breaking news to share. The fourth floor will be opening up in less than an hour, but I have received a tentative draft of the leaderboard. Would you like to see it?"

"Yes! Yes, we would," Donut said, hopping up and down. All semblance of anger—and her usual posh television persona—had fled. The crowd roared.

"Bear in mind, this won't be official until the next recap episode, and as you all know, things can change quickly in the dungeon, so this might shift. But I can reveal this is the current working copy. Nobody knows the exact formula for the leaderboard. It's a mix of views, favorites, levels, and money earned. But the list usually matches pretty well with the most popular players in the game. Are you ready?"

"Carl," Donut said, shaking with excitement. "We're going to be on it. I just know it!"

Odette waved her hand, and the top-10 list appeared.

CURRENT LEADERBOARD:

1. Lucia Mar—Lajabless—Black Inquisitor General—Level 29– 1,000,000
2. Hekla—Amazonian—Shieldmaiden—Level 28–500,000
3. Prepotente—Caprid—Forsaken Aerialist—Level 27– 400,000
4. Florin—Crocodilian—Shotgun Messenger—Level 24– 300,000
5. Miriam Dom—Human—Shepherd—Level 27–200,000
6. Carl—Primal—Compensated Anarchist—Level 27–100,000
7. Donut—Cat—Former Child Actor—Level 26–100,000
8. Ifechi—Human—Physicker—Level 18–100,000
9. Li Jun—Human—Street Monk—Level 25–100,000
10. Elle McGib—Frost Maiden—Blizzardmancer—Level 13– 100,000

Donut squealed with delight. "Carl, we're in the top ten! And Hekla is number two!" She turned to the audience. "I love her. She demonstrates such dignity. Such grace. I can't believe that ugly Lucia Mar is number one. Isn't she just awful?" The audience laughed.

"Who is Prepotente?" I asked, reading down the list. I knew Florin was the crocodile-headed dude with the shotgun. Miriam Dom was the goat lady. I didn't know Ifechi. Li Jun was the Chinese guy from the Maestro's show, the one I'd helped save from the troglodytes and brindle grubs. I was happy to see him on the list. I hoped Zhang and the others in his group were doing well, too.

"Carl, is that who I think it is?" Donut asked, pointing at the final name.

I nodded. Holy shit. Wheelchair-bound, dementia-suffering Mrs. McGibbons, one of the residents of the Meadow Lark Adult Care Community, was on the list. She was only level 13, having started the third floor as a level one. How in the hell had that happened? I hadn't talked to Brandon in several days.

"That's our show, folks! Tomorrow we will have an engineer from Borant on to discuss the ins and outs of this new, exciting level. I don't yet know what it is, but rumor has it, we'll see something that's never been attempted before. We'll also have a pair of crawler special guests. They're not on the top-ten list, but these up-and-comers are quickly becoming new favorites. Here's a hint: They're twins!" The crowd roared.

The audience faded away. "I really need to talk to you guys, but I only have a few minutes," Odette said. She didn't pull off her mask like she usually did. "I'm going on my own interview in five, on a different program. We'll be live-commenting on the opening of the floor. I'm going to get flak for not asking you about the assassination attempt, but Borant said it was off-limits. And Mordecai has reiterated that point several times."

"Do you just, like, watch him all day?" Donut asked.

"I do," Odette said, as if that was a perfectly normal thing to say. "As much as I can. This next floor is going to be especially dangerous." She looked at me. "Be careful with that gauntlet. It has the power to summon the war god Grull if you use it against any of his celebrants. They'll start appearing on this floor. And King Rust has apparently just spent a lot of money on a deity sponsorship. The Skull Empire doesn't usually purchase those, so it might be an attempt to get to you. I don't know which god they've sponsored, but if I was still a gambler, I'd bet on Grull."

"Can the god get to us if I don't accidentally summon him?"

"Probably not. Not on this floor. Ask Mordecai how that all works." She paused. "He has a lot of experience in the subject, unfortunately."

Lexis entered the room. "Katia, dear," the production assistant said. "Can you follow me, please? I need to show you the return procedures. Donut, you can assist if you'd like."

"Uh, sure," Katia said, getting up and leaving the room.

Donut paused, looking between me and Odette. It was obvious Odette wanted to talk to me alone. I moved my head, indicating for her to leave. She looked as if she was about to object, but then she thought better of it.

"Bye, Odette," she said as she and Mongo followed Katia.

"I don't know what the next floor's theme is," Odette said, watching them leave. "But based on what I'm hearing, momentum-based crawlers will have a strong advantage, so keep her around if you can. But I called her out of the room because I wanted to warn you."

"About Katia?" I said. "She seems harmless. And Mordecai really likes her."

"I don't think she's in on it. Not willingly. I'm talking about Hekla. She's not evil. Or psychotic like Lucia Mar. However, she is very practical. And cunning. She does not have your sense of justice, which makes her dangerous. I've watched her some, and she's becoming obsessed with the idea of getting Donut to join her gang."

"Hekla seems great, but I don't think we'd work well together. I can only handle one huge personality at a time, and Donut fits in that slot pretty well."

"Based on her conversations with her now-former guide, I don't think she wants you in the party anyway. She thinks you're unstable. But she knows about Mordecai, thanks to Katia, and since Mordecai is part of Donut's package deal, she wants Donut in the party so she can have access to a permanent manager."

"I don't think Donut would ever leave me," I said, looking at the door.

"No, I don't, either. Not as long as you're still alive."

I felt a chill rush through me.

"But again, I don't believe Katia is in on it. And she likes you. I can tell."

"Why are you telling me this, Odette?" I asked.

She chuckled. "I'm glad you're still following my first piece of advice. I lied earlier when I said I was paying an exorbitant amount to get you two on the show. When I bought your rights, it was very early, and you were very cheap. I paid less for the entire season of interviews than one pays to get you two on right now. If you die and Donut joins Brynhild's Daughters, my contract is voided. You two are still my highest-rated guests. In fact, I think that top-ten list is bunk. You two should be numbers two and three."

The top-10 list still floated there in the middle of the room.

"Odette," I asked, reading the list again, "what are those numbers at the end of each name? That million and 100,000?"

"That's just the bounty," she said. "It's how much other crawlers get if they kill you. Now I must leave. Be careful out there. I'll see you after the next floor collapse."

Odette faded away, leaving me alone, bobbing slowly up and down with the waves.

"Fuck," I said to the empty room.

BOOK 2 BONUS MATERIAL

BACKSTAGE AT
THE PINEAPPLE CABARET

PART TWO

GRANDMA LLAMA

RUN. RUN, MY LOVE. I'M RIGHT BEHIND YOU.

Grandma Llama's eyes snapped open. The yellow temple. She'd been dreaming of that place again, and of her husband's last words to her. He'd smiled as if to reassure her. There'd been a flicker to that smile, though, and she'd seen it. He'd smiled, said he was right behind her, and she'd never seen him again.

She blinked, disorientation momentarily overwhelming her. Where was she?

Oh, yes. She remembered now. They were "backstage." She pulled herself up onto all four legs, her old bones creaking and cracking. The lava sac in her throat gurgled like an upset stomach.

The yellow temple was only a dream. That place wasn't real. The other llama wasn't her husband. She didn't even know him, except in the dream.

The only other llamas in here with her stood nearby, talking. She sighed at the pair of young soldiers. Was this really it? Her empire dwindled down to this?

Just her and two bad llamas, both of whom were idiots.

"I can't take this. I'm gonna lavaball them," Tea Bag was saying as he stared off at the group of goblins.

Grandma knew this was coming. It'd been days since they'd come "backstage," and they still didn't have answers as to what this strange place really was. The gang—if one could call three llamas a gang—was getting antsy.

"You will do no such thing," Grandma said, cracking her neck.

"Not yet. We'll have our revenge when the time comes. If you lava in here, like a real lavaball, you'll set the carpet on fire again. Then what will we do? We'll all burn for sure this time."

"We gotta do something," Medium Arturo said, standing next to Tea Bag. "They stole our stash, and they're tearing through it all right in front of us." Both of their tails wagged in angry unison.

They weren't wrong. There'd been a constant cloud of smoke over the group of goblins since they'd arrived here. The distinctive stench of product filled the air, though it'd been starting to ease over the past day.

Across the way, one of the goblins with a pot on his head made a rude gesture in their direction.

"Yes, we'll do something, but not yet," Grandma said, trying to keep the frustration from her voice. "There's three of us, and there's 23 of them, including two shamankas and several of those bombers."

She'd been trying to keep it together. She had to be strong for the soldiers, even if there were only two of them. The goblins had murdered her son, and now they were flaunting it right in front of her. They'd stolen their product, murdered dozens of llamas, left, come back, and murdered her son.

They'd ruined everything.

There would be a reckoning. If it was the last thing Grandma did, she would have her revenge. But they had to be smart about it.

"We can take 'em," Tea Bag said.

"We can't. And if we could, then what? If we just randomly attack the gobs, all the others in here might not trust us anymore. Then what're we gonna do? You see those kobolds and dingoes? They'll tear us apart. And I don't even know what those floating brain things are. We don't need to be earning new enemies. Patience, both of you. We'll have our retribution."

Of all the groups in here, the llamas were clearly the weakest, and the fact these two nimrods didn't realize it was terrifying to Grandma. *This is my fault,* she thought mournfully. *We were so focused on the plan, we didn't spend time making sure the llamas weren't goddamned idiots.*

Medium Arturo spit to the side, and the fluffy carpet sizzled. It was marked in multiple places here where the llama's caustic spit had burned holes. Above, the magical floating automaton thing let out an angry metallic shriek. It did that every time Arturo spat. The three of them watched the floating machine for a moment before Arturo turned back to Grandma.

"I mean no disrespect, Gran. But you ain't the one in charge no more. Youse retired, and they laughing at us."

Grandma Llama pictured herself melting Arturo's idiot face off. She would've done it, too, if there weren't only three of them. She took a long, deep breath. The lava pouch in her throat gurgled.

"Listen, you godsdamned imbecile. I *am* in charge. I've explained this to you I don't know how many times. My son was a decoy. I'm the one really in charge. I've been the one in charge the whole time. You know this. You knew it before we even got here."

"If youse in charge, then why'd I gotta follow the orders of King-pin, then? Why he give me the product to sell? Why'd I have to pay him at the end of each day?"

"What does 'decoy' means?" Tea Bag added.

She just looked at them. Above, the circling automaton made a shrill noise and zoomed off toward a danger dingo that was squatting as he prepared to crap on the carpet. The floating disc tried to herd the monster toward the designated bathroom area. The creature growled and snapped at the floating disc and continued to poop.

They'd been here for over two weeks now. Every day, new groups of monsters came, though it was starting to slow down. Some of these monsters were frighteningly strong. The first floor of the dungeon would be long collapsed by now, and Grandma suspected enough time had passed that they were actually on the third floor. That's where these new monsters were from. Fewer were coming now, but the ones who did come were big, angry, strong, and very, very

confused. The most recent—a strange, muscular ogre creature wearing what looked like a spotted bathing suit—hadn't moved from
where he'd appeared. He just rocked back and forth, muttering
something about worms and ice cream.

The room was large. Large enough that she counted almost a
thousand steps from one wall to the next. Despite the hundreds of
monsters in here, the room still seemed empty. Voices echoed when
they were raised. There was a ceiling, but it was too high. Those
from the first floor were all terrified of the open space.

What do you want? That's what the voice had asked her as she
stood over the body of her son, needlessly slaughtered by the goblins.
This wasn't part of the plan. He was supposed to live. He was supposed to eventually really be in charge. They were building an empire, getting stronger so they'd be allowed onto a deeper floor. They
wouldn't attack crawlers unless they were attacked first. That way
they'd be safe.

But they hadn't been attacked by a crawler. Goblins. Goddamn
murderous, product-addicted goblins.

There were no doors in the chamber. No way out. It was a massive rectangular room with metal walls covered in a lush carpet that
smelled brand-new. Grandma only knew what a carpet was because
of the dreams. The yellow temple. She'd been dreaming of that place
a lot lately. She'd been a guard in the dream. She and her husband.
The yellow temple that smelled of lilies and new, soft carpet. There
was a young elf girl in the temple, and she'd brush Grandma's hair.

About fifteen of the round robots floated around the room. Most
of them spent their time angrily beeping at those who made messes
outside of the designated mess area, and then they'd swoop in and
clean it up afterward if it was something they could fix. They couldn't
fix the carpet, though, but they still beeped angrily.

Twice a day, the robots would drop sustenance biscuits and wa-
terskins all around the groups. A rat-kin brute had grabbed one
once, and he'd been electrocuted the moment he touched the flying
thing. It hadn't killed him, but it singed the fur off of both of the

large creature's arms. The muscular rat hadn't been right in the head since. Even now he paced back and forth, occasionally slapping himself in the face. Nobody dared fuck with the robots after that.

The groups remained segregated, building little camps and territories in the dimly lit room. There were the goblins. The kobolds with their dingoes. The rat-kin. The brain-with-tentacles things. The scat thugs. The chilly goats. So much more. Most were in groups of about three to five. The goblins were by far the largest group.

Recently, the monsters started coming in singles. There was the ogre. A succubus woman. A minotaur.

Nobody had fought yet, but Grandma knew it was only a matter of time. The rat-kin and the brain things didn't like one another. Also, the succubus and the minotaur clearly knew and hated each other. The raccoon-headed scat thugs would kill them all, given a chance. And what was worse, they had a mage in their group. A trash princess. They were known to be both dangerous and insane.

These were all "smart" monsters, Grandma noted. All, except maybe the dingoes, could speak. Yet most of the groups didn't talk to one another. They'd all marked off a little corner of the carpet for themselves and sat there sullenly, waiting for something to happen.

This, Grandma realized, was how they'd been trained. It's what happened in the dungeon when things were going normally. At least that's what happened on the first floor and, as she understood it, on the second floor, too. She also knew something changed on the third floor, and the monsters there didn't realize they were in a dungeon. Hence, the wild confusion of the newcomers.

"That one is kinda sexy, though," Medium Arturo was saying. Grandma blinked, turning her attention back to her two soldiers, still peering off at the goblins. Arturo's long llama tongue lolled from his mouth as he licked at his face. He made a strange, just awful groaning noise as he stared at one of the two goblin shamankas.

Grandma shuddered. She cursed herself for the thousandth time that of all the llamas to be stuck with, it was these two nimrods. *Most* of the llamas were idiots, but these two were just next level.

"*Very* sexy," Arturo continued, whispering the words like he was trying to be seductive. "After we kill 'em all, maybe I'll ask that one out."

"How are you going to ask her out if she's dead? You think everything's sexy," Tea Bag muttered.

"I don't think you're sexy. I don't think Grandma's sexy." His eyes turned to regard her. "Well, not too sexy anymore. But I wouldn't turn her down. I like aged meat, if you know what I'm saying."

Fuck it, Grandma thought as she started to spin up her *Kick* spell.

And that's when the lights of the room switched on. Everyone stopped what they were doing and looked up. The room had been dimly lit before. Now the light was so bright, she could see from wall to wall. The carpet glistened in the brightness, dotted with hundreds of stains from the monsters. All the talking and grunting throughout the room instantly stopped.

A notification came. The first one since they'd arrived:

The third floor has concluded. Please stand by . . .

One of the flying discs lowered and hovered in front of Grandma. It made a beep.

"Grandma Llama. Please follow me. All others remain until she returns."

They all looked at one another. The metal things hadn't spoken before. The voice was strange. Male. Metallic. The voice was similar to that of one of the dungeon admin folks, but different somehow, more formal.

"Fuck that," Tea Bag said after a moment. "If you want a gran, you gotta get your own. This is our gran. She's the mom of the Kingpin. Where she goes, we go."

Across the way, a robot hovered in front of one of the goblin shamankas. The other shamanka was shouting, likely dropping the same sort of protests. Grandma turned her head about the room, and she saw the same scene playing in a few—but not all—of the other groups.

"Tea Bag," Grandma said, "leave it. Stay here and don't set anything on fire."

———

GRANDMA FOLLOWED THE ROBOT TO THE WALL OF THE GIANT ROOM. She felt the eyes of the unchosen monsters on her and the procession of others. She suddenly felt the need to stand tall and proud as she walked. *Show them who you are.* She passed the red-skinned succubus woman, who glared up at them from her spot on the carpet. Grandma winked at the demon creature.

A large door magically appeared as she approached the wall, and she hesitantly trotted inside, the robot remaining outside.

This was just another, smaller room with a much lower ceiling. The floor was tile, not carpet, and her nails clomped loudly. It was the only sound in the room as the others shuffled in behind her. The walls were made of the same metal as the rest of the building, and the light here was muted. The air smelled cleaner, too, more fresh than anything she'd ever experienced.

Though that wasn't true, was it? She thought again of the yellow temple from her dreams. Of the window with the large, open sky. Of the elf girl with the brush and the kind words. Of her own husband, whose name she couldn't even remember.

There were now ten of them in the room. In addition to herself, it was the piercing-covered shamanka, one of the rat-kin brutes, the trash princess mage, one of the floating brains, and a few others. Nobody spoke. They all glared at one another, all nervous.

The goblin had her arms wrapped around herself as she stood in the back of the room, shaking.

Grandma regarded the goblin, and she realized that the small creature was already suffering from withdrawal. It was still early stages, but the signs were clear. She'd been waiting for this. She

didn't want to strike against the goblins while they were still tripping on product. But in another day, once they were all fully in the
throes of withdrawal . . .

"Okay, everyone. Gather around," a new voice called into the
room.

Grandma's attention whipped to the front. At the creature who'd
just suddenly appeared. Grandma gasped and took a step forward.

It was her.

The girl from her dreams. The elf who'd brushed her hair and
tied it with ribbons.

But no, she realized after a moment, disappointment overwhelming her, it was a young female elf, but it wasn't the same elf. Just
similar.

The rat-kin was the first to speak. This was one of the brutes. He
clutched a spear and brandished it menacingly at the elf. "Where the
hells is we? You been keeping us here for ages with no explanations.
No nothing. And your stupid food machines been giving us crap to
eat. They burned all the fur off Jimmy James, and he ain't been the
same since."

The floating brain thing waved its tentacles in amusement. It said
in a singsong voice, "It was quite the upgrade for Jimmy James, I
must say." The thing didn't have a mouth that Grandma could see.

The rat-kin brute turned to the brain and growled. "Imma pull
your danglies off and use them to jerk off your mom."

"I'm sorry, what?" the brain asked.

"That's what your mom said," the rat-kin replied.

"What? What does that even mean?"

Waving his spear, the rat took another step toward the floating
brain, which responded by floating up toward the ceiling and splay-
ing its tentacles, making it suddenly look like a massive flower. The
rat dropped his spear and grabbed his head and started to cry out.
Grandma felt a slight push against her own brain from the psionic
attack, but she pushed it away. Luckily it was only focused on the
rat-kin, who'd fallen to his knees.

"Oh gods, oh gods, it hurts," the rat cried.

"See, that's what *your* mom said," the brain said, a hint of triumph to its disembodied voice. "That's how you use that insult, you putrid column of syphilitic pus."

"Everyone," the girl said, "please, stop, and pay attention."

The rat screamed anew as he powered through the pain. He picked up the spear, turned toward the brain upon the ceiling, and pulled his arm back, aiming for a throw.

"Uh-oh," the brain said. "Listen, Larry. Let's talk about—"

The spear flew true, but the moment it hit the brain, the spear burst into a group of bugs. Moths. They flew about the room, settling against the ceiling.

"My word," the brain said. "That was unexpected."

"What did you do to my good poker?" the rat demanded of the brain, shaking his fist. "You'll pay this time, Nigel."

The brain's tentacles stopped waving and now hung limply. "I'm clearly not the one who did that, Larry. That was druid magic."

"Everyone, shut up," the elf said, the politeness slipping away. "I swear to Nekhebit, if you don't all calm down, I'll turn you each into a pile of dung beetles, and we'll start this over with a new group of mobs."

"Do you . . . do you all have names already?" This came from the goblin who spoke with a shaking, scared voice.

"Of course I got a name," came Larry the rat-kin's reply. "Why wouldn't I have a name?" But he trailed off at the end. "Wait . . ."

The question surprised Grandma, and she thought about it for a minute. *Did* she have a name? She was Grandma Llama. Her son was Kingpin.

But, still . . . those weren't their names. Those were titles. Well, Grandma Llama was a title. Kingpin was a title. But Tea Bag and Medium Arturo *were* names. They were stupid names, but they were names. Why did *they* have names and she didn't?

You do have a name. You've always had a name. The elf. She called you Miss Beautiful, and she called your husband Mr. Handsome. But Miss

Beautiful was just a nickname, wasn't it? And it wasn't the only name she'd ever had.

She remembered it all in a sudden burst of clarity, all at once. It was like she'd been kicked in the throat, and she gasped as the memories overwhelmed her. It had come so fast, so violently. She usually didn't have a name or title at all. But when she did, it was always something different. It was only for the last ten or so seasons that she was Grandma Llama. And the drugs . . . the blitz sticks. The toilet meth. The whole manufacturing facility. That was new. Well, some of it was new. They'd been selling and making drugs for many seasons now. The meth was new this season.

What? What?

She felt like she was going to pass out.

Who am I? *Who am I?*

She wasn't the only one undergoing some sort of epiphany. Everyone was suddenly very quiet. Even Larry the rat-kin had a strange look on his face. The brain named Nigel had floated down to the floor and was just sort of pulsing there.

"Oh, good," the elf said, looking about. "Thank you, Rory. That was easier than I thought it would be. You just saved me a significant amount of trouble. Everyone, just fight through it. That disorienting feeling will go away in a minute or so."

Grandma had always known she was a monster that had been "made" by the dungeon. She knew where they were and the purpose of their existence. But she hadn't known that her mind, who she was, her memories themselves were also being changed. That's what they did to those on the third floor and deeper, not on the first and second.

She thought of her son. The Kingpin. Not *all* of them had been made by the dungeon. He had been born. She remembered giving birth to him. Yet . . . She felt ill all over again. When had she become pregnant? Who was the father? Was it her husband from the yellow temple? No, that couldn't be. The timelines didn't match up. Her child . . . he'd been born, the season had changed, and he was suddenly an adult. That's when they decided to make him the decoy while she remained in charge. It was part of the plan. She remembered coming up with the idea, but now that memory evaporated. The plan *hadn't* been her idea. It was just there when he'd shown up.

Her mind continued to spin. The revelations slammed into her one after another like a volley of arrows.

The yellow temple wasn't a dream. Oh gods. Those were real memories. She'd been a guard at a "blessings reward" room once. She'd been safe, and the crawlers were always happy to meet them. Her husband was real, and they loved each other. Until . . . until . . . She remembered now. A crawler. A bune, the race was called. A small floating lizard. The crawler had killed the elf girl when she tried to stop him from stealing all the water from the blessings fountain. Her husband had faced the crawler and told Grandma to run. She had run away. She'd spent the next few days wandering aimlessly and weeping, not sure what to do. And after, when the next dungeon started, she'd changed. Her husband was gone.

That happened a lot, she now realized. Things would stay the same until a crawler came in and ruined it all, and then it would all change. If someone died, they were gone forever. But sometimes there would be new ones there to replace the ones that had been lost. It was so confusing. It didn't make sense.

Next to her, a little lizard thing with a long tongue was on its hands and knees, vomiting on the floor. One of the robots appeared out of nowhere and made a shrill noise.

The elf watched this all with a strange smirk on her face. With the wave of her hand, a chair appeared in the room. It grew up through the floor and was made of vines. The elf sat in it and crossed her legs. She leaned forward. "What you're all going through right now is something called a memory breach. There are normally protections in place to keep this from happening, but they degrade over time. The food and water you've been given has sped up the process. I was going to pop the bubble myself, but Rory did it for me. When this happens, the normal procedure is for you to be killed and your bodies thrown in the recycler. But obviously that's not what's happening here. We need your brains fully functional to accomplish our task."

"You're not a dungeon admin. Who are you? What is this place?" This came from the trash princess. The raccoon mage gasped the words.

"Think of me as a game guide. Not one for crawlers, but for monsters like you. I will be the one helping you acclimate and guiding your training and leveling from this point forward. My name is Menerva, and you ten are my Dungeon Master Generals."

Training and leveling? Grandma thought. *Dungeon Master Generals?*

"Okay, but where is *here?*" the trash princess demanded.

The elf grinned and held out her arms. "We are backstage at the Pineapple Cabaret."

Everyone just stared at the elf.

"What the fuck is that?" Larry the rat-kin finally asked.

The grin on Menerva the elf's face didn't falter. "My friends, it is your salvation. The backstage area is the dungeon's 17th floor. The last one before the big boss room one floor down."

The goblin—Rory was her name—stepped forward. "The . . . the 17th floor? We're skipping the others? How? How is this possible? Why us?"

"Okay, everyone pay attention," Menerva said, leaning even more forward in her chair. "We are currently backstage. That means we are in a place where crawlers aren't able to go. We are under the influence of the system AI, but this isn't a dungeon floor. You don't have proper interfaces, but that's going to change in a crutch."

"AI? What's that?" Larry asked.

"It's the god," the trash princess replied. "The god that makes the magic words."

"That's the dungeon admins, stupid," Larry said. "The untouchables. Like Damien and the fish people."

The raccoon looked as if she was about to launch herself at the rat-kin, but Menerva held up a hand.

"All will be clear in time. Just listen for now, and you can ask more questions later. If you don't know already, the dungeon has 18 floors. Right now the crawlers have just finished the third floor, and the fourth will open shortly. As a rule, the season's showrunners must have plans for every floor before the season ever starts. Six of those floors are predetermined by tradition. Those floors are 3, 6, 9, 12, 15, and 18." She held up a finger. "But only one crawler has ever made it past the 12th floor. As a result, we've had many, many seasons where 13 through 17 have never even been seen by the viewers."

"Viewers?" Grandma asked. She just blurted the question out. Menerva ignored her.

"This is where you lot come in. Because these later floors are never utilized, every showrunner just resubmits the same plans as the previous season. As a result, these later floors have been the same for a very, very long time. And frankly, I don't believe even the current showrunners know what these floors are. Nobody looks at the plans anymore."

"Why don't they just lower the number of floors, then?" This came from the brain, who remained on the tiles, pulsing. Nigel.

"That would probably require someone with better planning skills to put this all together," Menerva muttered. She continued. "Anyway, *this* floor, the 17th, is the final test the crawlers must pass before they face the great Scolopendra. On this 17th floor is where they will face monsters from all the previous floors, but in reverse order of strength. So you guys from the first floor will be the strongest. But we can't just give you super strength and levels. You will slowly train your way up so you don't accidentally kill yourselves. As for the floor itself . . . it is to all be self-contained in this room."

"The floor is here?" Nigel the brain asked. "Here in this empty warehouse with the fuzzy floor?"

"That's right."

"Well, that's not very exciting, is it?"

Menerva smiled and then snapped her fingers. A column of something—ice?—appeared growing from the floor underneath

Nigel, raising him up in the air. The brain made a yelp and floated away.

"As soon as I can trust you not to murder each other, you ten will be given the power to build anything you wish. Your task will be to build a mini dungeon, a mirror of the first floor, to test the crawlers. The only rule is that there must be a clear path from the entrance to two different exits. What you build around those paths is up to you. I will be helping you, but you will be building the entire floor yourself while you train. You have all the way up until the point the 16th floor is finished to build and design the floor."

"But crawlers never make it past the 13th?" the trash princess asked.

"That's right. And it usually all ends on the 10th. Sometimes on the 9th."

The raccoon made a grunt. "Then what's the point? If they ain't really gonna come, then why do we gotta do it?"

Menerva grinned. "A long time ago someone thought it would be a good idea to program this second-to-last floor to be self-building. All of you were plucked away by the AI just before you were recycled. You were saved, and your duty is now to build this floor to the best of your ability even though nobody is ever going to see it. It needs to be done because they say it needs to be done."

"Yeah, I got a question," Grandma asked. "If this so-called floor exists every season, and crawlers never get there, then where are all the other monsters from the previous seasons? What happens when the season is over? Where do we go?"

"Why, you go into the cabaret. We are backstage now. Once you're done with your duty, you get to join the others in the beautiful place. A place of forever safety and no crawlers and no danger. You get to go to the Pineapple Cabaret."

"Really? Do you really mean it?" This came from Rory the goblin, who'd moved from the back of the room to stand right in front of Menerva. She fell to her knees in front of the elf. "We'll be safe forever?"

"Forever and ever," Menerva said, holding her hand out over Rory like she was a priestess bestowing a blessing. Rory started to openly weep.

Menerva's smile grew even larger, but Grandma saw it. The flicker. It was the same smile, the same flicker her husband had given her. *I'm right behind you.*

Grandma was filled with a terrible, terrible sense of alarm.

PART 3 WILL APPEAR AT THE END OF
THE DUNGEON ANARCHIST'S COOKBOOK.